Grady-O'Hare

A NOVEL BY TERRY O'NEILL

ISBN: 1452866910
ISBN-13: 9781452866918

DISCLAIMER

Grady O'Hare is a work of fiction. Excluding historical characters of the Indian Wars period, all characters are fictitious. Any resemblance to real persons is coincidental.

DEDICATION

This book is dedicated to the freedom loving people of the United Sates. Their love and respect for the founding principles of the country and reverence for those who have shed their blood and given their lives in the furtherance of that great cause. God bless you all.

ACKNOWLEDGMENTS

I wish to thank my wonderful wife and companion for life, Pamela, for her putting up with my absence in pursuing this effort. For her encouragement, love and thoughtful editing. My longtime friend and associate, Craig Cabot, for his reading of the early manuscript and thoughtful contributions. And to many friends who have encouraged the work to completion.

COVER PHOTO CREDITS

Bay Bridge-photo by Philip Greenspun
Power Wagon-photo by Jim Allen
B24-Courtesy of the Collings Foundation
www.collingsfoundation.org
Wagon Train-photo by Bill Wilcox
Modoc Indians-Siskiyou County Museum
Grady-O'Hare Ranch-Michael Keith
All Others-Pamela O'Neill

CHAPTER 1

Scott's Bluff, Nebraska-1869

He slid down off his horse just slightly unsteady and reached into the saddle bag for a bottle of whiskey. The horse, now quite used to the pattern prepared to sleep on its feet until his master's escapade was complete; in the morning.

It was Malcolm Everett's Friday night custom to come into town from the Platte River Ranch, the largest cattle and horse cutting ranch in that part of Nebraska. It spread from just west of Bridgeport along both sides of the Platte in a long ribbon taking up the best pasture on both sides. You could generally tell if you were on the 'PRR' in summer. If it was green, you were, if brown, you weren't. The outside perimeter was often stair stepped as sectional land tends to be, and lately the acquisitions had been adding onto the north bank.

He was a powerful man in every way. He'd bought politicians and destroyed them, killed men with his bare hands. He had been in the 'land acquisition' business for nearly 30 years. He'd sold horses to the army, to ride or eat. It didn't matter to him. With an initial spread of just over 4,000 acres, the PR Ranch now encompassed nearly 17,000 acres and employed 41 men. That didn't count the sheriff, doctors, freight men, teamsters and various tradesmen whose businesses were inextricably linked to the PRR.

The Ogallala Saloon and Board was packed. The local ranch hands were paid and it was time to go to town; some

1

to get drunk, some to whore, some to wake up in jail. But one would die. The keys on the honkytonk piano were flying, and it was getting warm in the saloon. Not enough women- too many men. There would be a problem, sure as hell.

Every other Friday Malcolm came to town. He hated the pay day visit as there was competition for the whores. His age and weariness had begun to take its toll. Sometimes, he would just spend the night in town. He drank for his own reasons and preferred doing so alone. The bar always bored him in a short time; stupid people acting stupid, he thought. He was old, but had the money, and the girls all knew it. He hitched the chestnut out back and came up the back stairways, a habit, drawn from shame he felt when he thought of his church upbringing.

As he walked the few paces to the stairs, he stopped to take in a shapely figure under the stairway lantern. Not a whore's clothes, he thought, but several times he had found a lady waiting for him. With brawling sounds emanating from the saloon, the raucous cowboys, workmen and drifters all were having a time of it. This might be someone new. Her face was partially shaded from the lantern light, but he could see a pleasant bone structure, thin lips and a strong nose. He strained to see better, but the dark and the drink obscured the more detailed features.

"Well, good evening, m'am."

"Good evenin' to you, sir. Are you looking for someone in particular, or would a handsome man such as yourself be available to a lady?"

The sound of her voice was soft, inviting, and his spirits lifted some, as she moved a step closer to him.

"Oh, I'm quite available. I have a room here, and a bottle of fine whiskey. Would you be kind enough to join me?"

She smiled and turned to start up the stairway to the hotel rooms. He followed, observing the furls of her dress in the shadows ahead of him.

One year earlier

John and Melissa Brennerman had come to the plains from the east, as the nation elbowed its way in a westward expansion. The country seemed full of itinerant dreamers; men with a passion, a dream, a quest. Some for land, some gold, or adventure-all for wealth. Farming, of course, was the slow and steady way to wealth, if you didn't starve first. Many succumbed to disease, the cold, or heat, droughts, Indians, highwaymen or simply an accident too far from anywhere or anyone to help them. Mostly they were middle class that pushed west with savings, their possessions and the dream.

In a land rush auctioned by the United States, John Brennerman had done well by circumstances of good horsemanship, a keen eye for land and luck. Section 4 was 640 acres blessed by God's hand. The east boundary rose gently above the plain about 150 feet. In a world of flat, it gave a tremendous view. Several small springs dotted the hillside down to the 550 acres or so of flat Nebraska top soil on the bottom-soil that could grow anything. These springs supported a flourishing stand of oaks, locust trees and a massive walnut tree 80 feet tall and a drip line as wide. In the northeast corner was a tremendous spring gushing forth from a rock formation. Within forty feet, the spring ran a creek six to eight feet across. In the early spring, it tore into its banks refusing to be contained, then receded gently through the summer, maintaining a respectable flow all through the dry fall. The creek shot straight down the gentle hillside, through the middle of the section of land. John and Melissa's first project after constructing a shelter, which nearly killed them when it collapsed in a wind storm, was to put in irrigation ditches. They already had nearly 200 acres of the bottom land in irrigated pasture. The small herd of cattle was growing fat and in number, while goats, chickens and a friendly pig rounded out the barn inhabitants. A new home had been started and one large room sufficed for now, but the plans were for something far grander. Melissa's garden was huge and bountiful.

After endless dawn to dusk workdays, they sat on the small covered front porch looking into the western sunsets that washed over their land. The creek crashed down the little hill then meandered across the flat bottom land in slow sweeping turns. The sweet evening breeze arrived to cool their brow and delight their souls with the smell of moisture laden grass.

"Isn't it beautiful?" she said. Her gaze reached far into the west, where the Rocky Mountains thrust upward and met the crimson and gold sky, crowned with the azure blue that only lasts a few moments.

"Yes", he said slowly. "Tomorrow, we'll start on the south side ditch works. If we can work that ditch just right, comin' around the hill, I think it'll put 120-150 acres into irrigation. Mel, I'm thinking about putting some of that ground into hay. The rest should go into corn." This, he spoke with self affirming determination.

She moved alongside him at the railing of the porch, still transfixed on the sunset; put her arm around his waist, inside his wide suspenders and patted gently on his love handles.

"Just shut up and look at that", she said softly.

"Sorry", he said.

Yes, it was beautiful. God had blessed them and there was that sense that the future was bright. It seemed they had carved out a place in the world for themselves. It was lonely, and sometimes forlorn, but their love and devotion to each other was all that mattered to them. They were unconditionally committed to each other. She loved him beyond words and measure.

Without noticing exactly when, the grey had crept into the sunset. Gone was the crimson, fleeting quickly was the gold. The beautiful blue, so intense, now muted to pale hues.

"I'll fix us supper" she said, and headed into the cabin. John stepped down off the porch and walked out a dozen paces or so. He searched the horizon for nearly 360 degrees and found no inch of it disagreeable to him. Nowhere in his view could he see another man's home, or a building. Just range cattle from the Platte River Ranch, or a few strays, some deer and antelope. He relieved himself and walked back to the cabin to wash for supper as the stars were coming out.

Months passed quickly, with two people set on a dream and working daily to bring it to reality. Soon it was their third spring. The water shooting from beneath the rock formation was running a torrent and you could hear it from the cabin, not fifty yards away. They had survived another winter. The seed corn had come in and the south side ditch was nearly complete, thanks to a mild winter. Mel had finished the breakfast dishes and she was counting in her head the calendar days, as only women do, and began to smile to herself. John was down on the bottom, about a half mile away. She felt her stomach and smiled again. At lunch she rode out to where the ditch was nearing its end. John stopped work and eagerly prepared to eat a sandwich. The day was warming up nicely. The sky stretched forever above the checked table cloth that lay on the open ground. She laughed as he attacked the sandwich as if famished. He looked perfect to her then and there, unshaven, sweat stained hat, sleeves rolled and his suspendered breeches. The pale blue eyes sparked as he winked at her, indicating his approval of the meatloaf sandwich on fresh baked bread and his appreciation for her.

"I've got a surprise for you, when you've finished" she said.

He only nodded with an unbelievable mouth full of food, cheeks bulging. He grabbed his canteen and swilled. An inquisitive smile peeked at the corner of his mouth, as he searched her eyes.

"What might that be?"

"It'll keep 'till you're finished" she teased.

His smile broke widely, as he detected her trying to conceal her own. She pursed her lips trying to hide what was to him an overpowering radiance in her whole body. God, she was so beautiful. Heaven seemed to have made her for him. He gulped again at the sandwich, making quick work of it. He'd play along.

"Somethin' special for dinner?

"Nope"

"Somethin' from the Sears catalog?"

"Nope." "We got a new critter in the barn"

"Not even."

He munched down the last of the sandwich and cracked a large dill pickle in half. He crunched half in his mouth, pulling the other half back out. She leaned back and let the sun drench her face and closed her eyes, but she couldn't stop the smile from creeping, then engulfing her face again.

"You got somethin' goin', I can see that." he said.

"Nope."

"We got something going, John Brennerman"

His brow furrowed, as he searched her face for what she hinted at.

He swallowed and then stuck the other half of the huge dill pickle in his mouth, thinking and looking. Then, with the pickle sticking out of his mouth, his eyes opened wide and his eyebrows shot up. Holding the big pickle in his front teeth, he talked around it.

"We're gonna' have a baby!!"

He was on his feet as if a snake had crawled up to him, looking at her to see her reaction. She rolled her head back and laughed.

"That's right. We're gonna have us a baby."

He pulled her up to him and looked at her in a way he never had before. She was never prettier than this moment to him. Joy and happiness welled up inside of her.

"And if you'll please take that stupid pickle out of your mouth, you can kiss me."

He did. He held her and kissed her over and over until they were both laughing, crying-rolling on the table cloth. Then he loved her as never before under the open Nebraska sky, which stretched from the beginning to the end of time.

As spring turned to summer and the dry cropland melded from green to golden brown, their skin tanned and hair bleached. The south side ditch now irrigated nearly 180 acres-more than they had thought. Their bodies were honed in the manner that only daily work-hard work-physical work can do. Muscles in the back, legs, and abdominal core become rock hard when every movement is with weight, every lift is with the back, no machinery beyond the basic wheel and lever. So much to do to build something from nothing. Nothing is done unless it is instigated by your own body. So often, the most menial tasks a hundred years hence, spanned a day or more of hard work and took numerous attempts and iterations before success. But each failure brought innovation and creativity. The motivation was success, wealth, and sometimes ....survival.

In the evenings they sketched plans for an addition-a bedroom. The little cabin on the knoll-top would have to grow with them. The cool evening breeze lazily whisked their hair as they sat on the front porch and looked over their little piece of heaven.

On the morning of July 14, 1868 a single horse buggy could be seen making its way along the dirt road, which served as the main road through that part of the valley. It turned onto the smaller road that led only to their place. Someone was coming to visit. The irrigation had been set before dawn and the ditches were flooding. John had repaired a wagon, wiped his hands and watched the approaching visitor.

They could see a well dressed man with expensive boots, smiling broadly. He pulled into the yard and stepped down, a spectacled man, doffing his hat to Melissa,

"Mr. & Mrs. Brennerman?"

"Yes, welcome", said John.

"I'm Sandeen, Robert Sandeen."

They were curious, but having made an early judgement that he represented no threat, they reverted to their natural inclination to welcome strangers. A visitor in a place so sparsely populated was always welcome. There would be information from town, and the outside world which they remained happily oblivious to for long stretches of time.

"Won't you please come in?" said Mel. "What brings you out our way, Mr. Sandeen?"

"Good news." They all walked into the cabin and sat at the small table. John and Mel looked at each other.

"I'll fix some coffee and bread for Mr. Sandeen," said Mel.

"No thanks, don't trouble yourself, m'am"

"Its no trouble, I'll just be a minute."

She went to the open cupboards for the coffee tin and shook it.

"I'm a lawyer in Ogalalla. I represent a client who is interested in buying your property".

"Mr. Sandeen, the property is not for sale," John said squarely.

Sandeen smiled in complete expectation of this response.

"I certainly understand. You have a beautiful little place here. I can see that you've worked hard. That's a beautiful field down there below the road."

"It's not for sale."

"Mr. Brennerman, my client is willing to be more than fair-generous even, and trust me, he is very capable-financially speaking." He smiled thinly. Glancing at the waist of Melissa, "Surely an industrious man, such as yourself, could take a good offer and make quite a stake somewhere, maybe California. This can be a might harsh land out here, especially if young ones are coming." Mel glanced at him, uncertain of him for the first time.

"Look, Mr. Sandeen, we mean no disrespect to you or your client, and I'm sure he could make us a generous offer, but we're simply not interested."

"I'll cut to the quick. I'm prepared to offer thirty-five dollars per acre."

"No."

"Forty."

"No."

"Fifty."

"No." Sandeen set his jaw, and the eyes shifted to anger. He sighed regaining inner composure. "Mr. Brennerman,..." and here his countenance changed to almost pleading, a fearful furrow in his brow ...., "Please consider very carefully what I'm about to say. My client is the largest ranch around this part of Nebraska." Now they knew who the buyer was-Malcolm Everett. "He is intent on owning this property. It fits perfectly to his other holdings and future plans. I can't tell you how wise it would be to accept the next offer. You'll be a substantially wealthier man. My final offer is sixty dollars per acre. That's $38,400, about twice what it is worth."

It was a very handsome offer and he was right. It was twice what the place was worth. He looked at Mel. Sandeen's face was set, but beneath the surface there was a hope-no, almost a prayerful anticipation of 'yes'.

"I'm sorry Mr. Sandeen, but I don't think it's in the cards just right now."

Sandeen sighed and stiffened his chin.

"I'm sorry too."

He rose and put his hat upon his head. With a slight nod to Mel, he moved to the door. John rose to see him to his buggy. They both stood on the small front porch, Sandeen looking down the slope and across the Brennerman place. The ribbons of water like a skeleton framework gleaming on the land, and the irrigated portions, brilliant green. The small herd of cattle down in the northwest corner were working their cud, bellies full. Sandeen took the sweet smell in deeply.

"I understand, Mr. Brennerman," he said without changing his gaze.

Sandeen climbed up and without another word turned the buggy around and headed down to the valley road.

"That was a heck of an offer, Mel."

"Yes, it was, but I'm happy here. I don't want to move. I have everything I've ever wanted; I have you and I have your child and we have this place-a place we've built with our own hands. When I was a little girl growing up in St. Louis, I dreamed that life could be like this for me. It never was before. And then when you fought in the war, I wondered if life would ever come back to me. Well, now I've got what I want and the last thing I'll do is sell it." He held her in his arms and kissed her on the lips. He said nothing-just looked into her eyes.

"Well, tomorrow Skip Johnson is coming over for the spring calves. There are several I need help with. I need you to make the run to town tomorrow for supplies."

And so another long day began, and a long list of supplies was made.

At first light, the wagon was hitched, with two horses and what cash they had. Some credit was needed but their credit was good, anywhere in town. Mel climbed on board. John climbed up and kissed her.

"See you later. I love you."

"Love you too."

It was 14 miles to town and would take much of the day to load up and return. As the sun rose above the hills at her back she drove the horses into the long morning shadows on the road. In the distance were the Rockies. All around the plains and bluffs, the eroded formations of sand produced castles driven out of the earth. No one else was on the road. She would be in Scotts Bluff in about three hours. On the ride in to town, her mind wandered as she took in the scenery. Not a religious person she would quickly confess the existence of God. What else could explain all she saw and felt. The miles and hours passed pleasantly.

As she rounded the bend, Main Street came into view. Shopkeepers were sweeping and taking on supplies from the freightmen and teamsters drove their wagons through town. Some headed out west to supply Fort Laramie, some south to Denver. She rarely came to town. Most of the suppliers knew John Brennerman and that he was married, but didn't know his wife on sight. Men toted sacks, and dollies rolled along the wood plank sidewalks with barrels of nails, powder, flour and whatever else. She enjoyed the little town. Folks passing through on the Oregon Trail spent several days resting and taking on stores. Whole wagon trains were often encircled just out of town in preparing for the next leg of their long journey.

It was busy the hour most stores opened. Her first stop; hardware and general merchandise. "Avery's General Store", the simple black and white signboard announced. Henry Avery signed for delivery of a shipment of grains at the store front while young strapping men hefted 50 pound sacks into the rear of the store. Probably his sons, she guessed. Across the street the Ogallala Hotel and Saloon stood as the largest building on the street. At the far end of Main Street, she could see the little white church, with its pitched steeple and bell tower. She looked back at the Ogallala Hotel and Saloon. Seems that should be in Ogallala, not in Scotts Bluff, she thought to herself. Two men exited the saloon while two others walked in to take their place. "Breakfast, Lunch, Fine Dinners", the sign read.

Turning to her affairs, she pulled the wagon alongside the raised plank sidewalk and set the brake. Walking into the store, the variety and efficient display of so many items struck her at first. She had only been in the store once before, about a year ago, but she recalled it as sparsely supplied and somewhat dingy. Today, it seemed brighter, as the morning sun shot beams onto the floor through four large windows. Each sunbeam displayed airborn particles dancing in the light. She retrieved her list and presented it to Mr. Avery, who with no more than a grunt had summoned the two boys from the back. They were there immediately, doffing their hats to the lady.

"I'm Mrs. Brennerman, John Bren....."

"Oh yes, I thought I recognized you. Sorry I couldn't place the face, Mrs. Brennerman. How is John?"

"Fine. Working the calves today." He quickly dispatched each boy to the necessary errands the list produced. They took off like shots.

"How's that place of yours coming along?

"Well, actually, we hope to add onto the house in the fall, after harvest."

The boys were quickly filling the wagon and coming back into the store for more.

"Well, you come see me when you get ready, as I've contracted with a new lumber supplier-good quality, straight boards-no knots."

"We'll do that."

"That'll be $37.18 Mrs. Brennerman."

"I can give you $25, but I have more errands to run. Can I put the rest on credit?

"Absolutely. John paid off the bill last time he was in. Your credit is just fine with me. I'll get you a receipt." And he turned to the counter and pushed several long fingered keys, and the cash drawer slid noisily out to him.

She finished her errands by noon and picked up a newspaper: The Denver Post. She thought, that'll be a treat for John.

Now fully loaded, the wagon pitched more, its springs hard bent under the weight. The horses looked back at her as if inquiring if there was any more to be hauled.

"That's it. Let's head for home." She coaxed them, with a flick of the reigns and they pulled a wide U-turn on Main Street and headed back through town.

Once out of town, she reached under her bench seat and moved the rifle aside to grab a lunch basket of dried fruit, jerky and water from a canteen. The horses plodded along, knowing the way and needing no guidance or encouragement.

She let them plod at their own pace, slowly watching the land pass by, noting some deer and a mix of antelope grazing. The occasional willow trees marked a springy area, the occasional oak or locust dotted the mostly barren landscape. It was fresh, open, and theirs.

After an hour or so she turned onto the valley road. It had not been named and didn't need one. Everyone knew it and it was the only way to access their property and the few other small holdings that the Platt River Ranch didn't already own.

———

At lunch, John had just finished eating when he stood up to put his plate in the sink. Outside the window a shadow shifted on the ground and then was gone. His demeanor changed instantly, though neither panic nor indecision was in him. Without hesitation, he took two steps toward the gun cabinet, put his army issued Colt .44

revolver in his pants and loaded the double barrel shotgun. He kept against the wall and peered through each window as he edged alongside it. There it was again. The hair on his neck stood up as the shadow fleeted by. He listened intensely, hearing the soft crushing of dirt beneath a boot. Now stillness. Silence. A small gap in the siding near the corner had always let a razor thin line of light shine across their bed. It went dark, then lit up the bed again. He pulled back both hammers on the shotgun. Taking two steps he flung the door open, shoving the shotgun around the corner without exposing himself, and pulled the first trigger. The gun nearly ripped his arms off from that angle as he heard a scream and someone hitting the porch decking hard. He rolled through the doorway looking in the other direction. Voices were yelling and he heard someone running behind the cabin. He went left, around the front porch and down the side of the cabin. A man lay dead, with much of his face missing. He was moving quickly, around the next corner of the cabin when a man stood at arm's length-wide eyed, a pistol in his hand. Shock. His finger squeezed the trigger, but the shotgun muzzle was already parked in his gut point blank. John pulled hard on the second trigger without hesitation. The body kicked violently backward one boot on the ground, the other cart-wheeled in the air, as the handgun discharged without effect. John crouched low against the building and reloaded. Adrenaline now raced through his body. In the barn a Henry rifle sighted in on the corner that he would be coming around and waited patiently.

John listened hard, trying to hear past the blood coursing into his brain and the shots having blasted his ears. People don't realise how hearing in a gun fight is impaired. Worse, vision can become narrowly focused. His experience in the war taught him to expect this and his training kicked in. He noticed four horses tied up beyond the walnut tree up toward the big spring. Two more, he thought. As he edged to the corner, a shot fired and the corner lumber on the cabin splintered above his head showering his eyes with debris. He fell back to safety and cleared his eyes. It had come from the barn and he definitely had the wrong guns. Too far to be any- thing but luck for a handgun, and the shotgun was near the end of its killing limit. No way to get into the house for a rifle without becoming a sitting duck. Where the hell was the other guy? He scampered back around the rear of the house and looked at the man he had shot a minute ago. Most of the lower torso was missing. Incred- ibly, he was still alive, but not breathing. He had almost nothing below his ribs, which stuck out. This man looked at his ribs as if someone else's, then died. John quickly moved up the hill using the cabin as cover from the barn shooter. Where the hell was the other one, he thought? Two down, two to go.

———

Mel could not hear the gunfire, still seven miles away and upwind. She was feeling beautiful, as all in her world was right. It was a stunning day, brilliant blue sky, a breeze that slightly cooled to the perfect warmth of the sun. She felt her stomach and smiled inside. How wonderful to have John's child.

For several years they had tried, and she had begun those fearful thoughts that can bring any woman to despair. Fears of barrenness, of emptiness and failure to her husband. Self-doubt had crept in. But now all was wonderful. She looked to the sky and thought that she could feel God touching and blessing her. Her fears, now removed. Life beginning to finally come together. The last two years of John's enlistment in the Union Army were so difficult. His letters were all she lived for.

His company had chased General Lee all the way to Appomaddox. He was camped on the huge field outside the courthouse when America's most bloody war came to a close and the armistice signed. After his discharge, he made it home ahead of his letter. She had been glued to the window beside the front door of her parents' house, waiting. How awful that waiting was. Every day he did not walk up the pathway from the gate or no letter arrived was pure hell. It turned her stomach, until she learned to contain that debilitating dread. She sat there, as every day, watching the passers by. Each day more men in uniform filled the street. Then the day she had waited for. Her day. Their day. The street was full of men coming home. He carried a small duffle, no rifle, just his sidearm, a regulation Colt 44. He had hardly closed the white picket gate behind him when she flung open the front doors, the tears pouring down her face-unable to speak. He dropped his duffle and outstretched his arms. God, she was more beautiful than he remembered. She ran to him, gliding off the porch. She just shook-quaking in his arms. He, kissing her over and over as if wiping all the fear and dread away with his lips. He tasted the salt of her tears and held her for a long time.

The horses ambled along. They would be home well before dark-no problem. She pictured him in her mind, and as a soft breeze blew by, she thought she caught a wiff of his smell, John's smell; the unique scent of him that left her surrounded in her own love for him. She threw her head back and laughed. She shook the reigns to spur the horses a little faster than their plodding pace.

––––––

The tree he took cover behind pitched bark and splinters as several shots hit the trunk simultaneously. He quickly glanced. Rifles from each corner of the cabin flashed as he jerked back. The tree was thick but barely large enough to protect him, given the angles of the shooters, each at about forty-five degrees to his cover. He knew that if they both came at him, he would likely lose. He might get one but not both, coming from such angles. Two more, then three and four shots hit the tree. He swung the shotgun and blasted both barrels into the right corner of the house. The men yelled at each other, taking cover. John slithered up to his feet, behind the tree and reloaded. He charged toward the left corner-bringing himself in very close to the building on a dead run. As he traversed the apex of the angle of the building, his enemy came into view. He had just reloaded. John saw the muzzle flash as his shotgun rang out. He fell down. What the hell happened, he thought. Had he tripped? The man he shot had blown back into the boards of the house and crumpled to the ground. Another shot rang out and he felt an intense pain in his back. He looked down and his right femoral artery pumped blood a foot into the air. My God, he thought, I can't move. He had been shot in the back, the bullet ripping into his spine at the top of the lumbar vertebra. His arms were crawling to his gun, dragging his body, quickly bleeding out. Don't lose consciousness he thought. Then he stopped and grabbed the pistol in his belt and rolled over. The man came at him crouching, his rifle raised. Another shot and John felt it in his lungs, the taste of black powder smoke filled his mouth and he exhaled a gasp of smoke and oxygenated blood. The froth dripped down his chin. His head slumped to the dirt and he stared into the ground before him. He heard the sound of the Henry rifle cycling another round into the chamber.

"Mel! He gasped into the dirt. Oh God Mel, I'm so sorry. I love you". The final shot ended his last thought of her.

Quickly the lone cowboy, pulled the bodies into the house and torched it. He set fire to the barn and stringing the horses of his men behind his own, headed off uphill to the open country behind. As he crested a saddle about a mile away, he turned and watched the black smoke rise in a wayward column against the blue sky.

————

Mel was lost in her thoughts of the coming child, when she saw the smoke from far away. She still couldn't see the cabin, but it was coming from their place. It had to be theirs. There was nothing else near it. She snapped the reigns and the horses knew to give it all. They took off. She drove them to a lather but long before she got there, she could see the cabin and barn were gone, coming up the valley road. Desperately she looked for movement. Oh John, she cried to herself.

"Oh God, please don't let there be anything wrong with him." Nothing. Damn it, nothing but the animals in the pasture, the horses out of the barn stood by, waiting for her return, it seemed. As she turned up the road, her horses were played out with the heavy load. Up the hill they trudged, no amount of whipping could spur them faster. It seemed they went so slow. Her heart raced. All the buildings were on the ground now smouldering. The rock work foundation on the house remained and there was the rubble within its small confines. Up the hill the horses pulled, but it was slow, as her eyes raced to and fro down to the pasture, up to the spring, searching the ground, the big walnut tree. Where was John?

She jumped down in the yard and ran in several directions, this way then that. Then her eyes stared into the cabin rubble. She walked slowly toward the smouldering foundation and smoking heap, her hand over her mouth, as she saw the mere corners and edges of the remnants of the things that had been a part of her life that morning; a frame, part of a chair, a frying pan in the dirt.

Something was unidentifiably out of place. Then her mind grasped what she saw. She walked forward into hot debris and saw the remains of four bodies. Her brain reeled but without traction to reality as she looked. Was one of these John? Who were these people? Why were they in the house? My God! my God! What has happened? As if clubbed, she bent violently at the waste and vomited everything in her. There were no tears, as the shock precluded any emotion. She wiped her mouth and looked back upon the four corpses, now just charred remains of humans in fixed repose. One man had separated in half, and another was missing a skeletal shoulder. A slightly larger man, was missing part of his head. Her eyes gazed upon the last, a man intact. She looked down at his feet and saw the smoking boots, or what was left of them. On one boot lay the brass grommets of John Brennerman's boots. One clinged hopelessly to the leather, the others in a neat row in the dirt.

Oh God no!" she cried and fell backward, staggering out of the rubble collapsing onto the ground. "No, no, no no, no," she cried. For a time she went insane, as the animals looked away, somehow sensing her pain. She fell to the ground and heaved up bile as tears streamed down her face.

As the shock took hold, the brain had seen all it could bear, she collapsed into a catatonic sleep, as the last wisps of smoke were carried on the breeze of the plains. The dress between her legs filled with blood as the last vestiges of John and Melissa Brennerman's hopes and dreams slipped away.

She awoke near dark and barely survived the ride back to town. Several weeks in recovery would heal the physical health issues, the loss of blood. The emotional scarring was deeper. She was a broken person, an angry woman. Left unable to care for the place, the livestock sold together with the land to Malcolm Everett.

Sandeen had returned and apologetically offered $20 per acre and $2,500 for the livestock.

"Done" was all she said.

"I'm so sorry" he said, and he meant it.

The Sheriff opened an investigation, but they had no clues, or didn't say what they were, if they had any. People talked, but no one knew.

She left for Denver and tried to start a new life, but she was barely functional, hardly able to concentrate, and subject to the spontaneous crying that she simply could not stop. After several months in Denver, one day, a letter arrived, without return address, from Scotts Bluff. It simply stated that Malcolm Everett had ordered his men to burn them out and was responsible. There was no proof offered and it was unsigned and without distinguishing marks. She had suspected it all along and was near certain. Now she believed.

Anger and loathing as she had never known welled up in her and revenge became her only friend and confidant. She began to plan. There would be repayment. John Brennerman would not be murdered and then no one found guilty. Everett's lost men were said to have gone to Montana seeking better employment. Some said criminals passed through. Some said Indians. There was no proof, and worse, it seemed not to matter to the Sheriff. There was little investigation, and what had begun stopped when she left for Denver.

Months Later

On the back stairs to the Ogallala Hotel and Saloon, the shapely mistress quietly climbed, followed by the heavy bootfall on the board steps of the man behind her.

"First door on the left, my lady." he said brightly, considering his prospects. It was his customary room, prepaid and held aside for him. Later, one of whores would come back, if he did not show himself in the saloon in due time. She turned and walked through the door. He followed and closed it behind him, throwing the latch.

With feigned spring in his step, he crossed the room and set the bottle on the table and drew two glasses from a cupboard. He took off his coat and gun belt. Melissa Brennerman, carefully removed the hat that had shaded her face under the lantern and stared at Everett, a thin smile pasted on her lips.

"How 'bout a drink, to take some of the nip out of the air?"

"Yes, I'd like that." He poured a healthy shot into each tumbler, and offered one to her.

"Cheers" Their glasses clinked cordially. He swallowed hard. She sipped and set it down.

"Let me acquaint you. I'm Malcolm Everett, but you just call me Mac. I own a goodly sized spread east and south of here; called the Platte River Ranch. You may have heard of it." She nodded in the affirmative and smiled pleasantly. "Well......... we run some cows and a little horse flesh. It's a good operation. My wife and I built it up over the years, may she rest in peace. Wonderful woman, but I've been alone now for nigh on four years. It's terrible to lose someone you love."

"Yes, it is."

He took another gulp and poured his glass. He clinched his jaw and exhaled hard as the slug of whiskey hit home.

"I must say, you are a pretty thing, now that I can see you. What's your name?"

As she had planned. "Anita. I'm new; just been here a few days. I'm on the Oregon Trail headed back east."

"Oh, you been to Oregon.... California, then?" he inquired.

"Never made it past Utah. Ran into money problems. Besides, its hard on a single woman in that country. I've made my mind up to go back to Kansas City, and find me a city man."

"No question about it," he agreed with her. "It's a tough life out there. A beautiful woman such as yourself should be taken care of, protected and provided for. There are a lot of bad folk out there and they pay no mind about the finer gender of mankind." He paused. "Excuse me," he stood up and went into the water closet. She quickly poured the drink into a spittoon on the floor a few feet away and returned to her chair. She eyed the gun hanging on the post of the bed. She felt her thigh and the knife and the leather strap that held it in place. She heard him use the chamber pot, then clear his throat and spit, as old men do. He returned, looking at her and saw her beauty, the strong features of her face, rather thickish eyebrows, intense brown eyes and the brunette hair pulled up behind her head. The slender nose and thin lips gave her a character that spoke of an athletic, if not significant, woman. He was increasingly certain, this was no prostitute. He cocked his head as if to understand who was really before him. He'd had many women, and in this very room-his room. Unable to quite put it to rest, he felt she was someone more and that the story she told was undoubtedly not true. He grunted to himself, as the alcohol took hold. "What matter," he thought. "I will bed her and the truth...? What do I care?" The certainty of his thought produced a crude impulse in his loins. He eyed her empty glass.

"Let me fill that for you". He poured both glasses heavily, as he stood before her. They clinked glasses again in the facade of a toast. He drank hard. She sipped and set the glass on the small round table.

She undid the buttons of her velvet jacket and he saw her chest heave under the white lace of her blouse. He looked into her face. All pretense ceased. He unzipped himself standing before her. She collected her thoughts, knowing this or some moment like this would come. She forced a smile and stifled the utter hatred for him filling her mind. Was this the moment? She rose standing next to him. No. She needed him more vulnerable and her less so. His eyes blazed as she said, "Let me get undressed". They both began to undress, quickly throwing the clothes across the backs of the chairs. Now, he was naked and lying on the bed, partially covered by the blankets. Her mind raced as removing her undergarments would quickly reveal the 7 inch knife, strapped to her thigh. She had skinned deer, delivered animals, and trimmed a lot of beef with that knife.

"Mac, would you turn out the lamp?"

"You're awful shy lady, Miss Anita."

"I haven't done this before..... not like this," she said as if a confession quietly to him. This only excited him more. He reached over to the bed stand and submerged the wick into the base and the room went dark except for the ambient moonlight from the windows.

She pulled down her petticoat and in the darkness felt the handle of the knife. The strap still tight on her thigh.

"Now be gentle with me," she said. This disarmed him as he realized this is no whore. This is a woman in desperate straights doing what women have always done in such a state.

"I'll be gentle.......... yet firm," he sneered in the dark. She walked to the bed and could make out his shape. He was leaning up on one elbow holding the blanket open for her. The knife in her hand was concealed at her right hip, her grip intense as her left knee pressed down onto the mattress. Was this the moment she had waited for, that she had thought about, dreamed about, for months? Was it now? Was it now? Her brained screamed the question. She breathed in deeply as his hand threw the blankets over her legs. No. Not yet, she thought as she slid the knife under the pillow and laid down beside him. Instantly his hands were upon her, groping. It was all she could do to restrain herself.

He rolled on top, smelling of body odor and whiskey. His stench was reviling to her. Her hatred was uncontainable as she detested him and herself for what she was doing. She could feel him now between her legs, his arousal complete. He came down hard on her lips and kissed her crudely. Without thinking, her hand came out from the pillow and aimed for the middle of his back, directly at the spine. She punched the shank through him, toward herself with all her might. Her strong sinewy arms driving the blade through to the handle. It would pass through the spinal column severing the nerves to both legs, as he jolted into a frozen posture. She felt spittle or blood drip onto her face. Frenzied, she shook the handle and shoved it back and forth, then up and down. The spine popped and the arms collapsed, he laying on top of her. Frantic, she pushed on him and clambered out from beneath him. The knife still in him. Was he dead? The dark shape lay still. Quickly she made her way around the bed and her fingers fumbling with the match, lit the lamp. His back was to her, the handle protruding from the middle of his spine. There was surprisingly little blood. She grasped the handle and pulled it, but it emerged only grudgingly. His whole body jerked spasmodically as the knife gave way.

She circled the bed and looked at him. A look of astonishment and confusion gripped his face. His eyes staring at her, questioning. Of his own weight, he rolled slowly onto his back making quiet gasps, his features frozen. His limbs useless. She regained her mind after that moment of frenzy in the dark and now looked upon the man who had destroyed her love, her hope, her joy, her baby, indeed her life. Now somewhat settled, she walked over to him, the knife in her hand and got on her knees on the bed over him.

"Do you hear me?" she whispered to him. He didn't move, but she perceived the slight reaction in his eyes and brow.

"Good". I'm going to take from you what you took from me-everything. His brow and eyes looked more confused than ever and evoked desperation. This is for John Brennerman,.... my husband. You murdered him. I'm going to murder you."

In his eyes he attempted to struggle, but nothing was connected. She could see him mentally acting, crushing her, striking her in flight or fight mode, but the arms lay limp, the legs only trembling their last sensations. He was bleeding to death internally. "So I'm sending you to hell, you bastard." She put one hand over his mouth and pinched his nose shut. The eyes bulged, frantic in the comprehension of his own death. She straddled him on her knees, staring down into his eyes. Bending down close to him, her anger seethed out through words she could not control or recount and poured them into his face. He stared back understanding this was the end.

"Mr. Everett!" called a voice and a rapping at the door. "Mr. Everett are you in there?" Mel glanced at the door and saw the shadows of feet at the threshold. She froze for a moment. It was one of the whores, coming to see if tonight it might be her turn. Quickly, Mel rocked the bed softly, the springs began to creak and she moaned in soft but exaggerated tones. The head rail began to softly tap the wall. The woman listening at the door turned at the rhythmic creaking of the bedsprings and sneered to herself, walking away.

Now she turned her attention back to him, whose eyes were in total panic, complete fright, then a flickering of the eyelids and jerking of the torso. She stayed on him through his struggle, soon feeling the life ebb from beneath her hands. He lay naked, spread-eagle on the bed, the horrific stare on his face.

Quickly she toppled off of him and dressed. In minutes she was complete. She turned and looked at the body in the bed. The knife! Where was the knife? She flew to the bed and rifled the blankets and the knife tumbled out. She put it back in its sling and headed for the door. Slowly, she cracked the door open and listened to hallway noises. The piano was raucous downstairs, men traded taunts loudly, across the bar room. Glasses clanked followed by an eruption of cajoling and catcalls. There were no steps in the hallway. She stuck her head out slightly. Assured the hall was empty, she turned and locked the door with the key and took a few paces. Then outside on the back landing she checked the alleyway. Several drunk men hung onto each other two doors down. There was Mac Everett's horse. She looked the other way. Nothing. Quietly she tiptoed down the stairs and onto the dirt, skirting the buildings in the shadows. A block away, on the fringe of town, she came to her own horse tied to a tree. She mounted and turned the horse towards Wyoming and dug her heels into its flanks.

CHAPTER 2

There was no sleep that night. She had ridden west into a cold night with a three-quarter moon. An early snow left a sprinkle on the road, illuminating the wheel ruts, as two black parallel lines in the moonlight. She stayed on the main road, riding all night and the next day toward Fort Laramie. She camped the following night-exhausted. Afraid to make a fire for fear of the highwaymen that were known to prowl for vulnerable travellers, she distanced herself from the road by half a mile and bedded down. Provisions were slim; jerky and bread, but it was going stale. Water was plentiful, but the late Fall nights were cold, and without a fire, she was near frozen by morning. She slept with a Colt 1849, no lady's pistol, but small enough to fit her hand well. It packed cross-draw on her left hip. She was a good shot with pistol or rifle, but the gun was new to her. The Winchester 1866 rifle was slung on the saddle, the same rifle with her in the wagon the day her life went up in smoke. No belongings. Everything had been sold except what was on that horse. Her funds had been deposited in the United States Bank at Denver. She carried five hundred dollars, a handsome sum, disbursed between the saddle, the gear and the undergarments she wore. The knife was packed in the saddle bags-handy like.

She was exhausted emotionally and physically, having lacked a decent night's sleep for two days as she rode into Laramie.

Finally, she fell into a deep sleep, exhausted and spent. Cold and huddled in her blanket, she descended more deeply. She had been tormented for months now. It was worse at night -in the dark. The visions and dreams came to her. They oppressed her, body and spirit. Over and over again she was running to and fro searching for her beloved John. Then she would see them; the four charred bodies sitting at the table as if engaged in some parlor game. Then the other segments of this bifurcated dream came into focus with her suddenly mounted on top of Malcolm Everett. His bulging, frantic eyes, pleading with her. The gasping and drooling spittle bespeaking the frenzied brain realizing his impending death, as she suffocated him and waited. Waiting, finally the squirming struggle for life had left him. She could not hear in her mind, nor remember the words she spoke into his waning visage. But it seemed not her, but an evil thing possessing her. Coursing through her, it only used her tongue to speak. Then she would awaken, drenched in sweat.

A few miles out of town the debris started by the side of the road. The weary and overladen dreamers on the trail had begun to discard their belongings, having failed to provision themselves with what they needed. Instead, they had brought what they had. Now stood an upright piano here, and dining set there. A little further, a roll top desk and art work. Unnecessary things. Foolish things, all quickly turning to firewood in the elements. No doubt their former owners had ideas of coming back for them; a temporary and inappropriate end to what adorned their houses in the east. But the traders of Laramie were no fools. The price of the right goods; food, lamp oil, guns, ammunition, oxen and proper clothes were dear-very dear. Every tradesmen had already bartered for pianos, furniture, art and the like. They were worthless. Good furniture-warehouses and sheds being full, was dumped on the side of the road. Here, many decided to turn back, before they approached the Rockies or the Wasatch Mountains.

The horse was tired and hung its head, overworked and underfed. Her mind set, she would sell the horse and book passage, if she could find a wagon train going west.

Given the season upon them, she hoped to find one taking a more southern route, though all would be bad as the winter approached. Mountain passes were on nearly every route and it just depended on weather and guts, or stupidity of the trail boss as to their attempted crossing.

The California and Oregon Trails followed the same track through Wyoming from Laramie to just east of Fort Bridger near the Green River. There, several alternative routes were available: The Oregon Trail by several variations travelled west, while the California trail tracked southward to Salt Lake City, the Mormon capital. From there, across the great Salt lake and Nevada. It looked increasingly doubtful to make it over the Donner Pass to Sacramento before Spring. But maybe.

She rode in and inquired at the Land Office of availability on wagon trains.

"There's two trains in town, m'am, well they're out of town, about a quarter mile south. You'd have to check with each trail boss. There's so many folks dropping out, others taking up their places, I can't keep track of it m'am. Have you got a wagon?"

"No. Only a horse."

"Well now I don't mean to be disrespectful m'am, but that is not gonna cut it. If there is a place in a wagon with some family or other, you'd be obliged to pay them above what the wagon train wants for service."

"I see. Do you have any idea what it would cost?"

"Cost to where?"

"California. Sacramento to be exact."

"Oh, you gonna go find yourself a rich miner, eh?"

Mel smiled indulgently. "Do you know the cost, sir?"

"Not really, but I've heard rumours of $400-$500."

"That's a dear price to pay."

"Not as dear as those who've tried on their own."

"Yes, I'm sure that's true. Well, thank you much for the information."

"Good luck, miss."

Mel rode south out of town toward the two encampments of wagon trains. As she approached she could smell the meals being cooked on several fires, in both camps. Her stomach reflexively began to growl. She suddenly realised she was famished as the smell of fresh baked bread passed her nose. A boy fetching water in a pail by the creek which bisected both camps, walked before her, lost in his own thoughts.

"Excuse me young man."

He looked up startled.

"Yes, m'am."

"Do you belong to one of those wagon trains?"

"Yes m'am."

"And which one would that be?"

"That one." He pointed to a circle of wagons with appended wagons to the outskirts, perhaps fifteen in all. The other camp was larger, maybe 20-22 wagons.

"Who is the boss of that train?"

"Mr. Butch Jones."

"And when is your train departing?"

"Day after tomorrow."

While the boy wasn't much for words, he was certainly of a helpful spirit and confident in every answer.

"You are a most helpful young man. I just wonder if there is any room in the wagon train for another person?"

"You gotta' wagon, m'am?"

"No. Just a horse"

"Well then I reckon, no. But that wouldn't be my decision. You could ask Mr. Jones."

"And which one is he," as she spied the conglomeration of wagons and milling people darting in and about them.

"That's him m'am, over there greasing that axle for the Spencer family."

"Thank you, young man."

He squinted up into the sun behind her as she rode past, making a straight path to Jones. Dismounted, she walked toward the two well worn boots sticking out from under a Conestoga.

"Shit!" Came an exclamation. "Well you low down, no good, sonofa......" Mel cleared her throat. All paused. Then the boots clambered and the body wriggled like a turtle trying to right itself. A middle aged man, grey-wiskered, with grease up to his wrists rose to his feet. His sweat weathered hat apparently affixed to his skull.

"Yes m'am, can I help you?"

"You are Mr. Jones?"

"Yes."

"I seek passage on your wagon train, sir."

"You alone?"

"Yes."

"Gotta wagon?"

"No. Just a horse." She was becoming exasperated at this singular question.

"How much money do you have?"

"How much do I need?"

"Where you goin'?"

"Sacramento."

"Five hundred dollars."

"Three hundred."

"I said five."

"Three and my horse. And I can cook, mend, doctor and shoot, not necessarily in that order."

He looked long at her, up and down and into her eyes.

"That horse isn't worth but a hundred and fifty."

"Is it a deal?"

"It's a deal if you can find someone to ride with, Miss........

"Grady. Melissa Grady."

"What'll that cost?"

"Not my business." He started to walk away, wiping his hands-mucking off the grease. "Mr. Spencer, you're gonna' need a new axle. It might make it to Medicine Bow, but by South Fork, it'll be dust. I'd prefer you fixed it here instead of on the trail. I've greased it good, but its gonna' give way. Its just a matter of when.......... and where."

"Mr. Jones", interrupted Mel, "... just exactly what am I getting for my money?" He turned back to her.

"You're gettin' to Sacramento, but I ain't sayin' when." He left her standing beside the wagon as he made his way to the next, discussing preparations with the inhabitants.

Mel stood there in the presence of Henry Spencer, a sober but kind looking man. The clothes he wore were worn out clothes of a more elegant vocation. About fifty years old, his wife and two children were nestled in the wagon; a boy of 12 or so and a young girl of perhaps nine. She was pretty, but distrustful of any stranger. The boy was more curious.

They were each looking at the other. Mel felt herself as if a chattel on display. Indeed, she was being sized up. The trail ahead winnowed out the weak, the incompetent and the unlucky. Henry Spencer looked at her trying his best to see if she was any of those.

"M'am, I'd like to offer you a ride, but we're pretty full as you can plainly see."

"Yes, I can see that." She turned to walk away, unsure of what comes next. Perhaps the other wagon train.

As if reading her mind, "The other train is full up m'am—more than twenty wagons and only three trail hands." She stopped.

Spencer looked down, then at his wife, a somewhat sickly appearing woman who nodded prayerfully.

"M'am". She turned. "It would be rough, but if you could see your way to buy an axle and some food and supplies, maybe we could make a go of it. You'd have to sleep on the ground, but we'd share what we could. We're Christians and expect to be held to account. But this is a good time to turn around if you're having any doubts at all, Miss."

Mel turned to him and smiled.

"Let me see if I can get that axle. Have you got a list of supplies you need?"

He smiled back. Yes m'am,I do. That axle is a sixty-four incher, with three inch spindles."

"Let's see that list."

She saddled up and headed for the traders. Butch Jones, was enjoying the butt of a cigar several wagons down the line, but he saw that she was headed for him.

"Mr. Jones, I'll be with the Spencer wagon. We'll bring the axle along and extra provisions. I'm gonna' need this horse 'till we get to Sacramento. Its yours and another fifty dollars when we get there. I'll be back to settle the rest of our affairs this afternoon. He said nothing. Nodded and spit flecks of tobacco from his mouth.

She returned with the axle and supplies and paid Jones his due. The next day there was a bustle in the air, as everyone readied their gear, made last trips to town and mailed letters back east. Mel stowed gear, made closer acquaintance with the Spencers, including winning over both children. The spare axle was lashed to the sideboards of the wagon as the time for its replacement had come and gone.

The following day, the camp broke in the dark hours of morning and were an hour on the road when the sun filled the eastern sky and lit the canvas wagons in a halo of light.

The country was beautiful, the mountains dotted with only the most determined of conifers, moving downslope to forests of junipers with scattered pine. Fall colors lighted the stream corridors with hues of yellow, bright orange and dapples of red. The sage seemed fuller after Fall showers and cooler temperatures.

It was a mix of boredom when the road was good and incredible back breaking work when it was bad. In places washed out, they feared the axle wouldn't last. But it did. There were blessings and curses, hardships and laughter around the campfire at night. The trail hands often bantered and traded good natured insults with each other. This acted as something of comic relief for the train members, who never lost sight of the fact that their fate could be upon them any day.

At night, when all fell quiet and sleep came to the tired train, Melissa Grady tossed and turned fitfully. She had been tormented for months now. It was worse at night in the dark. The visions and dreams came to her, oppressing her; body and spirit. Over and over again she was running to and fro, searching for her beloved John. Then she would see them; the four charred corpses as if sitting at a table engaged in some parlor game. She felt herself shaking her head; "No! No!" Finally dispelling the horrid image, the next dream sequence began in what seemed an unconnected dream. It came into focus, with her straddling Malcolm Everett on the bed, in the upstairs room at the saloon. The frantic fear in his bulging eyes as she suffocated him, one hand over his gaping and drooling mouth. The other simply pinching off his nasal passages. He, in helpless paralysis. She could not hear nor remember the words she spoke into the desperate eyes, but it seemed an evil spirit possessed her. It was as if evil itself coursed through her and spoke through her tongue. She would then awaken in a drenching sweat. At once a feeling of relief that it was a dream, but quickly followed by the oppressive dread of a terrible truth.

The Spencers had become close friends, as only those who have been hurt or sick in close quarters with each other or having shared a treacherous path together can be. The children adored her. She helped with their reading and just spending time with them as Mrs. Spencer's health worsened and she rarely came out of the wagon. She taught both the kids to shoot, and the men remarked to themselves of her many attributes. Often Mel would ride her horse alongside the train along with the trail hands, whose respect she had earned.

On the morning of October 12th, the train ambled toward Rock Springs, where the Oregon and California Trails separated. The kids of the Spencer wagon were bored and decided to walk along the wagon as it slowly ascended a steep but small rise through a narrow ravine. The road passed through a particularly rocky section and the forward wagons churned up rocks and turned over others in a dusty and rattling procession. Henry Spencer was lucky as the axle had held. He would repair it tomorrow as the train planned on resting for a day at Rock Springs to let the animals graze. Jonny Spencer was throwing rocks at imaginary Indians as he walked along. Mrs. Spencer wasn't feeling well and lay in the wagon, while Henry held the reigns and Mel sat next to him, talking. Margaret Spencer had just turned ten years old the day before and they had made a small but adequate celebration. She had decided she nolonger wanted to be called Margaret. It was proclaimed that henceforth, all would call her Maggy. So far, they were doing terrible, each calling her Margaret then correcting to Maggy. She would set her hands upon her hips with a stern jaw and a squint in her eye, exasperated. This would make the trail hands practically fall out of the saddle, laughing. She was walking alongside the wagon, by Mel, twiddling with a pig tail and listening to her father talk. The wagon negotiated a tight turn to the right, when the right wheel climbed upon a jagged cobble sized rock and then slid off it. A sharp crack sounded followed by the quick sound of splintering wood. Instinctively Mel grabbed the bench as the wagon jostled for footing. In a flash, she was hurled forward and to her right, out of the wagon. Instantly she was on her feet spitting dust and grit from her teeth. The dust, having turned to a fine talc, formed a cloud at the front of the wagon. She ran back. As she looked down, Maggy lay pinned beneath the wheel. Her leg, with a compound fracture, stuck up through the spokes. And the wagon rested fully upon the wheel. She heard screams and men yelling. There was sudden commotion and men came running from the wagons as all halted. The axle had given way.

The hub of the wheel crushed her abdomen and the look of panic and shock was upon her. Mrs. Spencer clambered out the back of the wagon as Henry jumped to the ground. Immediately the men began to lift the wagon which sat on the wheel which was crushing the life out of the Spencer's little girl. At first it would not budge, and the women screamed louder. As more men came, they were able to lift the wagon and slowly Maggy was pulled out. Her leg gushed blood just below the knee where it made two right angles above the ankle. As Mel looked at the trail hands, she saw them look at each other in a look of sad resignation. But each man did what he could.

Butch came riding back and he dismounted on a dead run to them. Maggy was hyperventilating and going into shock. Mrs. Spencer was hysterical, and Henry could only hold her back hoping the men could do something for his precious daughter.

"We could dump everything out of the front wagon and get her to Rock Springs in a hurry," said Isaac Spoon, one of the hands. The trail was so narrow, no wagon could pass another.

Butch, thought quickly. "OK, lets do it." He reached his arm under Maggy to lift her, when she blurped a mouthful of blood onto her dress. Butch started to make his way to the front wagon about a hundred yards up the hill. Other men ran past him to clear it and make ready for a dash to Rock Springs. He covered the ground at the fastest walk possible.

"Now you just stay with me, darlin'. We're gonna take care of you," Butch implored. Her eyes full of fear searched his for the truth. She sobbed and whimpered. Her leg was mangled and bleeding profusely. They would have to tie a tourniquet at the front wagon. There was a good chance she would lose that leg and Butch knew it.

"Don't you fret, O'l Butch is gonna' get you to the doctor. You just hang in there with me, Honey."

Maggy's head started to sag backwards in his arms and her eyes began to roll. He was going as fast as he could. Up ahead, men threw the gear out of the front wagon to the side of the road and the Mulroonys, who owned it stood by in apprehension, seeing Butch coming. They all knew Maggy and loved her as their own. Isaac Spoon sat on the bench seat and looked back like a relay runner waiting for the baton, the reins in his grip. Frank White, another trail hand, took off like a shot on his horse to make sure the doctor was there and ready in Rock Springs. Butch finally came up to the wagon when Maggy's head snapped forward and she vomited blood to where it pooled in her dress and ran off onto Butch's vest. As he raised her into the wagon, she went limp. He gently set her down and listened to her little chest. He couldn't hear anything. He stood up to observe if she breathed. She was still. His face fell as he softly pulled back on her eyelid. The pupil was fixed and dilated. "Maggy!", he snapped. But she lay in the stillness of death. Butch hung his head as Isaac looked back through the wagon and realized Maggy Spencer had passed on. All their energy, so intense a moment before, now must dissipate and be replaced with despair. Butch looked down at her, and her face seemed like a little angel to him.

"I'm sorry little one. Forgive me." His throat clutched and the small facial muscles of his upper lip quivered under the large moustache. He wiped off her face with his kerchief.

Slowly he stepped out to the side of the wagon and looked back down the line. The Spencers were coming pell-mell with the other men. Then Mrs. Spencer's eyes met Butch's at twenty yards and she knew. His shirt covered in blood and the side of his head, where he listened for the heartbeat of the child. She collapsed as Henry tried to catch her.

The train held there for nearly two hours. People talked and spoke kind words of young Maggy. Jonny was stunned into silence and Mel just held him in her arms, rocking back and forth. Henry had no chance to even mourn as he was fully in despair as his wife apparently went insane. Some people gathered and said prayers. The gear was stowed back in the Mulroony wagon and the Spencer wagon was repaired in complete silence. At last, the train moved off out of the narrow ravine and cobbly road ascending to a new plateau. It was enough for the day. The men went about their chores in thoughtful silence. Camp was made and little Maggy Spencer was laid to rest by the trail. A small cross inscribed with her name and terminal dates was affixed. White and yellow wildflowers adorned the small mound of Wyoming dirt.

The next morning the train moved on. A week later, they left Evanston heading through the Wasatch Mountains to Salt Lake. Anna Spencer was alternately in catatonic depression or highly agitated and hysterical-screaming. When it was bad, Henry was forced to restrain her, binding her hand and foot while a rag silenced her wailing and screeching.

Butch Jones took Henry aside one night.

"Henry, I ..... I."

"I know, Mr. Jones. I'm not unaware of the effects of my wife on the train."

"Yes sir. That would be the problem. But I want you to know that........, that,..... Well I feel terrible for your loss and I..., I take responsibility." Here, Butch choked up a little, then cleared his throat. He looked square into Henry Spencer's eyes. His own, tearing up. His mouth working to find his words. I should have replaced that axle in Medicine Bow. This thing didn't need to happen."

Henry let the words rest on his mind for a moment and put his hand straight across to rest on Butch's shoulder.

"Mr. Jones, I thank you for your words and appreciate your sensibility, however, such things, in my view, are never solely the act or negligence of a single person. I accept this as an act that a merciful and loving God was willing to allow. I do not pretend to understand Him, and don't expect to. It is enough that His grace and mercy in my life are sufficient to bear me through this time of loss. I have a son. I need to attend to his upbringing. That is my aim. I've decided to leave the train at Salt Lake to care for Anna. I believe there will be help there for her."

"Yes, sir", said Butch. "Your a good man Mr. Spencer. I appreciate your understanding." He turned and walked off, wondering how a man so freshly cut by a loss such as his could still call God loving and merciful. He saw Henry as a stronger man than before. Stronger than himself.

Three days later, the train pulled in to the outskirts of Salt Lake, amid a bleak and cold winter scene. The land was cast in black and white and its starkness was chilling to the soul. The Spencers broke off from the train. While they rested for two days, taking on supplies and making repairs, word had come back that Anna Spencer had been committed to an asylum. Doctors held little hope for a recovery and told Henry Spencer to go on with his life. He did. He and Jonny rejoined them as the camp was breaking up.

Many were now virtually broke or had little funds left. They had provided their wagons as best they could for the push across the desert. At this point they tracked south to the Overland Trail through Nevada to the Sierras.

Mel showed her worth to the whole train, not just the Spencers. She set a broken arm, put in stitches, made rabbit stew to die for, including shooting the rabbit. She hunted when she could get time and produced one deer and one antelope. This was a big hit as anything new to the diet was welcome. Despair came often as breakdowns, sickness and accidents occurred. Every challenge was met by overpowering determination of the trail hands whose job it was to see these people through to the end. The emotions of the train ranged at every incident from despair at the outset, to ecstasy at the deliverance, with long patches of boredom and drudgery until the next event.

Though she was pleasant and joyful among the parties of the train, many came to realize she bore a burden of great weight. Though they never said anything to her, over the long trail, many of the hands and other parties had heard her incoherent pleadings in the night. The fitful sleep she often endured. First came the soft whimpers, as men turned away to sleep. Then repeating herself, protesting and pleading, thrashing about, then finally drawing herself upright in her bedroll looking around to see if she had disturbed the others. Partly out of fatigue and partly out of respect for her, their reposes feigned sleep. But they felt the tug that good men feel at the distress of a beautiful woman.

Sometimes, as she sat there drenched in one of these episodes, she would look up into the starry night sky-so dark, with stars like beacons burning into her eyes, she would taste the salty knot of tears in her throat and plead in a whisper; "God help me! God help me".

———

It seemed you could smell Butch Jones' nasty cigar at the back of the line. In a cold November morning about sixty miles out of Virginia City, Nevada, she rode up along side him as he had permitted her to do from time to time. The train's attitude was good, they were nearing the end of their journey, at least for awhile, it being too late to cross the Sierras. The group was tired and needed rest and temporary employment to replenish funds. If you still had any of the nice eastern furniture, here, it would bring a good price. But most of it had long departed, left as overt trail markers and testimony to a despairing mind.

"Looking for fresh company Miss Grady?"

"No. I'm looking to get ahead of that nasty plume of smoke from that wretched cigar."

"Surely you can find a breath of fresh air out here in all God's creation?" Indeed the sky was huge. He smiled at her, the reins easy in his hands.

"Mr. Jones, when you're upwind, you're *all* that's upwind." She smiled wryly.

"I just don't want folks to get lost" he looked over at her, with half a wink in his eye. Mel wouldn't let up.

"Butch, a blind man could find you in a feed lot." At this he laughed aloud. "Well, young lady, another day or two, and I'll be gettin' myself a bath and some barbering. Then we'll see. Maybe you would like to join me for dinner".

"I'll think about it." They rode along together for some time, remarking on the passing landscape, and sometimes in silence for long stretches. They enjoyed riding together.

"What will happen to the train in Virginia City?" She asked.

"Hard to say. We'll take a break. There's day work in the mines. Some will spend a few months and be ready to go in March or April when the pass opens. Some will stay and make their home. But if they've made it this far, most will never turn back. Their future is out there." He nodded to the west. The Sierra Nevada rose, imposing upon the clouds and sky, a monument to an unknown future.

Four days later, they pulled into Virginia City. The train camped outside town creating its own makeshift community. This, along with several other wagon trains too late to cross the Sierras. Labor contractors came through looking for able bodied men to work the silver mines. Soon, it was Christmas. Several found permanent housing in town, certainly much more comfortable. On the coldest of nights, train members were welcomed in, but the quarters were small. Mel took up quarters in a cheap rooming house in town and worked two restaurant jobs.

She checked on her funds and had them wired ahead to Sacramento after a withdrawal to help her get through the winter. Word came later that Mrs. Spencer died and they never knew why. She had sunk into the darkest of depressions and just seemed to run out of life. Mr. Spencer was offered a job as an interim pastor at a Baptist Church. The previous pastor had died young of pneumonia.

She decided to pay him a visit and found him deep in the study of the Scriptures as he prepared a sermon. He rose at the knock on his door and they hugged closely when their eyes met; like a father and daughter.

"Come in, come in," he beckoned.

"Its nice and cozy in here......... Er, do I call you Pastor or Reverend, or.... something else?" She had, of course, been to church as a young girl. It was a pleasant enough, if not too boring an experience. Her father, however, had his own theological program of "how it all works". Soon enough, he disagreed with his Pastor, and left for another church. He church-hopped for a season and then concluded it was not worth the effort. His children, including daughter number three, Melissa, concluded the same. So her response to things of faith or religion was a sort of skeptical friendliness.

"How about you call me Henry. And yes, the congregants have provided well my heating needs. Apparently wood is plentiful, as is the labor to cut and convey it to my door. I'm glad to see you Mel. I hear you're moving on in the spring."

"Yes, that's my plan". Henry, I wanted to stop by and tell you how sorry I was to hear about Mrs. Spencer. I was also wondering how Jonny was getting along."

"He suffers, as do I."

"Yes, of course. How foolish a question of me."

"No. Your inquiry shows the good heart that is in you, Melissa. I thank you for that. Jonny is in school and quickly made several friends. He misses his mother and sister." At this Henry Spencer's face tightened in obvious containment of grief and his eyes welled up. "And so do I. Yet we will both go on because that is what we must do. We are sustained in the strength of Christ and his suffering for our sins. If he can bear that........ then I can bear this."

She sighed. "I admire your strength, Henry".

"It's not mine, Melissa. Didn't you believe me? It is His strength that sustains me."

"Yes, I suppose. I mean, I understand that. But I just wanted to come over and visit and tell you before I leave in the spring, how grateful I am that you brought me into your wagon and your family, and I'm so sorry for the things that have happened to you." At this she, surprising herself, began to sob, thinking of young Maggy in Butch's arms, and her simple grave by the side of the road and those little yellow wildflowers.

"Mel, I'd like to invite you to church this Sunday. The preaching is expected to be lousy, but the pot-luck afterward is very likely to make up for it." He smiled.

"Thanks, but I'm just not a church person."

"I understand", he smiled again, nodding slowly in the affirmative. "Was there anything else I can do for you?" He looked directly into her eyes. It looked to her that in his eyes was the revelation of all her bad dreams. That somehow he knew her terrible secret. The truth of her sin. He, of course, had heard her in the nights. He waited in silence for her reply. For a moment she wanted to burst upon his shoulder and cry out for relief of her torment, for her terrible deed to be removed from history. But this she stifled.

"No. I know you're busy. You have a sermon to write." She put on her best smile. "I just wanted to thank you again for everything you did for me."

"You are welcome and you are always welcome in my home and in my church-church person or not." They hugged at the door and she stepped down onto the porch and onto the street.

"Mel", he called to her from the porch. She turned back to him.

"Yes?" As she held a smile for him, in his mind he raced through several things to say; about forgiveness, and about not letting whatever she carried 'eat her up', but it all sounded too preachy to his own inner ear. Holding her there, staring, he finally said, slowly and deliberately "God loves you, Mel." She acknowledged this with a small grin, a cursory nod and a wave goodbye. She turned and walked up the street.

By early February, the train seemed to be disintegrating socially. Butch Jones spent the winter in a boarding house, exchanging telegraphs back east, lining up the next wagon train. It seemed overland passage was changing. The stage coach was increasingly popular, though more expensive. It boasted an average of 70 miles per day. The wagon train sponsors were having trouble getting new subscribers for the next train. There was talk it might be the last. Butch sat in the hotel bar and thought; "Lord, this world is movin' faster and faster." Though people knew the railroad was to connect in Promontory Utah, estimated in another year or so, they could not comprehend the change this would bring.

At first the fares would be exorbitant and largely confined to the rich. But within months, as the rigors of trail life were compared to the ease and speed of railroad travel, the seats filled. As they did, the prices dropped and train cars were added. The prices dropped again. Soon the railroads were making money hand over fist. A chapter of American expansion was closing and a new one was beginning. For Butch Jones, he sensed an end to what he knew. He was feeling older than ever. Perhaps he should just quit the trail life he'd known. Virginia City was a pleasant place. Maybe he would be among those who stayed.

In late February, he rode out to the camp. It was a remnant. Two working wagons, the rest had been cannibalised or abandoned. The opportunities for ready work in town had caused many to give up on going further, at least for now. For several days he tracked down those he could find to see who would be finishing. After all, he 'owed' several of them all the way to Sacramento. Within a week, only three of the party was willing to go on to California when the pass opened. But one was too sick and another was splitting up due to marital problems. After checking with the sponsors, it was decided to rebate part of the costs to those who had an interest in going further. They made things right by each individual. Most were just happy to have survived and called themselves 'square' with Butch Jones. A week later, he received a telegraph message that the partnership had dissolved. Opportunities looked better in other investments. There was no need for him to return to St. Joseph Missouri, where it had begun. He was free to do as he pleased.

Mel had lived as cheaply as possible, saving her funds in the bank for land in northern California. This had been her plan all along. Butch Jones sat at her table one morning for breakfast and told her the options, as the train was now defunct. She delivered his steak and eggs, and poured his coffee in a fine china cup. It looked ridiculous in Butch's fat, calloused hands. Between her other customers, she found a minute to sit at his table.

"You don't owe me anything, Butch," she said. It's not that far and the trail is good, come spring."

"Well why don't you just keep that horse of yours and we'll call it good to here?" He forked a too large piece of steak under his walrus moustache and chewed in overt movements of his jaw. She smiled at him. "That's not necessary. You can have him, if that's 'right'."

"Frankly, he's pretty worn out. Kinda like me. I was hoping not to bother with him." This was not true, and they both knew it. The horse, older for the wear, certainly had life left. Butch figured he wouldn't need it and the gesture to Mel was worth it to him.

"What are you gonna do, Butch?"

"I got no job, no pressure. I got a little money I've saved. The company quit on me, but they were fair. And gimme a little severance. I'm thinking of that Napa country. Pleasant climate. Hear they're growing wine grapes there. Don't know much about wine, but there ought to be some work for an old hand. Good soil, plenty of water. I guess I don't really know."

"Damn it", he said quietly, as a piece of runny egg yoke fell off his fork into his lap, onto his best trousers.

"You never could eat at a table", she said, chiding him. He stabbed the errant egg particle and without a thought, buried it into the wide lips under the big moustache. She chuckled at him. "I've got customers," and she grabbed the coffee pot and made rounds.

Butch Jones, got up after paying his bill at the table. He was about to walk out the door, when Mel came through the kitchen partition and saw him. He turned and looked at her fondly. She walked up to him. "Goodbye Butch." He said nothing for a long moment. She instinctively rose up to hug him. He wrapped his big arms around her and squeezed. She held him for a still moment when her heart realised she had not touched a man like that in a long time. Feelings engulfed her and her face flushed. He set her weight back on her feet and looked at her again. "Goodbye Mel." He walked through the door and down the street.

She felt empty and more alone. She cleared several tables and finally Butch's.

In the spring, the trail had opened, and the slow migration of people lifted like a tide and moved west. Again the road was full of travellers. The high country of the Sierras took her breath away.

She was like a child as she watched the stunning forests, heavy laden with snow-like a winter dreamland pass by. In one moment she could see only an ice wall, then suddenly a hundred and fifty miles out across the forests of the Sierras to the San Joaquin Valley below, and this magical place called California. She was finally here. The immensity of space, the sugar-like sparkle of the crystallised snow on the branches of the tallest trees she had ever seen, left her mesmerised.

Never had her eyes seen such space, such grandeur. Never had her mind realised a world so full of nature. It seemed the trip across the plains was a vast expanse, but it was largely empty. It was a scenery devoid of much that mattered. Now it seemed the landscape was full. It was a stark contrast to the emptiness she felt inside herself. She quietly said a prayer to God. She felt so alone in so vast a place. She spent a night in Placerville and continued on the next morning.

CHAPTER 3

Sacramento, California

The snow of the Sierra high country gave way to the foothills with its vast forest of Digger Pine, a scrub conifer which
extends downward in elevations to the oak woodlands.
These, in turn, overlooked the rolling hills which grace the
rim of the huge valley of the San Joaquin. This is the geo-
graphical interior of the central state. From Bakersfield
and the Tejon Pass of southern California, northward to
the ascension of the Klamath Mountains above Redding,
is one of the great fertile valleys of the world. Rimmed by
the coastal range to the west, the mighty Sierras to the
east, the Tehachapis on the south and a mix of Klamath
and Cascade Mountains on the north.

Science and geology tell us that the earth's mantel, its
thin skin, floats on a softer, hotter core of magma. This skin is
comprised of plates, broken and moving alongside of and
against each other. Nearly imperceptible except within
geologic time, or an earthquake, these tectonic plates
are responsible for much of the earth's surface features.
When two plates collide such as the Pacific plate and
the North American Continental plate, one plate dives
beneath the other in a subduction zone. As the relentless
and massive pressure continue, mountains are thrust up
along the line of collision. The breaking, compressing and
thrusting in slow motion of mass on an astrophysical scale,

has no parallel on the planet. If the pressure and movement of these massive sections of the Earth's surface pulse in its energy, it could produce a mountain range, a valley, then another mountain range, like the heaped impurities in a boiling pot.

The creationist refers to Genesis to recall the work of the Creator in establishing His firmament. That the Biblical Flood and the receding waters of its aftermath are responsible for much of the features of the Earth's surface.

The aboriginal man says only that 'it is'. He recognizes a creator as well as the forces by which He works.

The three take increasingly less explanation, inverse to their spiritual connection to it.

As Mel's horse walked along the road descending into the Folsom area, she was amazed at the activity. Roads ribboned this way and that over the rolling hills. In the distance was the Sacramento River in the center of the valley, with settlements growing like urchin along its banks. There were wagons and horses on the road and bustling talk of gold and commerce, opportunity in El Dorado County. She heard the steam whistle of the short line from Sacramento to Folsom.

It seemed the pace of the world was faster here and there was the compulsion to hurry, as if your future destiny was around the next corner; waiting in the next town for your arrival. In two days she arrived along the banks of the Sacramento River, in the city of the state capitol. The bustle was infectious and it made her want to hurry to her own future and get away from her past and the dark pall that cloaked it when she recalled it. To leave her past far behind, forgetting its terrible truth, she sought out the train schedules at the depot, for the trains heading north. Keep moving forward was her only thought. She was disappointed to find that the track was still being constructed. She could go by barge up the river, or stage or horseback. She elected horseback.

The climate was delightful, seeming a month further into the year than just a few days earlier, crossing the Sierras. The horse, buggy and wagon traffic was heavy going north. She rode with several groups consisting of families. Most were from San Francisco and told her of one of the most beautiful places in the world, Berryvale, at the base of Mt. Shasta. On her third day, she awoke in the town of Willows and started northward again. At about noon, the morning haze had lifted sufficiently off the valley floor. Like a chimera, she strained to see what appeared a distant snow capped mountain, far away. At first it seemed an illusion hanging in the air. Perhaps, an unusual cloud formation, she thought. Within the hour, it was crystal clear-the most magnificent mountain she had ever seen. It was magical, as the travelers from San Francisco had said. They were heading up to a cabin on the upper Sacramento River. A little place they liked to call Sweetbriar.

At Redding, she rested for two days, bathing and relaxing before her ascent back up into the mountains. This time, the Cascade Range, but first she would trek through the lower Klamath Mountains. These, mere foothills to the mountain that loomed before her everyday from her hotel room window-Mt. Shasta. There was still snow on the ground in late spring, in Berryvale this year, reports had said.

Well-provisioned, and having bought new boots, a woolen skirt and leather vest, she packed a mule behind her horse and started up the trail alongside the Sacramento River toward its headwaters and that ever-looming white peak, which consumed her northern horizon. The waters of the river quickly narrowed and became loud as the earliest spring runoff was now in the river. Tumult, and white water were frequent descriptions as she advanced ever upward. The broad expanses of the Sacramento Valley, lying between its namesake and Redding, fell behind to what was now an ever changing canyon before her.

The vegetation now virgin timber. Ferns began to peak from the trunks near the river's edge. On her first day up the canyon she had seen a bull elk, two cinnamon colored bears, a bobcat and too many deer to count. Fish were jumping in the river. She stopped to talk with a family of anglers who told her this was some of the best fishing in the land. There were trout of several varieties, salmon and steelhead. They fought hard and tasted even better.

As her first day in the canyon came to a close, she camped, as she often did, by herself. The long shadows quickly engulfed the river and canyon into an early twilight. Her rifle was handy and her pistol nearly at hand. Yet, she felt at ease. She felt as if approaching a destination of great excitement but also rest. It must be what heaven is like, she thought, as she watched the day turn to night from a large rock overlooking the river. The last light of day, glimmering on the waters. For a moment she thought of the Big Spring in Scotts Bluff, and the water cascading down through her and John's land. She wept to herself.

Near the end of the second day, she was completely charmed by the continuing explosion of flora and fauna in the canyon. Wildflowers bloomed in the well watered, nearly misty environment, never far was the crushing sound of the upper Sacramento. As each day passed, the spring melt in the high country fed the river and it grew more rambunctious. Sometimes she would stop and hear the unmistakable sound of large granite boulders being rolled down the river bed, crushing and jostling the smaller cobble in their path. As she approached the small settlement of Crag View, she yet again gaped at the site of shear granite and limestone cliffs, rising 3,000 feet above the river, only a mile or so away. The shear vertical walls sprung from the virgin forests 1,500 feet below. The geological anomaly was called Castle Crags. Years later, it would become a park and monument. But this day, it was a holy gate to a land she had dreamed of and was now at its door.

The next morning she rode into the river hamlet of Shasta Springs, a glorious waterfall already gaining a reputation for its restorative properties. Here, entrepreneurs were building a resort. The sound of saws and hammers, and the calling of men to one another in a purpose greater than themselves. Indeed, the energy was restorative, and she began to feel some of the slag upon her weary heart give way. Like new skin from a healing wound, her heart was tender, yet hopeful. She stayed an extra day and fished for the first time in her life under the tutelage of a wealthy man's teenage son, who fancied himself a true danger to any fish in the river. She had cast the line poorly and let it drift down into a small eddy. She leaned to her young teacher, without talking her eye off the line to inquire what happens next, when the pole jerked violently and was nearly torn from her hand, bending in a fierce arc.

The line sung as the fish ran downstream against her cries of "uh oh, oh no! Oh no!" The young lad jumped and hooted, then immediately guided her to setting the hook and turning the fish to wear him out. He spoke to her, but not too much, letting the pole do the talking.

"He's gonna be a beaut", he said.

"Maybe you should take the pole."

"No m'am. This is your fish. You can do it."

Several other men fishing nearby paused to see this beginner struggling to keep the fish on. They knew by the pole action, she had a nice fish on.

"Pole up!", the boy yelled. She instantly obeyed. Her adrenaline kicked in and she found the strength after six or seven minutes, to continue to reel the fish in. Several minutes later, the fish and fisherman both exhausted, the young boy reached down and pulled up the line to reveal a twenty inch rainbow trout. The boy stood gap jawed.

"Lady, that was beginners' luck. But congratulations!" It seemed she had held her breath the entire struggle and now she exhaled to the applause of half dozen men who had stopped their own fishing to watch this right of passage, remembering their own in days long past. They looked up at her with smiles and clapping hands. She nodded sheepishly, acknowledging without words her silent induction into a special club. A sense of camaraderie and connectedness lifted her.

She spent the night in the cabin of the young man's family. She had never tasted fish so good. The cabin had a rough hewn deck overlooking the Shasta Springs, several hundred yards away. The sound, the way the spray painted rainbows within the canyon, ever changing opened a calm place inside her. Never had any place so captured her.

The family she stayed with was packing up, heading back to Marysville, where they had a large ranch and were planting orchards. She packed up her horse for the final push up the hill to Berryvale. Soon, they told her, she would feel like she was at the top of the world and never closer to God. They knew the area well and thought she would love it, but beware of the winters, they cautioned.

The next day she filled her canteen with the fresh waters of the spring and started up the road to Berryvale, a place formerly called Strawberry Valley, due to the plethora of wild strawberries. About two miles above the falls, which is the Shasta Springs, the road began to ascend steeply. Her spirits rose with the land. The road began a set of switchbacks. Ascending from the cool of the river canyon, the air warmed considerably. It struck through brush fields, out of the dense timber of the canyon. The horse and trailing mule plodded their way, burdened by the load of all her belongings in the world. She kept looking upslope. She had seen the mountain every day before she had come to the springs. But now the land rolled like a shoulder before her and she could not see the gigantic snow capped peak. Ponderosa Pine were scattered on the south slope of the brush field. Some were four and five feet in diameter, and nearly 200 feet tall. The manzanita was eight to ten feet tall. The trail switchbacked again bearing a more westerly route up through and across the brush. She came to a large andesitic boulder along the road and looked back down the canyon. She could see ten miles back down the canyon and from ridge to ridge for the first time. Somewhere, out of her view, to the southeast was Mt. Lassen, the last volcano in the Cascade Range. To the southwest was the back side of the Crags-still magnificent but not so stunning as when standing at the foot of it's throne. She turned her gaze back up slope and began to see the top of the peak she had sought all morning. She decided to walk, so dismounted. Her boots, now broken in, were comfortable. Everything was fitting right. She set her wide brimmed hat back on her head, and feeling the sweetness of the cool air on her wet brow, tugged on the reigns, bringing her animals along behind her.

The road sometimes resembled more of a trail but at all times was easily passable. It remained steep. She trod at increasingly faster pace as she sensed the trail approaching some kind of a summit. She saw a volcanic cinder cone five miles away. Mt. Shasta now fully engulfed the entire sky and landscape to her right. On the left, snow capped peaks rose above the timberline. All around her was a profusion of manzanita in pink blossom, with those monumental trees placed like chess pieces on the table. She was perspiring now, as she compelled herself forward. The summit lay only a hundred yards away. She was nearly there. The animals were no drag. They seemed as desirous to get there as she. Now only fifty yards. Still she had no perception of the landscape beyond this summit on the trail. The cinder cone was miles away. What sat in the gulf between this summit and there? It occurred to her, that spring might be giving way to summer prematurely, as she felt the pores of her skin open and she began to sweat profusely. The woolen skirt, now seeming a bad choice of clothing for so warm a climb. Now only ten yards, and small remaining patches of snow lay to the sides of the trail. Her blouse now wet under her arms and she felt the perspiration on her legs. The trail went up in near steps over several rocks. She came to the summit and stared down into a snow rimmed valley about three miles wide and perhaps five miles long. The white blossom of strawberries appeared in the warmest of its micro-climates. The pink manzanita blooms graced the hillsides that weren't already thick with forests of evergreens. Lush pastures were well on the their way to freedom from the winter's snow which bound them. The great color battle of spring between green and white-the green now seemed to have the upper hand.

She could hardly breath, not for the arduous climb but for its stunning beauty. She felt a cooling breeze which seemed to emanate from this little valley. Indeed it did. It kissed her cheeks and she pushed back the hat which held onto her neck by a string. The air felt like a crown upon her head and made its way through the woolen skirt to refresh her legs. The horse came along side her, and the mule stepped up on the other side. The three just stood there, basking in light and air from heaven and staring into the earth's version of the same.

—

CHAPTER 4

Fort Klamath, Oregon-Spring of 1870

Major John Putnam sat at his desk as the new trooper approached.

"Corporal J.P. O'Hare, reporting for duty, sir." His boots snapped as did his salute to the major.

"At ease, Corporal".

"Yes, sir." His feet parted instantly to shoulder width and his hands tucked smoothly to the small of his back.

"Welcome aboard, Corporal, we're glad to have your kind here at Fort Klamath. I've gone over your record. Your bravery is not in question, with three citations, but the mess with Greshum at Laramie......," at this, Putnam's consternation was plain. "Well," he continued, "we have enough trouble with the Indians around here. We need cooler heads than Greshum. You were there. What the hell went wrong?"

At this, O'Hare recited the story, for which ample military reports existed. The incident at Laramie was tragic.

A hunting party of Sioux Indians had meandered along the Platte River, about 12 miles west of Fort Laramie. This group of 14 Indians had been tracking an Elk, but had lost the tracks, going into the river. There was some alcohol that came out at the campsite that night. It seemed to brighten their spirits after the discouraging day of hunting and tracking. Seven of the men had taken squaws and had children while seven were young braves, yet unattached. The old men were telling stories around the fire.

The stories were of the old days, before the white man came. No towns had to be "skirted". It was all theirs. As the early evening shifted into night, the stories, owing to the drink, became more personal. These were great hunting conquests, fighting or sexual victories. One such story brought howls of laughter and accusations of its teller being less than honest and greatly exaggerating himself.

Soon the pipe came out and they smoked their hemp and drifted to an easy place, no longer caring about their empty stomachs and poor hunting. The pipe went round and round until they sat in the silence of their stupor looking into the fire and then the starry night above. One of the young braves got up and walked out to go to the bush.

"Jojo, your stuff always makes me have to crap", he said over his shoulder.

The others laughed at him. Walking a short distance into the darkness, he felt the contentment of the drug as he found a bush and pulled down his pants. He could see his fellows around the fire thirty or so paces away and obscured by the sage and brush. He began to focus, like a cat, as it was cold and he wanted back by the fire. He jolted and nearly fell into his own mess when a monstrous head broke through the sage bush at his immediate left. He startled and yelled out of the fright and surprise. His comrades back at the fire cracked jokes. "Perhaps Floating Feather needs help". They all laughed, but Floating Feather came flying into camp with his pants half down. This of course, drove them from mere laughing to rolling on the ground, gasping for air, in hysterics.

"A beast, a monster!" he cried out.

"Now, he brags about his crap", retorted another, and they rolled over yet again in uncontained laughter. They would compound yet another joke upon poor

Floating Feather, and each one, only drove them further into hysterics, until it had run its course. This, while he tried to recount what he had seen. But the men rolled on the ground laughing. Then, a huge ox nosed its way into their camp. At first, they were startled and sobered quickly. They called out and circled out into the darkness, but the poor beast was alone. It had strayed from a wagon train of emigrants nearly three miles away, back toward Laramie.

Soon, realizing this apparent good fortune, the merry band was celebrating with huge hunks of meat turned on sticks over the fire. They celebrated into the night and fed themselves enough for several days. They finished the liquor and partook of the pipe for several more rounds.

In the morning, an emigrant and the trail boss of his wagon train, out searching for the ox to pull his wagon, peered through the brush. The Indians were passed out around the smoldering fire. The men saw the gored ox not far away. They quietly retraced their steps back to their horses and rode quickly to Fort Laramie to report the Sioux had stolen an ox and eaten it.

Lt. Greshum took 29 US Army soldiers with him that morning. The Indians heard the army's approach and naturally braced themselves; their own rifles at the ready. The army came upon the Sioux as they were breaking camp having carved the ox for travel. Lt. Greshum accused the Sioux of stealing it, but they protested their innocence, as indeed they were. The emigrant stood by expecting the Army officer to make things right. Greshum, for his part, wasn't believing the Indians. He was singularly fixed on his military career. He was too young for the Civil War, and so sported an opportunity to prove himself a valiant soldier and worthy junior officer.

Slow Foot offered the emigrant his horse, a beautiful Palomino, well worth the ox. But Greshum's countenance gave no sign of grace or forgiveness. He gave a pre-arranged nod to his Sergeant as he walked away from Slow Foot, and the soldiers opened fire on the Indians. When it was all over, all of the Sioux Indians and twenty one of the soldiers lie dead. All for an ox, taken by accident or fortune, and after having been offered fair remuneration. Senseless.

O'Hare said, "No one had told me about a plan to fire on them. It was insane. But after the first shots, the Indians were firing back and they fought hard to a man. It was a full-on gunfight in seconds. Greshum should have been court-martialed, not promoted."

Putnam puffed on his cigar.

"Idiot. But we don't need any loose canons here. We've got a Modoc chief on the warpath, so to speak, and perhaps rightly so. Keintpuash is his name, though some of the locals and the foreign media call him Captain Jack. The Modocs entered a treaty back in 1856 under Chief Schonchin. But the government keeps throwing more Indians into the reservation to a point, they can't survive. Schonchin is fairly happy with the treaty. He is eating. But now this other chief, this .....Captain Jack is put out with the United States government. He is gaining in his following among the tribe's members. The whole mess is starting to stink. A bad winter and starvation will hit the Modoc. They've proved to be the most ruthless and barbaric of any of the local tribes. I've read the reports with the skirmishes in the last 20 years-dismemberment of children, mutilation of women. Damned awful stuff. I've got a few more years until retirement. Corporal, I'd like to finish them without another Indian war."

Putnam's cigar gesticulated as he shifted it to the other side of his mouth.

"It'd be a hellovalot easier to keep peace around here if the politicians and some of these generals would keep their word. Sometimes ...., well,........," he stopped himself here. "O'Hare, stow your gear and get acquainted. Be ready. You're going on patrol tomorrow to Lost River. I've got a bunch of young recruits and I need a soldier of your experience. Lt. Johnson is seasoned and will lead. Dismissed."

Corporal O'Hare saluted, turned on his heels and marched out, putting on his hat as he closed the door behind him.

He mustered the following morning at day break and was second, behind Lt. Johnson as they left Fort Klamath. The large timbered gates closed behind them and they headed south along Klamath Lake and across the basin which was comprised of two seemingly incongruent land forms; high desert and swamp. The shallow lakes were a haven to millions of migratory birds. Flocks of them darkened the sky at times. Countless "V" formations of geese flew along, and then, as if on signal, descended rapidly through the sky to land on vast lakes hidden behind tall rushes and "toolies". It occurred to Lt. Johnson this land had not changed since the beginning of time. Edmund Johnson was a sensible junior officer. He had enlisted in the Union Army and now finished a career, like his Major and hoped to retire in the local area. Land was plentiful. Lord knows, he thought, there's plenty of water here. The patrol made their way around the big lakes. The terrain was open, nearly treeless except along the river and creeks. The Lost River started just north of the California border and ran west into the Klamath basin and eventually into the river of the same name. They circled over by Bloody Point, a rock outcrop which was the site of several Indian ambushes, and scores of murdered immigrants. They patrolled past the Island, a prominent rock outcrop in a flat basin, rimmed with hills of juniper and sage. To the south, some fifty miles loomed the frozen north slopes of Mt. Shasta. Its snowy peak a landmark in the dead of August heat.

They met with a peaceful clan of Modoc, spearing fish in the shallow lake nearby. It was a fact of Indian "management", when there was food, the tensions eased. When it lacked, or there was distilled spirits around, the situation could turn volatile in a minute. One never felt at ease when the Indians had been drinking, and the army looked with great disfavor upon those that sold or traded it to them. It imperiled the settlers nearby and some of the trains on the Emigrant Trail, though the traffic on this trail was thinning out as the country moved to faster modes of transportation.

The head of this clan, Top Hat Charlie, was pleasant to the soldiers and they furthered good relations by handing out salt taffy to the children, and trying to find occasion to laugh during their conversation. Laughing was good. Staring was bad.

That year and the next passed without significant events with the Modoc. The patrols went and came back-never a shot fired in hostility. The soldiers came to be familiar with these Indians and learned the unique physiognomy of names. There was Hooka Jim, Top Hat, Little Jim, Big Jim, Steamboat Frank, Stink Foot, Scarface Charlie, Boston Charlie, Shorty Mike, Little Ellen, Strong Mary, and the like. They would note the small changes in the lives of the Indians. One morning in April of 1872, they came upon Steamboat Frank and his clan, cleaning fish by the lake. Frank was looking morose as usual.

"Where's Strong Mary?" (Frank's wife), asked Lt. Johnson in a familial way. Frank shrugged his shoulders in an uncaring gesture.

"Mary live now with Stink Foot." Johnson tried to look sympathetic and twisted his face to appear confused by this news. Frank seeing this, replied. "Strong Mary hit Frank." At this he took off his bowler hat which was crushed and filthy to reveal a chunk missing from the pate of his skull.

"Fry pan hurt Frank." Stink Foot and Big Mary now together. That OK with Frank. Good bye to them."

The soldiers tipped their hats to hide their grins but others genuinely felt sorry for Frank. Big Mary outweighed him by 35 pounds and was six inches taller.

Their lives, like the lives of all men, were a mixture of the daily monotony of carrying water, finding wood for fuel, and catching or foraging for food. At times their personal lives would erupt into drama of life and death or marital peril, only to subside once again into the ongoing routine of making do.

By the Summer of 1872, Captain Jack was off the reservation. He had moved back to Lost River and claimed that the Treaty always allowed him to keep that home. That he was not compelled to live on the reservation. The Chief, Jon Schonchin, saw it otherwise and this created rifts within the clans of the Modoc. Local settlers in the Tule basin were increasingly fearful of Jack. Sensing their fear, the Indians were quick to take advantage, requiring impromptu tolls and gifts and whatever petty charges they could justify for trespassing, hunting and fishing, since it was all the Indian's land. It wasn't so much the trifling costs, but his accosting nature and bearing that the settlers feared. At this time there were several other bands of Indians breaking off from the main tribe. One band lived up Hot Creek, yet another, up Butte Creek. Both were comprised of Modoc, along with some renegades of the Klamath River, or Pit River tribes. All had their fill of the reservation living and failed promises of the federal government.

In July of that year the Indian Agent at Ft. Klamath, Mr. L.S. Dyar, Mr. Ivan Applegate and Col. Elmer Otis petitioned the U.S. Government to have the Indians removed and placed on the reservation, peaceably if possible, forcibly if necessary. The commission of Indian Affairs granted their petition.

Lt. Johnson received orders from Major Putnam to go out to disarm the Indians, who had refused to meet with the Indian Agent. On the morning of July 29, the patrol of 24 men left Fort Klamath. Corporal O'Hare rode at the rear point and kept his eyes open. The men sensed the increasing drama in their part of the world. News was had that correspondents from the San Francisco newspapers were arriving. There was a surreal apprehension in the air. Putnam chewed more cigars than he smoked. He cursed under his breath sensing the path of his career to retirement would be neither quiet nor peaceful.

The air seemed heavy. Perhaps it was the morning sun's effect on the shallow swampy lakes rimmed with reeds and 'toolies' that gave a mugginess to it. Visibility was likewise hampered in the early morning hours as the mist rose. By mid morning the haze had lifted to a canopy four or five hundred feet over the basin, casting a beige glow of light across the basin floor.

The patrol rode into an Indian camp believed to be Jack's. Curly Bart and Bogus Charlie were in the camp, near the fire ring. Scarface Charlie was at the bank of the Lost River, eighty feet away. All eyes turned to the approaching cavalry. The soldiers were scanning left and right to a man. O'Hare dropped back searching along the banks of the river, occasionally turning to look behind.

Lt. Johnson, normally an amiable person, seemed in no mood for play. He dismounted along with a sergeant and private at his side and strode directly to Bogus Charlie.

"Where is Captain Jack?"

"In his tent."

"I want to see him."

"What for?"

"I have an order for his arrest."

"What you want him for that?"

"That makes no difference to you. Which tent is his?"

At this commotion, Scarface Charlie walked up from the water's edge at an even pace, but with his revolver in his hand.

"Sergeant, disarm that Indian," ordered the Lieutenant. Sergeant Buford Smith, advanced three paces toward Scarface and demanded Charlie's weapon.

"What for I give you my gun?"

But military people did not feel compelled to answer questions or justify their demands.

Sgt. Smith demanded a second time but Charlie refused. At this Smith pulled his own revolver, cocked it and pointed it at Scarface Charlie's chest, dead on. Charlie cocked his own pistol and stared into Smith's eyes. Peripherally he saw Smith squeeze the trigger and he deliberately fell backward instantly toward the ground and fired, the bullet striking Sgt. Smith in the throat with an upward trajectory that lifted him momentarily, returning him quickly to earth, less the back of his skull. Charlie crawled back toward the water, while pistol lead flew in all directions. Squaws hit the ground as taught. Captain Jack was just coming out of the tent to see what the commotion was about with no more than a blanket wrapped about his shoulders. He quickly hit the ground, pulling the blanket over him and escaped the melee, passing as a squaw. It was supposed that Scarface was killed as nearly every soldier unloaded a volley at his position. But not so. As other Indians joined the fight, the soldiers found cover some forty yards distant. The volley went on for two hours before the Indians effectively retreated, seeming to vanish. The Indians lost two braves, a squaw and a half-breed girl of nine years old. Smith died instantly, and four others were wounded, two mortally.

The same morning a group of settlers had formed, tired of the do-nothing government, and were ready to effect the safety of their families. They had come to the camp of Top Hat. He was there with Big and Little Jim, a renegade of the Klamath named Pock Face and Hooka Jim. The settlers requested their guns and promised there would be no trouble. They would be safely escorted back to the reservation. There was beef, and bread to eat on the way. They would be given flour and more beef when they arrived. Given these assurances, they surrendered their arms, but had just begun to do so when the shooting erupted at Captain Jack's camp, within earshot.

All thinking turned to betrayal and paranoia. In an instant, guns were drawn and the Indians began to fall. The settlers retreated to cover as the Indians took up positions. Squaws lay prostrate, except for Little Ellen who raced across the camp to her tent with Hooka Jim's baby in her arms. A stray bullet struck the child as she ran and she dove into the tent only to realize it was dead. She then appeared at the entrance, sullen and in a trance, and slowly walked toward her husband, Hooka Jim, uncaring of the hot lead that whizzed by her from all directions. She was but several paces from the tent when she was struck from the rear directly in the heart and fell dead.

At last the settlers retreated and both parties fell back to consider the situation. One settler, Jack Thurber, who had the best of intentions in coming to the camp, was stunned as he walked through the camp after the guns had fallen silent. The fighting he supposed was over, was not. He was killed by a single shot. The Indians had retreated as well and were now incensed at the apparent act of treachery. Hooka Jim, who hardly needed incitement to barbary, was maddened by the loss of his son and Little Ellen, his wife. He was determined to avenge by murdering settlers. At his leading, the clan made haste along the river's edge to the nearest settlements. The newspaper accounts later told accurately of their rampage.

William Neese and Joseph Penning, were riding their horses unaware of the morning's affairs. Both were shot,

Neese dead and Penning severely wounded. At the sub-sistence ranch of the Brotherton family, the rampaging Indians appeared next. Mr. Brotherton and his son were slain in the yard, without a word said. The frantic Mrs. Brotherton, with two small children barricaded herself in the small house and defended it with her life. She was rescued two days later. The private war moved on to the next habitation where a Mr. Kendrick and his hired man were killed. And then a man named John Schroeder, apparently traveling through the area, was murdered. A Mrs. Boddy had no idea, when she was unclipping clothes from the clothesline, that behind a linen sheet would stand Hooka Jim, his knife covered in the blood of her three young sons which lay behind him. She would have screamed at the horror of this spectacle but his knife severed her windpipe in a single thrust, nearly decapitating her.

Fourteen settlers in the Klamath Basin were murdered that afternoon before armed parties, not the army, were mustered and gave them reason to flee. They retreated to a geological formation known then as the 'Stronghold'.

Foreverafter known as Captain Jack's Stronghold, this thick lava flow was perhaps ten square miles of natures finest fortress. An upheaval of brutal rock, slag and basalt, this foreboding terrain was jumbled and tumbled in elevations of ten to twenty feet in height. Fissures created paths through this impregnable table top of rock and pillars and columns could conceal a person five feet in front of you. An Indian could walk in total silence upon its surface, ambush at will or hide for an eternity virtually in the midst of his enemy's camp. A more inhospitable or treacherous respite to attack would be difficult to imagine.

Worse yet, for the United States Army who would ultimately be tasked with the routing and capture of these Indians, was its tactical advantages. The approaches were from the open terrain along the lake coming up to the stronghold. For five miles distance, the Stronghold braves and warriors could see all tactical movements of their enemies and could reposition themselves in the countless natural fortified positions. What would later be learned is that the Modoc had another singular advantage. The sound of the soldiers gathered and drifted up to the Stronghold. And, after twenty plus years of dealing with ranchers, settlers, immigrants and soldiers, the Modoc know every command uttered by the several officers who would eventually attack them. It set up one of American history's most publicized Indian Wars. It would come to dominate the papers of every eastern city. Even the capitals of Europe were caught up in the Great Modoc Indian War. Captain Jack became a celebrity in print.

The general nervousness and apprehension reached unbearable levels for the settlers along the Lost River and the Tule Basin area. Fourteen had been murdered, more terrorized and no one had been arrested. No one knew where Jack and his ruthless Modocs were now holed up. It was the not-knowing of their whereabouts that drove the anxiety. No one felt safe.

John Fairchilds had one of the largest ranches in the area. Thousands of his cattle roamed the area. He had treatied with the Indians, bought land from them and was sought by government officials as the local expert. John Fairchilds had sat at the table with both Chief John Schonchin and Captain Jack. He was among those rare individuals that two feuding parties, at total odds to each other, completely trusted. His ranch played a part in the discovery of where the Indians now camped.

A Mr. Samuel Watson was a guest at the Fairchilds ranch one night, but pushed on the next day. While riding along the Lost River, he came across Bogus Charlie and Scarface Charlie, who told him about the fight. As a guest of Fairchilds, they told him to go back. If the other Indians found him, he would surely be killed. Wisely, he set off at once to return and rode into the yard at Fairchilds just past dark and informed John Fairchilds of the news.

At nearly the same time, the Hot Creek band of Modocs had received their own intelligence and dispatched an Indian rider to Fairchilds. He rode up and talked, expecting Fairchilds to have all the answers as to why this fight should have happened at all. John took pains to explain the more elaborate system of governance that existed. He simply didn't know the why of it. He managed to secure from the Hot Creek band an agreement to stay out of the fight for the time being. The next day Fairchilds and Nate Beswick left on a tour of the area. They found the scene of the fight at Captain Jack's camp. Upon returning, the young Indians who worked on his ranch had learned and now told Fairchilds where Capt. Jack was hiding. The next night John Fairchilds and three friends rode to Jack's hideout, an impenetrable cave location within the lava flow. They talked late into the night and slept there unafraid of their hosts. Jack could not understand why he was attacked. He wanted only to live in peace at his camp on Lost River; his home. He did not want the soldiers to come after him, because he would fight them. He had murdered no one (which was true). The murders were on Hooka Jim and his band, in revenge for the killing of his own son and wife. Jack wanted peace, but if war came..., he would fight to the end. He asked the men to convey this to the army. That there was no need for further bloodshed with him. But he would not return to Yainox, the reservation.

They left the next morning and having found the army, saw an amassing of several companies, and a large group of volunteers. They were preparing to send out scouts. Rather than see these men lost, they told their story to the commanding officer, a Captain Jackson. Fairchilds and P.A. Dorris warned them not to go up there, but in the arrogance that sometime pervades military men, they smirked. Asking how many Indians were up there? Fairchilds replied only forty five or so, including boys and old men, but the number wasn't the point. Jackson was warned there would be the loss of many men if he went up to the stronghold.

The media increased as tensions did, and not surprising a new commanding officer was sent for the glorious ousting of Captain Jack, Colonel Frank Wheaton. Preparations were made throughout the fort and among the soldiers to take the stronghold.

Corporal J.P. O'Hare, knew that Fairchilds was respected among the Indians and also knew the land as treacherous. Newspapermen pawed at Wheaton for an interview; his outlook on the great upcoming battle. He was far more gracious to the press than his men. O'Hare cleaned and checked his weapons and then went through some of the rookies, making sure their weapons and gear was ready. As O'Hare passed by the Headquarters, Wheaton had just finished talking with the press. Putnam was at the far side of the covered front porch. The cigar, somber, unmoving in his normally animated mouth. He glanced at O'Hare. Their eyes met, and conveyed what men of a like mind can say to each other without words. Wheaton was slapping the backs of the press boys, begging that he had to get back to work. He had a war to conduct, a victory to bring home. O'Hare and Putnam broke their stare. J.P. went back to the barracks thinking of Greshum, and the pompous bluster riding out to the Sioux Indians at Laramie. He looked at the young lads, so eager for the fight, shining their metal, talking nervously and quick to joust with one another-a means to dispel that ever-welling energy inside. He wondered which of the faces he now looked at might not come home. He had a bad feeling about this mission. He was always amazed that no matter how much preparation the military did, the execution of any plan in battle so quickly degenerated to chaos, and the thing needed was not brought, or existed at another part of the battlefield where it was not needed. There is an inherent inefficiency to warfare.

Finally, when they could take no more preparation, the orders came down. They were to attack on January 17th, a Friday. The volunteers, under command of junior officers would advance to the east of the stronghold while the Army 2nd Infantry advanced to the west. When they were south of the stronghold, turn toward each other and junction to the south of Captain Jack. This would create a line of infantry men east, south and west of Jack and Tule Lake would be the fourth element of containment. He would be boxed in. Lt. Barnard took the volunteers along the east flank to within two miles of the stronghold, but had already lost two men and several wounded. The Indians could see everything, and anticipate much of what was to happen.

A thick bank of fog enveloped Wheaton, trying to advance southward along the west flank. It was so thick, he would have delayed the assault, but there was no way to get a messenger to Barnard and the east flank. You simply could not see more than a few feet in front of you. He must attack as Barnard would be doing so. Onward the men marched seeing little but the man in front of them.

The Indians knew this terrain. They knew where they were and where the soldiers must come. They listened. Soon, emerging from the fog was the creaking and clacking sound of gear on the backs of men and horses. Shots rang out and men fell, but the army could see nothing. Nothing. The Indians quietly moved positions, setting up the next attack.

The march on the west flank slowed to a crawl, lost in the tulefog. Soon the minds of the men began to see Indians in the fog. They fired into nothing. Fear began to grip them as the column, instinctively moved more slowly. Wheaton, at the front of the column, fell victim to what the mind did to the other men. But he pushed on. The trail, barely visible, moved over a slight rise, and then the next volley of gunfire erupted. Four more men killed, five more wounded. Their screams muffled in the fog. Medics came and rendered their best. The wounded were evacuated to the rear. Wheaton's right hand raised to signal a halt. He called his officers together. It was decided to go back and around the lake and catch up with the progress of the east flank. The order was given and the column reversed. And then another volley. Bullets whizzed by for half a minute. Horses fell crippled and had to be shot on the spot. Two officers wounded and four more men killed. The column turned and fired into the fog bank. It was answered in silence. Several of the young men, all privates in rank, were hunkered behind their dead horses and were frozen in fear. O'Hare, lay on the ground, listening. Wheaton now advanced to what had been the rear and now lead the orderly retreat. Lt. Johnson, shuffled over to O'Hare and gave orders.

"Wheaton wants you as a rear guard to protect the retreating column. Take two men and stay here. If there is no advance by the enemy, leave in thirty minutes." J.P. looked at Johnson as if he had just given him a death sentence. Perhaps he had. Two young privates, Mathew Ferris and Zeke Bradshaw, were summoned from a few feet away.

"Get your rifles, canteens, and ammo and get over here", whispered O'Hare. He got their heads close to his, like a father to his sons. In the quietest of whispers, placed them within ten feet of each other. One behind a rock, the other, a dead horse. All weapons loaded. All at the ready. They stared into the dense fog. Sunlight must be breaking through as the pallor of the air took on a sickening yellow and brown mist.

In the rocks, less than one hundred feet away, the Indians listened intently, seeing in their minds, the actions that every sound reported. Patcheye, Shacknasty Joe, Boston Charlie, with two renegades crept slowly toward them. Their weapons ranged from a bow and arrow, to civil war muskets. But Patcheye silently levered a shell into his prized Henry rifle. Without a sound, they began to move in closer, hoping to wreak yet more terror on the retreating column. With the smoothness of water over a rock, they slowly poured from hiding and advanced in silence of the fog.

———

The volunteers, led by Capt. Barnard, advanced into a bowl rimmed with rocks, with a flat sandy bottom about one hundred yards in diameter. Though only three miles distance from Wheaton, they had been in the sunlight all morning. It was hot and muggy. They had not seen an Indian and had received no fire for nearly forty-five minutes. They mistakenly assumed they had flanked the Indian stronghold and now were behind them. Their other mistake was assuming that Wheaton would be in a similar position instead of circling around and following them trying to catch up. Barnard broke for water and food, for fifteen minutes, but it was not to be. The men had no sooner brought out their canteens and rations, than they took fire from 180 degrees. It was a poor place to stop. Without cover, it was a route and the entire force was lost, except for two men who miraculously escaped on horseback.

Just as Wheaton and his regiment was emerging from the fog along the lakeshore, he was met by two riders, the frantic remnant of Barnard's doomed force. A retreat was ordered back to the staging camp, where supplies, artillery and reinforcements could be had. Unfortunately the press would also be there. Within twenty-four hours, Wheaton was replaced and General Canby was put in charge of the assault.

———

It had been about ten minutes since the last creak of the column had turned to silence. Not a word was said among the three soldiers whose job it was to cover the slow retreat of their comrades. At even the short distances between them, features were obscured in the thick fog; a hat, a beard, a rifle. Yet somehow, one sensed the fear in the others as well as oneself. Their ears prickled with sensitivity. Their eyes strained to see further into the blank wall of fog than they truly could. And what they could not see, the fears of their mind delivered up.

In the fog, only forty feet away, slinked the five Indians, stalking in a low crouch. Their rifles pointed exactly where the trail would be that had been used by Wheaton. The Indians squinted into the fog, as they approached the soldiers doing the same. They moved in total silence, when Boston Charlie stepped on the slightest of sage twig, dropped by a nest-building bird last spring. The "click" froze everyone. The Indians looked across to each other. A look of disgust toward Boston Charlie.

To the soldiers, it too, sounded like a branch being ripped from a tree. Fingers tightened on the triggers. Zeke thought his heart would jump out of his chest as he aimed down his rifle barrel into the nothingness of the fog. Zeke and Matt looked at O'Hare. He pointed at the direction of the sound and nodded his head affirming what they heard. As the zephyrs of air swirled in the fog, now heating up, they would form more and less dense pockets of moisture. Some the columnar size of a man. Matt Ferris nearly squeezed off a round at what he thought was an Indian creeping up on him twenty paces away, only to have it evaporate. Zeke and O'Hare did the same. Their throats dry, barely breathing, one for its noise and two, as their chest constricted in fear and dread.

Patcheye motioned for Boston Charlie and one of the renegades to spread out, in a flanking maneuver to each side. He sensed someone, a presence was out there. While the three Indians advanced now to within 30 feet, the flanks were advancing on the three soldiers.

O'Hare saw another chimera of swirling mist form ten paces out, when the fog, now only fifty feet thick above the earth allowed a shaft of sunlight to break through to the ground. O'Hare focused down the sights of his rifle when, like ghosts, the three Indians appeared. Patcheye emerged at the end of his muzzle and the rifle discharged, blowing him backwards from his walking crouch. Zeke fired immediately. Matt's rifle discharged. Bullets ricocheted off the rocks around them. The renegade fell. The men drew their side arms as there was no time to reload their army issued rifles.

"Stay down" ordered O'Hare. He could see Matt Ferris, laying prone behind his dead horse. Zeke Bradshaw moaned, "I been hit! I'm shot. Ferris got to his feet to come to Zeke's aid when the renegade stepped out of the mist and shot him in the head from ten feet. O'Hare wheeled around and fired once. The Indian, hit in mid chest, dropped the rifle and staggered back. O'Hare grouped two more shells in quick order nearly adjacent the first, the force propelling the dead man backward. Zeke moaned again. O'Hare rolled over to reload his rifle before going to Zeke. As he did, Boston Charlie, seeming a pillar of lava rock, advanced to nearly stand at his feet.

His rifle pointed quickly at O'Hare, who hadn't seen him until the movement. Seeing the muzzle, O'Hare batted the rifle away with his own empty weapon. At this, Charlie drew his knife and flew through the air at him. There was no time to draw his pistol. O'Hare rolled back to his right as Charlie recovered and lunged again. The men struggled for control of the knife, rolling on the ground until wedged into the lave scoria. Its sharp edges gnawing and gashing their skin.

Charlie made no slow forceful moves, but rapid slashing and stabbing. O'Hare had blocked each, but odds would not prevail that defense much longer. Finally O'Hare gripped the knife. Charlie then kneed him in the crotch, once, twice, and again. O'Hare, felt his strength ebbing as he could not answer the force of this man. Now Charlie pressed down on him, the knife at his heart. Both men, with gritted teeth, grunted to prevail upon the other. Charlie leaned into his face, sensing victory and spit into O'Hare's eyes, which did blind him, and for a moment he sensed defeat, when his head pitched forward sharply into Charlie's now broken nose. Charlie saw stars for a moment. O'Hare felt the strength go out of Charlie as he slumped to the side. The Indian was stunned for only a moment. On his knees, he shifted his knife and lunged again. But the moment was all O'Hare needed. Charlie lunged into the .44 revolver's muzzle. It was his last act. Both men, now on their knees, faced each other at arm's length, the adrenaline wave cresting as O'Hare unloaded the revolver into the Indian until the cylinder clicked empty and then collapsed himself, holding his genitals in agony, grateful to be alive. If there was another Indian. O'Hare was as good as dead. This he accepted. He was completely spent.

The day's fighting was but a skirmish in a war that captivated the nation and more. Howitzers were moved into range and the stronghold pounded relentlessly, though it did little more than break the broken and fissured lava into smaller pieces. There were delegations sent and attempts at peace and armistice. It was not to be. Captain Jack held off three thousand soldiers eventually amassed against him for six months, with forty six Indians capable of bearing arms. Over 150 soldiers were killed or wounded. General Canby, came to be one of the latter commanders of this affair, was slain in a peace meeting with Captain Jack and Scarface Charlie, along with a well regarded Christian preacher. Despite the warnings of Fairchilds and others, to carry concealed weapons to the meeting with the Indians in their cave, they did not. Canby felt it unworthy of a soldier's honor as he had agreed to no weapons. The Preacher, stated he trusted in God. Both were murdered as the Indians had no intention of peace and came with pistols. The men's bodies were stripped naked and thrown down onto the course and jagged rocks, a mangle of flesh, their appendages in sickening angles. The Modocs lost six of their own in the entire war.

The Great Modoc War ended that June when, after several Indians were captured, they agreed to double cross Captain Jack and lead the soldiers to him. He had left the stronghold trying to make his escape into the Pit River country to the south and east. He was caught and surrendered without a struggle. Seeing his own betrayal, he hung his head and understood fully the doom of his people. Jack's trial was held and he and six others were convicted and sentenced to hang on October 3rd 1873. Several received clemency for their assistance in catching Jack. The death sentence was commuted for two others the day before the execution. Those two died in Alcatraz where they served their remaining years. Captain Jack and three others were hung, and a chapter came to a close in the American west.

The rest of the war was anticlimactic to J.P. O'Hare as compared to the day of the skirmish and his fight with Boston Charlie. Zeke survived a wound to his shoulder. They had walked nearly four miles when a patrol picked them up.

After the war, things settled down in the Klamath Basin. It turned out to be the last great Indian War, if they could be called such at all. His enlistment was up in a month. He rested on the porch of the barracks at Fort Klamath and thought about his life thus far.

He was born in County Clare, Ireland in 1842. The memories began at about three years old. It was the time of the Great Famine in Ireland. So many starved, all were ungodly scrawny. He never saw a person that wasn't sallow until he was nearly ten years old. He hadn't thought people could have a plump or full body. Hunger was constant in the small fishing village of Kilconnel, near the Cliffs of Moher. Here, a mighty wall of Ireland said 'no further' to the sea. Seven hundred feet straight up from the ocean to a table top of emerald green with cut facets at the cliff's edge.

The little village of Kilconnel with its drab huts and thatched roofs dotted the landscape of gray rock and deep green pasture. The smell of the sea was constant, its spray often drifting up to the little cottages. Men walked the roads on their way to menial tasks and meager outcomes, their tattered and soiled suitclothes and ties incoherent for the tasks at hand. The countenance of their faces saddened by deep etchings and furrowed lines, cheeks gaunt and sallow. Their eyes vacant and ashamed. Crude animal carts, dung in the road and the bog fires smoldering in the cold houses, were the constant. Smoke drifted from their toppled chimneys. There was poor and then there were the Irish; starvation poor in their own land. The depression was unyielding and the Irish weather a burden on men's souls. But he remembered, as in a dream, a summer day.

One day. It was beautiful. The emerald had come to life bathed in warm sunlight. Wildflowers sprung up in unfettered displays everywhere. The dark cloak over the peoples' faces seemed to lift and there were smiles. That brought him to recall that same day, his pa had brought him to the cliffs. Little Jonny thought if he stared hard enough to the west, he might see the faint outline of America. And then the clouds returned. The beautiful blue sea turned gray reflecting the clouds that were drawn like a blanket over it. As the sky shifted to the foreboding gray, the sun broke though in several shafts of light upon the sea, in random locations, miles apart. This shimmering with great intensity contrasted sharply with the dark clouds surrounding each. They were as spotlights upon the surface beneath its ray. He squinted against their brilliant reflection, though all else was turning dull gray. The boy looked out across the ocean. From his thousand foot high cliff, they looked like stepping stones for God himself, bathed in the light of heaven, showing the way across the great ocean.

He remembered sounds. Most often, it was the terrible coughing, wheezing. Many times a quiet sobbing, or wailing like a Banshee. His younger sister, Kathleen had died, at the age of nine. An older brother, got into constant trouble with the law. In a drunk, he killed an Englishman and was imprisoned for life. Jonny O'Hare, as he was known there, had hardly known his older brother. He remembered the sounds of the music. It had captivated him. The neighbors and 'uncles' and 'aunts' would come. They sat on the wooden kitchen chairs and stools with their fiddles and flutes. The bodhran drumming steadily, while the concertina and other instruments played at fevered pace. Immediately, someone would stand up and begin dancing in the small living room. A neighbor, an old man, whose name he'd long forgotten, if he ever knew, began to jig. Small quick steps, like he was dancing barefoot on hot coals. He shuffled as he danced within the tiny space in the room, yet seemed unhampered. People clapped to the beat and looked on, smiling. This seemed to sustain their souls while the paltry provisions sustained their bodies.

By 1858, now a young man, he'd had enough of Ireland's gloom, and worked his way on a freighter to Quebec. He worked for three years as a longshoreman, a bartender, and did some prize fighting, but decided to move on to America, emigrating to the U.S. He crossed into Minnesota where he was dubbed an illegal alien. Like many Irishmen, he was offered citizenship for a five year stint in the Union Army. He survived the American Civil War without a physical wound. But it would be wrong to say it left no mark upon him. He had developed the habit, when remembering the terrible battles and the inhumanity he'd seen, of giving his head a quick shift, like a twitch. In this, he accomplished dislodging the image seen in his eyes. It would bring him back to the present.

It was the Spring of 1874. Having no greater force in his life than the momentum of his soldier's employment, he stayed on in the army to fight the Indians of the west. He had fought for the United States for thirteen years: First, to quell the great secessionist movement and save the union from splitting apart. Then taming the west from Indians and outlaws. While these lingered on, he could see that their days were numbered. Times were changing. He had given perhaps the best years of his life to a country he was not born to, but whose promise, of freedom, and the unfettered pursuit of what a man deemed his happiness, was nowhere else existent on Earth. He had some savings and there was the opportunity of homesteading still in the west, but the door of history was soon closing. He and many others sensed and understood this. The nation had come across the continent and run into the other ocean. This was it. This was the last of it.

In the distance to the south he had seen the great mountain, Mt. Shasta. Sometimes he could not take his eyes off of it as he rode on patrols. He saw it from the north which looks entirely different from any other angle. While always appearing the snow capped volcano that it was, every different vantage point of the compass presented the mountain in a new form. This giant's base was twenty to thirty miles across on some transits. Its peak, over two and a half miles above sea level. The valleys that lie at the toe of its lower slopes, Butte Valley, Squaw Valley, Shasta Valley were at 2,500 to 4,000 feet elevation. Rimmed with timber these valleys pay homage to the barren glaciered slopes of its peak. The mountain was a composite volcano, made up of andesitic material, the same as the Andes Range of South America's west coast. The plate tectonics were, in fact, very similar; part of the Pacific Rim of Fire. Mt. Shasta had two principal peaks, the peak itself, and a craterous mount, sitting at the peak's shoulder like the head of a Siamese twin. Jonathan Phineas O'Hare wrote out his resignation letter that night and ran out the short time remaining for his military duty.

On the day of his discharge, he rode out the gate in his civilian clothes, amazed at how few possessions he had. He had stopped to say goodbye to Zeke Bradshaw. Zeke had healed well from his wounds.

"What you gonna do, J.P.? You don't know anything but soldiering."

O'Hare smiled at the youth. "I want the same thing as everybody else, lad. I want a place of my own; enough to support myself, a few cows, a big garden. I never want to be hungry again. I done that in Ireland and enough is enough of that. Maybe I can find a creek or river that I could do some fishing. I haven't fished since I was a boy. I'd like a little place to just be left alone, and see what comes of it."

"You're dreamin' J.P. I bet you're back in the army in six months."

"Don't be holdin' your breath on that, lad. There is a lot of good land around here, but time is runnin' out. It's getting bought up and homesteaded. It's time I did somethin' with my life besides doin' the biddin' of Uncle Sam."

"So, where you heading?"

"Just a little south of here. I'm thinking of the Mt. Shasta area. The Shasta Valley is warmer, a little easier on these older bones, ya know." He smiled at the youthful man, with a bit of a sparkle in his eyes. There was a brief silence.

"I'm off," he said plainly and advanced to shake hands with Zeke.

"I'll miss you, J.P.", he confessed.

"You'll get over it. You take care of yourself, and if your down that way, you be sure to look me up."

"Yes sir, I'll do that."

CHAPTER 5

Mel Grady got off her horse and anxiously marched into the Berryvale Post Office, run by Mr. Sisson. Sisson looked up and smiled at her, a letter between his first two fingers. She lit up and advanced to him grabbing it like a child does candy. He chuckled. The letter was from the United States Department of Interior. She tore off the side, careful not to damage the contents.

When she had come into the valley she had stayed at the boarding house of Mrs. Claudia Smith, a widow. Mrs. Smith kept a clean and comfortable house, and was reasonable in her charges. But the primary advantage to staying there, was that Claudia Smith knew everybody and everything about everybody. No gossip was too small for her consideration. No detail escaped her sharp eye. She was very pleased to know her new boarder, but seemed a little too inquisitive of Melissa's past.

Mel got to know many of the townspeople right off. She worked various jobs and spent considerable time looking over the local area. She had had several callers among the single men of town, but none seemed to her liking. This, to Claudia Smith's frustration. Mel had finally settled on a half section of land, after many visits to the property, for $16,000. A 320 acre parcel near the lumber mill in the next town later developed by Abner Weed. The Shasta River flows from springs in the mountains behind this property. These were glacier carved slopes above the timber line. The water crashed down some 4,000 feet in elevation and, hitting level terrain, roared across this land. The land itself, was natural pasture, for about two hundred acres, the rest was timber, mostly Douglas Fir, Incense Cedar and a little Ponderosa Pine. The spot was a little cool, being north exposure, but she'd learned it would produce the best timber growth. Most of the timber land was gently slope. What she sought now was the government land to either side of it.

Mel had applied to homestead Sections 16 and 21. These were adjacent to her half of Section 17. Rough and unspoiled sections, each 640 acres in size. They were comprised of pasture, rimmed in tall timber with streams and creeks traversing them. The pieces fit together in topography, in water management, in seclusion and privacy and she saw that it could be the place she had dreamed of.

She unfolded the letter which advised her of her award of the request for Homestead grant, together with the terms and conditions of same. She let out a hoot, heard for a mile. Mr. Sisson just chuckled. As she rode to her place of boarding, she began to make plans. All the pieces seemed to be coming together.

———

O'Hare rode south through Butte Valley, the mountain before him, looming larger by the hour. The terrain rose up fifteen hundred feet at the south end of the valley through timber and chaparral. The ground cover was a native grass, with sage and brush undergrowth beneath the conifer trees. As he moved southward there had always been ridges or smaller mountains in the foreground to obscure the lower parts of the mountain. Now he descended the rise, called Mt. Hebron Pass. The magnificence of the mountain stood naked before him. Soon, the road broke upon an expansive view of the alluvial fan, some twenty miles across. Lava flows of pyroclastic material formed gnarly ridges like giant fingers protruding outward from the base of the mountain. Below and between these two-hundred foot high ridges of jagged lava flow was the uniform slope of the alluvial fan carpeted with six foot high manzanita brush and pocked with tall conifers.

It was good that his horse watched the footing on the road as J.P. was often nearly hypnotized watching the cloud formations at the summit of the mountain. Clouds formed and dissipated rapidly; their shadows falling and dancing on the glaciered slopes near the peak. Then running quickly down the slopes to dissipate into nothing as the cloud evaporated. He was transported in his mind up to those slopes and could not turn his gaze away.

He arrived in the town that would later be named after its founding industrialist, Abner Weed. The weather continually warmed through the early Spring, but on any given day, the ever present clouds could form at the top of the mountain casting over all who worked and lived beneath her slopes, the coolness of the mountain air. When the sun broke through again, its warmth penetrated clothing to your skin.

O'Hare was camping along the Shasta River where a creek came into it, below the Bowles ranch. He went into town, only a few miles away, nearly every day, making inquiry into work and availability of land for purchase. In the taverns, there was talk of the railroad someday coming up from Sacramento. Massive machinery was arriving for the mill as the world evolved from animal power to steam before their eyes. It was a glorious age of progress and western man achieving ever greater dreams, forged the engineering to make them reality. As any new innovation developed it quickly adapted to innumerable uses that often confounded even the original mind that created it.

For thousands of years man lived, worked, created and improved his lot primarily under animal power; bone, sinew and muscle. The primary tools of lever and wheel had changed little in three thousand years of human history compared to what had happened in the last twenty-five. And, this, as nothing compared to what was about to happen.

As he rode the area, scouting it out, he would sit on his horse looking over the land, mountain and valley before him. He saw man's footprint upon the landscape. His energy here was infectious. A moment of silence when the wind did not buffet the ears, you could hear the big saws at the mill. Teamsters, with specialized wagons hauled huge logs, by ox-team to the mill. The smell of fresh cut fir and pine permeated the wind. Everywhere were the pale blue columns of wood smoke from the fireplaces and stoves of the residents and businesses alike. Where man was, there was a clearing among the trees, wood debris and a cabin. Wood was the commodity in abundance. It built everything everywhere and its slash and waste heated all of man's various enterprises. Enterprise ruled and waste was sin.

In early May he had found 160 acres, not far up the river from where he camped. He rode out and saw a somewhat cobbled piece of natural pasture. About half of the land went up a steep slope and was thick with fir and pine. Four thousand dollars was the price and it was fair. It had some mushy spots where springs pooled up and the river crossed. There were gray boulders clustered incoherently in the pasture. By what force or cause, he could not guess. Finally, he thought, I'll get a place to fish. He looked into its waters, about 30 feet wide and three feet deep and could see trout, shimmering along the gravely bottom. He investigated and eventually applied for a homestead for a section and a half, adjoining him. He bought the 160 acres that day, cash on the barrel head.

By the end of May, he was camped on the property, and with two other men, had felled enough timber to start his log cabin. He chose a site up on the hill, overlooking the land and with a direct view of Mt. Shasta which seemed to take up the sky. He and the men tapped into some springs higher up the hill for water, even though he had not been awarded the homestead on the parcel-yet.

In the morning the men worked, pealing the logs, notching them and constructing the levers, bracing and pulley systems to hoist them into place. Late in the afternoon, O'Hare rode or walked back into the homestead parcels. These properties were dark with thick trees, gullies and ravines unseen except from within them. One day, they stopped work early and he went off to explore the back areas of what he applied to homestead. As he walked, small rivulets trickled down every hundred feet or so crossing the path forged by animals and trod by only him. The further in he explored, the more magical it seemed to him. A ridge broke upslope on his left, as he walked. The trail rounded its toe and then opened into a hidden gulch perhaps only 600 feet across but he could not see far upslope. The humongous trunks were dark, their bark a half foot thick in places. Every twenty feet in every direction going up the draw, these giants stretched upward to the light. They were thrice anything else he had seen in the area. He walked to the nearest and stretched his arms, but they barely arced halfway around the trunk. He stepped back several paces as if punched, realizing the true size. His mind struggled as their scale and his own seemed incongruent. Slowly, he arched backward tipping back his hat to see the tops, felt vertigo and fell over. He started giggling like a child and then broke into laughter, then raucous laughter, finally grinning in silence, laying in the thick bed of pine needles. On his feet again, he began to count, but stopped at over a hundred and still could hardly see up the slope.

He knew he was well onto the property, no danger of having walked beyond what he intended to acquire. As he looked again up into the canopy, he made rough estimates. It was nearly a hundred fifty feet up the massive trunks to the first branches, entwining their fingers with other trees, diffusing the light to a soft glow on the forest floor. He could not understand his own tears which welled up being in the presence of so stately a creature of God. It was like he had been touched by something out of this world; a childlike giddiness that had escaped his youth in famine-struck Ireland, and at his mature age he felt young and blessed and ran back down the trail. He had never felt that kind of excitement. It was wrapped in his own desires of wealth and dreams, but it was also a spiritual episode, in that he felt like God had personally touched him, for the first time in his life. "Could it be?, he thought. Could I possibly end up with these magnificent creatures?" He slowed to a brisk walk back down the trail, but his feet hardly touched the ground. He was determined to say nothing of what he had seen. Not until it would become his... if it would become his. It seemed, his life a strange journey, the pieces were all coming together.

———

She emerged from her tent, surveying what seemed a semi-permanent camp. Food was hung in a sack, slung over a tree branch where bears couldn't get to it. Various lines ran from tree to tree. A good slug of wood was chopped, split and stacked near a sturdy table. The fire pit was improved with an improvised cooktop of strong mesh. The tent was standup tall and roomy inside, made of heavy canvas.

She stretched like a cat and yawned at the early morning light. Soon the men she had hired would arrive to begin the laying out and construction of a cabin. As the sun rose above Mt. Shasta, the tall fir and pines cast their long shadows across the dewy meadow. A herd of deer grazed only a hundred feet away. A large buck with a massive rack watched Mel, as his does moved slowly, their small mouths munching along the ground continuously. As she exhaled the yawn, her breath could be seen, but the day would warm quickly as it was spring. The smell of wet sage and pine filled her nose. Standing for a moment she heard the rushing of the creek still some distance away. She moved about to fix herself some breakfast.

The cabin would be small, something that could be finished quickly, but would suffice for a year or two. Then, she thought, something bigger, or just add-on to it.

Soon, the sound of a wagon rumbling up the suggestion of a road could be heard. Two strong men and two boys, their sons, hopped off. The wagon contained string, stakes, hatchets, hammers, falling saws and rip saws, rope and other tools and materials.

"Mornin' m'am", said Jimmy Hooker, as the other men went straight to designated chores of unloading.

"Good morning, Mr. Hooker. I'm glad to see you're on time."

"Oh yes, m'am. That wouldn't be a problem. We'll be here just past first light. The boys have their chores to do before we come here."

Mel smiled, approvingly. "They look like fine boys".

"They are, m'am, young men, really." They were probably 13 or 14, but seemed all business and needed no direction from their father.

"Have you decided on a spot for the cabin?"

"Yes, right over here would be just fine".

"Yes, m'am; good sun, close to the water, protection from the wind by those tall pine over there and not too much road to build. Yes, m'am, this'd be a good spot. How big she gonna' be?"

"I think 20 feet by 40 feet will be adequate for now."

"Will that include a porch, or such?"

"The porch will come later and be added on."

"Very good, and I'm guessing you'll want the front door toward the mountain?"

"Yes, with a large window looking up to it. And I want to see it from the kitchen sink when that gets put in."

"Don't blame ya' a bit, M'am. That's just the way we'll do it. And the outhouse?"

"Over there."

"Very good, m'am, downwind, yet close enough in winter."

It was exciting to see the project getting under way; twine being strung along the perimeter, digging for a corner stone, and trench for the rock foundation. Before they had begun, the four of them stood together and prayed. Though a willing participant, she joined in more out of respect for these men. She would grow to enjoy this simple moment in the morning and found herself listening more to Jimmy Hooker's straight talk with his God.

Within a week, the boys had the foundation in place while the men had felled enough trees to saw the logs into lumber. They had hauled them to the site by oxen. It was a slow process. They were sorted by size and cut to length. Soon, the latest innovation in portable mills would be along to custom mill the logs. It was breathtaking to consider the savings in work and time.

As the days turned toward summer, their length extended to what would be late night in the winter. This gave her time to explore; sometimes on foot, sometimes on horseback after a day's work. This day the men, finally exhausted, had packed up and were gone for the day. She decided to explore along the base of the adjoining canyon. She rode for about a mile then came to a large creek breaking from the hillside and dashing across the meadow, through the mixed conifer and deciduous trees that painted its banks. She tied her horse to a tree and the animal immediately began grazing at its feet on lush, tall grass. She wore boots which came past her calf and men's breaches, disdaining dresses while working with the men on the property. The sound of the creek rose in a natural crescendo as she approached a outcropping of rocks massed at the foot of the canyon where the creek broke free.

Something suddenly caught her attention in the corner of her eye. Two hundred feet below her was a handsome horse, a chestnut, well saddled, but no rider. Instinctively, she crouched down slipping into cover behind the rocks and overlooking the stream and terrain below. She scouted the area around the strange horse, but saw nothing. The horse was deep in tall grass of its own and paid no attention to her. Then, a voice.

She could not make out the words, for the stream noise, but instantly heard the tone of a man displeased. He now approached the far bank directly opposite the horse. She crouched a little lower as the man put his fingers in his mouth and attempted to whistle a shriek. She could barely hear. Whether the horse did, is uncertain. But he did not acknowledge it, his nose buried deep into the grass and smell of warm earth.

Now the man, paced up and down the bank, seeing the horse and its intransigent grazing. Clearly the horse had waded across the rushing stream without him. All the cajoling fell upon the horse's deaf ear. This man was slightly larger than average, more tall than husky, but not skinny. A beard and full mustache, dark hair combed back on the sides to a ducktail at his neck, with a flash of gray at the temples. He seemed good-looking to her. He now stepped into the creek gauging its depth and flow. His first attempt went poorly and he backed up the bank and started walking upstream, towards her. She crouched lower, then wondered why she was behaving so. Perhaps it was that she was nolonger on her land? But whose was it? Was it this man's? He came closer, then started in across the stream again. He was clearly calculating his options. His horse grazed in blissful oblivion. He tried again, but the rounded boulders, tumbled by the swift current were too much.

He stood for a moment looking around strangely. It appeared he had seen her, but... no. He sat down on the bank and began to remove his boots, his shirt, then his trousers. As she peered around the rock, he removed the long underwear, worn year-round by many men and stood buck naked on the bank of the stream. She could not withhold a smile as he tiptoed down to the stream, his boots and pants, a bundle on top his head held by one arm. He was a handsome man in every regard, and she longed for her husband afresh, as she had so many times in the last year. He was still cussing his horse as he let out a shriek as his manly parts submerged into the rushing stream. She laughed out loud, her hand covering the wide smile on her lips. Now he seemed to float a bit downstream, only his neck above the froth. Slowly he emerged on this side; first his chest, belly and then a considerably diminished manhood. His footing clearly tenuous, he struggled both to retain balance, yet get out of the water quickly. It amused her to watch this cold, wet man tiptoeing rapidly, 'ooching' and 'ouching' across the rocks, cussing that horse every step then, suddenly:

"Oh, ooh, oh, ah,-Shiiii......!" And 'kersplash' he went, his boots and bundle of dry clothes, back into the frigid water. Immediately, he regained the soggy possessions and threw them all onto the cobble strewn bank and fetched himself to dry land. Shivering and cramping up, he addressed himself to a flat rock in the sun. With his wet garments, boots and grittied buttox, he sat, then slowly prostrated himself upon the warmth of the rock.

She watched for some minutes as an interested woman might. Who was this, she thought? Perhaps a neighbor? Was he married? Probably, and with a family and all.

Was he kind, and as funny as he seemed? Or was he stern and poorly tempered? Could he be a future friend, or just a strange man passing through the countryside? Could he be her lover, like the love she had with John Brenner-man? She stole a last long glance as he lay openly naked upon the large rock, his body warming to the sun and sky. Slowly, she crept back down the rocks and quickly made way to her horse and walked it beyond a small stand of trees before she mounted and rode back to her camp, thinking of him.

Jonathan Phineas O'Hare, shook and shivered on the hot, flat rock, waiting for the sun's heat to overcome the blue clammy skin of his body. Some shivers ran through him like convulsions. Then finally, it broke through and he began to feel his body release the grip on his chest. Slowly it relaxed until he could breathe naturally. He sat up, grabbed his clothes and wrung them out. He glanced over his shoulder to the horse that had given such grief. The horse looked at him as if to say; 'Why, whatever happened to you'?

His brogue broke through. "Let me tell ya' laddy, you ever d' this again, they'll be squirtin' you out of a glue bottle."

He dressed partially in the wet clothes and rode the horse back across his creek and gathered the rest of his belongings then headed back to the unfinished log home.

———

On the Fourth of July that year, there was a celebration as in every town. A town hall had been built with donated lumber and labor. The festivities called for games for the children all afternoon, with an open style kitchen for the town potluck and a dance in the afternoon and evening with fireworks after dark.

Bring something, eat something, was the plan. The food was laid out on long tables and it kept coming from the horse-drawn wagons, or out of the mess that had established itself in the hall. There was roasted pig, steak, bar-beque ribs, chicken, corn, homemade breads of several kinds. Peas, beans, carrots and potatoes of a dozen different dishes. The pies were unbelievable; plum, gooseberry, cherry, strawberry, rhubarb, peaches and mincemeat. There was homemade ice-cream. The older folks marveled at the food and ate with gusto. The younger men and women, who came off farms and ranches, now saw each other as potential suiters, future husbands or wives. They ate less and watched more, gaggled into groups where they whispered silly things among themselves then laughed aloud.

Then there was the dance. It was country dance, or as some called it; contra dance. This was an event when people stopped the long days of grueling work; building businesses and ranches, roads, flumes, constructing buildings, logging and creek work putting in irrigation ditches. Now they came together as a community. Young women prepared themselves in the morning for the young men who bathed, trimmed hair and presented themselves as readily as the young ladies. Husbands and wives cut loose and danced, occasionally erupting in jigs or dances of their home countries. Cider was spilled liberally and some boys got hold of a bottle of rye whiskey behind the town hall. The party went into the night as the musicians played banjo, guitar, several fiddles and fifes, drum and base. A young man dazzled the crowd with a harmonica solo. Another brought them to laughter with a juice harp.

Melissa Grady still lived in her camp tent, though the cabin was making progress. She pot washed her clothes and hung them straight as she could. Though her dress was plain, it was clean and fit her well. She stunned men. One glance of her healthy tanned face and arms, well proportioned breasts, a graceful neck squaring to her straight shoulders excited them. Men just wanted to fall upon the crotch of her neck and kiss her. Her trim body and long hair pulled back to a pony tail generally stopped all male conversation mid-syllable as she passed by. It had been a long time, but she felt ready for a social event. She had seen the posters for weeks. She loved to dance. Tonight, perhaps she would.

J.P. had worked a typical day on the home. Its walls nearly complete and framing on the roof now beginning. At one end a massive fireplace of river rock stretched to the would-be ceiling and proceeded as a chimney up through the yet-constructed roof line. He was looking forward to the Fourth of July celebration and a break from the work. There was an eagerness to see other people in the community after days of near isolation.

He now made his way from his horse to the table of food, which having been plundered all afternoon, retained ample selection in all category of dishes. He had not seen a spread like this-ever. Old feelings from Ireland nearly brought tears to his eyes as he looked at the food. Such bounty, he thought. His empty stomach called forth, so he grabbed a plate and started in. Thirty feet down the table, the plate was filled as high as it was wide. It could hold no more, but he longed to sample it all. The women were back in the hall mess and talking about the prospects for the younger men and women. The men smoked cigars and talked of business as the evening finally cooled and the early stars shown. There was talk of the gold mines in the west part of the county; Scott Bar, Sawyers Bar, Humbug and Greenhorn. Millions of dollars were pouring out of this area, but here, it was primarily timber and ranching.

J.P. grabbed silver and napkin and looked among the dining tables for anybody he might know. He was sight familiar with most, but had not really gotten to know many of them yet.

Mrs. Terwilliger asked Mel to ferry out some more mashed potatoes from the mess. She grabbed a big spoon and the pot of mashed spuds and headed to the serving table. She stepped through the doorway and out toward the tables, aware of the hidden glances and turning heads of the men. She walked as only a woman can, who sees all without looking. And, in that knowledge, holds herself in such a way, making her even more desirable to men. She was in that state of consciousness and posture, approaching the table when a tall man, his back to her quickly turned and nearly ran into her. It was him. The man at the stream.

She nearly dropped the pot as she stood looking at him. She stared into his face a moment longer that she should have; a chiseled jaw line with soft eyes and early crow's feet. Their color a luminescent blue against coal black hair, swept back along the sides with a shock of gray streaming back over the ears.

"Pardon me" was all he said as he too stared longer than comfortable, yet only for an instant. 'My God', he thought. 'What a beautiful face.' Like any man, he scanned down her body in an instant, making all necessary assessments. He could neither aid nor hinder this momentary compulsion and she tracked his eyes instantly. Awkwardly they stood there. He offered his plate forward to accept a serving as if in a military mess hall. She glanced down then back into his face, a faint smile at the corner of her mouth.

"Sir, there's no room on your plate."

He looked down at the heaped food, well mingled and spilling, then back at her.

"Maybe just a wee bit on top?" He smiled back.

She plopped a spoonful of the spuds, forming the summit on the mountainous plate of food.

"Perfect", he said, unnecessarily.

"You're quite welcome", she said just as unnecessarily.

He sat at a nearby table and watched as she retreated back into the hall with the empty pot. She was aware of only his eyes watching her.

CHAPTER 6

The celebrations had concluded from the Fourth of July. No forest fires were set, though there were some head-breaking hangovers among the youth who had imbibed that bottle of whiskey.

The next week seemed more full of gossip than usual in town as folks talked about the young ones. Apparently there was one proposal of marriage and one married fellow so upset his wife with drinking and carousing that he was sleeping in the wood shed. This produced ample chuckles and small talk on the wood planked sidewalks of town.

Melissa was hard at work helping as she could, the men charged with the building of her cabin. It was coming along fine. The roof would start that week, and hopefully the windows would arrive from Yreka, about 25 miles north. She was often relegated to fetching and holding this or that while the men did the critical construction. Yet she was pleased and learned quickly. She could nail off the siding and trim boards with a hand saw. She would always provide a meal at noon day. Quietly and respectfully, she would bow her head as Jim Hooker said a quick but fervent grace upon the food and then plowed-in.

She had learned from Mrs. Terwilliger that the man she met was a Mr. Jonathan Phineas O'Hare, formerly a soldier in Fort Klamath, now a hopeful rancher-timberman on the property north of hers but separated from hers by yet another half section of land. More importantly, he was single. She had enjoyed thinking about him; knowing that he was a neighbor. Sometimes she would burst out giggling at the thought of him at the stream that day. Her workmen looked confused and wondered what was so funny, but she just waved them off. But something about him froze her when he looked into her face at the big dinner.

———

"Whoa! Whoa!" Yelled Bill Short, as the huge log, lifted high into the pulley system to set as a ridge beam. A center post drove up through the floor to break the 70 foot span in half. The weight of the log was near the breaking point of the braces. The block and tackle creaked and groaned under the strain-everyone ran well out of the way as the makeshift crane tried to swing the big log into place. After a moment of stillness, they crept back into place, the log dangling in the air over them. With ropes tied to the end, two men slowly pulled one end of the log into place near where the chimney was constructed. There, its notched resting place on a huge log post stood ready to receive it. "Slowly!" Bill Short yelled as the massive log slowly came to rest in its place. Then the other end was coached into its place on the post midway through the beam length. It fit perfectly and an audible sigh of relief was heard along with back slapping and shaking of hands all about the crew. Jon O'Hare was visibly relieved and someone produced a flask of whiskey and all partook in ceremonial goodwill.

The day was done and the men began to pick up their tools. He retreated to a makeshift office in a corner of the open floor, covered by a canvas stretched across a corner of the structure, still open to the sky. His desk was of sawhorses and an old door laid down upon them. He had been thinking about her. He had even started once to go visit, as a neighborly gesture of course, but had retreated, thinking it perhaps too forward. When the crew had vacated, he was left alone to sleep on the expansive open plank floor.

He gazed up into the stars and thought of her. He imagined dancing a beautiful slow waltz with her, their eyes never parting. Her cheeks and skin perfect. Her face, a work of art from God above. He imagined her laughing at his silly jokes and foolishness and then she was at his arm, looking at him proudly. He imagined her in bed, loving him, giving herself to him and he to her in passion and intimacy. He imagined her, in a yard with children playing and laughing, the log home in the background nearby. He beneath the long covered porch smoking a pipe; happy, fulfilled. He rolled over in his bedroll and spoke out loud to himself.

"You'll never sleep, if you keep thinkin' o' her, boy." He sighed and tossed and turned until the day's work overcame him.

As the Summer progressed, he received the land with the tall trees as a homestead. But the happiness he thought it would bring seemed dull now. Only the thought of seeing her again excited him. He had gone to visit in August and he was well received. Her workmen were there, finishing the small cabin which was nearing completion. It was a bit formal. He felt stiff and somewhat awkward. She so captured him, that he found it difficult to say anything though he had never been accused of being a shy man. Certainly not in the army. But she simply froze him in his tracks. Everything about her hands, face, hair, legs, her back, shoulders, her smile, her eyes, all captured him in a sense of perfection. He dare not let his stare linger upon her small rounded rump, or he cramped in his private area.

His log home, though shaping up to be a very respectable home, was going much slower than he thought it would. He had hoped to have it enclosed by now, but it would be a race into winter to get it finished.

In October, he received an invitation to a house warming party at Melissa Grady's new cabin. Friends and neighbors were invited to the small gathering-about 25 guests.

It was a Sunday afternoon. Folks showed up with food and several with musical instruments. As the crowd gathered, she realized how small the cabin was, yet all fit inside, though snugly. After a large meal was served about dusk, some men started a good sized fire outside and the music began to play.

She had watched him as he blended in easily and comfortably with others. Most, he knew; tradespeople from town and some of the other neighbors. While he may have been uneasy in her direct presence, there was nothing like that in his manners with other men and women. Soon, he was encircled while engrossing a small crowd in some story which was provably false at its conclusion, but had all listeners laughing and clapping their approval even so. He laughed with them and at them and his laugh was infectious and could not fail to make her smile and start to love him. When their eyes met, even for a moment, her chest warmed and it seemed that her face went flush. 'What was it about him?', she wondered. As the evening wore on, the townsfolk loaded into their buggies and headed back home. Some of the neighbors stayed a little longer.

Finally, near finished with her obligations as hostess, she removed her apron and went out to the fire and stood next to him while an old Irish aire played solemnly. It was sad and his eyes were fixed into the fire as she came alongside him.

"Did you have a good time?" she asked.

"It was lovely. The food was grand, and I'm enjoying the music." Feeling a little easier, having the conversation started, he pressed on. "You were wise to have a small home built first. You'll be set for this winter. I'm more than a bit behind in my overly grand estate. I'm guessing the first snow will be on my plank floor."

"I've seen your home from the road, it will be beautiful when it is done. My workmen are finished here. Perhaps they could help you?"

"Yes, perhaps. But its a bit of a budget problem."

"I understand," she nodded and stared also into the fire. Here, the conversation stalled uncomfortably. The fiddlers, which were two, struck up a fine, slow waltz. In unison, Mel and Jon turned to each other and asked the other to dance. They completely interrupted each other, then laughed at themselves for their common sentiment.

He took her hand formally and they stepped toward the fire. There in the dirt, they waltzed to the firelight and the melodious strains of the two violins. She was light in his arms and he, strong. As they turned and stepped, in perfect harmony, the firelight revealed her to him as the most beautiful creature that graced the earth. He no longer cared or was conscious of his eyes piercing into her soul. She looked upon him as a most handsome man, but it was his eyes and his smile that unlocked her heart and that heart lay open before him. Turning and stepping, the light changed its view of each, but their hearts were as in an embrace, wordlessly, spinning slowly in each other's arms. She drew near him and smelled him at his collar. The same rush she had sensed as a wife in love came upon her, and she lingered there.

All too soon, the song came to an end. They separated, he bowing and she a curtsy. The musicians began to pack up with the other remaining guests and started home as the workday would begin at dawn for most, and before then for some.

He didn't want to leave. He wanted to stay with her awhile longer. She busied herself with her departing guests. He stayed by the fire until only the two of them remained.

In her mind, there was a certain discomfort. She wanted him to stay. But there was sensitivity to perceptions by others. Him being there at all could create rumors difficult to dispel. She walked over to him at the dimming fire.

"Jon, thank you for coming. I'm glad to know we're neighbors. I, uh, er, would you like some of the leftovers? I've got more than I could ever eat before it spoils. And there is pie that needs a home." She smiled at him.

"Yes. I'd like that. I don't have much in the way of cooking over there as yet."

"Come on in and I'll fix you up." He followed her in through the door. She moved swiftly as if she'd known that kitchen for years. Bundling half a loaf of bread, some chicken and fried potatoes and a quarter of an apple pie. He stood stiffly. Finally, advancing toward her, he spoke.

"Melissa, I just want to thank you for inviting me. I'm glad we're neighbors." He spoke honestly, "...And I am really pleased to see you again." At this she stopped with the food and turning around, faced him. "And I, you, Jon O'Hare." He stepped forward to her. They stood there frozen in the moment. "And, ..., and you are so beautiful," he said. He then reached his arms fully around her and drew her up to him and kissed her. Her lips burrowed through the thick mustache and beard, finding his lips, kissing him tenderly and embracing him, pulling his large shoulders to her. The kiss was long, unhurried, and tasted like clover honey to both. They separated for breath after a moment and fell back into each other, kissing hard and tasting, inhaling and squeezing. Oh yes, there was something there.

The temperature suddenly seemed to spike as endorphins rampaged and blood pressure throbbed within them. They forcibly parted, knowing they must. She exhaled and put her palm to her forehead as if checking her temperature, turning back to the leftovers. He just breathed heavily beginning to comprehend what this woman could do to him.

"I'd best be going." he said.

"Yes. I think so." she replied.

She finished preparing his bundle wordlessly and set it into his hands.

"I'd like to come calling on you." He requested.

"You'd better." She replied quickly, smiling at him.

"Tomorrow be all right?"

"It depends."

"On what?" He asked quizzically.

"On whether or not you intend to get that house of yours built before winter. You can't be callin' on me all the time and expect to get that mansion of yours built."

"Mel, I've been livin' in tents and on bedrolls since I can't remember. One more winter wouldn't matter, if I could see you every day."

Her mind flashed back to the questions she had about the naked man crossing the stream with a bundle of clothes on his head. Then, she had wondered what kind of man he was. Now she was finding out. He was better than she had hoped. She raised up to kiss him quickly.

"Now you gotta' scoot."

He wanted to tell her something, but words just seemed jumbled in his brain, so he let them pass.

"Good night." He stepped back through the doorway. A partial moon barely lighted the way, but he knew the road home. He galloped, hardly feeling the road beneath the fall of the horses hoofs. He spurred the horse on and caught up with the earlier retreating guests just as the road forked between his ranch or town. He bid them all good night again, and they, him. He was grateful to have caught up with the buggies as this would no doubt spare much gossip and protected Mel's reputation for which he now felt some duty.

———

The moccasins padded silently on the big pine needles and the buckskin trousers slid along the sinewy muscled legs. An arrow, with an exceptionally well carved obsidian head, was notched on the string. Silently he crept through the most magnificent tall trees he had seen. Raised on the other side of the mountain, Chiksha Ka had left his homeland after the Army troubles with the Modoc. Pit River and renegade Indians had brought sorrow and trouble to his land; the land of the Shasta Indian. A beautiful woman, in her thirties, hid with two young boys, a toddler and adolescent, back in the trees. This young man had followed a deer through the woods. It had led him to this place. As he looked up into the trees, his heart was moved. Then the doe stepped out from behind a tree forty paces away. He watched without motion, not even a shifting of his eye, until the deer turned its attention away. Slowly the bow raised and was drawn. Its hind was toward him. He was ready now. He let out the slightest of a "pssst" from his lips. The doe raised her head, inclining itself toward the sound, exposing its flank. But the arrow's flight had anticipated this and struck between the second and third rib, directly into her heart. She collapsed to the ground, kicked twice and was still.

It was good. They had lived on fish for several days while they traveled from the east side of Mt. Shasta, up Butte Creek and along Antelope Creek. That area was heavily volcanic. These were the sacred grounds of the Shasta. But recent history had dislodged many who sought only peace and their continued way of life. For Chiksha Ka, he, though young, could feel the change of history beneath his feet. He knew that the old ways of the Indian would pass into the way of the white man. His father was an elder of the tribe and leader of his clan. He had told his son of a dream. The land would be ruled by the foreigner. Their life adapted, though the vision saw many Indians vanish.

Early missionaries, had for a time, tried to convert the tribe. Although some converted, the mission, in general, had failed and they had moved on. But not before teaching some of the children of the leaders to read. Chiksha had learned to read and had acquired the basic education, knowing some history of the white people and a crude understanding of the world beyond that of the tribe. Of Europe and Asia, and closer; Mexico and Canada. Yet, he desired to live as his people had lived and wanted this for his young sons. His heart was constantly torn between the love of the old life, the land and its ways, versus the knowledge of the world as it was becoming. He saw, in accurate terms, his own people's place in the movement of history and it was unkind.

Until he could be more certain of his eventual relocation, this was a good place. He marveled at the size of these trees. At sunset, the lighting within this forest had a soft glow as it was diffused so high up. He set up a small fire for himself, and prayed, singing out to his tribal spirits; giving thanks for this place and for the deer who's life he took. He softly padded the ground to a drum beat in his own head and raised his arms to the sky looking at the crowns of these magnificent trees. He sang, danced quietly and prayed in his fathers' tongue for the peace and protection of his family. That the ancient ones would guide him in the way he must go. That they would show him the path.

———

The days were getting shorter and the nights cooler. The fall colors came late to this country as warm weather could sometimes linger late into the year. Again the wispy columns of wood smoke were seen throughout the area. More than in the early Spring.

Jon O'Hare was running out of money. His plans did not anticipate the amount of labor required. He had all the raw materials. But without the means to convert a raw material into a useful thing, it remained as God had left it. The fledgling herd of cattle did well, fattening on the lush pastures, and a dozen of the cows had given birth. The herd was growing. But to sell them to pay for labor would set the herd back the year it had just progressed.

The workmen had been paid, and many had given him additional labor out of their friendship and respect. But they too, were driven by the economic necessities, and those were never more clear to men than when winter approached. Food and supplies must be stored up. There could be weeks on end when one could barely leave his abode let alone, earn a living. At that point, all effort was aimed at surviving. Food, water, warmth: All else was ancillary.

Jon had managed to build a good sized root cellar during the summer and kept some supplies in there. It was dug into the hillside a hundred feet from the home and made of stacked river rock and local cobble, with mortar. The simple pitched roof, dove into the hillside, resembling a mine shaft entrance. A gravel floor allowed any water to drain out beneath the door's threshold.

The rains would come any time now. He had already spent several nights in the root cellar. He considered his dilemma as he looked up through the partially completed roof of his home to be. He thought of Melissa constantly.

He had pushed hard to finish the roof, forsaking many of the visits he would have made to her. Several times she had come over with food. They had talked of their pasts; their childhood, siblings and parents. Then school and the things that had shaped their adult life: the army, her marriage. He had asked many questions of John Brennerman and of their marriage. She was honest and told him plainly of her love. Each time, she would look at him and her eyes told him that yes, she was capable of that kind of love for him. She sensed that he, like any other, must question if he could ever be as good as the man in a woman's past, whom she loved. She skirted carefully anything that might lead to her dark secret. He, sloughed off much of the time spent in the army as boring or with humorous anecdotes. He did not like talking of the killing, the bloodshed, the scalpings, the massacres he had seen or had come upon. They would remain as his private hauntings. He simply revealed that they existed and she knew he would talk of them as and when he felt like it.

Her nightmares continued with periodic respite. At times she thought she was rid of them, only to have several nights in a row that disturbed her greatly. Often she preferred a sleepless night to the darkness and torment of these terrible episodes. She worried about how this could be kept from Jon, if they were to marry, as seemed hopeful. She felt a sense of bondage to these dreaded dreams. She could not control nor escape them and this depressed her.

It was the season to prepare for winter. Men hunted for extra meat as those with gardens had already preserved much of that harvest.

Jon O'Hare followed the hoof prints of a white-tail buck, about 160 pounds he guessed. Not large, but this was a case of volume; put as much in the cooler as you think you'll need....... and then a little more. He had adequate supplies of grains and flour, salt and beans, coffee and such. Mel had brought over preserved asparagus, green beans, a sack of onions, some potatoes, canned fruit and some jelly. He bought a tin of something new in town made from crushed peanuts, a thick paste. This, he relished.

The buck had tracked along the contour of the hill, staying inside the tree line for cover. He couldn't see the animal, but it was only a hundred yards ahead of him, on a well worn trail. Jon was fifty feet further upslope paralleling the trail. He tried to stay off it, to keep his scent and prints away. The ground was moist from the heavy dew and he could see the prints every place the ground had been saturated.

The picture of Jon O'Hare was narrow and telescopic in the wide eyes set above long wiry whiskers. Silently, the feline pads touched the ground. Its bony shoulders flexing with the terrain it crossed. A two hundred twenty pound mountain lion was reduced, no famished, to a mere 180 pounds and now tracked him about forty feet upslope and only a hundred feet in back of him. Intently, this cat would freeze and hunker down as Jon made his way across the hillside, between trees and through small thickets of brush and sage. The cat would move with uncanny speed and close ranks upon him, then freeze into motionless camouflage amongst the boulders, brush and dry grasses on the hillside. Hunger gnawed in its belly and it began to salivate.

Jon sensed the buck's nearness and began to crouch, moving more carefully yet quickly. The big cat, did likewise, sensing the energy of what was to come and now closed to forty feet behind and twenty feet above his prey. The pupils dilated as he could now pick up the scent of his prey. His stomach was beyond hunger. It ached for food. The cat locked on visually and began to move as only cats do; when they stalk their prey and attack is imminent, perhaps seconds away. It moved at the brink of silence, closing rapidly upon its food. The launch into chase and kill only an instant away.

Jon looked out across the valley and remarked in his own mind how beautiful this land was. The rich green of the conifers, bordering to the pastures with yellows, gold and crimsons of the birch, oaks and alder trees along the streams. Like ribbons of color flowing out of every gulch, making their way across the green felt of the valley's pastures toward the Shasta River which would collect them all and then deposit them into the mighty Klamath, thirty miles north.

His mind lingered as his eyes took it all in, and then he saw it. The buck was as he expected, medium in size, a nice three point rack. It was only fifty yards away and profiled to him. An easy shot. He raised his rifle and took aim from behind a scrubby juniper tree.

The cat closed ground quickly. This was it! Twenty feet, fifteen, another stride. Jon caught something out of his peripheral vision and began to turn, but too late. He was paralyzed for the only moment that was his. The picture in his mind made no sense. A cat was in the sky above him. The fawnish brown of its fur against the deep blue sky and black lips pulled back revealing yellowed fangs bearing down on him. The ears pealed back flat against the wide head. Whiskers and pink tongue, hissing. The vile breath stinging his nose as strong forearms stretched out to him-claws extended. And then this, the strangest of all. A shaft of wood sticking from one side of the cat, just behind the shoulder, through and out the other side. Its gleaming point a deep red against the blue sky. Instantly, the cat fell upon him and they both tumbled down the hill. His rifle thrown from his hands, discharged as it banged against some rocks. The buck took off. All went dark.

His eyes clicked open, flickered, then shut down again. Some timeless moment later, they clicked open again, fluttered, then he groaned. Finally realizing his status, moccasin feet were but inches away from his face. 'The cat! My God, the cat!', his mind raced. He tried to startle himself and sit upright, but the shoulder he relied upon gave out and his face crashed into the dirt again.

"Slowly" came a word in clear English.

Without getting up, he looked up and saw an Indian standing over him. This sent an involuntary shot of adrenaline through him and he struggled to sit up. The Indian made no move, but just watched him. Stunned, he sat on his butt and surveyed this scene. A few feet away lay the mountain lion. A hole through its ribcage into the heart had pumped volumes of blood in the few seconds the cat had lived past his lunge through the air. The arrow had struck home as the forearms had extended to the zenith of their reach and the hind legs had launched the cat into the air.

And slowly, it did come to him. He saw and now understood. His shoulder was bruised badly, but otherwise he was fine. A small concussion from hitting the ground with the weight of the cat on top him gave him a queezy feeling.

"You are good? came a question.

"Thank you", the response. "Yes, I think I'm okay." The Indian nodded to the dead carcass over his shoulder.

"The hunter was being hunted."

"Yes, I guess I was." He looked at the Indian with obvious questions in his face.

"I am Chiksha, but my Christian name is Billy." This always amused O'Hare. It appears the entire Indian nations who had acquired Christian names by missionaries or ranchers or trappers seemed to fall into but a few names.

Charlie seemed the most popular, then Henry, Bill or Billy, Tom, a few Mikes, and then the rest.

"Well Chiksha," he said with perfect inflection, "I owe you. Thank you."

"You call me Billy. It's fine with me. You live in the big log house? The one with a little roof?"

"Yeah." They both laughed. "I'm Jon O'Hare", and he extended his hand to the Indian who took it easily, and shook it firmly.

"You are not Modoc, or Karuk." Are you Pit?

"No. I am Shasta."

"Are you traveling through or do you live here?"

"Good question. Right now, I am camped here. I am in the big trees, the giants."

"Oh, I know them," Jon replied.

"You sit, while I work." Billy said, and he turned his attention to the cat. He had it skinned in what seemed a single minute. He held up the full skin, which lacked the trophy type head for the more utilitarian cut as a garment, a cloak. He held up the skin and said something prayerful to the sky. He reached down and offered O'Hare a hand up. They walked back to the log home. The woman and the boys following out of sight up in the woods. Billy kept track of them peripherally and inconspicuously. O'Hare hadn't a clue.

Jon O'Hare was amazed at the English this Indian possessed and his education. Though only equivalent to perhaps sixth grade, it allowed him to converse freely with him at any length lacking very few proper words, which the Indian had learned but forgotten from disuse. They arrived at O'Hare's cabin in progress and took shelter in the small portion that crudely enclosed the kitchen area.

A small bandage was put on Jon's head and he rigged a sling to relieve the pain in his shoulder, which would be much improved within a few days. Feeling obliged, he offered Billy several canned goods. There was some salt pork. He pulled out an opened bottle of whiskey. He thought about all his experiences with Indians and drink, but felt safe with this man. After all, he already owed him his life. He swilled on the bottle and passed it to Billy, who did likewise. As they traded snorts, they began to relive the only experience they had together; the cat. Soon they laughed and seemed as long friends. Then it struck Jon.

Still feeling obliged to Billy. "Let me fix you a sandwich."

"I remember that word, but forget what it means."

"Simple. Anything you put between two pieces of bread is a sandwich."

"I think I've had sandwich before".

"Not like this, O'Hare replied." He sawed several pieces of bread off the loaf Mel had baked for him. Then he got the canister of the 'wonder food'-the peanut paste out and spread it on thickly. Then another bolt of lightning hit his slightly feebled brain. Elevated from the several quick shots of whiskey, he rummaged through his supplies and with an "Aha!", produced a jar of Melissa's jam. He went about his determined task in the manner that half drunk men do. They perceive themselves moving with great efficiency and purpose as if on an errand from on high. To more sober eyes; staggers and stumblings.

"I've never tried this, so you'll be my Guinea pig". Billy's brow furrowed.

"What's a Guinea pig?", he asked.

"Never mind," O'Hare dismissed with a lazy wave of his hand. "It's not worth the explanation", he slurred.

Their friendship now budded openly as the alcohol breezed through their blood streams. Soon, O'Hare, produced for the first time in 'his' known history, what he thought was surely the culinary masterpiece of the wilderness; a peanut butter and jam sandwich. He offered it to Billy, who looked at it from several angles without touching it's guts and then looked suspiciously up at O'Hare.

"Are we to eat this thing?" He asked as he lifted the top piece of bread and grimaced at the gaudy red and brown concoction.

"I've had them both, just never put 'em together is all. Watch." At this he took a big bite of the sandwich and chewed several times. He stopped and Billy looked deep into his face as if determining if he would be ill or die. Then the gnoshing resumed with gusto, but he could not clear his mouth to speak. Finally drafting water from a ladle and barrel, he cleared his pallet and exclaimed: "You gotta' try this."

Billy could easily see the eager excitement on his new friend's face and took a zealous mouthful. He chewed, masticating twice, then stopped as if stunned, feeling his mouth become mired. A moment of panic set in.

"It's okay, just keep going", O'Hare encouraged. Soon Billy swallowed the sweet and salty mix of dough and gulped some water. Now relishing the sandwich, he quickly finished his, while O'Hare mused about the possibilities of going into the peanut butter and jam sandwich business. This, of course, lasted only until they both passed out; the whiskey bottle emptied and peanut butter and jam smeared on their faces.

Up in the woods, the woman sighed and looked at the young boy. In her native tongue: "Sometimes.............., your father,......," and this she just left in mid-sentence.

CHAPTER 7

In his stupor, O'Hare dreamed of Melissa. He was kissing her. She was kissing him wildly, even seductively. Her tongue seemed to lash out at him. She was forceful and persistent. He turned his head to breathe as she penetrated his lips. She was wet and steamy. His resistance finally awakened him to his border collie, Pete, licking Jon's lips and cheeks, yet another fan of the peanut paste and jam.

Soon, they were both awake. The pain returned to the shoulder and a headache was added to the injury. Billy begged off and said he was going back to his camp for the night.

"Hey O'Hare, do want help with this house?"

"I can't afford to pay you."

"I didn't ask for pay. Just let me live, hunt and fish here."

O'Hare smiled, and the Indian liked the smile.

"Okay with me, Billy. I could use the help. Have you ever built anything?"

"No, but it won't matter. We will finish it."

O'Hare shoved out his right hand and they shook firmly. Billy grabbed his bow, quiver and cat hide and disappeared up into the woods.

——

That winter was mild and drew a collective sigh of relief. The depletion of wood fuel and food stores was withstood by all but the foolish.

Mel was often out on horseback surveying how best to irrigate the pasture land from the creeks which broke from the gulches on the steeper side of the ranch. She planned to bring the water around the toe of the hills, skirting the pastures along the contour. While all the pasture was green and wet in Spring, she had learned how quickly it dried in July. By August her cows could destroy the turf, rendering it a dry tuft of roots. For now there was plenty of grass, so they moved on. They fattened well in the summer and fall. As the herd grew, she knew she must take hold of the water resources that were hers and develop them.

She had found the Chinese to be good workers. As the mines in the western county stalled or played out, the excess labor found demand in the valley which was growing with farms and ranches. Some Chinese families pooled their funds and started businesses of their own-often laundry or food.

While prejudice exists and always has, most were accepted within the towns and among local businessmen. When human needs and wants for any manner of goods or services were unmet, there was a natural inclination to accept and appreciate those, of any color or creed, who recognized the need and set forth their own capital and effort in an attempt to satisfy them.

And so the towns grew one business at a time. Sometimes in a flurry, occasionally with great fear and hesitation. Often an enterprise was unsuccessful. The doors closed, but another would open using the carcass of the last enterprise as a discounted foundation for the next.

Individuals unencumbered by external restrictions were left to create the world they desired. One life at a time. Their only limitation being the capital at their disposal, the God-given capabilities of each and the tenacity with which they pursued their dreams. Ownership of property was paramount. Whether real or chattel, it commanded the utmost respect and there was little tolerance for any abridgment.

Families plied their cumulative skills and labor, including that of their children against the constant challenges of a stubborn yet bountiful nature.

Accident and misfortune, man's constant companion since the beginning of time, did not slumber here. Reports of a cabin burning down were among the worst of winter news. There, all would be lost and the unlucky family, if they survived, prevailed upon friends, neighbors and the church to sustain them in charity, or debt until the spring, when they would begin again.

But accidents could be less dramatic and still be fatal; a fall from a horse, the single misplaced swing of and ax, a sleeve caught in machinery, a slip of footing deep in the woods or an errant gunshot. All were everyday possibilities. Such news of others often met an offering of prayer for God's mercy on the unfortunates and a silent prayer of gratitude that it had not been them.

Mel and her Chinese laborers had also worked on fencing over the winter. The small cedar had been cut and split for rail fencing. Rocks, which were all too plentiful in some areas of the pasture, were dislodged from their stubborn holdings and stacked into meandering walls two feet thick by three feet high. Much of these fortress looking walls were of a volcanic rock with abrasive surfaces and edges. They stacked well, adhering to each other by their cleaved sides and surface friction.

She decided to fence out the stream from the pasture, protecting the fish as there was ample stock water in other sources.

While she worked tirelessly during the day, she busied herself by night in the economics of her dwelling; sewing curtains, making what she could and shrewdly purchasing what she could not make.

New inventions appeared in the stores in town of every manner of household item. Anything that could be made of a better material, an innovative design or that would save the slightest bit of repetitive labor seemed to have been thought up.

Night or day, busy or resting, she thought of him. Jon had visited sporadically but his arrival was the delight of her week. The ebb and flow of her own work week began its crescendo the day before his visit on Fridays. The ingredients obtained, she baked his favorite pie, which seemed to change with every introduction of a different filling or flavor. She would prepare them a meal with plenty for him to take home. They talked for hours and it had become obvious to both that they were well suited to each other.

Christmas had passed with uncharacteristically mild weather, but with just enough snow for children's dreams. Snowmen, and sleigh rides through the country seemed the recreation of the season.

Jon and Mel rode their ranches encouraging each other with ideas and viewing the progress each had made. She was clearly the more organized and her labors' fruit, more apparent.

He too had done some fencing but much of his and Billy's efforts focused on the log house. Thanks to the weather and Billy's help, the roof was finished in January.

Now enclosed with two bedrooms a kitchen and dining room open to a large living area, it was habitable. More grand yet was the plank floor whose long lengths lead the eye to the end wall where the massive rock fireplace stretched through the log beams above them.

Billy had introduced his wife and young sons after a short while, his trust in Jon now sufficient. Jon liked Billy's wife who went by the Christian name of Sarah. Though her English was not as good as Billy's she learned very fast as did the boys. Still, the family would sometimes revert to their native tongue when discussing something among themselves. It was Billy's goal to somehow adapt to the work he saw emerging while holding on to that which he revered in his own culture.

Still rough and unfinished, when the house was weather tight, Jon brought Mel over and cooked a dinner for her. Sarah helped. It was venison steaks, biscuits, stewed tomatoes and mincemeat pie. The meal was one of many to come over the rest of their lives. They could not have known their lives, so recently crossed, would establish friendships and family ties that would last for generations and require love, honor and sacrifice.

Sarah and Mel hit it off as often happens to women when two men of like mind and character find each other and bond in values, ethics and outlook. Billy and Sarah's boys loved Jon, who played with them more readily than their own father. They adored Mel, even more and pouted when they were 'shooed' from her presence, to go play or do chores.

After that first dinner in the big home, Billy and family retreated to their camp, which was to be improved with a modest cabin of its own in the spring. The fragrance of cedar wafted throughout the house as the fire was stoked with split logs three feet long. He lit a cigar and stood before the fire, staring into it. He silently recognized a moment of accomplishment. He had seen this very moment many times in his mind, but now it was here. He toked on the stogey and blew a smoke ring up toward the high vaulted ceiling, appreciating what he saw and felt.

Smoothly, her arms came around him from behind and she caressed his back, her arms folded against his belly.

In his heart he also knew how empty this and every other vision and dream would be without her. She completed him. She was the compliment of his body and soul. He put his hands over hers and she closed her eyes, exalting in the simple embrace, the crackle of the fire, his smell and the form of his body in her arms.

He whispered something, but she could not hear for her own private thoughts denied any interruption.

"What?", she said, asking softly. He whispered again the same thing, by syllables and tone, she could tell. But again, she could not hear. Now somewhat perturbed in a cute way.

"What did you say?"

He turned within her embrace and looked into her eyes in a way he had not before. He stared deep and long into them as she noticed his slow descension. He came to rest on a single knee, holding her hands in his own. He began to kiss her hands, the backs, then palms, left then right, then the backs again. Her heart raced at this touching and she bit her lip to stifle the welling emotions.

His back warm to the fire, he looked up into her face, the fireglow dancing on the strong, yet beautiful features of her face. She looked like an angel looking down from a warm and cozy heaven.

"I said, marry me, Melissa Grady. Marry me and make me the happiest man in the world. Marry me and complete me; bear my children and I will be your man forever."

Her mind seemed to race, but could not find traction. She was instantly transported into her own future; the happiness that might be hers, the hope and fear of bearing his children, the fear that her secret might be known, and the hope that somehow it might be banished from her life. She was lost in these thoughts as he waited, looking up to her face.

"Well...?", he asked after several long moments.

She took his face in her hands and knowing her answer, put her fingers through his hair, coming to rest them again, cradling his face.

Slowly she got down on her knees with him.

"Yes, I will marry you, Jon O'Hare. And if you love me as I know you can, I will be the wife you want. You will complete me. I love you so much."

"And I love you," He proclaimed. They kissed tenderly before the fire. They hugged and cried some as the realization that they would become man and wife took hold. Jon vacillated between being giddy at the prospect of being a husband and a father, and then to sternness as his mind foretold of the sacrifices and planning that would be involved. Within three minutes his mind was concerned with several generations down the line and she just laughed at him. Then he burst out laughing with her.

He insisted that she spend the night. The bedroom would be hers and he would sleep on the floor by the fire. The other bedroom was full of stored materials and goods. They toasted with several glasses of wine and talked deep into the night. They suddenly realized that if they could buy the land between them, they would assemble one of the best ranches at this end of the valley. She had 960 acres and he had 480. With the half section of 320 acres between them, they would have 1,760 acres. Four creeks flowed into the Shasta River which ran though the combined properties near the downslope boundaries. The sixty or so acres of the 'tall trees' way in the back, was known only to Jon and Billy.

They parted late, into the early morning hours, kissing good night. They would be married in the spring; the sooner the better. She could not wait to write to her parents, now aged and unable to travel the distance. Soon, she would be the center of news in the community. They would be a couple. She started planning the wedding and her dress and all the incidentals.

Jon threw down some blankets and a pillow on the floor. Pete, lay at his feet like every night, his chin resting comfortably on paws. His brown eyes darting from Jon to the bedroom door with every sound that emanated from it. Jon lay back, his head in the palms of his interlaced hands behind him on the pillow and looked up into the beams and logs running at right angles through the upper space near the roof. Not entirely by accident but with hope for a quieter result, he farted and it seemed so loud on the plank floor, that he felt compelled to call out.

"Pardon me," he declared. She heard that and decided it best to ignore this indiscretion. When, of a sudden, a gastrointestinal event in him culminated in a tremendous eruption, fluttering the floorboards again.

"Sorry" came the monotone.

"Stop that. You're doing that on purpose." She yelled from behind the bedroom door, stifling a giggle.

"Well, not exactly. But, dear, if we're going to be married it won't be the last time you'll hear it." This humored him in an adolescent way.

"Well, that certainly gives me something to look forward to", she dripped sarcastically at the door. At this, he smiled, as Pete's eyebrows raised, his chin planted between his paws, anticipating the next banter.

"Now, I know ladies do not participate in this 'sport', but try to have compassion on the more brutish gender."

A last eruption and she protested "I heard that".

"That was Pete," he lied, as Pete, on hearing his name raised up, seeming to defend his own manners.

She smiled and shook her head, going to bed but not to sleep for her mind traveled through a new and vibrant future, bright with color and hope. Soon Jon was snoring.

She listened and realized how much she wanted to just be with him; to lay in his arms, to be held by him and rest on his chest. She felt that they were invincible, together. They were a team, a partnership forever. But she must wait to lay with him. The very thought drove her slightly mad.

Her thoughts turned then to John Brennerman, a man she had loved with all her heart. She cried at the thought of losing him and how he died. He was such a good man. And now her tears were in letting him go; the last of him. The secret part she had held on to. It was time to live; to love again, to give her own heart a chance at happiness. Slowly, she let a memory of him walk away into a dimly shrouded fog. He looked back as if to understand and then turned and stepped into eternity. She tried to stifle the sobs but it shook the bed. Then, images of Jon O'Hare walked into her life. He was bright and radiant, full of life and he offered that life to her. She stepped toward his visage and accepted that new life. She held onto him tightly never wanting to let go. Finally, sleep came to her.

———

The winter continued mild and so drew comments and compliments at nearly every light conversation. The towns-people were most happy with it. The farmers and ranchers were too, but it wasn't long before worry talk began about a "no rain" and 'what if' scenarios on a deficient snow pack in the high country. Jon figured he could do nothing about it and disliked wasting time talking about the things he had no 'say' in. February saw the start of the big barn, with a place to stack the hay and get animals out of the wind and the weather. He had been surprised at the windiness. Some days, the wind seemed to roll off the 14,000 foot mountain, gathering speed across its barren upper slopes. When it hit bottom it sometimes snapped trees three feet thick, like matches, especially when they stood alone without the protection of a forest. Down in the pastures, it came 60 to 70 miles an hour. With gusts, nobody was willing to guess at. A barn was necessary for the animals. So back into the smaller forests he and Billy went to fall the timber for the logs. They selected them with care for the size, length and taper: Douglas Fir.

They were becoming quite adept at logging, having learned the falling as well as the hauling aspects. Billy seemed to understand a tree on its insides. It became as a science for him, how a tree would cut, how it would sometimes twist on its stump, according to its grain, and fall in the precise urgings of the cuts and wedges driven at the stump. He could put a tree down within a few degrees of a selected placement, where it would not damage the others growing nearby. Some of the day workers Jon hired to help Billy would make puny bets, as none had any sizable coin, on where a certain tree would fall. Billy would set a stake out 50 feet or so, sticking up about four or five feet high. Invariably, Billy would fall it and drive the stake or bust it to pieces. This the men loved to see, even at the cost of their wager.

The spring of 1878 came in nice, about mid-March. The date was set in June for the wedding and things began to happen at panic pace. Mel could hardly focus on ranch projects for the details of the wedding. It would be simple and held at the ranch, as O'Hare's place came to be referred. The dress was being made by a seamstress in Mt. Shasta, and they took care of the food themselves. All the neighbors and a good many townsfolk were invited.

A chance encounter in late February solved a particular problem: Who would marry them? Jon was setting rocks as footings for the posts of the pole barn, logs actually, when a horseman rode into the yard. Older, gray whiskered, he wore a long coat, had good boots and a wide brimmed hat. He was a local preacher, new to the area and was out and about, getting to know the people.

He rode straight over to the work and introduced himself to Jon, while the others kept working.

"Browny Wells", he said, sticking out his hand.

"Howdy Mr. Wells. Jon O'Hare, pleased to meet you. How can I help you?"

"Mr. O'Hare, you just call me Browny. All my friends call me that. I'm new to your beautiful country and I'm out getting to know the folks hereinabouts. I'm the minister of the Presbyterian Church in town."

"Oh, so it's Reverend Wells then is it?"

"Browny will do just fine sir. And I'm guessin' from your brogue and look, you'd be Catholic Irish."

"Well sir, Irish, yes and I was raised Catholic, but no, we never went to church that I remember. I'm probably more heathen than anything else," he smiled broadly to the preacher. Browny smiled back just as widely and seemed to light up.

"You are in luck, my boy. It so happens I'm beginning to preach on the Gospel according to John. There is no better place to see God's love for man and Christ's work upon the cross. It will be an education for you Mr. O'Hare that could carry you into the hereafter."

"Well, Browny, I'm awfully busy with the here-and-now. I don't see that I'd have time to worry about the hereafter just now. I've got a barn to build and a house to finish and a wedding coming......"

"A wedding!", cried out Browny in exuberance. "Who's getting married?"

"I am". Browny stuck is hand out again and shook even more vigorously in congratulations.

"And who is the beautiful bride to be?"

"Melissa Grady."

"I don't believe I know her."

"Neighbor, really."

"You don't say. That'll be right handy. Where's it gonna be?"

"We'd been thinking here. No offense to the church, mind you."

"No offense taken, Mr. O'Hare. The Lord said 'Go forth and populate the world', and that, we should do. If there is anything I can do, please let me know."

"Well I guess there is, come to think on it".

"What's that?"

"Reverend Wells........"

"Browny, please," he corrected.

"Browny, spending no time in church doesn't necessarily mean I don't believe in God."

"I understand, son."

"I think Melissa and I would like a man of God to marry us. Would you consider doing that for us?"

"My boy, I'd be delighted, but I would like to meet with you and the Mrs. to be sometime soon to discuss some particulars."

"Of course."

"You name the time and place and I'll be there. Or, you could drop by the church if you're in town."

"I'll be in touch, or we'll drop by to see you soon. If you'll pardon me, I got work to do, but nice to meet you Mr. Browny."

"Likewise Mr. O'Hare. God's speed."

"Thanks. So long."

CHAPTER 8

Jon and Mel looked at the small white building with the steep pitched roof and steeple over the front door that rose another half story above the roof. He helped her out of the buggy and felt her clammy hands, a cool sweat upon them. Her jaw clenched ever so slightly as she straightened her blouse and addressed the small cobble walkway to the front door.

"I feel so awkward, Jon. I haven't been to church since I was a little girl. Are you sure we should have a preacher do this? Maybe a Justice of the Peace would be good enough?" All her comments came in rapid succession, more as thoughts than conversation.

"It'll be fine, Mel. He's a nice man, doesn't seem too 'preachy' to me. I run into him at the store last week and he was in work clothes. You wouldn't know him to be a preacher, to look at him. In Ireland, we were afraid of the priests as kids. I don't get that feeling around Browny." They walked toward the door, on which was affixed a small placard. 'Browny is around back unless it's Sunday.'

She exhaled giving herself another minute before meeting this 'preacher'. They stepped down off the side of the porch and followed a well worn path to a small house in back of the church. As they neared the rear of the church building, they heard an eruption of men laughing and gaffawing at each other. As they rounded the corner, a half dozen men sat gasping painfully for air, beet red with laughter. One lay rolling on the ground on his back, stamping the souls of his boots, desperate to breathe. Another was slapping his floppy hat on his knee alternating between bending over and stretching to the sky as he walked around in a small circle, his face contorted in laughter. Another man was bent at the waist and appeared to be dry-heaving in the corner of the yard. In the center of the men stood Reverend Browny Wells, with a shovel in his hand and an awful stench emanating from the ugly slime that rose half way up his right leg to just below the knee. He walked like a man with a wooden leg.

They were a group of men in the church of all ages, set to dig a new latrine for the outhouse. The old one had failed and this prompted the diligent crew to their task. Browny in the first shovel full, had found the old system, covered by a rotten timber. His shovel pierced the remaining strands of fiber on which his own weight had stood and down he went. He deftly managed to catch himself and limit the disaster, but not before submerging his one leg into the noxious goo.

Even Browny was smiling at his very bad luck, gimping across the yard to a hand pump well and a bucket where he would begin the treacherous chore of cleaning up.

"Good afternoon," he called to Jon and Mel. "Pardon me, I'll be just a little while. You folks are welcome to have a seat in my office. I'll be right with you."

"All right now," he called to the men. You know where the old one is. Go on out further and find a new spot and get to work." This was said as among friends, committed to a common chore.

"I've got business with these folks. Lord knows I've done the hard part for you." At this, they all laughed again and grabbing picks and shovels moved out away from the buildings. Someone wisecracked how Browny might have got his name and they all erupted in laughter again.

"Hardy Har Har," he mocked them and gimped to the hand pump water well.

Mel was introduced to Browny. Everyone smiled politely and seemed overtly friendly, though keenly aware of awful odor. Browny then excused himself to clean up, while he bid them to wait in his office, which was the kitchen table in his little house out back of the church. Soon he returned and offered them water or coffee, which they declined. They chuckled again at the condition in which they found him. It was good-natured.

"Well, let me say, congratulations once again to both of you on the upcoming marriage. I am honored and would be happy to marry the two of you. I usually talk to younger couples than you, but my basic 'speech' is the same for everybody."

He went on to ask of any past marriages and offered his condolences to Mel for John Brennerman. He questioned them about their past church experiences and their reported faith. He cited the need for the give and take in the marriage, the responsibility to forgive when wrongs and offenses occur. "And they will", he said. Mel had questions about the wedding itself and these Browny answered and the 'details' were worked out. Finally, Browny got around to what seemed to be the thing he wanted to discuss the most.

"Probably, the single most important piece of advice I can give you is a simple statement. But in following it, you'll be prepared to handle any storm in your life, you'll manage the tragedies, you'll grow with and "in" one another, you'll share in the blessings and bounty this life can give. No man or government can own you. Nothing can stop you out of fear or threat. It is the single most empowering gift in the world." He sat silent for a moment lost in his own thoughts, a wide smile breaking slowly across his face.

"Well, what is it?", asked Mel.

"Here it is: Center your life around Christ." They seemed a little disappointed, but still curious and he went on.

"Look, everybody worships something. Usually its the person in the mirror. Sometimes its a husband or wife or children even. Some people put their land, cattle; their wealth as the thing they think is most important. Everybody puts somethin' on the top of the 'totem pole' of their mind; some 'thing' or person in their life. I've seen folks put just about everything up in the "top" position. I've seen bright people put their own smarts at the top; their fancy degrees. I've even seen preachers and rabbis put their knowledge of scriptures at the top. Anything and everything will fit up there and that's the problem. There is only one thing; one person who belongs as the most important thing in your life and that is God."

Jon considered this and then asked. "I knew there was a God when I was a small child. But as the years have gone by, I've begun to doubt and at times, I've flat out denied, at least in my own mind, that he existed at all. I've seen so much that it begs the question."

"As have I, Jon. Before I took up the collar, as they say, I spent some years bounty hunting. I've seen some things that nobody should have to look at. I've done some things I can never repeat to anyone but God." At this, Melissa stirred and a sliver of hope crept into that place deep inside her that cried out, a place where she constantly pressed against the bars of her prison cell. Browny continued, "Most of those things are what man does to man."

"But God allows it!", injected Jon.

"Yes, He does allow it. You're right. And if you're gonna' ask me to explain to you how God sees fit to do things or not, I'm afraid you're asking the wrong man. The Bible says, we cannot know His mind. The nub of it is, that we cannot fathom a mind that is outside of time, within time, and sees the end of all things from the beginning. You'd think birth pains were a terrible burden to a woman, and they are. Sometimes fatal. But then, afterwards, new life is born-a precious child comes into the world. You trying to judge the 'rightness' of her pain, without knowing the end result would be pretty stupid. Yes?"

He went on, "Knowing that God exists should not be derived from considering the actions of men. Look instead at creation; the stars and planets perfectly in order. Consider the water system of this planet, the birth of a child, all of God's creatures, wonderfully made, perfectly adapted at the moment of their creation."

"But God allows natural disasters; floods, famines, hurricanes", Melissa countered.

"Most famines, not all, but most, and I've studied them, are man made. But there is no question that there are natural disasters. Nature simply erupts and destroys man and what he has built. I speak only for myself here, but since you ask, I'll offer my own thoughts: God created this world, the Earth, its processes, from geology to botany. Those systems spend much of their time in seeming harmony as to our lives. We use the water and sun and soil to grow crops. We fish the rivers and lakes and think; Isn't this grand? We husband animals and fashion livelihoods for ourselves, quite impossible without these resources. Then something happens that upsets us, within our time and space reference. Perhaps, a flood, perhaps a drought, a swarm of locust or earthquake. But aren't these processes those that have been in place and produced the planet we live on? The sphere by which we are sustained. The answer is yes."

"I guess I've always believed in God, said Melissa, but what if I can't......., what if something is between us. What if I couldn't go to heaven?"

"Couldn't?", Browny asked.

"What if I .... , shouldn't go to heaven?"

Jon looked at her quizzically, but Browny pursued this.

"If going to heaven is solely about what we do on this earth, then none of us is going. You need to understand this. Going to heaven, spending eternity with loved ones and friends in the presence of God is about what you *believe*, not what you have done. But let me say this: Once you've made a decision on the belief question, once you have professed that faith, if it is true within you, it will change what you do and who you are. In fact, it will change everything; how you think, your priorities in life, how you act toward others. It will transform you. The "belief" question is this. I'll just come to the quick of it. Who do you say Jesus Christ is? That's it. Who was He?" Browny looked at each of them alternately, then settled on Jon.

"I'm just not sure. I know what you'd like me to say; that He was son of God. But I just don't know, yet."

"Fair enough. And if he *was* the son of God, and if what he said *is* true, would that be important enough for you to make a relationship with Him the most important thing in your life?"

"I suppose it would. If.....it was true."

"How about you Melissa? Who do you think Jesus Christ was; a good teacher, a Rabbi, a wonderful Samaritan or philosopher? A revolutionary, perhaps? Or was He the son of God?"

She turned to Jon. "Could you please let me to speak to the reverend for a few minutes, Jon?" He looked surprised, but calmly said, "Of course, dear."

Jon went outside and looked up into the treetops and the blue sky above the little white church and sighed. As he looked down, he was thinking, while scratching his boot in the dirt, rolling a pebble under its sole.

"Reverend Wells"........., "Just Browny", he interrupted. "Okay, Browny........ I am curious about something you said."

"What exactly?"

"You said you had done things that you could never repeat except to God."

"That's right".

"Are these things..........., well I'm certain they are terrible, but........., are they crimes? I mean,................, what would you do if........ Oh, I'm sorry. I'm making a fool of myself. Good heavens, I can't even talk. I'm wasting your time." She stirred as if to leave.

"Please. Don't go," he intoned. "When I told you I couldn't say these things except to God, it is true. But I can see in your heart Melissa that you are deeply troubled and I would like to help if I can." Her chest constricted with emotion. "I hope you can. I'm desperate", she whispered, staring at him intently.

"When I was bounty hunting, I tracked a man who was wanted for murder of a stagecoach driver. There was a robbery and it had gone bad. Anyway, there were no eyewitnesses, but circumstantially, he was a very good suspect. I finally caught up with him on a dark, warm night in August, part way up the Rockies in a remote area, up Idaho way. My partner fell sick and I had left him behind in town. I was on my own."

"I watched through the window and saw he had a woman and boy of about twelve. They were clearly family." Browny looked down at the table and sighed, his eyes inflamed momentarily by visions he saw. His lips were pursed slightly, but shy of a whistle as his lungs deflated and a look of grief swallowed his face. Suddenly he rose and turned to stare out the small window above the table. "I can't".

"Please........... I think I need to hear this", she said. "Please".

He swallowed hard, and looked out the window, transporting himself far away. "I'll only say the 'what', not the 'how' of it. When the sun rose, I had finished the second grave and my man lay across his horse, tethered behind mine.

When I got to the Sheriff's, they told me another man had confessed to the stagecoach killing. My man was innocent."

Melissa sat, motionless, her own tears, gliding down her cheeks, her eyes closed. Softly, she asked "What happened next?"

"I walked out the back door of the jailhouse and vomited. And then there was an inquiry, which absolved me of any wrongdoing, as there was a legal warrant and bounty and he drew a weapon. I spent the next six months in a drunk."

"What about......., what about......, the others?", she asked.

"That is enough, for now. Melissa, it wouldn't have made any difference to me what the "law" said. Was there justification? Yes. Was it right? No. Not in God's eyes and not in mine, but I did what I did."

"Melissa, God is a God of forgiveness. What Jesus did on the cross was for my sins and yours. You may not believe it now-today. But if you study in my church, before long you will come to know that this is the great big truth and it is more important than anything else. Christ died for my sins that night. Melissa, He paid the price for your sins as well. All of them, even the ones you think are so big that there can be no forgiveness. It is Satan that accuses us; that never let's us forget. It is he that torments us with the sins of our past and says ' you cannot be forgiven for *this*. And in those six months of drunkenness, I battled with demons, real demons, and Satan had me convinced that I would have to die to pay for my sin. I was so tired of fighting those demons, I found myself with my own pistol at my head, crying like a baby, but unable to pull the trigger." Mel was sobbing into her handkerchief.

"A pastor took pity on me and took me in. After he flushed the whiskey out of me, he began to teach me. As

I learned, and prayed and studied, in time I saw for myself what I had been blind to all my life: God is the most important thing and Jesus is the way to Him."

"Oh Browny, I've done something so terrible, so shameful, I cannot bear it any longer." She was crying, her shoulders quaking and shuddering. "I have wrestled with demons, of guilt and shame and I'm afraid. I'm afraid this will ruin my marriage to Jon."

"When was the last time you prayed. I mean really prayed to God or to Jesus, by name?"

"I don't know. I can't remember-a long time ago."

"Would you like to know that you are forgiven by God?"

"Yes, oh yes, but how can I know."

"You'll need to accept this by faith, for now, because of His Word. But I know that in time, you will, as you say it, 'know'. You need to confess your sin, not to me........., no, no, but to God directly, intimately, truthfully, and fully-holding back nothing, for it is pointless-He knows everything. He was there. The secret you thought you couldn't share, is something He already knows. It is Satan, who can bind us and keep us in spiritual bondage because of the dark secrets we keep." He sat down across the table from her and grabbed her hands in his.

"Are you ready to begin life anew?"

"Yes."

"Then pray this prayer with me. Afterward, I will leave you to confess to God. But know this; I can see who and what you are. I don't know what you've done. But there is no condemnation from me. Now, here we go."

Here, Browny slowly, thoughtfully made up his own version of the sinner's prayer. He spoke each line as it came to him and then paused for Mel's repetition of it.

"Oh Jesus, I am a sinner and I have sinned greatly in this life.

I believe you are the Son of God and that you died on the cross for my sins.

I have run from you long enough and I quit that running today.

Come into my life, Jesus, and guide me by your spirit. Show me the way.

I will make you Lord of my life."

Mel repeated each line after Browny had spoken it.

"Now I'm going to leave you......, if you want, to confess, privately." She nodded her understanding. He rose to go.

"No," she said suddenly. "Stay. I want you to hear this."

"Are you sure?" Melissa nodded. "Very well then" and he sat back down. "He waited in silence. Then it came-like a flood.

"Oh God ...., and Jesus........." ", she blurted. "I don't know how to do this, she sobbed, but I know you were there that night. I confess to you that I killed that man. I was so filled with anger and hatred at him for what he did. He took my man and he took my baby", she wailed. "Oh God, I'm so sorry. I'm sorry. Forgive me, Jesus. Forgive me." She wept and shook, uncontrollably and could speak no more. Browny came around and held her, and the tears fell.

Jon thought he heard crying coming from the little house, but felt no need to investigate. Whatever it was that prompted Mel for privacy with Browny, he sensed was being dealt with. He stayed out and pondered further what he had heard. He realized that the entire premise of his life was based on, whether he wanted to admit it or not, that Jesus was *not* the son of God. How could he explain his life otherwise. Because if....., if Jesus was who he said he was, then that fact, indeed, all His teachings, would have to rise to the greatest import to him. He determined then and there that he would at least make the effort to learn, to find out within the bounds of his own intellectual ability, who Jesus Christ really was. It might take some time, he admitted to himself, but he could no longer go through each day indifferent to a firm answer to that one all-important question; one way or the other. He looked back at the little white church, as he had absentmind-edly walked some distance away. He looked at the little belfry and thought, this place will do. Browny would be an acceptable teacher. In his own mind, he felt a certain comfort around Browny that he didn't feel around most religious people. He turned around and walked toward the church and little house behind it.

Browny had listened to Mel as she poured out her story to God and him. He could feel her whole body wet with emotion and heat through her dress as he gently com-forted her. He whispered to her that God had forgiven her. That her secret was safe with him. It would be between him and her, and God, of course. The legal implications would be left to fate. Was there a moral justification to what she did? Probably, but not certainly. Was he truly the guilty man that destroyed her husband, child-her whole life? Probably, but not certainly. Would man's law solve anything except its need to adhere to itself? Would it seek and find justice in its outcome? Probably not. Browny knew, as he felt her quakings begin to subside that there are some questions, some burdens, we carry. Though God's forgiveness is certain, our own ability to forgive oth-ers as well as ourselves is miserly-stingy. It was our com-plete inability to "let go". That was the problem.

As she looked up at Browny, a smiled forged its way through the swollen red eyes and the salty spittle that clung innocently to her lips.

"Thank You", she said, but he just looked into her eyes and they both knew they shared something special, a spiritual bond, broken in pride and self, and lifted up in grace and mercy.

"Welcome to the family of believers. But this is more a beginning than an end. I'll just offer a bit of advice. The most important thing is a personal relationship with Christ, so begin to spend time with Him. Set aside some time each day. I like early morning best, but pray and open your heart to Him. Ask for guidance and wisdom and strength to accomplish whatever He would lead you to do. Lastly, have faith. Believe. Trust. You have no idea how powerful it is."

"So now then, let me just invite you to church next Sunday. We've got some wonderful folks-all sinners mind you." They both laughed, and a lightness came into her heart that moment that she could not explain. It felt like it was going to explode in her. Inside her, the darkness was lifting, while Browny mumbled along about the church times and the congregation. She couldn't hear it because this powerful washing of her soul and spirit was flowing from her feet up her legs to her chest. This lightness she had not felt-ever. When the feeling welled up through her chest into her throat, she spoke.

"Thank you. Thank you, Browny." She turned toward the door to see Jon who was coming through at that very moment. She ran into his arms practically knocking him back out the doorway. He hugged her and felt that vibrancy inside her and it was palpable. She was saying she had Jesus. He was stunned but felt an easy happiness for her. Looking at Browny, he noticed that the older man had tears. Tears flowed down his red cheeks against the gray whiskers, bushy white eyebrows.

"I reckon we'll be at church on Sunday. What time?", he asked.

CHAPTER 9

Jon and Melissa met on the road and went to church that Sunday, and most every Sunday for the rest of their lives. They met and formed many friendships in that church. They learned from Browny, and though not at first, but later, became daily readers of the Bible. Jon became a Deacon years later and Melissa was increasingly active in the women's ministries.

The wedding was a beautiful June day. Though they had planned it at the ranch, they changed it to a church wedding. The little church burst at the seams with friends, the congregation which had become very close to both of them, merchants who knew them as individuals, delighted in the prospects of their marriage. Billy was the best man and Sarah was the maid of honor.

The buggy ride home to the ranch was surreal. She sat close to him. The sky had never seemed so blue, the white cirrocumulus clouds, lined up in straight rows, marched across the western sky like an army paying homage to them. As he turned to her, her bonnet against the sky, the green eyes were deep and wonderful, her cheeks blushed, those bold eyebrows he loved, the wisp of hair on her neck was nearly too much for him. How could he love anybody so much, when most of his life he loved nothing at all. It was as if he were awakening to life for the first time. He was alive; fresh and everything was new. He owed it all to her. Well, to her and God too, he thought.

Coming to the log home, it looked like a castle for a prince and princess within their modern world. Ribbons were tied around the columns on the front porch and flowers decked the door way, guiding to the door itself. He offered his hand as she stepped out of the buggy and he swooped her off her feet. Before she knew what happened, he marched up the seven steps to the porch. Across the threshold, and they both began to smile. He kicked the bedroom door open and she giggled and then he threw her onto the bed and she bounced, with a stifled squeal then a laugh as he landed playfully alongside her and then atop her. He kissed her down her neck and his nose filled with her most heavenly scent and he was completely overcome by it. She nibbled on his ear. Both of their bodies flushed, awash in a hormonal tide that swept all else aside. Instantly they were up and pulling off their clothes.

They turned to each other naked, without shame. Her body was beyond his dreams. She was gorgeous, shapely, her smallish breasts perfect in his eyes. "My God, you're beautiful." He said and meant it. She looked at him and said, "Oh my God. You're so ...., and they came together in that moment in an embrace that lasted the rest of their lives. They never parted emotionally from that kiss forward.

They lay down as husband and wife and gave to each other all that they had, holding nothing back. The fulfillment was total, complete. They did not leave the house for three days. They tasted and smelled and rolled in each other's arms, coming to an intimate knowledge of each other in innocence and joy neither had expected. They prepared their meals, drank some wine, read from the Bible to each other. They shared their hopes and dreams and they gave their fears to God and let Him carry them. Nine months, to the day, Connor O'Hare, came into the world, happy and healthy. Melissa wept with joy and praised God for the blessing of this child. Jon, looked at the boy, unwrapping the blanket from its wrinkled face and puggish nose, and went to his knees at her bedside. He gave himself to Christ without reservation.

———

The 1870's passed into the 1880's and with that decade came the Union Pacific Railroad, linking California to Oregon. Seventeen tunnels were dug through the mountains between Redding, California and Ashland, Oregon. Scores of wooden bridges were built. Up the Sacramento River canyon, the tracks crossed and re-crossed again, this famous river, a trout fishing paradise in the region, but an agricultural boon in the downstream region of the valley, all the way to San Francisco Bay.

The railroad was deeded every other section of land throughout the region, by the United States Government. The railroad had lobbied hard and donated even harder. This would be the price of linking a nation together. And link it they did. The engineers worked seven days a week as did the crews; blasting, logging, grading the road bed for the tracks. The trains themselves hauled much of the material to the rail's end, where older forms of labor carried the steel and supplies to their place. The land given to the railroad was often traded or sold, as the engineers saw where the line must go. They hired locals to log their own land if it had timber that could be used on the tracks. Sometimes for ties, sometimes for tall trestles that spanned hundreds of feet through the air. It was used to brace the tunnels. Massive amounts of labor, lumber and steel were produced and precisely placed for an end result years away, yet they knew it would come to be.

One such logging firm was Jon O'Hare. Billy was his lead faller and he had hired two dozen other men, trained them and got contracts with the railroad. Sometimes they were logging on railroad land. The fees were lucrative, but Jon had to reinvest into more wagons, ox-teams, saws and cables. They custom made their own axles and wheels to take the enormous weights and carry them across rugged ground. At the start of the 1890s, the towns of Siskiyou County were all being served by the railroad. Grady-O'Hare, as the ranch was known had grown, first with the parcel that had separated his and Mel's place and then by adding additional timber lands in the back and more pasture stretching out across the valley. It had been a very successful decade.

At the large dining table, sat Jon at one end, Mel at the other. On the one side sat Connor, Liam, William and Festus. On the other side sat their daughters in age; Sarah, Rachel, Deborah and Melinda. Pete was an old dog, mostly blind now with glossy blue cataracts. He spent his last days being loved on by the children who thought of him as the senior member of the family, worthy of their adoration and entitled to their respect.

Billy had long left his buckskins in a trunk somewhere at the house in the big trees in the back of the early ranch. Sarah remained healthy and in addition to Little Bill and Charlie, she had given birth to Melissa and Alexis. Billy and Sarah's children were physically beautiful children, with thin dark features and bright eyes and teeth. They laughed easily and were excellent in the Weed school, which grew rapidly with the burgeoning population.

The town grew as well, administered by its namesake, Abner Weed, an extraordinary lumber man and industrialist.

The Grady-O'Hare Ranch now encompassed over 6,000 acres and had nearly 2,000 acres of pasture with free water. Its frontage on the Shasta River extended now nearly three miles on one side and both sides in several places. The cattle herd had grown to 700 pairs. A slaughter house was opening up in Gazelle, a small town, just north of them on the mainline tracks.

While much had changed; their prosperity, their family, their nation and their faith, the mountain had not. It was the constant. It oversaw all that happened in its shadows and hidden deep in its forests. From its peak it saw a nation building beneath the skirt of its lower slopes.

The O'Hare boys were excellent horsemen by ten years old and they grew strong under the weight of their chores; fencing, chopping wood, harnessing teams. When they got old enough "to do some good", they worked in the woods with "Uncle Billy" who was nothing less than a second father and sometimes the preferable one. The girls worked on feeding animals, mending clothes growing and preserving foods. All the children hunted and were excellent shots with rifles, of which each had one or more. Festus was enamored of the bow and arrow, which Charlie, Billy and Sarah's younger boy, had introduced to him. The two boys grew up together and seemed to have their own level of communication and appreciation for each other.

In Mel's old cabin, now at the other end of the ranch, Xing Chang and his wife, Ling, lived and worked as caretakers. Their two boys, Henry and Walter, helped with the cattle. They became local legends as cowboys. Everyday, Ling and Li, the daughter, came to the big log house and worked as domestic help. They were treated with respect and, in time, family adoration. They would act in obeisance at one moment but were completely comfortable scolding with authority the next. The house ran like a ship, with order and camaraderie.

Grady-O'Hare was home to all; three families, fifteen children in all.

Jon and Mel walked out into the pasture one spring evening near dusk. Their gaze easily fell upon the focal point of the southern horizon, Mt. Shasta. The pink alpenglow of its snowy slopes washed them in its tinted hue. They had struggled and fought and built, and failed, and built back, and now their future seemed so certain, both here on earth and for eternity. The crickets and bull-frogs along the creek were loud as they made their way back toward the large home, the soft light of the oil lamps peeping through nearly every window.

They basked in one of those moments not often enough taken in life, when William came running through the pasture, the cows parting for his important errand.

"Pa, a rider just came by, says we're at war with Spain. They're asking for volunteers in town and lots of the young men are signing up. Oh, and he also said Browny died of a heart attack, real sudden like."

Jon looked at Mel and they made their way back quickly, the ethereal pink glow of the mountain top fading into the dull gray of night. Darkness came quickly.

The death of Reverend Brown clutched them both. They were surprised by their own strong feelings for the man and what he had come to mean to them. For Melissa, he was special. He was the man who helped set her free; the man who pointed the way, not so much by his elegant sermons, but by the quiet certainty of his bearing and the knowledge that he knew his faith and lived it every moment. He was not pious and sometimes not even serious, but he knew *Whom*.......to have faith in. For him, there was no doubt. Brownee walked the walk. She would forever be grateful to him.

—

Liam stood in line with the other local boys, the man at the desk stood stiffly in his woolen uniform, medals bristled on his chest and his hat cocked on his head.

"We'll make quick work of this war, boys. You'll be back in time for Christmas is my estimation."

The young men gawked at his medals and strength of his bearing. One by one, they advanced.

"Age?", the soldier asked. The answer was uniformly "eighteen". One lad said sixteen at which point the room fell silent, while everyone held their breath and gave him a chance to amend this error.

The boy quickly corrected himself. "Eighteen. I meant to say eighteen." The soldier raised an leery eyebrow, cleared his throat from somewhere beneath the full mustache and pointed to the signature line without further words.

As Liam walked forward to the solitary desk in the town hall, he looked back at his friends in line, the boys who grew up on the ranches around him and sons of farmers and merchants. They peered around each other and encouraged him in their faces; eager and determined; smiling in the presupposed victory. Soon they would be war heroes. He thought he was finally besting his older brother Connor, in the silent but unspoken rivalry for their father's love and acceptance. Connor seemed always ahead of him, never a chance to 'catch up'. Now he was making his chance. He would be a hero in his father's eyes and one day, the old man would look at him with that certain look which gave love, pride, acceptance, and that welcomed him into the brotherhood of men, like no other look, from no other man.

"Age?", barked the soldier.

"Eighteen", came his reply and he signed his name.

———

The training had been brief and seemed boring, insufficient and nonsensical all at the same time. It seemed that important information always came through clusters of men, whom he hoped repeated the instructions accurately.

His father had been angry and his mother cried when he had joined up. He pleaded with them not to worry. His father seemed resigned and understood. Melissa briefly relived the days of waiting at home for her first husband to come home from the war.

"Keep your head down and your wits about, ya boy", instructed his father. Do what you're told, but don't volunteer. He had warned Liam and counseled him, but it was not until the day he left home that his father had shaken his hand. And that, being insufficient, bungled into an awkward hug.

"Be careful, lad. I need you back here."

"Don't worry Pa. I won't let you down."

Those were his last words to his father and he thought about them now as he gripped his rifle, after swiping his thighs with his sweaty palms. The Caribbean sun beat down hard upon them. He was still trying to get used to the humidity. Somebody had shouted a command, which not every one heard. Confused, half the men questioned those around them for what was said. "What? What?," everyone kept saying. But it was clear from the action of the men they were preparing to advance. He wished there was someone closer to him, but every one of the young men simply looked out across the open field in something of a determined trance.

He felt incredibly hot, all of a sudden, as if he had too much clothing on. The warm Caribbean sun beat down on the tall grass, hip high and waving, as if beckoning them forward. Inviting them into the lime green field before them. Currently, they were hunkered in a wooded area taking cover. The Spaniards were on top of this nondescript grassy hill. Hardly a bump on a map, Liam thought.

Everyone had been talking about Colonel Roosevelt and his wonderful manner on a horse. Liam shook his head and wondered how anything or anybody could be so confused as they were when they set sail from Tampa to Cuba. In that confusion half the men were left behind and all of the horses. Trained as a cavalry, they were shoved into the theater as infantry. With the Spaniards dug in at the top of San Juan Hill, their small expeditionary force seemed wholly inadequate to dislodge them. To fight on open terrain ascending a grassy hill with not a stick for protection seemed incomprehensible.

Suddenly the men to either side moved out, but he had not heard the command. 'By golly', he thought. 'There was Col. Roosevelt on top his steed, his pistol held high leading the men on the charge up San Juan Hill'. Bullets whizzed by. Men began to fall, but the column kept marching. They fired, but not with much hope of hitting the Spaniards who were invisible except for the strange sparkle of their muzzle flash. Roosevelt was steady on his horse, a huge target, yet fate seemed to smile on him. The infantry men fell all around him. Up they went, the thick grass almost entangling their boots. They had to stride through it. Now the Spaniards felt their approach and they redoubled the rate of fire. The man on Liam's left screamed and fell dead. The smell of gunpowder and blood filled his nostrils and the spray of blood seemed to float in the muggy air. 'My God', Liam thought, will any of us be left? More men fell. The world and the sounds of battle crescendoed, deafening then silence. The men approached the knoll top, but before they did, the Spaniards turned and fled. The Americans now in the Spaniard's old positions, fired at will at the fleeing army and they fell ingloriously. A last barrage and the men took off and waved their rough-rider hats in victory, as Colonel Roosevelt, complimented them and pondered the effect on the war and on his political career. "It was a bully good charge up the hill", he would later say. "A tidy little war", others would say.

A hundred feet from the top, on the ascending grassy slope, Liam O'Hare slowly let go the clenched grip he had on a tuft of grass, all red and slick from the blood pouring out of his neck. He tried to call for help, but his windpipe was severed. He rolled onto his back away from the warm sweet Cuban soil to look at the sky a last time. Blood spurting out of him, gush...., gush. He thought of the ranch and saw the cows on the pasture at dusk. He heard the bullfrogs down by the river. There was Mt. Shasta, he thought. And look-with a pink glow all around her summit and the clouds lit up in crimson and purples. Gush, gush. His mom called him in for supper from the front porch, like she always did. One hand was on her aproned hip, the other shielding her eyes from the afternoon sun, that she might see him in the pasture or near the barn. Gush, gush......

There was his Pa, in the big chair by the fireplace. He was reading a letter and tears flowed down his face. The paper fell from his hands and his head buried into his thick fingers. His shoulders shook.

"I'm sorry Pa. I'm sorry. I didn't mean to........," gush........ and his blue eyes went vacant as the tall blades of grass brushed his face, under the clear Caribbean sky.

For the nation, the Spanish American war was quick and largely painless. All its political and military goals were met. Roosevelt soared in popularity and became governor of New York before his successful run for the White House.

At Grady-O'Hare, the day was solemn. Two soldiers on horseback, came to offer the grateful nation's condolence for the loss of their brave son. His meager decorations and a flag were handed over. After coffee at the large table, with all the other children gathered round, they spoke in glowing terms of the reports of Liam's bravery. The O'Hares saw them off from the front porch that spanned the front of the log home. Melissa went to the bedroom and cried for several days. Jon was somber, speechless.

They dedicated a small plot of land overlooking the ranch, not too far from the home, for a cemetery. It seemed wrong to inaugurate it with a life so young.

Connor slowly took over the reigns of the ranch operations. He always conferred with Jon about the plans. He was ever mindful of new inventions and innovations. He was forever in the shop tinkering with new mechanical devices, or modifying them in some contrived new use.

In 1904, they bought a saw mill to produce their own lumber. The cattle market dried up and times became lean. The price on the hoof, was hardly worth the keep and the care. Then the San Francisco earthquake hit. After the devastation, timber prices improved as the city rebuilt, and then expanded into the south, north and east bay.

There is a time when an enterprise of which the core is one or two people realizes that the peak of performance has come and gone. Grady-O'Hare had grown magnificently under the care and toil of Jon and Melissa. It was a cattle company, and lumber company. But the years of work and toil, of risking and straining had taken its toll on both of them. Physically, Jon was worn out. An accident on a fallen horse had injured his back and put a permanent crook in it. It was painful for the first several years, but his body eventually became used to it and compensated. Mel enjoyed generally good health, but sun and wind, work and pain, had weathered her face-beautifully to be sure. But still, the years had taken their toll. It was a slow passing of the reins to the next generation. The two of them wanted to spend more time, that both knew was precious, together. Not caught up in the struggle for growth, not in the 'striving' mode. Instead, time, for them, was about simply doing the little things they enjoyed and making them seem bigger.

Jon and Melissa spent much of the time in their home garden, or going for occasional rides around the ranch. In time Connor, William and Rachel had all married and had kids of their own. The best days were when the grand kids came to visit. They saw the old white haired man and gray haired lady and seemed to wonder what their significance was. When the grand kids sat on their lap, they smelled old, like old clothes, and they didn't have much to say. Their eyes smiled, and so the children loved them. When they went into the large log home, they saw many animal's heads mounted on the wall, and a mountain lion skin hanging high up on the logs. They said that the lion almost ate grandpa, but Uncle Billy saved him. People told stories when they visited. They just talked and told stories, some were funny, some were sad.

Deborah was engaged, finally, after too many years in college. Melinda was a schoolteacher in Sacramento and never married. Festus, spent time in San Francisco and was smitten with the Pacific Ocean. He had signed on as a merchant marine and as far as anybody knew; still sailed around the world. Apparently without end or purpose. They would receive every so often a postcard from some exotic port. They kept a collection as some would stand vigil. They were from Brazil, Portugal, Egypt, Japan, Mexico, England and China. So they knew he was alive, but that was all.

The little church grew and then an argument started by some, but nobody could remember exactly what it was about, and the church split. Some stayed, others went to the Lutheran Church and others still, started a new Baptist Church which seemed to do well. Jon and Mel never lost their faith and the kids were brought up in the faith. They were less sure about churches, but attended regular just the same.

Jon was nominated to run for county supervisor, as he was well respected throughout the area and popular, but he would have no part of it.

San Francisco rebuilt, and the rattlings of war in Europe came with the newspapers. On May 1, 1915, The Lusitania set sail from New York to Liverpool. Off the Irish coast, near Kinsale, it was sunk by a torpedo from a German U-boat. The rattles turned to drums. To the ears of the white-haired old man, who often sat with an old Indian, listening to the radio, it seemed like a never ending story. Man's inhumanity to man. It's not that he didn't believe in war. Sometimes war would solve a problem when nothing else had or could. It was just that man's nature never seemed to change. He knew the country would go to war. Connor sensed this as well and capitalized by buying as many cows and horses as he could. Mules might also be needed, so he started buying and breeding work mules.

Billy's health was failing and so was Sarah's. Their children had left to work in the cities of Sacramento, San Francisco and Portland. They had kept their home in the tall trees. The last tree Billy fell was one of the tall trees. A special order from a hotel rebuilding in San Francisco. They wanted a 84 foot long 2' x 2' beam and posts of equal size to support it thirty feet high. It was hauled on a special train car and they were paid a handsome price. But afterward, Billy, said he would never cut another tree down.

War came with the assassination of Archduke Ferdinand of the Austro-Hungarian empire. But not before a letter arrived from John Brown & Co. From Clydebank, Scotland. The letterhead was of the RMS Lusitania, wherein it regretted to inform him of the loss at sea of Festus

T. O'Hare, an engineman. He had only been in their employ for six months, but their regret was immeasurable just the same. There was apparently no other kin. No wife or children and they apologized that it had taken so long to track them down. It seemed there was no insurance and so the letter of apology and condolence was all that was forthcoming.

A second grave, also empty, was placed in the cemetery and a small quiet service was held.

Jon and Melissa's daughter, Sarah, named after Billy's Sarah, died in the influenza epidemic of 1918. Everybody knew somebody who had died from this terrible sickness. Some local families lost several members. Sometimes, the children were left without either parent and put in state homes. Other times, the parents were left with no children at all. But no one was left untouched.

Connor and his wife Leah, now had four children of their own. They had moved into Melissa's old cabin and enlarged it. The families interacted on nearly a daily basis.

As Connor had foreseen, the price of livestock went up during the war. It was a terrible time, but lucrative if you sold to the government. They seemed insatiable and the prices proved it. The lean times faded quickly and the coffers of Grady-O'Hare once again filled rapidly.

Jon and Connor worked like a junior and senior partner in the operation of the ranch. Connor absorbing all that JP had learned. He appreciated what his father had built and created. Mel was always the emotional rock. Once, she was weak and tortured. Now, her marriage to Jon and her ever growing faith in the Christ that had paid the price to set men free, gave her strength and hope. Though she ached for the losses of her family, she held an optimism that was based on eternity-not this world.

This was also the period when so many things had changed in the country. There was now an income tax, for which President Wilson's name was generally thrown in with a string of expletives. Financial crises and various 'panics' had plagued the country, as every country, since its beginning. The government was a minuscule part of the economy of the nation, but it was growing ... every year. At the founding of the nation, the government spent between one and two percent of the what the nation produced. It had spiked up during the Civil War as all warfare is expensive, to thirteen percent, but then fell back. For decades it ran between two and nine percent of the nation's gross output. Now this war, World War I: 'The war to end all wars', took nearly 30 percent of GDP, and through the "progressive era" of the Great Depression never was smaller than 20 percent. It grew in its bureaus and offices, departments, regulations and committees. Laws reigned down like water from the sky, always on behalf of the people-or so it was said. Nearly a hundred years from the day the O'Hare family walked down the hill from the little cemetery, the federal government would be taking over 40 percent, without a great military conflict.

There was the new Federal Reserve System, passed on the eve of Congress' Christmas break in 1913, along with the income tax. The new system that would finally put an end to deficiencies of script. That would mollify the nasty swings of the business cycle. Those were the selling points. In came one of the most misunderstood of all quasi-government entities.

———

As the war came to an end, the country was on a tear to invent every kind of contraption imaginable; washing machines, toasters, ovens and stoves leaped forward in the design and technology. All over, roads were being built and paved and electricity was talked about, but still more than a decade away. Soon though, there were telephone poles were running alongside the county road and coming up their driveway of Grady-O'Hare. Telephones, though only 'party lines" at first were installed at breakneck pace, and toilets with in-house plumbing were becoming common. Change was upon the nation as it turned its muscle to domestic production. The automobile was coming to be more common and replacing the horse, even in rural America. Jon and Melissa had purchased a revolutionary device called a radio. Every evening, all would gather for a new nightly ritual: Listening to the news of the world, and then broadcasts of humorous stories or mysteries.

Connor had paid cash for their first car and soon after bought a truck. J.P. was willing to go for a ride but still didn't trust them. After a month, it got the better of him and Jon O'Hare took Melissa for a ride on the ranch roads. He never could find third gear so, generally he went very slow while the engine revved at top speed. Mel, always looking dismayed, as Jon had a huge grin plastered on his face. Connor just laughed and watched.

It was perhaps Jon and Mel's second or third time in the truck, when he finally got out of the granny gear and the truck lurched forward. Jon was unable to control it and destroyed a water trough, drove through the pig pen and dragged three hundred feet of fencing out into the pasture before he got it stopped. All to the frantic screams of Connor, Leah, their kids and Billy. They evacuated the porch on a dead run to the pasture to rescue the runaway rig.

Mel climbed out of the car in a jiffy and was yelling at Jon, accusing him that he'd tried to kill her.

"Good Lord, I'm never gettin' in that car with you again, till I'm good and ready for heaven." She went around in a bit of a tizzy, talking like that and then realized Jon was still in the truck. She fell silent and then called to him.

"Jon? Jon?" she repeated, as she strode to the driver's door.

He was sitting motionless, staring straight ahead as she approached and opened the door. Jon O'Hare was already in heaven. He stepped out of a sea onto a crystalline shore. He moved through a crowd of close friends who parted and made a way for him. It was as if he were a long awaited special guest. There was Liam. He looked but could not find Festus. They were all beckoning him forward sweeping him toward someone very special. There was such warmth, light and love. The feeling was indescribable. The airyness of his heart took his own breath away. He looked back toward the shore he'd just arrived at and then through a sort of window, a portal into the beautiful sea. In the stillness of its waters, he saw the scene he had just left on Earth.

He looked down and he was hovering over the hood of the pickup truck. He peered through the window and saw himself. What was left was a tired body that had loved and fought, had grown, and worked. A life that had seen men at their best and their worst, children had died and grandchildren grown up. A fortune made and lost, which once meant everything, and then nothing. He had lived without love for years too many. But had found a love in her, the woman now collapsing, that few men could know. He smiled thinking of her and her love for him. If nothing else mattered, he had been loved completely by someone-and that was enough. Everything else was already fading to complete unimportance.

He hated to leave her alone, but the moment had come. Not a day of his choosing, but one he must accept. His heart broke for her as he watched her crumple at the running board beside his still body. He began to float higher, receding backward. From across the field they came running when they saw grandma collapse. The boys and their wives. Pigs were running loose where he'd destroyed the pen and the fencing made a perfect "V" from the front of the truck back to the original fence line. He turned back to the welcoming gauntlet before him and walked into eternity.

"Where is He?, he asked. "Where is Jesus?"

"There is all the time in the world. Or, I should say: There is no time. You will see him very soon. First, we must get you settled in." An elderly man spoke to him these words as they walked along a cliff with the ocean to his right and what looked like Ireland on a beautiful and warm summer morning on his left. It was so green, so fresh, so clear. It was better than the best of it in his memories. He looked back across the ocean, and said: "Oh my God, I'm home."

BOOK 2, CHAPTER 1

It was in 1924, on a warm mid-summer night. Mel was in failing health and had been for some time. The love of her life had gone on and the sparkle in her own eyes had gone with him. She spent time in the kitchen, but more in her chair by the fireplace. Her favorite place was the rocking chair on the back porch. Here the view overlooked the pastures of Grady-O'Hare and then the ever dominant mountain looming in the eastern sky. Summers were best as the arthritis was more tame. Winters were difficult. She shuffled on a cane and there was a small hunch to her back. Her face was still beautiful, even if old; the nose bearing something of a crook in it. Her hair, long and gray, in a pony tail.

Lately, the grandkids had noticed and Connor as well, that when she sat alone, she would talk softly to herself, or perhaps it was someone else. She wouldn't do it, if she knew someone was present. She was still lucid and functional, just slow and limited in movement and speed.

That evening she sat in her rocker on the porch in the early evening. The sunset colors now washed over Mt. Shasta's summit. She rocked and as she did, the old boards on the porch, creaked along with her. Grandkids played games in the parlor, just inside. As they took turns on their board game, they listened to the soft creaking of the rocker. They looked at each other, as they heard 'grandma talking to grandpa again'.

Mel looked on at the world before her, one created by the God she knew and loved, and yet left the 'finish' to her. She and Jon had altered nearly everything in the view, and yet she saw clearly that it was so temporal. All the important things, He created. In the end, they had done little more than play in a sandbox, albeit on a grand scale. She rocked and as she rocked a song the Jon used to sing when he worked in the field came into her mind and she hummed. It was a pretty Irish ballad, but she was never sure what it was about. She just like the melody of it.

The tune was in her heart and her eyes and mind were filled with the wonderful view before her, but more than seeing, she was understanding it all in a sense of time-lessness she rarely glimpsed. 'Oh Jon, she thought. How I wish you were here.' Then she chuckled to herself out loud. Actually, I guess I wish I were there with you. Then she thought, for just a second, those old fearful thoughts. Those thoughts about that night in the Ogallala Saloon. Soon she would know if the "promise" from Jesus was true. She had garnered a whole lifetime of peace through that promise. A life that was hard and sweet, painful and blessed. How good it all was. Her mind turned as it did so often, back to Jon. 'How I miss you, my love'.

She heard a familiar footfall, on the porch nearby. It stunned her out of the reverie she had indulged while rocking and looking over the ranch. The footsteps approached, and she turned slowly to see who approached from the side. It was Jon.

The grandkids inside, were finishing their game and setting up for another. They noticed the rocking chair had fallen still.

Jon O'Hare was as handsome as the day she had first laid eyes on him; that day at the creek. He stood before her and held out his hands bidding her to join him. She took his hands and stood up, effortlessly, her breath taken away. Here he was, like that evening at the town pot-luck, like the night in her kitchen at the little cabin. She was speechless. "Oh darling! But how can this be?" He just smiled, his eyes gleaming and soon, she left the porch and was with him in a far and wonderful place. A place she had never been, neither clouds, nor earth, yet she was at home. There was an overwhelming feeling of well-being, peace. Not like anything she had ever known. She knew, and knew thoroughly now, that she was in heaven; that the promise was true-and kept. She had been forgiven. She was loved and accepted by her God, for all eternity.

———

America had experienced its first wave of progressivism. The Woodrow Wilson administration was its delivery. The activism of a federal government to meddle in the lives of its people was, on the surface, successful. Now there was an income tax, *ever so modest*, and a Federal Reserve Bank, that could regulate the terrible burden of the business cycle out of existence. That evil of freedom which continually produced booms and busts. Of course part of that activist government also cost the country a terrible war. And now finished with the nasty business of war, came a reprieve, while the country turned its attention to domestic production. The people became wealthy on the inflated value of assets; paper or real. Real estate, stocks and bonds; all were flying high along with the people.

People didn't see that; far from the business cycle being destroyed, it had simply become a creature of the politicians and princelings of the banking industry. Now the 'Fed' had the levers controlling the money supply and rates of interest, or at least in great measure.

But there was no denying the general sense of well-being, that all those material goods did render. Happily, men tucked their broker's statements and bank statements into neat files they were proud of.

And the material blessings were bountiful. More cars, more appliances, better schools, better steamships, better tools to make better tools. Air travel was beginning in its earliest phases of public usage. So many things had been invented and distributed into so many homes, that people thought, as in all booms, that they lived in a gilded age.

Over in Europe, things were beginning to deteriorate. Germany was straining under the costs of reparations from WWI, to France and England. Trouble was brewing.

On October 28, 1929, the New York Stock Exchange crashed, after several troubling episodes. The DOW tumbled, and the gilded age of the 'roaring 20s' turned out to be a thin patina covering a weakened substance. The reverberations were worldwide.

Americans had become soft and complacent in material if not superficial wealth. Now it crumbled before their eyes. The file folders in every house, once the source of pride, became little more than fuel for a fire. Most were wiped out. Homes were lost, businesses failed throughout the nation. Men and women were cast into the streets to sell their labor for whatever they could get for it. The soup kitchens became ubiquitous. Suicide of the well-to-do, was tragic and too common. The psychological blow to the people made them vulnerable to those sought power by the promise of restoration; by the showing of a government in control and ready, willing and able to help the 'forgotten man'.

Franklin Delano Roosevelt, a cousin to the former President Theodore Roosevelt, was a rising political star. His ascension to power was bold and calculated. He took office in March 1933, in the midst of the Great Depression. He formed his covey of trusted advisors, known as the Brain Trust. These men, like him, were progressive. They saw nothing that man did on his own, that government couldn't do better for him. If only he would give them the power. This was the second great wave of progressivism.

The election, under so terrible a time, appeared to give these men the mandate they sought and they wasted no time. They nationalized key industries and regulated nearly every industry in the nation that was of any importance. They created bureaus and inflicted bureaucrats upon those left who still produced something of value. From electrification to food production, they inserted themselves into the heap-usually at the top. They created a federal workforce to do public works and projects the 'princelings' deemed worthy.

They were collectivists-socialists is fair. Certainly their leanings were that way. Their disdain for private property and free markets was evident in every law they wrote, every mandate they made and every regulation written. There's was a world of power unknown in modernity to that point. But their economics was failed. Their philosophy, fatally flawed. Despite their power over money, industry and laws, they could not bring down the unemployment rates to numbers recognizable as 'normal'. Meanwhile, the federal debt mushroomed.

Over in Europe, things went from bad to worse, with inflation in the Weymar Republic of Germany, out of control. It would usher in a house-painter and failed artist; a socialists fascist by the name of Adolph Hitler into power.

———

Connor had run Grady-O'Hare for a decade, when the Great Depression made itself felt. The cattle herd thinned down as it wasn't worth a visit by the veterinarian to save one. They were heaped and buried in open pits. Still, he felt blessed to have resources to feed himself and his family. The gardens sustained them and large canning operations went on in the fall to put up food for the winter.

Debt service was the problem. Yes, the ranch had grown in the good times. Like many, much progress was made though the investment of borrowed money. Grady-O'Hare had piled up huge amounts of cash, but it had spent them as well. What was left was dangerously low cash reserves.

Much of the cash was used to buy out Deborah and her husband, Tom's, interest. They had gotten involved in an automobile dealership, but had to file bankruptcy. It was necessary to buy them out. Deborah and Tom only visited twice again, in their whole lives. Deb's branch of the family simply drifted away. Their children were city kids and liked it that way. But the cash was getting precious and the times were getting harsher.

William and Rachel, together with their children, were the surviving co-owners among Connor's siblings. Out of eight of Jon and Melissa's children, three remained alive or vested in Grady-O'Hare.

Connor would receive letters from his brother and sister, catching up on family matters and how the children were doing. He enjoyed this sense of connection, but there was often a statement slipped in, on toward the end, regarding a poor state of finances in the family. William, or Bill as they called him, started a small farm up in Tulelake. The government under, a new bureaucracy; The Bureau of Reclamation, had provided for irrigation water, and folks were staking out claims. World War I vets got priority, but there were enough parcels to go around. Bill and Dorothy his wife, were making a go of it and already had a small house in the little town and 140 acres just half mile down the road.

On a cold spring morning in 1933, the phone rang. It wasn't a party-line ring that he could recognize. It was Dorothy, and she was hysterical.

"Calm down Dorothy. What happened?" But she was frantic and he could tell the phone was being waved around.

"Dorothy! Dorothy!"

"He's gone!, she screamed.

"Who's gone? Dorothy!, Who's gone?" Connor could hear rustling on the other end and wailing. The telephone clattered, then a man's voice came on.

"Mr. O'Hare?" , he asked.

"Yes. This is Connor O'Hare." He waited, offering nothing more.

"Mr. O'Hare, this is Doctor Frederickson from Merrill. I am very sorry to inform you that your brother, William O'Hare, was killed this morning. He passed away about a half hour ago."

Connor was stunned and he asked flatly as if in a stupor: "How did it happen". "A tractor" Dr. Frederickson replied. Now that usually meant just one thing to ranchers and farmers; that the tractor somehow ended up on top of the operator. Normally, this occurred on hilly land, often the tractor would be 'side-hilling'. But the Tulelake Basin is flat as a pancake where its farmable, so this made no sense to Connor.

"A tractor?", he queried in disbelief. "How could that be?"

"Its just one of those things, I guess. He was taking the tractor to the other end of the field to pick up some implement for it. A sink hole opened up to the side of him and the tractor rolled sidelong into the hole. It crushed him...., probably immediately. Apparently there was some time before anybody saw him. There has been some reports that with all the irrigation now on the land, that several sink holes have opened up. This is the first time anybody has been hurt. Mr. O'Hare...?"

"Yes, I'm here. Please see to my sister-in-law, Doctor. I'll leave to come up there later today. I've got some work here, but you tell Dorothy, I'm on my way."

"Yes, that is a good idea. I'm going to sedate her now. The children are on their way home from school. They don't know........ She is very upset. Let me say I'm..., I'm very sorry for your loss, Mr. O'Hare."

"Thank you, Doctor". He hung up the phone.

"Leah!" he called out to her painfully.

———

After Bill was buried in the little cemetery at Grady-O'Hare, Dorothy had come to Connor. The finances were in poor shape. She had sold the farm and the house in Tulelake. She wanted a fresh start and had decided to move to Los Angeles with the kids. She knew that Grady-O'Hare was strapped for cash, but she offered her share, Bill's share, at a cheap price. She just wanted to move on with her life. Bank loans were difficult. So Connor sold a piece of timberland. It was unbearably cheap. Long Bell Lumber Company bought it. But it was enough to help Dorothy and the kids get on down to L.A., and try to start life over again.

When things began to sour, Connor had paid off some of the debt, but there was still a first mortgage and an operating loan from the bank. The buying of two other interests in hard times didn't help. He was making the payments, but just barely. A further downturn in economic conditions, and he might have to sell the herd for pennies on the dollar or nearly give away some timber.

Early on, Jon and Melissa had saved up some gold coins, adding to them from time to time. They were hidden in the ground behind the barn. The note on the operating loan was all due and payable on November 1, 1933. The depression was at its worst, or so everyone thought.

On October 24th, Leah had gone to town for some supplies and would retrieve the kids from school. Home alone, Connor grabbed a spade from the barn and went around behind it. He appeared to look here and there and then paced in a very specific manner arriving at a nondescript point and pushed the spade into the ground. Back at the kitchen table the coins were examined and counted; 231 coins, of which 212 were one ounce $20.00 gold pieces. The balance were smaller coins. He had sold another fifteen percent of the herd. Sold the last of his stock holdings at a terrible price. These, together with a further draw down of cash reserves, would come close to paying off the operating loan.

On November 1st, he walked into the Siskiyou National Bank and wrote a draft, handed over cash and then hefted the two bags of gold coins onto banker Leland Casper's desk. The office was partitioned in free-standing walls of good quality dark panelling with windows on three sides, so he could see out and everyone could see in, but not hear.

His desk was large and neatly adorned with a lamp and pen set, a telephone and notepad. He sat back into the rich leather chair, which rocked easily without squeaking.

"What's this, all your saved nickels?", Leland jested.

"No, sir. That is gold." He had hardly uttered the last word as Leland 'shushed' him and rose quickly to close the door to his private office and draw the blinds.

"What's the problem, Lee?" Asked Connor.

"This is illegal. That's the problem."

"What are you talking about?" Protested Connor.

"Shssshh. Not so loud, Connor. Gold is now illegal, at least in this quantity.

Connor looked stunned and was. "I'm sorry, but I'm not following you Lee."

"Didn't you hear, Mr. O'Hare?"

"Hear what?", he protested further.

"Back in May, I think it was, the President declared gold to be illegal except in small amounts and for art and jewelry and such. Surely you heard this."

"Well I remember some talk in the papers, but I haven't paid much attention to it and I've been awfully busy surviving and keeping the ranch going. I guess I missed the big notice. I sometimes go a stretch without catching up on things."

"This gold is illegal and I can't accept it as payment for the loan. It was supposed to be converted to cash back in May. Now it carries a fine of up to $10,000 and or ten years in prison."

Connor was dumbfounded at first and sheepish about having missed an apparently important event, but now his mood turned to a mix of fear and anger. He rose and leaned across the desk to the banker. "Are you telling me that I'm a criminal for owning these two bags of real money that my parents scrimped and sacrificed for?"

"I am". Connor returned to his seat with a thud and a look of disbelief.

"Well, I had counted on this to help pay off my operating loan."

Leland Casper leaned forward. "Connor, look.......... I'll take the rest of it and rewrite the loan for the balance owed and give you until next summer. Maybe things will be better by then. I've got faith in you and Grady-O'Hare."

"Thanks, Lee. I appreciate that. You know that we've got plenty of land. Its just that I hate to sell it under these conditions."

"I understand".

And now a new frown came upon Connor's face. "How the hell do I get out of here with this gold?" he asked Leland.

"I guess the same way you came in. Just boldly walk on out through the lobby. Nobody will know that it's gold."

"I guess that's right." He got his hat and shook Leland Casper's hand. He picked up the two bags and Casper opened the door for him.

An unusual feeling flowed through him and he hated it. He had always walked with a certain pride, wherever he went. He had never felt like he had to hide anything from anybody. But now he walked out of the bank and down the street to his pickup and knew he was a criminal; ten years and/or $10,000 fine mulled angrily in his mind. His head was still spinning as he drove home, the anger welling up inside him.

'Who the hell are these people to make real money illegal and phony money real?' It was Executive Order 6102, but its name didn't matter. It was the 'progressives' and their constant and continual encroachment into the real lives of the people they were supposed to represent, but lorded over instead. He talked to himself, occasionally yelling and slamming his hand on the steering wheel, as he turned off the county road and headed up the long driveway to the house. He could see Leah's car and the kids were already onto their chores. He shoved the bags under the seat for now and reburial later.

Leah was in the kitchen, as always, teaching Katie how to make another dinner. Their teenage daughter was already a good cook, and could do most preparation without any supervision. He kissed them both and then gave Leah a look behind Katie's back that said ' we need to talk'. Leah acknowledged with the slightest of nods, hardly missing a beat in the preparation of dinner.

After dinner, Joshua and Katie went upstairs to do their homework before coming back down for radio time, if they had finished.

"Have I got a story for you", he started. He related the whole story about the bank. "Leah, I never felt like that in my life; a criminal in my own town, my own country, and with my own property. Something has happened to this country. It's not that the economy is terrible that I mind. I don't like, but its their infernal cures that will destroy us. I never would have believed it ....", and he trailed off, unable to find the words.

It was Leah's turn. "I saw Janet Pierson at Shugg's Five and Dime. She told me they had a man show up out at their ranch to inspect their cattle. Told them they'd have to make some changes, put in more water troughs and vaccinate their herd. The man said he was from the Department of Agriculture. He came right onto their place; no invitation or nothing."

"What the hell is going on here?"

The depression withered on, and with it the American people trudged forward in an economic slog. The ever pervasive government grew under the collective wisdom of Roosevelt's 'Brain Trust'. The bureaucracies grew. The alphabet soup of the administration's latest programs grew. These, for inventing work, and under authority made possible by a court packed with 'enlightened' judges who found no effective limit on the federal government in a document designed precisely and strictly for the limitation of federal power.

Grady-O'Hare hung on, reflecting Connor's own tenacity and ability to make do and improvise, or simply do without. It had weathered the economic storm and showed the deep lines of character as in an old but comfortable face. The buildings stood, but were in need of work. The men who lived on the ranch seemed equally tired.

Finally, the rising tide of warfare in Europe was upon them. The mad man of Germany had come to power. He and the ever popular in America, Mussolini, had joined their fascist forces, nationalizing their industries, particularly war sensitive industries, and were all set to save western Europe for fascism and socialism, of which they both professed.

Communism continued to grow within the Soviet Union and China. Lines in the sand were being drawn. Hitler's blitzkrieg through Poland in 1939 is as good a starting point for the war as any, though its ideological beginnings were much earlier.

America stayed out, but as some have noted, there were economic interests in joining the war for America, as well as legitimate ideological and geopolitical ones.

Inexorably it was brought into the war in Europe and on December 7, 1941, after increasingly heated diplomatic exchanges as a prelude, Japan attacked Pearl Harbor, Hawaii, and the world, once teetering on total war, now plunged in headlong.

———

It was one of those spring mornings when the birds seemed to be on stimulants. Their incessant chirping; urgent, but happy. Warmth was coming to the mid-morning hours, even in the shade.

Connor O'Hare stood before the headstones in the little cemetery on the hill. The dry grasses between each, was their simple adornment. A small split-rail fence marked out a 50 foot square plot. He had been there nearly an hour. From time to time he turned his gaze across a beautiful timbered hillside and then down and across lush pastures, to a river several miles away. Then to Mt. Shasta-always the end point of the view. It was 1944.

Connor himself was tired and old, and he looked at the spot he thought he liked best. He would be next to his Leah. He looked again at how they were lined up straight and proper; Liam and Festus, Jon and Melissa. He thought for a moment how mom had just withered after pa died. She just didn't care any more. She was always talking about catching up with him, and she meant to. Jesus, she was a determined woman. Not far away was Billy and Sarah's graves. Their old cabin still stood, but it was now open to the sky. Last year a bear got in there and just tore the place up. Without a good foundation, it would eventually end up on the ground. He still liked going up there though, to the tall trees. They were more magnificent than ever, though a few more had been cut for special purposes. His father had told him not to cut those unless he got triple the price of the lumber, and for a cause he liked. He enjoyed seeing them used when nothing else would do. Structurally, steal had taken over the world. But some uses, particularly architectural requirements, demanded a special beam. Next to Billy and Sarah was Charlie, their second son. He pondered Charlie's life, like another brother to him; raised on the ranch. He was so good at anything athletic, hunting, riding, shooting. Yet, he never seemed to 'take hold'. He battled alcohol much of his life, so did many of the Native Americans. When the news of Festus' death came, Charlie became a crying drunk. It didn't make much sense, as he hadn't seen Festus in over twenty-five years. It must have been the time they spent as youngsters, playing, hunting in the woods. Festus loved the bow and arrow at which he became as good as Charlie. Neither man had ever felt more complete or satisfied in life than in this childhood friendship.

Billy and Sarah could do nothing. They would see him passed out in alleyways in town, sometimes when getting supplies for the ranch. But every time they brought him home, he sobered up, got fed, but was gone within a few days. He eventually shot himself. Everybody pretended like it was an accident, but most knew.

Connor looked down across the ranch far out into the valley again, and fiddled with the crease of his old hat, between his fingers. Making the dimples in the hat just so. The breeze blew warm on the strands of gray hair that fell across his brow.

The ranch had grown some, but they had to sell other portions to pay heirs; children of children. Some had apparently found a life in the cities, some all the way across the country. Yet, Connor had never really left there. Grady-O'Hare was his life. He knew where the soil changed, exactly where the river would flood. Where untapped springs held their secret.

The log house was added to and retrofitted with indoor plumbing and electrical wiring. He'd put two new roofs on. Hell of a job, he thought. The pastures and ditch works had been honed over the years to near perfection as everything that could be irrigated was irrigated. The outlines of the pasture creeping up into several of the gullies, conforming precisely to the contour line. The trees that were scattered along the edge, once small when he was a young man, now towered a hundred feet upward. Their tops swaying eight or more feet in the anabetic winds. They groaned, like the straining ropes on a ship tied to the pier.

The workshop had been built, but the barn needed serious work. He didn't feel like doing it. It was time to turn it over to someone. He hoped it would be Robert, his youngest son and the only chance remaining of keeping the ranch under family operation and ownership.

Seeing that land had to be sold to pay off heirs at every death, he had incorporated the ranch and issued stock, all held in the family. He was the largest stockholder and President. He was also the manager and principal ranch hand. He hired and fired, welded and fabricated. He fenced, and dug ditches, logged and branded cattle. The days were every bit as long as Jon O'Hare's, in the early days. Connor's produced so much more. The tractors, mowers, bailers, farm implements; all capital equipment making every man's labor more productive, more valuable.

On farms and ranches across the country necessity proved to be the mother of invention, indeed. Backyard mechanics and farmers repairing their machinery, invented tools and machines. The science improved with regard to seeds and fertilizers, all to one end, producing more "pie". Pie, in the sense of all that is produced. That aggregation of goods and services are a peoples' product. It is the result of their own creativity and productivity. It seemed to Connor that the politicians spent a lot more time figuring out how to divide up the "pie". All he'd ever asked of them was to stay out of his way, and to pay their bills on time. And even though there was rationing of strategic materials; rubber, tin, aluminum, fuel, steal, seething beneath the restraint were a thousand, no ten thousand new ideas, new ways of processing, from plastics to potatoes, new tools, and new management techniques. All would explode exponentially, when this war ended.

Connor looked down at the mud caked on the toe of his boots. Another war, he thought. The old man was right. Jon had told him: "It will never stop, not because we are so bent on war, but because evil will always exist and try as you will, all your compromises will fail. Why? Because it is evil and it is never satisfied. You can defeat it in the physical plane, within the history of this old world, but you'll never finish it off. It'll come back in another place another time, another tyrant, another megalomaniac, another ideology, religion or 'ism'. That's the problem, boy. Somebody a lot smarter than me said ' All that is required for evil to succeed, is for good men to do nothing', and damned if it isn't true."

He filled his lungs with the sweet air, the cedar lightly stinging his nostrils. He dropped his hat onto his head and it settle into its natural place. He walked out and closed the little gate behind him and headed back down the hill in the Willys jeep.

Earlier in his life, he and Leah had Joshua and Katie. Joshua had become a doctor and practiced in San Francisco. He married, but the marriage produced no children. He died young, of a heart attack. Katie married a farmer down in the Sacramento area and they had done very well. He grew row crops in the rich delta soil and had grown into a major operation.

Later in their life, they had a son, Robert. It was a frightful pregnancy and no one was certain how the child would turn out. Abortion was out of the question. Connor found a new foothold in his own faith, grafted from his parents' to begin with. Robert came out healthy, but Leah struggled. No doubt it cost her some years, he figured. The young boy was their joy. He was funny, a natural comedian and a ham at that. His enthusiasm for life was infectious. He was curious about everything and a complete sponge for information. Connor had gone through dozens of workmen and ranch hands. He never saw anybody catch on as quick as "Bobby". The kid was a wiz at anything mechanical. He could fix a radio, rope a steer, ride a horse as good as any he'd seen. There was nothing he couldn't do, and that was the problem bothering Connor. This was the boy to take over Grady-O'Hare. And now he was in Europe, flying his beloved B-24 Liberator. No doubt, kicking the crap out of the Germans. The thought of him being shot down; the thought of his not coming home, would probably mean the end; the end of it all. The dream, the life, the legacy, the heart and sinew that he and his family had given in the pursuit of something grander than what their own lives could ever achieve. He threw up a quick prayer to heaven without so much as standing still for it.

"God, please bring him home safe and sound-Amen".

———

173

He stared out the window and watched the tops of the clouds pass by just below the wings, illuminated by the moonlight. It had a dreamlike quality, except for the sudden jarring from the turbulence. The men bounced in unison in their seats, seeming bored as it was so common. The nose of the B-24 Liberator, showed a very shapely, American looking woman painted well. She was raising her skirt, seductively, revealing a shapely leg and an inviting look on her face. "My Girl", was lettered in script at a dashing angle below her. Behind it came rows of hash marks, in groups of five. The image flickered in the moonlight. There were seventy-seven of them. She was helping break the will of the German people and Chancellor Hitler.

Early that morning, My Girl flew out of Dover, across the English channel, to cross Belgium and on into Germany. Her glorious past had watched bridges collapse into rivers, fuel depots erupt and factories turn to rubble. Railroad lines, as well as the trains themselves, had been dismembered. Munitions factories, all manor of Hitler's industrial base from which he prosecuted the war to take over Europe had gone up in fireballs from the latest generation from Consolidated, the company that produced the B-24. Total production would end up at 18,000 of these emissaries of the free world. They went through several generations of upgrades. My Girl had played her role effectively.

The two men in the cockpit talked easily and bantered back and forth with the rest of the crew. Jimmy Caldwell, from Chicago, Illinois sat in the nose bubble; front gunner. Doc Henley from Pheonix, Arizona was top gunner and he was watching the stars peeking through the upper cloud cover. The belly gunner was Jason McCormick of W. Teaneck, New Jersey, 18 years old and new to the crew. Chuck Haley from Ogalala, Nebraska sat behind the cockpit, the navigator. Joey Hopper sat over the bombing sites next to the bomb bay doors. Up front, was Lt. Myron 'Ronnie' Dickinson, of Denver, Colorado-copilot. In the left seat was Captain Bobby O'Hare from some place in northern California nobody had heard of.

Through the gaps in the clouds below, the darkness of the channel had passed an hour ago. Another half an hour and they would be coming to their target.

The crew was well-seasoned, except for McCormick. They talked to dispel the nervous energy that every mission brought. They had had a long lucky streak, only once taking some machine gun fire. That was four months back and the reason why Jason was new to the crew. His acceptance came slowly as the men would have to let go of Mikey Jones, from Los Angeles, their original belly gunner. A likable guy, quick to laugh and buy beers. He was not easy to replace. None of them were, really. All were normal, everyday guys, street kids and farm boys, grown-up fast. And they took to it. Now they were liberating a continent from a tyrant, though they didn't spend much time thinking in those terms. Usually, it was the tight-knit camaraderie and the promise of going home that pushed them on.

These men knew each others' stories, their towns, lives, childhood friends, parents and sweethearts. They knew the likes and dislikes as well as the habits of each. Their voices immediately recognizable to each other without identifying themselves. This, even over the simple intercom radios and the loud metallic droning of the air frame and engines passing through the sky.

"How's it lookin' up there, Doc?"

"Fine, Cappy, just us and the stars."

"Good. Let's keep it that way."

"Hey Cappy, I think we just passed something down there", squawked young Jason.

Chuck, the navigator, chimed in, "That would be Antwerp."

"Not enough lights for a city that big" said Jason.

"Most are observing the blackout rules."

"Okay, we're gettin' a little closer now, let's cut down the chatter."

"How we doin', Chuck?"

"Right on course, Cappy".

The bomber squadron consisted of eleven B-24s, unaccompanied by fighters. The target was Dusseldorf; its munitions factory, a steel foundry which produced armor plating, two bridges across the Rhine and the docks and shipping terminals which facilitated the barge traffic on the Rhine River. Two planes were assigned to each target. The targets, mostly lined up south to north, were spread about a mile apart east to west. The plan was to fly eastward in the early morning hours, flying to a point about five miles south of Dusseldorf, then turn north and line up for the individual bombing runs. They would descend into the Rhine Valley at the crack of dawn breaking below the cloud cover that would hopefully shield them. Thus the bombardiers could visually see their targets and confirm their hits or misses.

The squadron maintained radio silence between planes. The weather reports had anticipated that they would have a cloud cover shielding them from the ground at 14,000 feet. The weather man estimated a 2,000 foot thickness. Thus they could maintain a decent altitude from anti-aircraft fire. They would stay at 11,000 to 12,000 feet. The plan was to dive through the cloud cover at top speed, right at sunup, with little time for the enemy to react. By the time they did, the bombs would be exploding all around them, and the squadron would fly up the Rhine for several miles then turn back west and back to Dover.

The radio crackled alive.

"Zebra Leader-follow me." That was all that was said. The lead plane tipped the nose down and to the right. In two columns, they followed, swooning down and to the right. Chuck looked over the shoulder of Ronnie Dickenson and watched the altimeter, as his stomach came up to his throat; 16,000, 15,000, 14,000. The engines were whining and straining as the lumbering airframes made their way down through the thick, water laden cloud cover. They jiggled and jolted in their seats, huddled in their leather jackets and caps. The clouds were lighting up as if someone had lighted a lamp. Beautiful colors flew by, as the sunrise hit first in the clouds above the earth. It was like flying through a pool of rainbows.

"Why do I always have to piss when we start one of these?" complained Ronnie.

No one answered him.

"Final !" crackled the radio. The leader now banked hard left, turning north only four miles south of Dusseldorf and the target zone. Bobby O'Hare called out "12,000". They all knew they should be breaking through the cloud cover. And with it, their visual exposure to the air defense network. They would then visually identify their individual targets and line up on them. At that point, they would only have a minute or two to get over them and drop their bombs. It was those two minutes that would tell them if they would go home or fall to the earth in a fiery aluminum coffin. The gunners all fully anticipated engagement with the Messerschmidts. With any luck, most would be on the ground. Any extra bombs should be dropped on the airfield north of town and thus help their escape back to England.

———

Corporal Hans Engst, was shaking himself after urinating, having just come on duty at the guard house on a strategic road crossing, four miles south of Dusseldorf. He had farted and then thought he heard a sound he had been trained for; the American engines in their bomber planes. Still holding himself, he looked up, the hair on his neck rising steadily. The gray puffy bottom of the clouds cloaked them. He saw nothing, but with each second, the droning became more recognizable. Hastily, he put himself back in his pants and ran to the phone in the guardhouse, his boots clunking the pavement hard.

At that moment air-raid sirens were lighting off all over the city. At the airstrip, north of the city, pilots poured out of barracks, strapping on their gear on a dead run to the waiting Messershmidts-always fueled and loaded with ammo, ready to fly.

———

It felt like going down a roller-coaster, everyone leaning against the steep incline. The gunners checked their belts and machine guns. Their turreted seats swiveling easily. Still they were in thick clouds, no visibility.

"10,000 feet" called Ronnie. They were still in the clouds; bumping, jostling.

Chuck was back at his detail maps. "Three miles to target, Cappy. We need to break loose here!" The bombers' descent tortured their planes. The engines could turn no faster. Still, they could see nothing.

"This is Zebra Leader. Drop down! Drop down! You're on your own!

"8,000 feet", cried Ronnie, looking over at O'Hare, for some sign of hope. Visibility zero.

"Hold on boys!" O'Hare said calmly, and he pushed the stick forward to the max.

"Two miles to target, Cap. We're gonna miss it. We're gonna miss it, damnit!"

O'Hare yelled, "Bomb bay doors open! Now ! Now! Now!"

The fuselage filled with wet icy cold air, and it blew through the entire plane in one second as the doors opened. But everyone was sweating profusely.

Ronnie shouted, "7,000 feet", over the rushing wind, nearly garbling all communication. Still in thick clouds-no visibility. O'Hare pulled back on the stick wrestling with the controls as all their guts felt like they would exit through their rectums and a sickening feeling came to all of them. Jason, in the belly gunner's bubble, was frozen as he looked out at the flexing wing in a sickening tortured movement. He closed his eyes expecting it to break free of the airplane and end this nightmare in a spiraling fall to earth.

Now, "6,000 feet" someone screamed, and clouds of explosives lit up around them as the anti-aircraft guns on the bridges were now fully engaged. They couldn't see, but they heard them and they started firing. "There", one cried, as the first bomber broke through the clouds. They were practically on top of the them. The guns targeted the planes as they broke through. People were yelling and running through the streets taking cover, even in this early hour. A cheer went up from the gunnery placements, as two of the bombers began to smoke. But the cheer faded quickly as they observed the metallic pellets exiting the plane in alarming numbers.

"It's all yours, Joey" yelled O'Hare to the bombardier.

"Thirty seconds to the target" yelled Chuck.

"Slide to the right, Cappy. We're off! We're off! Go Right."

O'Hare cranked hard right, and the anti-aircraft fire, or 'ack-ack' exploded all around them. They flew through several explosions and heard the leftover debris hit the plane and windshield.

"Ten seconds to target."

"Jesus, Joey. Its now or never."

"I got'em!"

"Drop 'em, Joey"

"Bombs away!"

The airframe lifted immediate with the shifting of ballast and reduced weight. The second and last string of bombs were prepared.

"I got more, Cappy. We couldn't get them all down on the target."

"Watch'em, Joey, let me know how we did."

All at once the fifty calibers lit up, all firing at three o'clock.

"Messers........, (garbled). Three ......(garbled). The aircraft literally shifted left, as all guns fired directly right at a squadron of fighters coming at them fast. Inside the gunnery bubbles, brass flew in a hurricane of casings as they tumbled through the small chamber and fell out the bottom slots.

"Yahoo!", screamed Joey, as he watched the bridge explode on the easterly abutment. The bombers behind them continued the destruction. The ack-ack, lessened somewhat as the fiery hell descended on the city. Secondary explosions at the munitions plant rocked them thousands of feet above. The problem was the fighters. They were at three thousand feet.

Up front, in the nose gunner bubble, Jimmy Caldwell, never took his fingers off his 50. Without wasting a movement, he would follow an enemy from right to left and when he reached the end of the turret movement, followed another one back left to right. He had shot down two within several minutes. And now O'Hare saw the airfield at one o'clock. Elevation, 2,800 feet. He guided right and told Joey to get the last string ready.

Every gunner was firing now in nearly all directions as the Germans were swarming like flies. Two bombers were going down and they watched them hit the lush

German countryside in a ball of fire. Several parachutes were reported. These would become POWs if not shot on sight.

Doc Henley, in the top gunner bubble had one 'kill' already, that exploded instantly. He also saw the bomber behind them take a direct hit from anti-aircraft. Apparently they, too, had bombs in the bomb bay, as the aircraft disintegrated before his eyes.

The next fighter squadron taxied into position on the main runway of the airstrip.

Bobby O'Hare pushed the stick down and the bomber began picking up speed again. It was responding better now. Much of its weight, jettisoned. Behind them, the city was aflame. Two miles dead ahead was the air strip.

In the control tower the German Colonel screamed his orders to get those planes off the ground.

My Girl was flying on the deck, 1,400 feet, coming fast and low. Bobby eased it down to 600 feet and poured on the gas.

"Jimmy, you take out that f—(garble) tower as soon as you see it!" barked O'Hare.

"Roger, Cappy."

Just over the treetops, a mile ahead, was the tower. The plane was too low to shoot at....., for now. In another ten seconds all hell would break loose.

Jimmy opened up on the 50 caliber, lobbing them over the tower then bringing the tracer rounds right on into the cross-hairs. The tower exploded. There were no more orders given. The first fighter was getting off the ground at the end of the runway, its wheels retracting. The nose, top and belly gunners all took aim and fired. Immediately, smoke poured from the engine and its flight sputtered before it burst into flames. Two more were on the runway picking up speed. Only Jimmy in the nose and Jason in the belly, had clear shots at them. The tracers caught up with each plane and they engulfed into flames stalling on the runway, their pilots obliterated. More Messerschmidts started down the runway, intending to steer around the debris and flaming hulks.

Now the gunners turned their attention to the ground guns firing at them. But their speed, low height and nearness, forced an overt swivel of the guns on them, making it difficult to aim.

O'Hare cranked back on the stick as hard as he could, his teeth clenched and My Girl groaned with the strain as she tried to put as much distance between her and the ground as possible. The plane lifted radically.

"Now, Joey. Now!"

"Bombs away!"

And the last fell out the bay doors, only a three-second drop to the ground. The hangars went first and the parking area next with several airplanes, exploding. Then a perforating line of bombs fell across the runway cratering massive holes and rendering it useless. The additional weight release helped as My Girl gulped additional altitude. The blasts from the ground pushed and jostled her in the sky. Young Jason in the belly gun was nearly sunburned from the instant blast. Hoots and hollers started coming across their intercom radios.

"Keep an eye out, you guys," yelled Ronnie.

My Girl banked left at 1,200 feet and headed over to the Rhine, descending down onto the river 300 feet over the water. This was their escape.

"How many are with us?" asked Bobby.

"I see three. No, four. No, wait,......five."

In a stately chateau, overlooking the Rhine, a refined looking woman looked out her window. Frightened children hugged each leg. Her view overlooked her own estate, gardens and vineyard down to the river's edge. Fisherman were out on the water and barges floated gracefully toward the terminal, downstream. She saw the dark plumes of smoke from Dusseldorf and knew that not only was the city seriously damaged, but that the war was lost. The Americans would not quit until it was over. In her mind, the only question was what would be left of her country. With these thoughts, a pall upon her mind, the surreal came into focus as My Girl flew into her picture, flying low and banking as it followed the turns of the river, in front of her.

They stayed low, flying across Belgium, tracking north of Antwerp on the way back. Everybody checked in. All were accounted for.

"We're not home yet, so keep a sharp eye," said Ronnie, his composure beginning to return to him.

"Jeez, Bobby, that was a hell of a ride. I think I need to head back to the stink pot." Bobby laughed. "I think it's too late for me", he said, and they both laughed.

Soon the intercom buzzed with reliving of the fight just minutes before. Immediately good-natured arguments over several of the kills started.

Tensions eased as the land fell away behind them. Eleven had gone out and six were returning. As the English Channel approached, the radio came alive. Lucky Lady, directly behind them had two injured. Holy Smoke was bringing up the rear. They had one injury, but none were critical. They started naming the planes that had gone down and who might have parachuted.

Doc Henley broke through, "I got two 'smitties' at eight o'clock high. I got one at one nine o'clock. Nope. Shit, they're comin", he screamed. All guns came around to the left side and opened up. The other bombers did likewise. This was nasty. They were coming fast, from up high and the sluggish bombers were broadside to them. Behind them, Lucky Lady was taking evasive maneuvers. So were the others. At least twelve fighters bore down on the slow flying caravan in the sky. Soon the sparkle of their machine guns was visible. Jimmy, up in the nose, had no shot. He would have to wait. Doc thought he would melt his barrels, casings rolling on the floor until you couldn't see the floor. Several ripping sounds tore through the fuselage, and the whistling increased.

"We took some, Cappy."

"I know. Keep firing!"

Ronnie radioed to Dover air field requesting help from the RAF. A patrol was about fifteen miles out and on their way. The 'smitties' flew over them, their first sweep complete and they began the steep banked turn to come at them again. Doc followed them and his 50 struck home. Jimmy finally got a shot up front and sent one home, smoking badly. Back in the pack, somebody was on fire, but still flying. The Channel was coming up. They strained to see their deliverers coming from the west, as the Luftwaffe fighter pilots banked up and around and were lining up on them for a second round.

"We've got to do something, Cappy. They're coming." With only 4,000 feet elevation, there wasn't much to do. Doc hollered, "Here they come, eleven o'clock high. I'm getting low on ammo up here."

"Keep on 'em, Doc," yelled Bobby, as he took the plane down and underneath the approaching fighters, forcing them to dive straight down and turn to follow him. It was risky, but better than being a sitting duck. The line of bombers behind them all went to evasive maneuvers in an attempt to stave off the onslaught.

The fighter was nose diving and O'Hare knew it. He banked the plane hard left back toward the channel. This forced the fighter pilot into a near spiral maneuver to try to catch the line of his machine gun up with the lumbering bomber. My Girl crossed over the shore, heading for the Cliffs of Dover-hoping and praying to see their rescuers.

As the Messerschmidt, straightened up, it could not maintain the steep pitch, but its line of fire was nearly crossing over the top gunner of the bomber. Inside, Doc Henley's grip on the 50s was white knuckled. He watched as his tracers kept going all around the nose of the fighter coming at them. The machine guns on the fighter were lit up and he knew he was the target. It was a shoot out. This German pilot was no slouch. Bravely, despite the G-forces and near vertical dive, he kept on them. In his peripheral vision, he saw the marker on the belt pass through the gun, indicating he was nearly out of ammo. He re-focused trying to hold the jumping gun on its target. Finally, the tracers hit the razor thin profile of the fighter. It started with engine smoke. The bastard kept firing, as bullets ripped across the fuselage and through Doc Henley, who collapsed in his harness. Two rounds went through Chuck Halley, only a foot away and the inside of the cockpit turned red with the spray of blood. The Messerschmidt flew past their nose a second later, on fire and plunged into the Atlantic, in a splash of pure white froth and yellow flames against the cold blue water.

Ronnie turned around and saw Chuck's body on the floor, a mess of blood and pulp. Doc was peacefully slumped, hanging in his harness; his Browning 50 fallen silent and the ammo belt having fed through the gun, to the last shell.

They now flew blind on top. "Jason, get up on top and take over that gun. Let me know what you see," said O'Hare. Quickly, Jason scampered out of the belly bubble and up to Doc's position, but seeing him, stopped his progress momentarily. He reverently slipped Doc out of the harness, and fit the bloodied equipment onto himself after setting up a new ammo box.

"All clear, up here, Cappy." O'Hare said, "Take her, Ronnie. We've been shot up on the left aileron." Ronnie took over and immediately felt the flawed responsiveness that O'Hare had held in check. The plane jostled on the takeover. Bobby went back to confirm the status of his two friends. Quickly done, he surveyed the damage to the airframe. Damaged but airworthy. He made his way back to the cockpit.

"There they are", cried Ronnie, gleefully. The bloody spray on the windshield formed rivulets and drained down in the cockpit wall. But through the hideous tint, he saw the RAF fighters approaching. They rose from the emotion of the death of their friends to a new elation and relief at their rescue as the enemy turned back to the continent. The RAF boys gave chase.

"Oh shit, we got problems!"

"What now", asked O'Hare climbing back into his seat.

"Fuel! He must have hit the tanks." Outside the plane, fuel gushed from several holes in the right wing tank. Ronnie and Bobby each looked out their windows.

"Right side", said Ronnie.

"Gain some altitude on a slow left bank, Ronnie. Let's put what we can in the left wing."

Slowly, My Girl climbed off the deck flying over the water and the slow left bank began shifting fuel. She resisted. The aileron was seriously damaged and made holding a bank difficult, as the weight shifted it became more difficult.

"I'll take it."

Ronnie let go of the stick. Ahead were the white cliffs of Dover, a palisade against the sea and menace from the continent. Right now, it was the target, so long as they got up and over the cliffs. It was going to be close. They were five miles out, about eight to the airstrip. The plane yawed and pitched and the stick came out of O'Hare's grip as it began to struggle to maintain elevation.

Ronnie Dickenson looked at the fuel gauge, the needle pegged on empty. They were under a thousand feet and the tops of the cliff wall were at seven hundred thirty-five. The altimeter, slowly gave up ground to the forces of gravity. My Girl was losing the battle for altitude.

"Here we go" spit O'Hare through his teeth. "Everybody hold on". In the nose bubble, Jimmy Caldwell considered the cliffs, a massive wall. It looked to him that they would fly smack into them.

A sudden shudder jolted them all, as the plane suddenly lost forty feet of altitude. Every sphincter tightened and no one breathed.

"We're too low, Cappy", whimpered Jimmy, as the right outboard engine cut out, starved for fuel, its propeller, coming to an abrupt halt. The plane shifted left and O'Hare struggled to right it, all remaining engines full, and pulling gently back so as not to force the damaged aileron into total failure. My Girl lifted ever so briefly.

"Let's hope there's no down draft at the cliff," said Ronnie. Two hundred yards to the cliff. The stick was pulled back all the way. My Girl groped for every foot of elevation.

"Oh shit!" someone yelled as the plane lunged downward again. Frozen, they looked at the oncoming shrubbery scratching out an existence in the cracks and crevices of the wall. They were frozen in seeing their own death. Terror seized them. Wanting to close their eyes to it, but unable. They were only twenty feet too low at a hundred yards, coming at 110 miles per hour. Jason's bladder emptied, as well as his bowels.

Atmospherically, the warming sun on the channel had simmered the air on the water that morning. A slight breeze blowing against the prevailing winds, cut a path across the channel and was energized by this warming air. The breeze, gusted to a light wind, bearing due west against the prevailing easterly flow. It was only a quarter mile wide, but directly below the flight path of My Girl. To either side, the prevailing winds blew from the Atlantic to the continent of Europe. But this particular swirl of air moved in the opposite direction until it was stopped abruptly at the cliffs of Dover and could go nowhere but up.

The jolt in their seat bottoms, was mistaken, in that moment for disaster, then they realized, she had just been given a miracle of God. My Girl climbed onto England's shore in a sudden lift of sixty feet as it crossed over the cliffs. God's little breeze had shoe-horned her onto the land.

Tears streamed down their faces, as they yelled and shouted, the smiles wide through blood, sweat and fear. They seemed not to believe in their own miraculous rescue. The pasture and crops passed below them, as the aircraft lumbered on at less than tree top level.

O'Hare continued to battle the aileron, as the left outboard engine sputtered to a halt.

"Just keep her in the air, Bobby," prayed Ronnie. The runway was dead ahead. No trees or buildings. Their elevation; thirty feet off the ground.

"Joey, get the wheels down, now!" squawked O'Hare. Joey, cranked hard and fast on the manual wheel crank handle.

"We've only got the left side, Cappy. The right's all shot to hell."

"Oh, Sweet Jesus, will this never end?", complained Ronnie.

The tower squawked they had them visually, clear to land, but only one gear down. Fire trucks standing by. Sirens came alive on the base as the crash team climbed into their vehicles and raced toward the end of the runway.

The altimeter said zero, but they were still flying, about 20 feet up. Jimmy Caldwell watched fence posts pass underneath his seat, as the right inboard engine began to sputter, and My Girl could no longer sustain flight. She plummeted the short distance to the ground as O'Hare pulled back one last time and the aileron gave way. The crushing jar jolted all of them as the plane teetered downward on the right, lacking landing gear underneath that side. The plane started to steer left on its one set of wheels, until the right wing tip touched the grass, just shy of the pavement. My Girl swapped directions and skidded rightward, now onto the tarmac, heading for the near-est hangar, which was emptying rapidly of all personnel. The crash crew now raced down the tarmac to the other end, where the plane was showering sparks and lacked any control whatsoever. In the cockpit, things were spin-ning as the two men watched, unable to do anything. First, the oncoming tower, then the tilting landscape, crossing over the tarmac, now a hangar and men run-ning before them. Now, a picture of farmland, and forest. Now, the tower coming around again. Vehicles coming with lights flashing, and My Girl spun as if she was in a slow waltz, finally coming to a halt facing the English Channel. Simultaneously, they unbuckled and clambered out of the plane and ran for the nearby field as the crash team administered foam and water.

Jimmy Caldwell stood looking back at her and then fainted. Joey was on his knees praying, and that seemed so right. Jason, Bobby and Ronny, half collapsing, did the same.

CHAPTER 2

As confetti rained down on New York City, America and the free world celebrated its victory and the end of that war. This was a war of incredible cost in blood and treasure. Here, the victory was sure-absolute, not "an acceptable political outcome". Even then, in the smoldering heap that was Europe, dormant seeds lived in the ashes. Simmering beneath the headlines of history was an intellectual and philosophical war well under way and about to spill out onto history's front pages.

It was the culmination of two schools of thought; one religious and the other, political. The political quickly jumped the fence into economics, as all things political must. In the mid-19th century, the writing of Karl Marx, V. Lenin, Hegel and others purported to have found the antidote to the economic struggle of life itself. They, and their utopian brethren, through collectivist mentality, declared they had found the answer. It was manifest in communism, or the more politically salable 'socialism'. The latter, a meaningless stepping stone to the former. And then, on to tyranny. The men who would ably refute them in the field of economics were Austrians and would later be known as the "Austrian School". They were men like Carl Menger, Eugen BomBawerk, and its most prodigious articulator, Ludwig Von Mises. Later, F.A. Hayek would take its theories and win a Nobel Prize in economics. But the world remained largely ignorant of these men and the theories they propounded. It didn't want to be bothered much by the science which sought to study the laws and precepts by which prices occur, values are understood and how finite resources are developed and distributed. Indeed, while men clamored over getting what they want, they thought it a bore to understand precisely by what mechanisms who shall get what.

They ignored the natural inclinations of man: First, the primacy of his individuality and second, his propensity to better his condition in all endeavors, by his own efforts. The communists substituted the collectivist notion of group struggle for those natural inclinations. Lulled by floral speech about caring for the good of the many, sacrifices prescribed by the benevolent ruling committees would guide-no mandate the individual's actions. But the subtext of the economics underlying such a creed is that those who support this system would be given the jobs. The wages of which would be at the expense of their brethren. It was a loyalty based system as opposed to a merit or market based system.

A contemporary Frenchman, Frederick Bastiat summed it up well, defining the state as... ' ...The legal fiction whereby everyone seeks to live at the expense of everyone else." And he exposed the great problem with another quote: "Everyone wants to live at the expense of the state. They forget that the state wants to live at the expense of everyone."

Underpinning this shift was another change in the paradigm that had existed in the western world for 1,500 years. In 1859 Charles Darwin wrote the book 'The Origin of the Species'. In it he advanced a 'theory', whose assumption, implications and conclusions would profoundly change the world. The theory of evolution, in time, would become assumed scientific fact; a gospel, in its own right. The Bible stood in direct refutation of Darwin's theory and by implication, the very existence of God was not only questioned, but dismissed as a holdover of unenlightened man, fraught with superstitious beliefs. Religion was said to be the opiate of the masses.

According to these "progressives", man was entering a new epoch, freed from the oppression of a God who would judge him, free now to create a utopia where benevolent rulers would summon from each according to his abilities and bequeath to each according to his needs. Here now seemed a scientific set of facts and principles that could finally put an end to a "judging" God, and deliver what was the power of the clergy into the new high priesthood, the men of science.

The clergy was able to mount counter attacks in the form of revivals, largely by the blessing of God's spirit upon the people of the United States. So, the battle was engaged. Eventually, the Scopes (monkey) trial seemed to bring this to a head in America. Science was pitted against the Bible, and the result was the beginning of a rapid decline in a meaningful belief in God, by its people.

On the economic front the truth was also presented, but very few ever saw it. While everyone had read and understood Marx, few had read any of the works of Von Mises, or Hayek, or many others. Theirs was a considered work, based on truth, how humans acted in economic terms. They warned of the collectivist mentality and what it meant to personal liberty and the national economy. They exploded its fallacies and 'economics by committee". Without the information that market prices provided, economic calculation was impossible. Thus, direction of scarce resources, be they natural or human, could not be determined. All economic calculation started and circularly ended at the committee. Its decisions quickly became governed by its own need for political cover, destruction of those who opposed it, or the distribution of spoils to its supporters and friends.

Connor had felt the uneasiness creeping upon him for years. During the Roosevelt period. The 'New Deal' was a turning over of the goodness and profundity of the U.S. Constitution, for a grab bag of social and economic programs which fed upon the fears of men and inclined them to dependency on the state. The culture and country were changing. He couldn't put his finger to it precisely, but like the earth shifting beneath him, the slow movement over time was perceptible and profound. It changed the values of the people. They cared less about others than they had in the past. Maybe it was because the land had been so harsh and life so fragile, that they depended more on each other, their neighbors, friends and family. They depended more and believed in a God who not only could redeem them for eternity, but rescue them from a myriad of hazards, dangers and threats to life. Without needing formality or formula, they had a sense of community. They knew they needed each other. Paradoxically their extreme self reliance did not preclude their commonality; their need for commerce, worship and fellowship.

Government was the most obvious sign. Its progressive growth, in scope of authority and pervasive intrusions, was menacing to men like him. The size of its economic draft was ever increasing, sometimes by slight increment, often by bold usurpation. The slow destruction that he felt of the country's currency and the imposition of the federal income tax during his lifetime was ominous. They promised it would never exceed two percent, but had long since surpassed that rate and had become a leviathan. Even those who had proposed and supported it said that no reasonable man would support it if its rate could creep upward. He had remembered, as a small boy the Panic of 1893 and again as a young man, the Panic of 1907. Both were precipitated by a series of bank failures after an overextended economy had contracted. The Federal Reserve System seemed to have stabilized the economy and abolished the dreaded business cycle with its customary expansions and contractions, but this was wrong. Terribly wrong. With the federal government ever more in control money printing, credit and taxation, certain people in the government assured the citizens that everything now was under control. This was short lived. The Great Depression destroyed any idea that government could control and navigate through turbulent economic waters. This was the longest and deepest depression the world had seen to date. The collectivist controllers were undeterred by their failures to direct the affairs of men and a nation. Increasing control through taxation, subsidies and the shear size of government was heaped upon the system. Yet, the nation would survive and did, but it was long and brutal and, in Connor's view, was made worse by the actions of government.

The military victory of World War II and the economic victory obtained by the war, finally ended the Great Depression. This only fueled the notion that man, through government, was invincible. The latest high priests of collectivist economics; John Maynard Keynes and Kenneth Galbraith, were anointed with the oil of approbation and the robes of academia. Watching these changes in his country gave Connor a slight scowl, which was accentuated by his sagging face.

———

Bobby O'Hare was back in the states, staying with friends in New York and he celebrated with the rest of the country. He would be coming on a troop train back to the west coast. From San Francisco he would take the train to Dunsmuir, coming up the Sacramento River canyon, where eighty years earlier, Melissa Grady had ventured on her own, looking for a new life. Where fifty years earlier, Jon O'Hare had furnished lumber to build the trestles and bridges across the river that carried the trains.

Connor was grateful the war was over. He sensed there would be a new beginning for the ranch. But Bobby would have to do it. He felt himself as little more than a tired caretaker. He lived alone with only a little daily interaction with the ranch hands. Yes, the country was turning a corner and the ranch would as well.

He poured the hot black coffee into the mug he had used for many years. As he finished pouring, the toaster sprang and delivered its product just the way he liked it. He set the coffee pot back on the gas burner, now off, and breathed in the smell of the slightly burned toast, which he then buttered. A small plume of smoke from the toaster wafted through the kitchen. His knife flicked some of the charred crumbs onto the red checkered oil cloth on the table. He bit into the toast, savoring the simplicity of its familiar smell and taste, as every morning.

He chewed slowly and deliberately, tasting the butter and feeling the crunch of the crust. He chased it with the strong black coffee and felt himself revive somewhat. This ritual was followed inexorably by the next. He grabbed the wire framed spectacles and strung them onto his nose and behind his ears. With both hands, he adjusted and torqued the frames onto his face just so. As every morning, he efficiently used his napkin to clean the crumbs from the table with the sweep of his hand and with the other, brought to himself, the worn and tattered Bible from near the salt and pepper shakers.

God, how he missed Leah. He missed her-especially in the morning. For every day, at the moment he awakened, for just that instant, he thought she was here, with him. He saw her and she was beautiful and happy. His heart soared in that moment. Both of them were younger.

This was always followed quickly by the truth of time and death, to which he submitted.

He let the Bible open to a random page as he did habitually. It fell open to Ezekiel. He thought to himself about the prophesies of Ezekiel. Particularly in Chapter 37 and 38. He turned there now and read again for the umpteenth time. As he read, he thought about how the Israelites had turned from God. Here was God, accusing them of '... even devouring their own children'. Here, God promised to cleanse His land and His people. He would restore them to Himself. There was that famous passage about the dry bones coming back to life.

This picture of rebellion and grace seemed to capture Connor. It spoke to him, as if he understood something more of what God was saying than perhaps other people. Clearly God was saying he was going to bring back the Jews into their land. He knew enough of history through the Bible as well as secular texts to know that this had never happened. Not since the return from the Babylonian captivity. He wondered whether there might be some other explanation, some interpretation that he was missing. Though never a Bible "thumper", Connor had always had an interest in the Bible, not only in bringing its guidance into his life in a practical way, but in eschatology, the study of future prophesies. Connor believed the Bible was the Word of God, and that was that. Readily admitting there were many things he did not understand, and there were mysteries he probably never would resolve. Yet he wondered how this detailed and extensive prophesy, which threads its way through these chapters, could occur. The Jews had been dispersed since 70 AD, and now the holocaust of Hitler's 'final solution' was hitting the front pages. How could so lost and vanquished a peoples be restored. Impossible, he thought.

He read on, all through Chapter 37, stumped that this prophesy was unfulfilled and would seem inevitably so. He closed the Bible and prayed quickly a rather rote prayer for the day, said his "Amen" and then rubbed the sagging, whiskered face. He didn't bother to shave everyday anymore. He would do so if he went to town or church, but not otherwise. I wish Bobby were here, he thought, for the thousandth time. He looked up at the calendar of farm implements; September 7, 1945. The war had been over three months to the day. Bobby would be home soon. The chair raked the plank floor as he scooted it back and helped himself to his feet. The screen door creaked on the return spring and then slammed loud back to the jam as Poncho, his ranch hand came into the kitchen and motioned to the coffee pot.

"Help yourself", said Connor.

"You coffee ees too strong, Señor Connor", as he grimaced at the first gulp.

"Well it suits me fine. If you don't like it why do you drink it? Its the same every morning. And every morning you complain."

"Eets Okay, no problema." He spat several grounds into the sink, and smiled at Connor.

"How are we doin' for water?"

"Bueno! Mucha agua. Ponds ees full."

"Well we need to get water up to the north end while we still can. This will probably be our last irrigation up there. The creeks are slowing down."

"Si, I did that this morning". He gulped more of the coffee. Connor looked at Poncho slightly perturbed, not because he'd done the wrong thing, but precisely because he'd done the right thing at the right time and didn't need Connor to tell him. This slipped under Connor's skin as yet another symbol of his no longer being critical to the operation of Grady-O'Hare.

"Dammit, Poncho, I didn't tell you to do that."

Poncho's eyebrows raised and his shoulders shrugged slightly. "You want I shut the water off, Boss?"

Now fully perturbed, "Hell no I don't want you to shut the water off *now*. It's going!" Poncho gestured helplessness as if there were no pleasing the boss. He reached to set down the cup, knowing the time in the kitchen was about to be over.

"Come on, let's go check the herd, or what's left of it." Connor grabbed his hat off the peg and headed out the door for the old jeep, a slight limp perceptible in his gait. Poncho smiled, following in his footsteps. This was how most days began.

———

The train ride was unbearably hot, coming up the Sacramento Valley. Major Robert O'Hare guessed 110 degrees. The train car was full of soldiers, sailors and airmen. Most traveled in uniforms which only heightened the discomfort. It would just be a few hours and he would climb out of the valley and the dreadful heat, back to the forested land and a more agreeable temperature, though still hot.

It was mid September, but the last heat wave of summer seemed unrelenting. At every stop men said goodbye to their comrades in arms, though most hadn't known each other before boarding the Oregon-Pacific Railroad car. They shared the common hopes and fears for the future, a common sense of horror and victory in the past and so they related, as all warriors can and do.

———

Peace was at hand. Factories were already shifting from war to domestic production. Around corporate board rooms, strategies formulated that would set the course of production for thousands of goods and services. Restrictions on strategic and raw materials were being lifted. There was, of course, more than a little apprehension among the men of war. Could they adapt? Did they have skills, other than military ones.

Those that projected an incredible rate of family formation and all its ramifications were correct. Tracts of land would have to be subdivided and inexpensive homes built and offered for sale with favorable financing-especially for G.I.'s. Men and women formed marital unions at unprecedented rates, and naturally, the birth rate shot through the roof and produced a demographic bubble that would do much to dictate the production, consumption and political power for their entire life span. These children would be known as the 'baby boom' generation, or as the decades passed, simply 'boomers'.

The country was about to embark on one of its most productive periods. Huge volumes of timber were needed to build houses. More concrete, more asphalt roads, more electrical and phone lines. New roads were developed at break neck pace. After President Truman ended the war, President Dwight Eisenhour embarked on an interstate transportation system, later referred to simply as the 'freeway'. This along with the manufacture of all things for domesticity. From toasters to ironing boards, stoves, radios, automobiles would quickly leap forward into production levels undreamed of before. Each would advance in design and technology. Soon, the plans would be laid for an interstate transportation system by the federal government. The best and brightest now turned their efforts on improving the quality of life by innovation and productivity. There was, of course, a spike in unemployment as industry could not immediately absorb the influx of men coming home from the war. But soon enough, it made a place for them.

Government too was ramping up. Never satisfied to go back to prewar levels of Gross National Product, the government was getting ready to explode with domestic programs. Never smaller-always larger; that was the operating maxim.

In Europe, the Marshall Plan was to be formulated and it would rebuild western Europe in large part and help establish America as both a powerful peacetime as well as wartime ally. There were always her detractors and they wasted no time in pointing out that the communists of Russia were equally responsible-no even more responsible for the victory in Europe. Quiet whispers in high places seemed to suggest that America may be the real threat. Didn't it begin to look like an occupation? Their presence suggested a long term goal, ostensibly to rebuild Europe, but couldn't there be ulterior motives? World hegemony?

In collectivist circles, America and its 'corrupt capitalistic system' was trying to parlay its military victory into world domination, thus subjugating the masses under the foot of an exploitative boot.

The socialists of western Europe had infiltrated into high places in the governments of Italy, France, Belgium, and the United Kingdom. Alliances of ideology were formed with the communists of Russia, and within a matter of months, the iron curtain would descend across Europe and the "Cold War" had begun. There was hardly time to savor victory before the next war was at hand. But this was not a 'hot war'. This war was between the ideologies of collectivism and individual liberty, between the economics of market based production and government controlled distribution, between the religion of enlightened science, and the Judeo-Christian faith.

———

Bobby O'Hare slid the window down and a blast of hot air engulfed him. With it, the smell of hot pine trees surviving the summer. The sap was running in the trees and he could pick it out of the pungent air. He loosened his tie, and looked around the train car. There were only a few soldiers left and they were passed out in uncomfortable positions in their seats, Their jaws sagged open. Suddenly, the girders of a steel trestle filled the window passing by, surprising him. They were crossing the Sacramento River. It looked a cool glacial blue, with frothy water bounding over its boulders. So inviting, he just wanted to dive in. He couldn't wait to get home.

The train wound its way up the canyon, stopping in Dunsmuir, the last passenger terminal. He hitched a ride quickly, from Dunsmuir to Weed, and found an old high school friend, Jock Hagerman, who gave him a ride out to the ranch. The bulbous '42 Plymouth passed under the heavy log crosspiece to the ranch gate-"Grady-O'Hare".

Connor was watching Poncho weld up a broken gate in the shop. It was towards the end of day. Sparks cascaded down from the welding which now was atop previous broken welds.

"Maybe you should buy a new gate, Señor?" said Poncho through the darkened welders mask he flipped up and down with the jerk of his head.

"Maybe I'll just get a worker who works instead of telling me what to do?" struck back Connor.

"Si. Maybeee" , replied Poncho in total disregard to the threat.

Connor heard gravel grinding in the yard and a car door slam. The shop was not well-lighted, and he covered his eyes coming out into the bright sunlight. He didn't recognize the car as it pulled away with a waving hand, but what was left behind was a man in a uniform bent over a duffle bag, who then stood up.

"Bobby!" cried Connor.

Bobby glided across the yard. "Pop!"

The two men shook hands as they were taught, then awkwardly, embraced each other. Connor's eyes watered up and he wiped them with a handerchief. His lips quivered in happiness, joy, and relief. He kept looking at Bobby, to be certain it was real and not a dream.

"Damn if you aren't a sight for sore eyes, boy."

"It's good to be home Pop." "Hey Poncho", he called out, as Poncho came out of the shop, removing the thick leather gloves.

"Señor Bobby!" They shook and hugged. "I can't believe he hasn't fired you, yet."

"Oh no, Señor Bobby. He fires me every week". Bobby laughed.

"Well, come on in the house son, let's get somethin' cold to drink." The three men talked incessantly as they clunked up the wooden steps to the porch and the screen door banged loudly behind them.

"Got, ice tea, got beer, got water. Didn't know you'd be comin' today." He wished there was more and he regretted he was so unprepared. The refrigerator looked so empty at a time it should be so full.

The men sat on the shady side of the porch and talked late into the night. There was no effort to pry into Bobby's war experience. It was more about the hopes and needs of Grady-O'Hare now and in the future. Bobby talked about maybe going to the school of forestry in Humboldt County, or a degree in agronomics from UC Davis or Berkeley.

Poncho was living in 'Mel's cabin', which is what they called the little house that Melissa Grady had built. He was there with his wife and three children, all in school. Connor was quick to talk of passing on the torch. There was no resistance. Bobby seemed up to the challenge though it was unclear how any schooling would occur.

The herd would need to be rebuilt. Bobby had ideas. He talked about a closed herd, completely developed and raised on the ranch, for a controlled, high quality beef. In the forests, he talked about detailed inventory of timber, and a management that would allow for some harvesting soon. He, too, thought the country would be clamoring for timber in the certain housing boom. At last, as he talked, he saw that Pop had fallen asleep, a peaceful countenance upon the whiskered face.

Poncho and Bobby rose quietly. Poncho bid good night and slipped off the porch to go home. Bobby sat and watched the old man breathing softly in the rocking chair. At last, he got up and gently stirred the old man, and helped him to the bedroom.

As the morning sun crested the Cascade Mountains, O'Hare sipped coffee in his old jeans, boots and a plaid shirt. He leaned against the post on the porch and gazed across the land. The air was sweet and a slight breeze came off the mountain, sweeping the pastures. It was good to be home, and he felt his life beginning anew, fresh.

CHAPTER 3

Bobby took over the reigns with his customary swiftness and certainty. The forest lands were surveyed. The pasture part of the ranch had been well kept. His interest was in creating and developing a herd of cattle as well as the timber assets. He was never able to go to Davis, or Berkeley or Humboldt for his forestry degree. Instead he wrote to the department heads and secured every textbook, devouring them at night. Soon, he foraged over the thousands of acres of timber for near perfect trees, and took their cones and seeds, planting them in a small greenhouse type of shed. He visited the tall trees many times, trying to understand their secret to growth, but more importantly, their clear timber.

When he found part of Grady-O'Hare's forest infected with powder post beetle, he immediately logged out the infected timber and sold it, buying new equipment.

He developed a plan for roads to get to each area of the forest, careful to protect the small creeks and streams and establish decks which could efficiently collect the harvested timber for transport. His goal was to create timber production that could be sustained over the life cycle of the typical timber native to the area. It was forward thinking and generations ahead of its time.

He researched neighboring and nearby lands which might be for sale. Instead of outright purchases which might deplete the coffers of Grady-O'Hare, he bought options to purchase, for much smaller sums. He trained an assistant to help assess the timber on the optioned pieces. Sometimes he would purchase simply the timber rights. But his preference was for the land as well. Making note of tree growth, by their rings, and noting parasites and infestations. He learned well the lessons of his books, and he often wrote letters with specific questions to chief foresters of corporations and forestry schools. Often he posed questions that others had not come to or for which there were no answers, yet. At this time, forestry, had not evolved to what it would become. Due to the relatively low stumpage prices, most forestry efforts were geared to finding the largest trees, building roads to them and getting the trees out and to market. Little thought was given to the future, to forest health.

He would often ride through the ranch in the old Willys jeep, with Connor alongside. They talked of the past and dreamed of the future. Occasionally, he got letters from airmen who had served under him. But these dwindled over time as life's demands crowded upon those men's time, making it easier to put away the years, once so profound and full of the intensity of life. This was a new life and most were anxious for it to overtake the old life, lived during the war. They were consumed with wives and scrubbed children, with getting an education and a career in place. Everyone felt the ascendancy of America upon the world stage.

But others saw that other battle; the seething discord. It crept out of the shadows of the corridors of power and onto the world stage. On March 5, 1946, Winston Churchill would say that an "Iron Curtain" had descended across Europe. The Soviet Union, an ally of the war, would become the new enemy. It had felt its own ascendancy-victorious at the conclusion of the war. The Marshall Plan, was engaged fully now in rebuilding western Europe.

Connor and Bobby attended to their business. Like so many Americans, they were tired of the world's affairs and yearned for the life that was unfolding at home. But history and world affairs care not for the weariness of those who would assume power or be thrust into world events. The ranch was becoming prosperous again. They were selectively logging some of the old growth and replanting. With the proceeds they bought more land or exercised the options they held. The cattle herd was showing some promise with a strong birthing in the spring.

They went to church on Sundays. When Bobby had seen a beautiful girl of Italian ancestry, he was smitten. Vera Gallino lived in Weed, where her father was a bookkeeper and mother raised six children. She was the fifth and by far, in his eyes, the most beautiful. She had smooth cheeks down to a thin jaw-line and handsome lips. She wore her jet black hair plainly, letting the curls fall upon her shoulders which raked straight out from her slender neck. Her eyes were a dazzling blue and everyone who noticed Vera at all, could not help but comment on her eyes. They seemed wet and brilliant. She had the waist of a butterfly and the legs of a long distance runner. Bobby never missed church, once he met Vera.

One Sunday, the Italians in the community of Weed, which were considerable, threw a big party. Tons of food, dancing, a big band played, along with some of the local blue grass musicians. It was very similar to the town hall picnic that brought Melissa Grady and John O'Hare together. Vera and Bobby had already known each other from church for several months, when the Italians threw their party. They danced together on the first dance, eager to touch each other. After several quick numbers, a slower song gave them a chance to sense each other more intimately, unhurried by the frenetic pace of earlier songs. In that dance, they both began feeling a sense of connectedness, yearning for the other. She had heard the stories about his flying in the war, though he never mentioned his feats or his medals. A war hero? He unquestionably was. She was not shopping for a war hero, but a man to give her a family. She sought a man who would be faithful to his family, to her, to the country, that shared her own ideals of fidelity and liberty and hard work and a better life for their children. She was infused with the hatred of her father for tyrants and collectivism. He had fled prewar Italy, with the clothes on his back and his children.

For Bobby, it was simple. She was gorgeous and he just could not quit staring into her eyes. It was embarrassing, but he was helpless. They parted from the crowd and strolled out into the moonlit night, talking easily about nothing important, laughing easily as they sought to be comfortable with one another. They talked about her siblings and parents, he, about his dreams for Grady-O'Hare. He told her about his projects and seedling experiments. Before he knew it, he was completely immersed in his dreams, explaining the decisions and ramifications of each step of various projects. She didn't mind. In fact, she loved listening to him talk about the plans he had; the dreams he was forging. He was invincible, so sure of himself. The energy and passion with which he spoke was infectious and she loved being infected by him. She thought to herself; this is a man going somewhere and I want to go with him wherever that take us. Where he goes, I will be with him.

He finally caught himself and realized how he had rambled on, when he noticed the way she looked at him, the way the moonlight reflected in those brilliant eyes. He brought her to him and kissed her passionately. She felt that same passion touch her lips and it was like an electrical current through her body. It took her breath away. He had never tasted anything so sweet, so intoxicating, so lovely as her. They pulled away and looked into each other, now differently, and then fell headlong into another kiss-long and pressing. They knew then, that night, that they were in love with each other. The time of watching the other from afar, was over. They would not remain as thoughts and dreams at the periphery, in the venue of hope and fantasy, but in reality, in the active present-touching and being together.

———

The courtship continued through the year and in the Spring of 1947, they were married. As if by tradition, they, too, used the ranch for the ceremony, and not a moment too soon. Nine months later, Vera gave birth to the first of five children; Danny, then Patrick, Matthew, Angelina and finally, in 1955 came Jon-Connor.

The spring of Danny's infancy was little more than the continuation of winter. Twelve cords of wood chugged through the wood stoves and fireplaces in the large un-insulated home. Connor lived in the closest bedroom to the kitchen and Vera cared for him as a loving daughter would. That winter had taken its toll on his health.

He was relegated increasingly to the house. He often arose before dawn and quietly stepped into the kitchen and began his morning routine. Vera, who generally ran the house in the morning was yet asleep. It was usually the smell of his singed toast that awakened her. Often she stirred and turned to look at Bobby sleeping, breathing slowly, deeply. Sometimes she snuggled against him, soaking him in.

It was the morning of May 14th, 1948. Connor awoke and sat stiffly at the side of the bed. He rubbed his sagging face and felt the whiskers. Every step through the day was an effort. He sat bleary eyed in the darkness and let his thoughts and consciousness come back to him. He thought of his beloved Leah.

His feet fumbled on their own for the slippers nearby and found them. He leaned slowly and turned on the small lamp on the bed stand and proceeded to get dressed. Every movement seemed to require a grunt or audial assistance. He put on an old flannel shirt, missing a button where it tucked into his khaki trousers, which were held up by worn suspenders. He put the slippers back on. As quietly as old men can be, he went about fixing his coffee, making plenty in the newer, larger, improved coffee pot. He whistled some incoherent tune in an airiness which had no tone. It was more like breathing rhythmically through pursed lips.

The toaster delivered up, just as he sat down with his first cup. The plume of smoke crept along the ceiling where it had accumulated for years on the paint. The aroma snuck into the rest of the house as he crunched through the blackened crust. He reached for his Bible.

He was reading in the third chapter of Joel, who spoke of Israel as restored to its land at the 'end of days'. Joel could not be speaking of the return from Babylonian captivity. That was already history several hundred years prior. How could this be so, he thought, as he washed down the last of the toast with coffee. It must be in the future, he thought. It was that same old nagging problem with Ezekiel.

The pictures and stories had been circulated widely of Hitler's final solution for the Jews. Names like Auschwitz and Buchenwald were now historical facts. Tensions had risen for two years, after Churchill's "Iron Curtain" speech and there were reports that Berlin may be divided. The Russians were accepted as the new enemy of freedom, of the West, and America.

He pondered these things for awhile, but mentally moved on. He said his prayer, as Vera woke to the toast. She rolled over to Bobby and, reaching beneath the blankets, grabbed him tenderly but intently. He responded immediately and awakened. He brought her on top of him. She put her finger to her lips for silence and then slipped beneath the covers. They were in the world of lovers-intimate. Soon her finesse and seduction excited him to near panic. Now she came up and kissed him and moved to straddle him, putting her finger to her lips again. He smiled. On that starry morning, Patrick was conceived.

Out in the kitchen, Connor had poured another cup and made his way to the living room. He set the mug down and rekindled the fire, now just glowing coals. It came to life and he stretched out his hands for its warmth, rubbing the arthritis from his knuckles. It was getting worse by the month.

He turned on the radio and stood by as the tubes warmed. The voice seemed to boom in the quiet house and he quickly adjusted the large knob on the left, lest it wake everyone.

The news reporter said something about history and his voice was excited. Connor listened but couldn't make it out. Carefully, he inched up the volume and bent forward to hear. The reporter mentioned the United Nations. It was something 'historical'. The reception was poor, so he adjusted the knob on the right. '...Ben Gurion, ... nation, and the Jew's', were spitting out the radio. He fiddled with it some more and bent his ear closer. Then he heard clearly.

"This is a historic day, a historic moment in time. By decree of the United Nations, the nation of Israel has been reborn". There were reports of Jews celebrating in various cities around the world, particularly Tel Aviv and New York.

Connor sat back in his chair in disbelief. He was speechless, motionless-stunned. It was hard to even swallow. He felt lightheaded as he comprehended God's word coming to pass in what had been a private battle in his mind over the Bible. Now it was so; in the stroke of a pen-in a single day, as the Bible had said it would happen. Israel

211

existed again. He now knew that His people would soon be restored to the land.

He felt his chest warm and tears of joy began to roll down his face, diverted only by its deep wrinkles. He began to chuckle in giddy disbelief, but then started tearing up again. I must tell everyone and wake them, he thought out loud. He tried to pull himself up, but something was holding him down. I must wake them he insisted in his mind. They must hear this and understand what this means. But the leadened arms would not budge. He looked strangely at his left arm, and flexed it slowly as if it were the problem.

Vera and Bobby lay quietly in each others' arms.

"I better get up and get going", he said.

"No. Just another minute. Lay here with me", she said.

They lay for several minutes, cocooned in their own world. They heard a clatter and looked at each other, questioning. Then, a clunking sound.

"I'll see", said Vera. She closed her bathrobe around her as she went out the door and to the kitchen where she expected to see some kind of mess. Finding it empty, she then headed to the living room, following the soft sound of the radio. As she broached the room, she drew her hand to her mouth.

"Bobby!" The tone meant -hurry, now! He flew into the room and saw Connor on the floor, still. The coffee spilled and the cup shattered. "Dad!" He yelled and jostled him. At the instant of his touch, all sense of urgency left. He realized his father had left him for good. He was in Heaven.

As Connor stepped onto the shore, he looked back into the sea of this life and watched the scene in the living room. There was Bobby and Vera in each other's arms, the fire burning brightly. He loved them so. He could see the spark of life in her that would be Patrick. The scene pulled away and he saw the home and then the ranch, then the valley and the mountain, all telescoping away. The long shadows of the mountains fell across the valley at dawn. Then he was in the atmosphere.

As he turned away from the water's edge, Leah was there to greet him. She was beautiful, young-they way he remembered her. He realized his own youthfulness and vigor. They were exactly as he had pictured them when he awakened so many times. Yes, this is where those images had come from; this moment. An incredible feeling of well-being and complete happiness engulfed him. Leah stood before him, holding out her hand, beckoning. He took it and they were running like children, like childhood friends-not laden with the responsibility of marriage or parenting. Joyfully breathless, he stopped her and looked into her yes.

"Is this.......?"

"Yes", she said laughing.

———

It was a private ceremony, after the memorial service at the church. Their family gathered in the little cemetery on the hill. Snow still hung in the forests above them, but was long gone at their elevation.

The fresh dirt next to Leah's grave was covered in flowers. Several long-time rancher neighbors were there and all the ranch hands. Poncho was inconsolable. He wept openly while his wife and children looked on.

At some unsent signal, they all meandered toward the gate. Bobby held it as they passed through, each speaking softly to him. Each offered as friends do, where little can be done at all. Last was Vera. She raised up and kissed him, with little Danny in her arms. He looked at the child and saw as much of Connor's face as his own.

He closed the gate and stood for a moment looking down the row of graves. The vacant space spoke to him, whispering that here was his place as well. The grave was patient but inevitable. Someday, his children would be here, doing this for him, for Vera.

She threaded her arm through his and they made their way down the dirt road behind the small crowd of friends.

"I love you", she said.

"I know".

CHAPTER 4

The 1950 Dodge Power Wagon was already aged by seven years, but was in amazingly good condition. It was not only a 'ranch' vehicle, it was the Sunday-go-to-town rig. It was a centaur of a vehicle; half jeep, half station wagon. At all times, the Robert O'Hare family could be transported in toto and in style. Its rugged motor, gearbox and four-wheel drive assured that it would always arrive at its destination. Whether hauling kids to school in two feet of snow, or muddy washed out roads, it always delivered the cargo to where it was going.

But this day was a beautiful late spring day. The air crystalline clear, the sky an azure blue. The Power Wagon featured not only its tank-like capability, but by special factory order, a woody exterior. Less than two hundred were manufactured. It was a vehicle that attracted attention going down the street. The paint was a deep red and the chrome grill spoke of grit and power. A metal visor extended forward from the top of the windshield. On the interior, the headliner was custom wood, tongue and groove maple, the dashboard, a no-nonsense steel, painted as the exterior color. The dials and gauges large, but few. Three bench seats filled the cabin interior. Four windows down each side, plus the rear and windshield gave ample visibility. Up front, on the custom bumper, reinforced by being welded to the frame, sat a heavy duty winch, strong enough to extract a small bulldozer from a muddy grave, if you had a good enough anchor.

The AM radio blared as the O'Hare wagon pulled into the Hancock Station for gas. The kids filled the back bench seats bouncing like pin balls. They were always excited to come to town.

"You kids simmer down back there," Vera said. As she saw the seat of Patrick's breaches and cowboy boots vaulting over the middle bench to the rear seat with peals of laughter.

"Patrick, you sit up and behave yourself". After a moment, Vera gave that look; "I'll come back there, and you won't like it", she said.

Bobby eased the wagon up alongside the pump and shut down the engine as two men hopped out of the office and headed for the car. Each had on a white uniform with a black belt, black leather shoes and a black bow-tie. A soft white military cap with black piping sat on their heads.

"Good morning Mr. O'Hare. Fill it up?"

"Please, Jimmy".

"Yes sir."

"Hello Kyle", said Vera to the other young man, who had already tasked himself with cleaning every one of the ten windows, starting with the windshield.

"Hi Mrs. O'Hare. Sure is a beautiful morning, ain't it?"

"Isn't it", she corrected "and yes, it certainly is. Are you working all day?"

Kyle worked feverishly. "Naw, just 'till three o'clock. Then going fishing with my dad up to Kangaroo Lake", Kyle answered.

"Oh, its so pretty there."

"Yes, ma'm, like to make you forget about the fish." And they both laughed.

In the back seat, the kids had settled down to just bouncing up and down in the seats. Angeline and Matthew stood mesmerized at the gas pump. It stood as a monolithic contraption giving forth energy, painted a brilliant red with white trim. It was steepled with a glass canister filled with the beautiful red liquid gasoline. An occasional bubble gurgled up to the surface. They watched the sunlight filtering through it. The smell of raw, pure leaded gasoline waft passed them and they took it into their lungs. They liked the smell and smiled at each other. Something about its chemical mustiness was satisfying. Matthew watched the numerical dial slowly spinning, cycling through its nine digits plus the zero. The gallonage dial spun frantically, while the dollar amount poked along. Examining the other numbers he could see the price was 23.9 cents per gallon.

Kyle had worked his way to the other side windows and he made goofy faces at the children inside. This started them giggling and endeared their favorite gas station attendant to them.

Nearly finished, Kyle came to an open window at the mid-bench seat, driver's side. So accustomed to making the squeaking sounds of cleaning glass, he deftly emitted sounds from his lips like a ventriloquist perfectly simulating the moistened paper towel he worked on the missing glass window. He feigned to dig hard at some obstinate bug on the glass. All the children watched as he worked out the problem, making the constant noise his fingers seemed to produce. Vera watched over her shoulder smiling. The children peered in closely as something seemed amiss. As they leaned in closer, Kyle suddenly roared loudly, his head sticking through the window into the back seat, his face an ugly grimace before bursting out laughing. The children screamed in terror, then in delight at his foolish antics.

Jimmy came to the window. "That'll be $4.72 cents, Mr. O'Hare". Bobby handed him a five dollar bill. "Keep the change, Jimmy. Thanks Kyle, good job on the windows." Kyle gave him an easy salute. The power wagon cranked over and started with a rumble. They pulled onto Main Street in Weed and headed to the grocery store, as they did about once a month to stock up on food and supplies in the other stores in town.

Invariably new inventions stood boldly in the display windows of bustling storefronts. Jack's Hardware and Sporting Goods was a huge store, well known for several counties around. The hardware was downstairs with a seemingly endless array of tools, fasteners, hardware an such. Upstairs was every thing a hunter, fisherman, or outdoorsman of any kind could dream of. A small area dedicated to coffee drinking, bantering or ribbing amongst friends, had old furniture and was centered around a wood stove. A coffee pot was always on. On the wall was a collection of mugs, hanging on wooden pegs. Each one had a name or insignia indicating its owner.

Behind the long glass counter filled with handguns and ammunition was a rack of hunting rifles and shotguns that extended nearly eighty feet.

Danny and Patrick especially loved coming to the sporting goods store. They bounded up the stairs two at a time. The smell of Hoppe's cleaning solvent permeated the place from the small gunsmithing area at one end. There was always someone looking at a long gun, checking the action and drawing to the shoulder looking for the right "feel".

For the children, the monthly trip into town was a welcome relief from the chores at the ranch. Before school, there were chores. After school, there were chores. On most weekends, there were chores. Once a month, after church, the boys lined up for haircuts. It was simple. Everybody got a butch. A kitchen chair was put onto the porch and an old sheet was wrapped around them. The newfangled electric clippers made even Bobby appear to know something about barbering.

This afternoon, in 1958, Danny sat in the chair and the clippers clicked to life-emitting its muffled buzzing sound. When dad touched your head with the clippers, your whole head vibrated and it made your vision jiggle a bit. Bobby readied to make his first pass.

Danny said, "Wait, dad. I don't want a Butch."

The other children looked wide-eyed at each other, then at Danny and Bobby, as if Danny had cursed the Savior. Their eyes expecting who-knows-what, in response. The clippers switched off. 'Uh-oh', they thought.

"What's wrong with a butch?"

"They're for......, for, squares, Dad." There was silence. A smile crept upon the side of Bobby's mouth.

"A square huh? You don't say?"

"Yeah, Dad. All the guys at school are getting flat tops at Myron's Barber Shop."

"A flat top, eh? Well, I don't know if I can do one of those."

"Can you, please try, Dad."

"Well, let's see here."

The clippers clicked back to life as the other children stared in amazement as something other than a butch appeared to be taking shape on Danny's noggin. As he worked the side shaving near the scalp, the children leaned to watch every move. Finally, Bobby backed away.

"There you go." And he handed Danny a mirror. Danny looked and then broke into a great smile.

"Perfect! You are so cool, Dadio", he quipped, discarding the sheet. The flat top was right on the money. As soon as Danny was pleased, the others chorused 'me too. I want a flat top', over each other's voices.

———

As a nation, the economy entered full throttle into the post war boom. The Korean War sealed the identity of future enemies as the communists; of all types and persuasions. China competed with the Soviet Union for menace of the century. The automobile became the symbol of American ingenuity and prosperity. Culturally the nation drifted away from the serious business of war toward self fulfillment and fun. Glamour, fashion and celebrity accelerated to near idol worship. Movie stars, athletes and the literati were in the ascendancy.

The kids grew up through Elvis, rock 'n roll, little league, the Beatles and the Cuban Missile Crisis. Life was good. Life was scary. But growing up is full time work, so school dances, first loves, close friends and finding one's strength and weaknesses were all navigated by the O'Hare children. From athletic prowess for the O'Hare boys to conquests of love and friendship by Angelina, the O'Hare clan traversed the years of puberty and entered into young adulthood.

Jon-Connor was slightly younger than the close age proximity of the other children, separated by a few extra years. He was average in size, but with a generous wit and talked as easily with adults as he played with schoolmates. His parents' friends would often comment to Vera, after JC, as he had come to be called, had left the room. Following some mature observation of human behavior; "Where does he get that from?", they asked with furrowed brows and a growing grin. The boy had brown hair and a band-aid of freckles across his nose and cheeks. His grin was infectious and he laughed easily. At times he was moody, almost forlorn. One day Vera watched him, at the fence, through her kitchen window. He was staring out across the fields, looking up at Mt. Shasta. His head perched in his hands, elbows on the timber of the split-rail fence. He was gone. Somewhere else. She didn't know where, but he was gone. He traversed the land between moods of private introspection and slapstick antics in the parlor. Two important moments had injected his consciousness and personality at a young age. One was a dream and the other, a waking thought.

———

He was nine years old and it was summer. It was a Sunday morning, before church and the house was still asleep. He had awakened early. It was near the solstice and so it was warming early in the morning. If there was any day, the O'Hares slept in, it was Sunday. He was in his shorts and teeshirt. Quietly, he slipped out the door, careful not to let the screen-door slam and stepped across the wooden porch and down the stairs to the lawn. It was fresh and the air clean, with the slightest dew barely clinging to the grass. It tickled his bare feet as he took several paces across the lawn-not even wet-only slightly moist. The sun was well up over the mountain. The cattle were lowing in the distance. He sat down, then laid on his back, the grass felt like a steam bath, relaxing him. He stared up into the blue sky and lost all peripheral vision of the horizon around him. Alto-cumulus clouds, puffballs, silently flowed together and then separated; kissing then parting from one another. He watched them materialize from nothing, then dissipate back into the same deep blue from whence they came. He was conscious of nothing except the clouds. Then he thought about God and heaven. He was staring intently into those thick broiling formations and imagined he saw God walking furtively behind them, just avoiding a clear perception of Him. His own machinations affected him, and he bolted upright staring with the intensity of looking at it through a rifle scope. He scanned back and forth unsure of what he had seen. Then slowly settled back into the warm, moist lawn, his fingers laced once again behind his head.

The dream had come on a school morning. Vera was calling him to awaken, but he could not-no he would not. The dream was too captivating and he didn't want to leave it. A beautiful lady, in colored robes had come to him and beckoned him, without a word, and he followed helplessly... willingly. Wanting to go with her. As he reached her, they were both immediately swept up into the air. They were flying. Yes! Really flying! The wind was comfortable on him and he was neither hot nor cold. Up, up and now they were perhaps a thousand feet elevation. He was tucked comfortably under her arm. His arms and hands outstretched. He laughed and looked up at her and she smiled back at him, knowing what he felt. Words could not say. As he looked down, they were flying over the most beautiful countryside, a patchwork quilt, like Ireland, but more than just light and dark greens. There were so many fields of flowers, entire patches of red and blue, yellow and oranges, blonde fields of grain and green ones too. Orchards and vineyards. He looked down upon it all and it took his breath away. It was too much and he was suddenly overwhelmed with joy, wonder, and peace. He looked up at her as if to ask with his eyes: 'Is this real?'

She stood over him, shaking him now. "Wake up sleepyhead. You'll be late for school if you don't get a move on. Breakfast is ready, so you best hurry up." He looked up at his mom as the confusion lifted and he came back into the reality he had known. But he never forgot that flight. Those few moments, flying, looking up into 'her' face. Looking down upon that magnificent land. Oh how he wanted to go back. But he never did.

———

At Grady-O'Hare, business had boomed. The name of Robert O'Hare became locally synonymous with integrity, competence and wealth. The ranch had acquired two additional neighboring ranches, and timber holdings well outside the immediate area of the ranch. Timber holdings included areas of McCloud, the Klamath River area, Dunsmuir and the Sacramento River canyon, Medford and Grants Pass, Oregon. Within the uppermost area of the northstate, Grady-O'Hare was recognized as a dynamic and growing enterprise as far south as Sacramento, the state capitol.

A phone call to O'Hare's ranch office from the U.S. Department of Transportation, would change the ranch forever and open an entirely new opportunity for enterprise. The federal government wanted to bisect a corner of the ranch with a new freeway, part of the national system. This particular element would be the major north-south interstate on the west coast. It would link Mexico to Canada through the states of California, Oregon and Washington: Interstate 5.

They would need land for the freeway and additional land for a rest stop. Bobby looked over the plans and asked if there would be an offramp for services nearby. The traffic engineers couldn't justify it with a small town nearby, but were willing to look at other reasons to justify one; recreational amenities, links to county roads, market roads for agricultural commodities and such. They wanted to send appraisers out to prepare an offer. O'Hare agreed to this preliminary step.

Overseas, the nastiness was brewing, that would become the Vietnam war. President John F. Kennedy, a moderate politician, was adored in the media and the public. He had invested the first few Americans into the cause. He would not live to see the disaster that the conflict would eventually mushroom into. He was assassinated in office. The country mourned. The war went on. While the military accomplishments went unheralded, the political will of the people was tested and found wanting. The era had changed and the counter culture emerged.

Music, spawned from folk and rock 'n roll, powerful and moving, lyrical and instrumental had bit deep into the psyche of the nation and particularly the young people. The counter culture hoisted itself up on a motto of sex, drugs and rock 'n roll, but this was naive. It was co-opted by other elements who saw it as a useful vehicle for their own agenda.

Leftists saw it as opportunity to change the politics of the country. The communist Vietnamese saw it as a means to undermine the country's willingness to fight. For many, they held onto a culture of personal irresponsibility for as long as life would allow. There ratcheted upward a disdain for all things religious, all forms of authority and rebellion for rebellion's sake became a virtue.

The media, of all types, saw their own ascendancy in the reporting of this watershed period and were generally sympathetic to the causes.

Color TV had become the standard, and the gory pictures of the war were coming home every night on the news. Bobby was often passing through the house to his office and stopped momentarily to see the images. They were brutal and honest, but he thought, counter productive. The kids were sitting on the couch before him, realizing an aspect of life far removed from the beauty and serenity and security of their own life. They were captivated by them and they listened as the war correspondent dressed in a safari shirt with an unbelievable number of pockets and buttons, cited the critical statistics of dead and injured.

"They'll lose this war, if they keep doing that", Bobby said with certainty, and moved on through the room.

"Doing what?" asked Danny.

"Keep feeding the public those statistics and showing the horrors of war."

"Why not, Dad, it's the truth."

"It may be a truth, but its not the only one and is certainly not the most important truth."

The news broke into a commercial. The jingle started up while a beautiful woman smiled broadly, showing a perfect set of snowy white teeth.

'You'll wonder where the yellow went, when you brush your teeth with Pepsodent..... Pepsodent.'

"If you want to know, come into my office", said Bobby." Danny sensed his dad's tone, and read it as ' you're my oldest son and I want to tell you something'.

His dad's office was simple and masculine. The walls and ceiling were of hand selected clear mahogany tongue and groove. The chairs, classic red leather and brass tacks. His desk, an antique overlain with a glass top. A bankers lamp of brass and green glass illuminated the desk top, when turned on, but left the face and eyes of the worker in shadows.

Danny was enrolled in the local junior college while still working on the ranch. Unsure of his vocational future, he took the general education path. Like his father, he knew no life that didn't include Grady-OHare in some meaningful way. He had walked and hunted every ridgetop and gully. Knew where to look for stray cattle, could walk straight to several snake dens and never needed a canteen as he knew every spring and when it dried up. He understood the irrigation system, which was in its own way, both simple and complex. On some level, he thought that his education was ancillary to his taking over the ranch some day. The more mature part of him said the education was vital to keeping and prospering the ranch. Deep inside he knew that no generation every really owns a property like that. All are caretakers to generations grow-ing up or yet unborn. At first, one thinks to himself of the possibilities of personal fulfillment. But its not long before the gurgling of the creeks and the swaying of tall trees in the wind sing a song whose lyrical essence is that; 'you' are the temporary one. The good ones settle in quickly to accepting that it is as much a burden as a gift. There is back-stiffening tradition and honor in holding a property such as Grady-O'Hare, a demand to grow it, if possible and an expectation to improve it at whatever the per-sonal cost. The shame and dishonor associated with the slightest possibility of losing it is an imponderable horror.

He plopped down in one of the two leather chairs ar-ranged before the large desk, as Bobby set down files on bloodlines of the bulls in the cattle operation and several properties which were prospects for acquisition. The prized information inside them was the estimated volume of tim-ber and road costs to extract it. He and his people were the best at what they did. This information was handled as if top secret. It was.

"This war is all wrong, dad. Nobody at school is for it."

"Really?....Nobody?"

"Well, there's a few guys who believe it's the right thing to do and they're joining, mostly the air force. Some guys are getting drafted and talking about high-tailing it to Canada."

"I don't care what the others think. What do you think?"

"I don't know. I think communism is bad, but its getting hard to see that we are the good guys. It's not like World War II, dad. It's different."

"Well, some things are different, but much is the same. When you give your word on something.... anything; should you keep it?"

"Of course. Our word is our bond."

"That's right. If your word isn't worth a shit, neither are you. That's what you've been taught. How is it any different for our country?"

"I don't know. I guess it wouldn't be. But the cost...."

"No !! It's not about the cost. The time to consider the cost is *before* you give your word. Once you've given it. .... You are committed. So don't give your word on a whim. Make damn sure you can and will do what you're prepared to promise, or........, just walk away, son."

"We've made commitments to protect and defend the south Vietnamese. Whether that was a good idea or not is now immaterial. We are at war with their enemies and frankly, that makes sense to me. They are our enemies; the communists. There are, however, several problems...., big ones."

Danny sat in silence as his father looked alternately out the window to the distant pastures, then swiveling around to look at him, when he wanted to make a point more personal.

Bobby continued, "The first problem is the way they are fighting this war. Politicians are in the middle of every war. Usually, they're at the bottom of it. But this one........, they apparently feel they know more than the military about how to win it. The problem is that the politician's goals aren't necessarily the same as the military's."

"The second problem is that our enemies don't have to deal with public opinion and that is a huge advantage. Consequently much thought, effort and intelligence is spent on affecting the opponents will to fight. This is always an asymmetrical burden on democracies, when they fight totalitarian regimes. You can beat the hell out of the enemy on the ground, but if you lose the, uh..., the public relations battle with the people back home, you're going to lose the war."

"The media in this country today is not like the media in World War II. It seems to me, they want us to lose. They show the horrible carnage that is this war, and all wars that were ever fought. They go over the statistics of dead and wounded and want to personalize them, so that the personal tragedy of every loss is felt. Son, I'm not saying that this isn't the truth for the family and friends affected, but this nation, hell, no nation will not be able to stand watching this every night."

"The only thing worse than fighting a war is losing one. And I'd say we're fixin' to lose this one. The unintended consequence of losing a war is immeasurable. Even if no one has to pay reparations, that is spoils to the victor, your allies begin to doubt and mistrust you. Your enemies seek to further their cause against you, having exploited your weaknesses. Evil people seeing strength in our enemies are more apt to become traitors or spies. You cannot fathom the true cost of losing a war, to say nothing of the demoralization of the people. There is also the collective shame and reluctance to engage the next fight which may well be far more valid and critical to the nation than the one just lost."

"It seems to me that the press so prizes its precious first amendment right that one day you'll see them divulge our military plans, maneuvers, tactics and strategy to everyone, including our enemies; all in the name of their right to print anything they can dig up. They value their 'scoop' more than the lives of our men. They will gladly risk those men's lives for their careers, for their Pulitzer Prize, but not for a cause like freedom. Not for a nation's honor."

Danny sat in silence, pondering the old man's words. They rang in his ears. He excused himself. As he shut the office door, the old man started in on the stack of files. It would be after ten o'clock that he would finish and climb gently into bed beside his sleeping Vera. It would start all over again at five in morning.

The file at the bottom of the stack was by no means the least important. It was a preliminary proposal to purchase from Grady-O'Hare, land for a public rest stop and a mile away, a set of offramps in both directions. The county planners were prepared to grant commercial zoning and the City of Weed was willing to furnish a water line, but not sewer. Behind the proposal was a set of drawings with plans for commercial site development. They included family restaurants, fast-food restaurants which were taking the country by storm, and several sites for new motels. Several other sites were considered ideal for service stations and a small market selling convenience items. Suddenly, a nearly insignificant portion of Grady-O'Hare's land was about to yield perhaps as much value as the rest of it combined. It was unfathomable. But letters of interest stapled behind them from agents of the motel and restaurant chains made it quite plain. It was so.

———

CHAPTER 5

Patrick, the second son, veered to a peer group of the fun-loving, partying types by his senior year in high school. He was bright, perhaps even brilliant in realms of knowledge that suited him; math and chemistry, but chief among them was a propensity to understand people and manipulate them to his own purposes. At this stage of his youth, he had no purpose and so he practiced these skills, hardly aware of them himself, on pointless pursuits of embarrassing others, glorifying himself in some group setting, though it would turn darker in later years. This night was a spring night when everyone one of the group of friends was looking forward to the end of school, graduation, a summer of fun and then getting on with their lives. The common thought was that they had endured enough of school. Taking a cue from some of their parents who chided them that school was not the real world, they interpreted it as less useful than true education actually was.

The politics of the war had filtered well through the school systems to all but the youngest of children. This group was decidedly of the opinion of anti-draft, anti-American, or at least American culpability in all things, and of social injustice. Patrick formed what was the intellectual pillar of the group, his obvious intellect, recognized by all. Yet they loved him, because he could or would indulge in their debauchery, drugs and drunkenness and this made them feel better on an unspoken level. It was he that set their worldview stakes into the ground. Yet another was a rejection of all religion as "an opiate for the masses". He would quip around a party campfire of pickup trucks and stupored youth.. "I've tried both and the opiates are far the superior." This to the laughter and the passing of joints and pipes of pot.

His history teacher was a profound influence in the past year and Patrick grew to think of John Harlow as a personal friend and peer rather than the traditional student-teacher relationship. John Harlow was young and popular at the high school-much loved for his anti-establishment leanings and what was mistakenly perceived as "free-thinking" that is to say non-traditional, no, anti-traditional. Invariably all history lessons came to a political point through his meandering lectures. Students were not encouraged to take notes so much as to listen and he was a charismatic lecturer. No glimpse into history could fail to reveal the social destructiveness and economic "unfairness" of capitalism and conversely, the egalitarian benefits of socialism.

There had been some talk among parents about his political leanings and the accuracy of his lectures, but the school administrator recognized his popularity among the students. He secretly shared some of the same beliefs though not to the same degree nor the fervency with which Harlow held them.

Patrick strode up the walk to the front door and knocked. It was a small house in Yreka, with minimal trim and simple lawn. It was unadorned in any aspect. He had parked a block away and walked quickly under the street lights so as not to be noticed or recognized. The door jarred open a few inches.

"It's me," said Patrick.

The door swung open but the body remained behind it. Patrick stepped in quickly and pulled off his sweatshirt hood revealing his long flowing hair which the girls adored and his friends thought very 'cool'. The room was dim, almost dark. The other person moved around, drawing blinds and curtains.

"Glad I caught you. There is a big party tomorrow up at Crawford Lake, everybody is gonna be there." The dead-bolt on the door slammed shut. "Everybody is trying to score some weed."

"Well, this is the best you've ever smoked. This is killer shit." The figure moved into another room and then came back in. Patrick heard the rustling of plastic as items were placed on the floor and a lamp was turned on revealing a dozen baggies of pot. Each was dominated by thick, pickle sized bud. Patrick smiled at the looks of the stash before him and then smiled through the low light of the lamp to John Harlow's face. Patrick opened a baggy and took its aroma into his lungs. He coughed.

"Wow! That is some strong shit."

"Its from Thailand. Its one of the few benefits of Viet-nam. Wait 'till you smoke it. But I'm warning you, a couple of hits and............," at this he suggested with his manner that you would be high... very high.

———

Danny walked quickly through the classroom door and went to his seat. He was late, and professor Fabiano Bresciani cocked a thick, gray eyebrow toward him acknowledging the tardiness. Danny broke an apologet-ic smile and sat down. The small Junior College in Weed was called College of the Siskiyous and was only a few years old. It was the only post secondary school in Siskiyou County. Most high school graduates went here to acquire their general education cheaply and stay close to home. Others attended here from far away as the area had incredible natural beauty and a ski resort had recently opened on Mt. Shasta. It was the late sixties and the culture was dividing along what appeared to be the lines of the Vietnam War; for or against. But it quickly morphed into pro-American versus anti-American, communism versus capitalism, collectivism versus individualism.

Fabiano Bresciani, called Fabi by his beloved family, had fled the communist ascension in Italy following the defeat of Germany and Italy. Back home, he was a family man teaching high school in a small rural town of northern Italy when Mussolini had come to power. Fabi's father, a vintner with a large vineyard and estate, had gotten on the wrong side of the fascists and had disappeared without word, witness or a trace. Fabi went into hiding with his family in a neighbor's barn and watched his family's estate taken over. He had separated his family, sending his wife and two children to the south, where they would meld into the large population centers. He remained behind, joining the Italian underground. He worked in the underground until the end of the war. When the armistice was signed, he prepared to reclaim his family's property. Here, he met with equal tyranny from only a slightly different point along the political spectrum. At the close of the war, there was a great struggle in most western European countries between the ideals of the western victor; America, and the eastern victor; Russia. Like so many other countries, Italy swooned leftward, having experienced hardships with the boom and bust cycles with capitalism.... 'Maybe communism would work?'

It seems more a condition of human frailties and faults that regardless of political-economic systems, the human vices of greed and want of power are ever present. Under such, 'who' one knows and is aligned with accounts for much, especially during a time of revolution and or dramatic change. It was just so in Italy as well. Alliances could mean tremendous gain-attaining more than five lifetimes could produce. Or it could mean a short drive out into the country and a single bullet in some old farm outbuilding. Someone well connected to the new emergent power system had moved into the Bresciani vineyard and, by the looks of the body guard, it could well have been old mafiosi. Only the frequent visit accompanied by armed troops, as observed by Fabi from several fields away, suggested there was a direct link to the power in Rome.

He now realized that he had fought and killed to rid his country of one tyrant only to watch another one ushered in with great pomp. Parades and promises were the order of the day. Fabi had snuck back to the estate and unearthed the last remaining stash of gold to buy passage to America for he and his family.

Arriving with little money, they had migrated to the small Italian community of Weed, as circumstances would have, luckily landed the teaching job at the new junior college.

Much of the faculty was young and it seemed to Fabi they sought too much to befriend their students rather than instruct them. Perhaps that is the way it is in American schools, he pondered. He was only in his early forties, but his life's experiences had prematurely grayed his hair and deepened the lines about his eyes. The expression cast upon his face by a habitually lowered left eyelid was a mixture of both maturity and sad resignation.

He taught political science, economics and history. His fellow professors recognized in him a deep conviction to what he taught. He taught what he believed and believed what he had lived. His knowledge life-lived and the book learning supplemented it, not the other way around.

To him, fascism and communism were not clinically dry classroom discussion topics, they were memories of running through the woods, Nazis chasing him and his underground compatriots, after ambushing a supply depot or an assassination of a high military official in his vehicle on an isolated road. It was the fear of footsteps under a shadowy street lamp during an operation. The complete panic when someone shouted "Alto" and rifles cocked.

It was watching the work of generations of his family, given over as payment for some political alliance. It was the questioning look on his children's faces as they began to understand the life they had known was forever gone. There was the clinking of salutary glasses amongst those who gave no blood, sweat or tears to that which they stood in occupation of. Drinking, celebrating and laughing; imagining themselves worthy and deserving of this sudden and extravagant wealth due their understanding and manipulation of all things, economic, political, indeed human, was superior to others. It was their understanding and finesse in the use of deception and coercion and, when necessary, violence. Finally, it seemed to them life had recognized their brilliance and given them their just reward. As Orwell had said. "In the Animal Farm, all animals are equal, but some are more equal than others."

Professor Bresciani paced slowly across the front of the classroom, considering his first words to the new class. His hands were in the pockets of his tweed suitpants. A cardigan sweater over his plain white dress shirt, revealed just a bit of the solid blue necktie knotted slightly to one side.

"The economics you must know to understand the world around you is not the economics of deep and complex mathematics. That will, no doubt, be a great relief to many of you." A chuckle rippled through the class. "Nor are the most important parts of it about elaborate charts and grafts, through statistical analysis. No. These tools of the economist only express the specific or aggregate actions of what we seek to understand. It is human action that is at the heart of all we do and hope to understand.

Now, let me say first, that many of you walked into this room and the only thing you knew about this subject is that it has been referred to as the dismal science. Nothing could be further from the truth. If you do not learn its basic truths, the laws that govern within it, what will be dismal, is your life or the life of your children within a few generations. I am not here to make you into academic economists. No. I am here to help you learn to think in economic terms. Far from being dismal, boring or unimportant as you probably now believe, your ability to think critically and appropriately within this sphere of your life will exert an enormous influence on how you do; financially, and in many other realms of your life. How you think individually, and vote, in this field of knowledge will greatly determine the course of your country, and, from what I can see, the course of the world for decades to come-certainly your life span."

Some students drifted off to their more meaningful world of sex, fun, partying, fantasy, family and escape in general. Yet others, including Danny, heard not only the words of Professor Bresciani, but the way he said them, his whole manner and aura. He was speaking to them personally, as well as academically, and it seemed he would be doing this whether he was paid or not. Danny took in what he said and throughout that semester learned from Fabiano Bresciani the key relationship of the individual to the greater economy. The link between economic calculation and human behavior; and its concomitant, between the state and the individual. He changed Danny and a few of the other students.

———

Bobby fired up the old Willys jeep and drove it out of the barn into the barn yard to let it idle and warm up in the morning sunlight. He gathered his forestry notebook, his scaling tools for calculating the volume of timber in a tree, compass, his old .45 in a side holster and his border collie, Lizzy and headed into the back woods of Grady-O'Hare. He idled slowly through 'tall trees' as in reverence to their magnificence. He passed by the remains of Billy's cabin, now a local legend with his great-grandfather Jon O'Hare. He saw wildlife scattering at the approach of the noise of his engine. A flock of wild turkeys took to air in a flurry of sound and feathers. A group of large bucks, with four and five points turned and watched him pass by. The border collie, riding shotgun, looked at him with a dog smile that asked "Can I chase 'em?"

The jeep wound its way in second gear up out of the gully in a series of switchbacks. The jeep passed though areas of young planted forests, areas of clear-cut open meadows and back into native woods. Across steep slopes and up long windswept ridgetops, the valley below, a checkerboard of quilted patches, green, brown and tan. Geometric shapes of land with the rivers and streams cutting across them without regard to manmade boundaries. He looked across the land and saw two golden eagles circling at his very elevation, scouring the forest floor below for mouse or snake. He could seemingly touch them. Up more switchbacks, he went further in, now in places only his family had ever seen, or a few lost hunters from adjoining government lands. Springs bubbled up and drained across the road and the jeep splashed softly and slowly through them. Now the road narrowed being beyond the last place the logging equipment had ventured to improve. Soon, there was no road at all and here, he stopped. He consulted the topographic map and compass and viewed a hillside about a mile away. It was off his property, part of the ownership of railroad lands which checkerboarded the entire western Pacific region. First, he would have to descend a steep slope, then cross an un-named creek and climb up the other side. He loved the days that he could be in the woods. The office days might be the more critical to financial success, but they could never satisfy his soul like a day in the woods. He was careful in the descent, knowing he was alone and a long way from the home. He had left a map and note as to his destination and intent to look at the property and its timber.

After descending for twenty minutes, he crossed the swollen creek on a fallen log, about six feet above the water. Lizzy complained at its first abutment, nervous of the height. Bobby encouraged her and in a flash she was across. He tousled her head and his eyes praised her bravery and she gloried in it. Now Bobby and his dog turned upslope and began the trudge uphill.

He arrived to find a stand of old growth, spotty, in some places but with several pumpkin patches. He began to take measurements and paced off plots to arrive at his estimations. He shared his sack lunch midday with the dog and completed his work by early afternoon.

They had crossed back over on the log and headed upward toward where the jeep was parked. He stopped for water from his canteen halfway back up the slope. The pooch had drunk deeply at the creek. As he neared the top of the deer trail he had been following, he could see the road edge above him. The trail rose at a gentle slope to broach the edge of the road. So with every step his view of the road and jeep parked at its terminus came more fully into view. The jeep completely visible, he stopped dead; frozen as he saw movement in the jeep. The dog was at his heels immediately sensing his master's tension. Lizzy ventured up, past Bobby to the road edge to see for herself, as Bobby tried to grab her. Just then, a bear cub tumbled clumsily out of the jeep it had been investigating. Bobby lunged for the dog, but it was too late. The border

collie seeing any other animal in its beloved vehicle con-
stituted a property and territorial crime of life and death
proportion. The back hairs pitched all the way forward as
she shot like lightening to the jeep and the silly cub on its
back playing with some piece of gear from the jeep in its
forepaws. But it immediately got to its feet, frozen by the
oncoming menace of the dog. "Sweet Jesus," cried Bobby as he climbed up onto the roadway calling the dog.
The cub backed up, not understanding what the dog was
about, but sensing an attack. The collie screeched to a
halt a few feet from the cub and frantically barked while
circling the animal, now trapped against the jeep. The
animal pawed at the dog, which quickly feinted and retreated but continuing its incessant bark and baying.

As Bobby approached the jeep, his heart stopped. Up
the road, fifty yards beyond the jeep was a large black
bear; a female in full charge. The dog's heart was pounding in its chest, having the cub trapped, it looked up to
see the charging mother. The dog sensed in the eyes of
the bear, that she was under attack, and quickly dove
over the side of the road; the bear in pursuit. The bear
showed amazing agility and speed, running downhill at a
full gallop. Lizzy was running just slightly beyond her own
ability to control, and tumbled head over heels, quickly
righting herself and then sprinting cross-slope, the bear
only a pace behind. Bobby looked on in horror, praying
the dog would not turn to face the attack. He called
at the top of his lungs and the dog responded by turning upslope to his position at the road's edge, where he
watched the chase, his .45 un-holstered, but useless for
now. The collie was flying on adrenaline, zipping between
trees, coming toward him, mother bear right on her tail,
not slowing the least. Bobby advanced to a Douglas Fir
tree, a few feet below the road, about sixteen inches in
diameter and steadied the pistol against it, taking aim at

the charging bear. He called again to the dog, not wanting her to stop, but Lizzy perceived her leading the beast back to her master and in her mind, she would not do this. Her brain overwhelmed by that thought tapped her physical exertion for only a moment. But that was all it took. She had slowed only a stride and the mother bear swiped her with her paw. The dog flew fifteen feet through the air, a sickening yelp coming from her collapsing lungs. Bobby's heart sunk as he let go the first round. It was a difficult shot and managed only to wound her shoulder muscle, but it turned the mother's attention and she now charged at Bobby, a ferocious growl from her spittled and drooling snarl.

He aimed at her skull and fired again, striking her, but it was not clear that it damaged her. She charged, now only twenty feet from the tree and he fired the third of eight rounds, and missed. He glanced at the jeep, only thirty feet away. but climbing just those four feet of steep bank to the road would have sealed his doom. She now charged toward his side of the tree and he quickly circled to the right and fired again, free hand, at five feet to the bear. The bear stopped at the muzzle blast only feet from its face but quickly was upon Bobby's position. He now circled back around the tree which seemed foolishly skinny and unable to offer protection. He scampered around the tree, maintaining it between he and the snarling bear. It was difficult on the steep slope and it was only his adrenaline that allowed him to move fast enough. At every emergence of the bear's terrifying snout around the tree, the .45 discharged in smoke and fire. The bear retreating momentarily. His mind counted two shots left in the magazine and here she came again. He could smell her awful breath, and his own fear of death. Again he scampered around the tree trying to sustain this insane dance of death, but lost his footing and fell backwards headfirst down the slope, sliding on the forest duff. He watched her come around the tree and charge down the slope after him. He slid to a halt and raised the pistol, aiming at her heart. The first shot hit her, but without effect. She kept coming, and was nearly upon him. It was over and he knew it. In that moment there was a quick thought of Vera, the kids, Jesus and God, Himself. He let go the last round. The bullet smashed into her front teeth and she shook her head furiously, blood and bone flying from her muzzle and fell toward him.

Her heart had pumped furiously chasing the dog, then, turning uphill to charge Bobby. One of the shots ruptured her left ventricle and another severed the carotid artery. She was bleeding out internally. Another shot had put out her right eye, but failed to lodge into her brain. She was full of fury to the last moment, which was a stumbling downhill fall toward her enemy. Bobby rolled to his right and her full weight fell beside him, nearly crushing him to death. All her sickening air expelled through her nostrils. Her head was almost beside him. The adrenal rush over, he was mentally collapsing, seeing that she was dead. Dark blood oozed from both nostrils the eye-socket and an exit wound near her ear. He rolled up onto his knees and breathed in deeply, allowing normalcy to flow back into body and brain. Remembering Lizzy, he got to his feet and stumbled unsteady, toward her last position. He saw her black and white body in a small shrub and he went to her. He knelt down to her and she looked up at him. A large patch of fir, the size of his hand was laid back, exposing at least two broken ribs. A puncture wound inside the larger wound bubbled red oxygenated blood. She was alive, but just barely. He holstered his .45 still welded to the grip of his hand and tried to pick her up with as little flexing of her body as possible. Struggling for footing, he made it back to the jeep and set her gently on the front seat and began the ride back.

She yelped a few times at unavoidable bumps and jars but was otherwise stoic. He talked to her the whole way down the mountain, assuring her and encouraging her. He pulled into the barnyard and headed for the kitchen phone to call the vet. Doc Jenkins was on his way. Bobby came back to her and picked her up carefully bringing her into the house. He put her by the fireplace, her favorite spot. She would recover. It would be a day and an event that he and Lizzy would share alone, together. It would, if even possible, further cement their mutual love and respect for each other. While Lizzy loved the kids and Vera, too, she belonged to only one man.

CHAPTER 6

Plans were going forward in 1967 to develop the land at the interchange of the interstate highway. Two different budget motel chains were developing sites and two fast-food restaurants were right there alongside them. A more upscale family restaurant was making inquiries to Bobby's office at Grady-O'Hare. Lizzy stayed close to him these days, more so than she used to.

Danny had done well at the College of the Siskiyous, but had decided to join the Marine Corps. His philosophy and ideals had turned decidedly pro-western and American. Not that he didn't see America's failings, but taken as a whole, its history as compared with any other major power, was unmatched and left little room for shame. He agreed to stay until he graduated with a two-year degree in business. He wanted to be in the Special Forces. Being a Navy Seal was the pinnacle of this. His athletic ability, smarts, and can-do attitude made him a shoe-in. He already knew a lot about hunting, surviving in the woods, and was an excellent marksman as all the O'Hare kids were. But Patrick less so.

Patrick fought incessantly with Bobby and Vera. He drove Vera crazy with his unending display of under performance. Bobby had all but washed his hands of him. He loved his son, but he didn't like him very much. The drugs had become more open, and Patrick justified them in social commentary by decrying the evils of alcohol and prescription drugs. Pharmaceutical companies were *the* drug pushers. The unfair legal system did more damage to lives than the drugs. Bobby could hear no more of it and demanded he leave the house, which he did. Bobby hoped his son would pass through this phase. Patrick was smart and got good grades despite his mediocre effort, so there was no problem getting a scholarship to U.C. Berkeley. There, he all but quit his classes the first year and became more active in the antiwar movement. His organizing skills, adeptness in arguing on his feet, and ability to throw in a humorous punchline, often won him the victory of the moment. But others were watching him and saw raw political talent. Something that could be tapped, something to be exploited.

In the waning days of the Nixon Administration, the Watergate debacle had fully born its fruit and the resignation was imminent. Bobby and Vera sat down to wearily watch the evening news, Lizzy at their feet, looked up at Bobby. They rolled their eyes at the apparent unraveling of their country. The TV anchor switched to the field reporter, who seemed to think and act as if he were in a live fire zone in Vietnam. But no. He was perched on the steps to the President's office at the University of California at Berkeley. There too, was the moronic; Hey Ho, 'fill-in-the-blank' chant, of people who looked more like third world transients than the sons and daughters of businessmen, attorneys, accountants and doctors, which they were. The reporter was mumbling through his setup and then the camera panned the crowd and at the top of the steps, the leader of the protest. A wild frizzy haired bearded young man leading the chanting crowd. Vera leaned forward, her facial features going numb, as if she could not comprehend.

"Oh God", she whispered to herself. She looked over at Bobby. She saw the redness in his eyes and she knew it was true. Patrick shouted angrily into the microphone while the sycophants around him cheered his every attack. Bobby got up and passed in front of her, walking out of the room. Lizzy followed at his heels, her head bowed as if shamed. He walked to his office and shut the door. Vera sunk back into her chair and sobbed quietly; partly for her son, partly for her husband. Soon she went to him and they wept quietly together, then went to bed without eating.

Patrick marched down the steps amid the pats on the back and encouragement of the crowd. It was his moment. So light was his head, that he had trouble feeling the steps beneath his feet. This defining moment was when he decided what he would be. The drug that was running through his body at this moment, was better than any drug he had ever tasted and he had tried them all. This was the one. The approval of the crowd. Its accolade of his words and validation of who and all that he was.

He stopped part way down the huge concrete steps. Before him were ten, perhaps twenty thousand students. He knew then and there he could manipulate them. Give them what they want, or at least, what they think they want, and they would propel him to power. Power, not just over them, but many more; oh yes, many, many more. He turned to the man who had been just out of the close up camera shots, but nearby. He looked into his eyes and this man acknowledged the look with the slightest of nods and a thin crack of a smile. 'Yes', the eyes said. 'I saw what you did. I can take you where you want to go.' Patrick smiled back. Then turned to the crowd and raised both hands as if in victory and the students and protesters audibly emitted a deafening cheer. Yes, this was a drug he must have again.

———

Matthew, the third son, was growing up a simple country boy. He loved the ranch, hunting and fishing. His best friends were the hired hands. He was happiest fixing fences, cowboying, or up in the woods, cutting trees, clearing roads. He could work any piece of equipment from bailers to bulldozers. He was intelligent, but neither well-read, nor inclined to subjects larger than he could grapple with using his own gloves. He had just gotten his driver's license and, having been a prudent saver, paid cash for the muscle car now parked in stall number four of the barn; a 1968 Pontiac GTO. The new 4-track Muncie Blue light and high-fidelity speaker system made it one of the 'coolest' cars at high-school. Matthew had his girlfriend, Sandra Lockley, a very cute blonde. They were a committed couple at a young age. They would eventually marry and live their entire lives together, never looking back at what might have been.

Jon-Connor, or JC as he was commonly called, waved good-bye to the station wagon leaving the barnyard. His camping gear was on the ground before him. He was still in his scout uniform and he had just returned from a camp out, but was nearing the end of that pleasant episode of his life. Next year he would get his learner's permit, though he had already been driving on the ranch since he was ten years old. He pulled his gear up onto the porch and started sorting it out. Vera came out to greet him and he gave her a big hug as always.

JC still had a special thoughtful quietness, but had begun to get along better with others and even began to achieve some popularity. This was difficult as he was something of nerdy young man. His older sister, Angelina, had become the homecoming queen and had the intelligence, good humor and maturity to match her beauty. This certainly didn't hurt JC's prospects in the school. Older guys were always being kinder to him than they would otherwise, in order to weedle a date with Angelina. JC realized this, of course, and was only too happy to get rides home from these guys, with his heavy books. It became something of joke at the kitchen table: This week's ride home for JC was next week's suitor for Angelina.

———

Cars were parked everywhere. The barnyard was packed. The edge of the long road from the county paved road was lined with cars and pickups. Tables from church were borrowed and set up on the lawn. Close to two-hundred people had gathered for the party. Most everyone from the little church in Weed, kids from high-school, coaches, students from the junior college where Danny graduated only last month. There were teachers and professors, neighbors and local people of power and prestige. After all, this was Bobby O'Hare's oldest kid. It was a beautiful summer day. A large pit had been dug with a backhoe by Matthew and a whole pig had been lowered onto the madrone wood coals and had been buried since sun-up. Several barbecues were working and a large permanent brick BBQ had a half side of beef turning on a spit. Checkered table cloths from the church adorned the long collapsible tables arranged in sets of two and three, with many rows. It was Danny's induction party. Several kegs of beer were chilling on ice set within galvanized portable watering tanks. No less than a dozen ice chests were scattered below and up on the porch with all kinds of sodas and more beer. There was a table of 20 gallon thermoses filled with iced tea and lemonade and stacks of Dixie cups.

Inside the old log home, reasonably but not completely modernized, every chair was taken and clusters of two and three were gathered in every nook and cranny. Danny breezed through the crowd accepting the congratulations from all and smiled indulgently at the ubiquitous warnings to keep his head down and not volunteer and such as that. With a couple of friends in tow, one being John Sergich, who was joining the Marines with Danny, they worked their way through the crowds and clusters.

In the living room, leaning against the mantel on the rock fireplace, was Professor Fabiano Bresciani, dressed in tweed slacks, a tie and cardigan sweater. Several other faculty members were there as well as two of Danny's old high school teachers. Bresciani sipped on a lemonade, while most of the others were drinking beer or iced tea.

A young man, believed to be also from the college, was animated in his discussion with another, slightly older man. The younger man had curly blonde hair parted in the middle of his head, and extending to his shoulders in length.

"This war is so stupid, man. How do we know that communism isn't the right way for the Vietnamese? We think we know all the answers; that our way is best. It's a bunch of bullshit. If they call me, I'm gone. I'm outta' here. I won't murder innocent women and children for some corporation's oil rights in the Gulf of Tonkin", he proclaimed in adolescent righteousness.

The slightly older gentleman, chimed in. "Josh, it's not just the military industrial complex we were warned against, by none other than General Eisenhower. No. The problem goes much deeper. Worldwide social justice is what we want, what everyone should want. I'm sick of seeing the super wealthy getting richer in this country, while the disenfranchised get poorer. It is the nature of capitalism to exploit the masses. To keep them poor while the powerful and wealthy get more so. Consider the industrial revolution in England. Children were made to work in the mines. They died of black lung and tuberculosis, for penny wages. There should be some equality, some fairness, don't you think?" said John Harlow.

"Definitely," said Josh.

"Surely, everyone wants to see children well-fed, workers fairly paid. Who would need to make a million dollars a year when so many can't even get decent medical care, are poorly housed and who suffer the shame of unemployment?"

"Capitalism is a bankrupt socio-economic theory which will be defeated by the masses who struggle for a decent life. The Communists will defeat them, which is why this war is so futile. But more than victory by the communists, capitalism will fall by its own self-destruction. Even now, it can only prop itself up by wars of aggression and imperialism. That is what America now stands for."

"Nonsense", said Bresciani. "I see no way of judging capitalism as a failure since there is neither place nor time wherein it has been tried with general purity. What we do know, however, is that its primary mechanism, the free market, is an absolute success wherever it has been tried. I would venture further to say that the greater the degree of its implementation, the greater the general well-being of the people. The United States was a good example of this in the last century and earlier part of the twentieth century. Hong Kong is a good current example. Unfortunately for the United States, there has been and continues to be a decided shift toward Keynesian economics and a collectivist mentality. This, of course, can only lead to one place if it continues; communism. That, only after it pauses for a decade or so with its half-sister, socialism. Oh, and by the way, I happened to overhear your remark on child labor. While the conditions were indeed deplorable, *by today's standards,* did you ever consider that taking their chances in the mines was preferable to a near certain death by starvation? I think you underestimate people's ability to make their own decisions, based on the facts they know at the time."

Harlow's eyes had begun to roll, mocking Bresciani. "So then, Professor, we can assume you miss the 'good 'ol days' of Robber Barons, that era of unbridled capitalism, eh?" Harlow began to effect that timed pacing as he did when he lectured his high school students, and looked around the room. Many had turned toward the two men-interested in their discussion.

Fabi responded, "That some men will be very wealthy is not unique to capitalism. It has been so since ancient times. That fact and those men are unimportant to the real question. What we must endeavor to know and understand is the means by which men acquire that wealth. Before capitalism and market economies, history would show us class systems maintained a wealth often created by no more than heredity, loyalty to power or a tribute for military conquest. What is unique to capitalism, which is an economic system, separate from political systems, is that it renders the consumer as the king. This is by virtue of his countless economic votes. Every time he spends a dollar, or declines to, he sends a signal through the marketplace. Only under capitalistic systems and their political concomitant democratic 'principles', does the smallest economic man wield such power. But only and precisely the power he has 'earned' by his dollars acquired. This is the system that rewards the men, making them wonderfully wealthy, when and only when they have satisfied the needs of their fellow man."

"Unfortunately many, such as yourself Mr. Harlow, attribute much of the human failures to capitalism. As if greed were its byproduct. Nothing could be further from the truth. In communist dictatorships, I assure you there is no less greed, no less corruption-indeed it is greater there. The means to wealth in such a system is purely about corruption, not production; party affiliation, not satisfaction of human needs and wants."

Harlow gathered himself. "It is as plain as the nose on your face, professor. It is there for all to see; your precious free markets and capitalistic system are being rejected by an increasing number of countries around the world. The Soviet Union is growing in power. They are not interested in conquering us. They simply wait for our inevitable failure and self-destruction. They are a patient people and they mean us no harm. It is we who are constantly rattling the sabers of war, exploiting oil and mineral resources of third world countries, corrupting their dictatorial governments who wholesale slaughter their own, while we turn a blind eye. All for the almighty buck. Someday, these chickens are coming home to roost." Harlow had his hands in his pants pockets, his light coat brushed back at his wrists. He rocked slightly on his heels, waiting for a reply. "Why do you suppose so many people are rejecting your philosophy and embracing ours, professor?"

Fabi chewed his cheek momentarily and looked at Harlow. "You pose an interesting question, Mr. Harlow. I think there are several reasons, but first let me address a premise you have alluded to without saying as much and it is a faulty premise at that. You have continually ascribed social evils to economic systems. I would suggest a more discerning approach. They should not be mixed. Economic systems are about the production and distribution of goods and services. They are about creating the "economic pie", so to speak. Capitalism with free markets simply creates more pie, and that pie is distributed according to meritocratic principles. That is to say, by those who have earned it. Your system, sir, produces less pie. Period. So you spend all your time and effort into redistributing it-usually according to a political calculation. Overtime, your system discourages innovation and risk taking; requisites of progress. And so, the pie will continue to shrink."

"I do not say that capitalism is inherently kinder or harsher, that it either promotes or discourages ethically good or bad behavior. It, like all economic systems is value neutral as to these things. I only contend that it produces more 'pie' than yours. When it comes to good or bad human behavior, philanthropy, charity, kindliness, generosity; I recommend the field of religion for guidance. I heartily commend you to the teachings of Jesus Christ, and what are generally regarded a Judeo-Christian principles of behavior. It is my personal belief, and I contend that history has borne this out; that the best of all multi-faceted systems, is a capitalism noted by free markets, under a republican form of government rooted in democratic principles administering to a people steeped in Judeo-Christian ethics and practicing their faith."

Harlow applauded lightly, deliberately slow, and softly in a mocking manner. "An eloquent speech, Professor. No doubt practiced. But I noticed you failed to answer my question. If all you say is true, why then are more countries moving in a socialistic manner and rejecting the Nirvana you preach? Umh?"

Fabby looked down and sighed. "There are three reasons which are interconnected. I'll try to explain them briefly. There are undoubtedly more, but these are the primary ones as far as I am concerned. First, there is an anti-capitalist mentality. This is a human and personal factor. As individuals, we have an inherent fear that if we must compete with others for the provision of food and shelter and whatever other material amenities that are deemed good or necessary, or we will fail. Or at least fall short. Markets are rather brutal in this regard in that they are no respecter of persons. You simply must satisfy the consumers of whatever it is you offer, be that labor to dig a ditch, or the ability to teach mathematics, or the manufacture of widget XYZ. It is a haunting fear and it is within most of us."

"Secondly, politicians viscerally understand this fear and play to it. They quickly convince the people that it is unfair to be subjected to the rigors of an economic system where they must compete with others in every facet of life. Rather, these politicians and potentates promise by infinite variations of a theme where all shall be gathered and put in a communal pot. It will then be allocated up by some metric in which every man believes he will do better than if he must struggle and compete for those things. It will fail, of course, based on the provable fact that under such a regime there is never enough 'pie' to distribute. And the system itself produces an ever decreasing amount of goods and services; the 'pie'."

"Thirdly, I would say there is an unholy but critical alliance between the politicos and the media. By that, I mean nearly all media. They seem joined at the hip in ways I admit I don't fully understand at this time. But clearly, the media, academia, the literati, the entertainment industry, artists, and most commentators of the culture all seem disciples of those who preach and promise something for nothing. As the old saying goes, Mr. Harlow: There is no free lunch."

"Bravisimo, Professor Bresciani! Bravisimo! Now, we don't want to spoil the party with this discussion, though I've enjoyed it, professor. Perhaps we can continue it at another time. No doubt it will remain topical for many years," said Harlow. He reached down and picked up his drink and lifted his glass to Fabi. "To Danny O'Hare", said Harlow. Everyone in the room joined in; "To Danny O'Hare".

Bresciani added "May God look after him."

—

CHAPTER 7

Danny went into the Marine Corps. After three years and only one tour in the waning days of Vietnam, he had become a sergeant. He was offered Navy Seal school and passed. He was a fine specimen of a fighting machine. His body honed to agility and strength. It was a rock. No less so his mind. It had been deprived and tested and had trimmed out all excess beyond accomplishing the "mission". He would spend his entire career in the military, seeing duty in future wars and clandestine operations all around the world.

Angelina became a teacher and returned to Yreka to teach high school and was favored among students and faculty alike. She married a young man she met at college and he came back to her small town with her to become a coach and woodshop teacher. They had a son and daughter, both of average ability, typical desires and middling accomplishments.

Matthew married Sandra and moved into a home built on the ranch, not far from Mel's old cabin. He worked with Bobby every day, but tended to stay on the livestock part of the operation, either the animals or the hay production. He and Sandy had three boys, all good natured, hard-working and dutiful young men. They were strong and helped work the ranch. This was needed as only one of Poncho's boy's, Pepe, had stayed in the area.

Pepe continued to work at Grady-O'Hare and lived in the cabin where he grew up. Poncho had passed away the year after Danny enlisted, and his wife soon followed him up the little hill to the little cemetery marked out by the low split-rail fence.

The ranch was stable as to acres owned, but the interchange development had brought a whole new level of wealth, beyond what they had believed possible. As it grew, they were willing to convert cow pasture into commercial real estate for the travel services industry. Ten sites had been developed. While the ranch prospered, Bobby began to have the same uneasy feelings that Connor had struggled with, as he watched the hand of government all around him.

Bobby saw that the country was changing. Aside from temporary interludes of conservatism and pockets of traditional thinking, John Harlow's world was coming to pass. Many new laws had come into effect; The Clean Air and Clean Water Acts, and there were the beginnings of a new political force that he was distrustful of. It was called the 'environmental movement'. While sounding harmless and childishly positive, there were details in the legislation which bothered him. Perhaps it was the smarmy names of the laws, which are often disinformation in themselves, that pried at his mind. He had engaged some of these so-called environmentalists in public hearings on timber harvesting, which had dramatically been controlled, as well as water issues. One of the more onerous laws was another benevolent sounding piece of legislation; the Endangered Species Act. The difficulty, the real problem, was that the laws could be reasonably administered, done in a way that would meet with little objection. But he knew that the danger was in how the details might be applied and what he read in the text of much of this body of law disturbed him deeply. The people he saw in the uniforms that would administer it, gave him little faith.

In his own mind, it came down to property rights. He took no subsidies and asked for none. Through the land development process at the interchange, he saw with each year, greater difficulty in accomplishing anything.

JC had graduated from the junior college and worked the ranch with Matthew and their dad. JC's interests covered everything from the cattle to the timber and he had a keen sense of the business, which Matthew happily avoided. He had learned the basics in the land development business watching his dad. At the age of twenty, he was drawing up plans to develop a roadside restaurant on one of the remaining sites. The idea was simple vertical integration. He would market the steaks, burgers and potatoes as local and the best in the world. Truly, they were very good. The fast food chains seemed to be springing up like weeds and doing well. But he saw a different angle than just a faster, cheaper burger. His would have unsurpassed quality and freshness. People could look across the landscape and see the cattle grazing in the distance. It would be part of the allure of the eating experience. Bobby encouraged the effort as a father would, but not certain anything would actually come of it. Stylistically, they would construct a commercial log built lodge, with two-foot diameter logs. It would be made of their own timber, milled and erected on site, with lodge furnishings, similar to the Grady-O'Hare homestead. Bridge bolts and steel plates would fasten some of the open hand hewn beams through the large dining room. This would be a destination restaurant, with plenty of room to park for trucks and travelers. Locals would come there to have weddings, events and special dinners. JC could see it all in his mind and as months went by, he worked on it all within his imagination, recognizing problems along the way and struggling to find their best solutions.

JC had also been working on a greenhouse project. But this project was physically existing. This was more a hand-me-down hobby of Bobby's. A new commercial greenhouse was built; 50 feet wide by 200 feet long. In it were their best efforts of seedling fir, cedar and pine. After, thirty years of gathering cones and experimenting with every soil, watering and seedling, they had crudely engineered species that grew fewer limbs, thus producing more clear wood. They developed a strain of cedar that grew faster, clearer and had a more pungent aroma. It was basic seed characteristics selection more than any genetic engineering. Occasionally, timber company foresters came by the house, sometimes for coffee, but sometimes for a formal walk through on the latest findings from the project. Much information was shared among these professionals.

The cattle herd was nearly organic and refined more each year in that direction. JC and Matthew worked on the potential to go into custom butchering and sell the choicest beef cuts to world class restaurants. JC saw this fitting well with his own restaurant plans.

Patrick drifted further from the family. There had been a terrible argument at a Thanksgiving dinner at the ranch. Patrick had married a woman from an elite New England family, with old money. They had met at Berkeley, she, smitten by the young man who was clearly a rising star. First, president of the student body, then a state assemblyman from Oakland, where the campus was located. He was a champion of the environmental movement and for the whole rundown of liberal political theologies, which included a devotion to Darwinian Evolution, and a nominal tolerance of all religion, but masking a fervent hatred of Christianity. That had been the blowup at the dinner. Patrick and Marie, his wife, had left vowing never to return. Bobby had stood on the front porch making certain they knew the way out, while the rest of the family sat somberly at the picked over table. It had been a disaster.

A gulf had opened between them that would change their fates.

———

By 1980, the country was in a deep recession. Inflation had raged, and interest rates had tried to stay ahead of the depreciating wealth of the currency. Partly because of the bill coming due for the Vietnam War, but equally so, an ever-expanding federal budget, increasingly gobbling up wealth. Gold, long at $35.00 per ounce shot up to $850. Silver, steady at $3.00 or so per ounce topped out at $50. Interest rates for mortgages could not be found under 15-16 percent. Real estate suffered and soon, the rest of the economy. Europe and Japan had re-emerged from WWII to be global competitors in many industries; automotive, electronics, steel. China was beginning to emerge along with other Asian markets.

The troubling economics were not the most important events occurring. President Jimmy Carter (1976-1980) had administered over the terrible economic condition. It ushered in a period of distaste for liberalism and birthed the administration of Ronald Reagan. But Carter sowed a terrible seed that would years later hand Reagan his worst day in office and set up a new era of world affairs.

The Middle East was a complicated place. History had shown it to be a place of ancient hatreds and spontaneous warfare; hidden agendas and declared intentions. Alliances were formed often from the old adage: "The enemy of my enemy is my friend". But like the shifting desert sands, those alliances evaporated like a mirage and quickly. The Islamic Revolution was growing throughout the Arab and Persian middle east. This was particularly true in Iran, where the Shah of Iran was a close western ally and supporter of strong US relations. Like all middle east dictators, he was less than benevolent with his enemies and those who would support them. Islamic clerics were rising in power in the streets of Tehran and threatening a full scale revolution. For an unexplainable reason, Jimmy Carter thought this was the time to support the young radicals and appease them by putting pressure on the Shah to resign. He arranged for the Shah's safe exile from the country, but insisted he must go.

Immediately, the Ayatolah Khomeini, a radical fundamentalist Muslim, who himself had been exiled to France, came back and took control of the country. If Carter thought his personal actions would alleviate tensions between the radicals and the US, he was terribly mistaken. On November 4, 1979, a group of Islamist students stormed the US Embassy in Tehran and took over fifty hostages. The marine guards were ordered to stand down and thus no fight was given. The "Iranian Hostage Crises" lasted 444 days and was the just undoing of the Carter Administration. Yes, a group of students had stood up to the mighty United States and taken their diplomats hostage, demanding money, public policy changes, national confessions and such.

Carter ordered a covert rescue operation but did not give it the resources necessary to be successful. Tragically, weather conditions-a sandstorm, caused a fatal accident in the remote desert staging area and the operation was scrubbed. The US had now been even more humiliated. People had died in the botched attempt. American will and moral was at a low point. This incident was, to date, the greatest victory that a resurgent Islamist nation had achieved. This Islamic 'nation' was not geographically defined. It was politically defined by their ancient aim, thwarted at the gates of Vienna in 1683 by the French, but now rekindled-hot, red hot. Whether Arab, Persian, Asian, Indonesian, African or European, Muslims were believing in and fighting for an extreme goal, an Islamic Caliphate. Called Jihadists, named for the war or struggle so articulated in the Quran, their holy book, they adopted terror as their weapon of choice.

During the hostage crises, the airline hijackings began. This crippled air travel during the already severe economic slump. Both Europe and America were victimized. The world seemed unready to believe that people could be so barbaric as to victimize civilians in a war the victims hardly understood. It would not be helped by the west's (Western Europe and the United States) reluctance to deal with it forcefully, or even frame the war in its proper perspective. The Jihadists were nothing if not patient and persistent. They would soon teach the west just how serious they were and how committed.

The Iranian Hostage Crises ended when Ronald Reagan took office. After several years, the economic cycle had purged much of the malinvestment and misallocated capital from the economy. It was beginning to rekindle a stronger stock market and general economic conditions began one of the great periods of productivity. Much of this was centered in technology innovation. Primarily, it was the computer. Once, a deep laboratory project, then escaping to the garages of entrepreneurs, hop-skip-and-jumping in large scale production, finally going into global production and distribution. One day soon, every business would be operated with them and virtually no home would be without them.

While the productivity of all workers in the world was enhanced and made possible through the technology, burning along under the surface was the fuse lit long ago. It would lead to an explosion some time in the future. Actually, more of an implosion. It was the incessant growth in the size and scope of all government. Not only was the federal government intervening in nearly every aspect of life in America, but the states, counties, townships and municipalities, taking their cue from 'Big Brother', sought also to control regulate, establish fees and licenses, permits and every conceivable means by which to extract money from the productive. And if America was bad, Europe was long ago absurd.

To step back a decade, prior to Nixon, President Lyndon Bains Johnson (LBJ) had declared war on poverty. He had used the good will of a nation and the political capital of an assassinated president (Kennedy) whom he replaced to pass a plethora of legislation for the "Great Society". Its goal; "... put an end to poverty in our time." It never occurred to anyone that "poverty" would be re-defined so as to always exist. Thus the need to fight the war was unending. Welfare, aid to families with dependent children, the laws of unemployment and disability all brought in the age of victimhood. Soon, even in the sixties, the welfare state was growing enormous. Let out of the cage during the great depression, it seemed shackled during the war years. But now, no more. Now it was being vested as a "right" and worse, all sense of social shame was wiped away, as if this were little more than the only alternative the people had. In the land of plenty, they chose paucity. In the land of the free and home of the brave, they opted for victimhood and entitlement.

All government entities were constantly raising taxes, complaining of the ever increasing demand for their services. This, while each election cycle they pandered to the masses offering ever greater and widening services; school lunches, preschool, health-care, subsidized housing, higher education, etc. They thought them up, offered them up, voted them in and taxed everybody who worked to pay those bills.

Perhaps the most damaging mischief of this era was the increase in regulation. No matter what else the public's attention might be diverted to, the increase in regulation of every sort, every political subdivision, from congress to the school board. From the state house to city hall. Local cities and counties developed elaborate planning and zoning laws. After all, wouldn't chaos be the alternative? States developed laws governing clean air, and water, historical and archeological preservation. Always, committees were formed, councils were created and dictates rained down. Agencies of all levels of government grew like weeds in a well watered, but unattended garden. It was not long before the simple act of getting a building permit became a maze of Byzantine hoops to jump through. Development was seen as evil, except of course, what the local government agency could coerce from the developer. JC saw this first hand.

———

Siskiyou County now had a Planning Department and Commission, like every other county, and many larger cities. JC, now twenty six years old and the operational head of Grady-O'Hare walked into the meeting. Bobby, the patriarchal head of Grady-O'Hare, had attended only one prior meeting and told JC that his attendance was unlikely to recur. He was so angered and sickened by the attitude of the bureaucrats, their tone of speech and the content of what they had said, that he swore: "I don't know why the hell we fought the war to rid the world of a tyrant, only to enslave ourselves to a bunch of tyrannical clerks. It would be better for them and me, if I never attended another meeting like that one." The one he referred to was an expansion of the offramp development and would involve just under seven acres of land. It was a small amount of the thousands of acres he owned, but to the agencies and bureaus involved, you'd think he was destroying the pristine habitat on which all God's earth depended.

Grady-O'Hare was converting some more of the cow pasture to the growing need for highway services. It seemed the offramp was perfectly placed at the right time of travel between Portland and San Francisco to seek meals and lodging. The established enterprises did very well at this location and the competitors had noticed. They all wanted a site at the interchange. Pepe tagged along with JC for friendship and moral support as they had talked about the upcoming meeting. It had been continued because Bobby had walked out in a storm, suggesting something about kissing and having a royal Irish ass.

Pepe and JC took their seats in the council chambers, newly constructed in the annex of the courthouse. A grandmotherish woman peered down at papers before her through the round lenses of her spectacles. Her mouth worked as she read the summary on the agenda item coming up.

She cleared her throat and rapped her gavel solidly once. "Our next item involves a proposed land use change from agriculture to commercial freeway. This is at the Old Highway interchange and the applicant is Grady-O'Hare. Is there anyone here to represent them?" JC stood.

"JC O'Hare, for Grady-O'Hare".

"Thank you, Mr. O'Hare. Please be seated, while we hear from staff."

A young man about JC's age scooted his chair closer to the table and then pulled the microphone toward him.

"Madame President, staff has reviewed the zoning change application and recommends denial of the application." Pepe whispered into JC's ear, "Glad the old man isn't here." JC rolled his eyes, knowing he was in for a long evening and shook his head slowly, affirming Pepe's comment.

"As you know Madame President, our county has recently adopted a policy of no loss of agricultural lands. Grady-O'Hare, the applicant, has exhausted the original lands zoned for commercial use and is now requesting 6.95 acres additionally to be converted to this use. We see no justification for this and note that if we do not draw a line here, there is no end to the potential conversion. Our first finding is that there is no compelling need to justify this zoning change."

"Our second finding...." JC stood up and addressed the commission. "I disagree that there is no compelling......," The gavel wrapped several times briskly.

"Mr. O'Hare, please take your seat and do not interrupt. You will be given a chance to respond at the conclusion of staff's findings." JC nodded an acknowledgment. "Easy does it, boss", said Pepe, sensing the burr of aggravation.

"As I was saying, our second finding is that there has not been an archeological study done on this. Should the commission wish to allow the applicant to proceed, we would recommend an archeological review." JC, was determined to keep his cool, but he was thinking, ' When the hell did this all start'?

"Our third finding is that the proposed future development, which is assumed given the request for zoning change, would violate the Clean Water Act, due to the existence of wetlands on the subject site."

"What the hell are you talking about?" shot JC, snapping to his feet. Pepe hid under the brim of his cowboy hat.

"That is not any kind of wetland. It is irrigated because we've put water on it from our ditch, and....," The President rapped her gavel continuously with a perturbed brow.

"Mr. O'Hare, please sit down. You'll get your chance to be heard." JC sat down slowly, as snickers and whispers rippled through the small audience.

"Madame President, that concludes our findings. If any of the commission members have any questions, we'd be happy to try to answer them." She looked both left and right as there were three members to each side, forming a slight semi-circle, concave to the audience.

"Any questions?"

The men and women of the board looked somewhat stupefied as if not having any notion of what to do or what would constitute a good question. Then a retired looking man, that Pepe had seen driving around near the ranch the past week spoke.

"Regarding the architectural study, is there any indication...", The person next to him whispered to him. ".... I'm sorry, archaeological, uhh archaeological study. Is there some indication of dinosaurs or something?"

The staffer smiled indulgently. "Well sir, we're not aware of any dinosaur bones or anything like that, though I suppose it is possible. These studies are typically about Native American sites, campfires, worship areas, burial grounds, etc. If found, we need to contact the local tribes for input in order to understand the significance."

"Thank you, staff." The man leaned back in his chair, apparently satisfied he had contributed to the discussion. Emboldened, a young man sitting at the far right side, whom JC recognized as a teacher at the elementary school, leaned into his microphone.

"I've driven by the proposed site many times and if it is not being irrigated by the owners, it is usually very dry. Does the fact that it has been irrigated, necessarily mean it is wetlands and to be preserved and protected?" This seemed like an interesting question, and Pepe and JC looked at each other.

The planning staffer enjoined. "The answer to your question is that: It depends. The classification of wetlands isn't necessarily about our perception of water sitting on the surface. If that occurs, you can be quite certain it is 'wetlands'. At the dryer end of the spectrum there are specific biological tests to be performed. Soil samples must be taken. Certain microorganisms present could result in a wetlands designation, even if water rarely sits on the land."

"Now hold on a minute.." Jumped up JC to the immediate and incessant rapping of the gravel.

"I will not ask you again, Mr. O'Hare! I will summons a Sheriff, here in the courthouse, and have you removed if you do no behave. We are almost finished here. Please continue, staff."

"Well I think I answered the question, Madam President." He looked to the young man who asked the question, seeking whether the answer was satisfactory. The man nodded in the affirmative.

"Any other questions?"

A pretty woman who sat next to the president had long, flowing brown hair and was attired in a sort of renaissance dress, with long dangling ear rings. She ventured to her mic.

"Has anybody considered how the septic systems would work, since they are not on a sewer? Water? How about the impact on infrastructure?"

The planning staffer pleasantly indulged these questions suggesting by his tone, they were thoughtful and appreciated.

"In all fairness to the applicant, these issues would be better brought up at the time when we have a proposed project, not just the zone change application."

The President of the Planning Commission looked to and fro to her compatriots and saw no further questions.

"Very well, then. Are there any comments from the public?"

JC rose. "Yes, ma'm, I have some comments." Her gavel rapped twice and she smiled excessively, showing her extreme patience was now wearing thin.

"Mr. O'Hare, you are the applicant, not the public. Our procedure is that the facts are presented by the staff. The commission members interface with staff. Then the public has an opportunity to comment or question. Staff may reply. Then the applicant may speak. Then there is additional opportunity for the public. Then the commission votes. Is all that clear to you, Mr. O'Hare?" He sat down silently, beginning to chew on the inside of his lower lip.

A gentleman at the rear of the audience stood. "Yeah, I've just built a new home..." He was cut off by the president.

"I'm sorry would you please state your name for the record?"

"...Oh, sure. Sorry. I'm Joseph Smirkum and I've just finished a home on a little parcel near there. I've watched that interchange develop over the years. When I finally finished my house, the lights from the vehicles coming in the parking lots shine right into my bedroom. Sometimes the truckers park there and take naps with their engines idling. It can be very difficult to get to sleep. I'd like to know what you can do about these nuisances. Also, it seems if you grant the request, there'll be even more traffic and noise."

"Thank you Mr. Smirkum. Staff, do you have any comments?"

The lead staffer cupped the mic with his hand while he whispered back and forth with one of his assistants. Finally. "Yes, we recognize, the issue, and can understand

Mr. Smirkum's concern. We're not sure what to tell him except that we agree, there will be more of it, if this zone change is approved."

JC was chewing the whole inside of his cheek, waiting for his opportunity to speak. He leaned to Pepe. "What the hell is the matter with these people?"

"Is that all?" asked the president. "Very well, then. Mr. O'Hare, it is now your turn to speak."

JC stood up. "I would like to address each ......," She interrupted him, "I'm sorry, but you'll have to state your name and that you are the applicant, for the record please." JC sighed, containing himself with what grace and patience he could muster.

"My name is JC O'Hare, for Grady-O'Hare Ranch, the applicant."

"Thank, you. Please continue," she said.

"I'd like to address each of the issues. First off, these guys (pointing at the staff) haven't bothered to look at the situation honestly. Their first finding was that there was no compelling need to add to the commercial uses that this zone change would accomplish. By what criteria could this possibly be determined, other than market criteria? I have in my briefcase, letters, from business that would like to build out there, several motels, a truck stop, restaurant. We couldn't support all of them, but we can support more than what is out there. Their desires are based upon the research they've done with traffic counts, gross sales at the existing businesses, anecdotal evidence, and professional expertise. That the current businesses are so successful is the best testimony as to compelling need. If need isn't based upon this kind of evidence and data, then what have you based your findings on?"

"Secondly, they "found" that there would need to be an archaeological study done. I don't know who the hell thought this up, but we wouldn't have the towns and cities we have, if you couldn't build on something that somebody else in prior history hadn't already discovered and lived on. It is the nature of scarce resources, like water, topography, tactical views and such. Now I don't know what exactly you're looking for. Indians had small campfires all over this country. Not every place they walked is sacred ground at my expense. I know that ground very well, I assure you, there is nothing significant on those 6.95 acres. It is just open pasture. Not a tree or a trickle on it."

"This brings me to my next point. This wetlands bullshit, sorry, wetlands issue is ridiculous. When my grandfather worked that ground up, early this century, he had to bring a ditch over there to get water to that pasture. I can dry it up to a popcorn fart in about two seconds." Giggles went through the audience.

"Mr. O'Hare, I know you are excitable, but please refrain from such verbiage."

"I'm sorry, but this is just bullshit. There are no wetlands, except the wet land we made by our own efforts. It is not naturally so. I don't know about how dry land can have a microorganism associated with wetlands, but I own and manage more acres than all you people will ever dream of. I know something about land and water, fish and people. I know real wetlands when I see them. What you're doing here is abusing a law you find convenient and flexible to your own purposes."

"Now then, to the young lady's question. The water, septic and infrastructure will depend on the specific development. It wouldn't be the same for a motel as a restaurant. So you'll get another chance at that."

"Lastly, as to Mr. Smirkum's problem: His problem was there before he built. He bought the cheapest little piece of dirt in the neighborhood. It was cheap for the very reasons he now complains about. But the motels and restaurants were there first. He is the last one to build and he's owned it for a couple of years so he knew damn good and well what it would be like. So I recommend he quit whining and buy drapes and ear plugs. That is unless, of course, this commission is going to take upon itself the task of freeing every man from the consequences of his mistakes." He turned to Mr. Smirkum who sat quietly. "Get over it, Smirkum."

"Now that I've responded to all of your so called issues and problems, let me tell you as briefly as I can why you should approve this zone change. In an area where good jobs, indeed any jobs are rare, you should welcome the employment. Since we've first developed, over forty-five people earn all or part of their living out there and its all income to the area from people traveling through. The sales taxes generated along with the motel taxes is over $600,000 per year. That's $600,000 more you get to waste and spend frivolously than you would otherwise have. Lastly, it appears, according to our tax bills that you are receiving $8.34 in property taxes from the 6.95 acres at present. Under similar development as what exists out there, we project developed values of over $4,200,000. That would amount to about $43,000 per year in property taxes received, when developed. Gee, let me think about this, $8.34 versus $43,000. Hmmhhh. Oh hell, you guys do the math. You don't need to bother us about school fees, as these customers won't be enrolling their kids, just passing through, dropping off a lot of money on the way. As to the infrastructure; we'll be paying for all of that when we develop. Trust me when I tell you that *you* won't do it."

"So you folks decide what you want to do." He turned to leave. "Come on Pepe." They were out the door in the hallway, the footfall of their boots in the hallway, heavy and quick.

The President of the Planning Commission, smiled at the other members and some words were spoken off the

record, their hands cupping the microphone. She chuckled, then she spoke into her mic.

"Are there any other questions or comments? Seeing
none, I call for the vote. All those in favor of the approval
of the zone change for Grady-O'Hare say 'aye'. All those
opposed, say 'nay'. It is unanimous. The application is
denied. Please send the applicant formal notification by
mail."

"Our next agenda item is approval of $16,000 for an
art project in front of the County Courthouse. We've received several proposals from local artists. Let's take a
few minutes and pass out sketches of the proposals to the
audience. This is an exciting project that generated a lot
of interest in the community. And I must say, our local artists have truly risen to the occasion by the looks of their
proposals."

CHAPTER 8

Bobby felt old and was generally in pain. It was his back. He grunted getting in and out of cars, or bed. The easy chair was not so easy anymore. Lizzy rarely left him, and like her master, her own back suffered pain. Her spine was beginning to rise up. She didn't chase cattle any more. Some days, Bobby hardly got out of his leather slippers. Vera had aged gracefully in the face, but the arthritis in her hands was getting worse. Her clothes were of another era, stuck in the style of her prime. She had been a good wife, a frugal woman, dedicated to family and home, ranch wife. She had given wise counsel to her husband when he asked for it and he knew it was wisdom as soon as she spoke. He later thought to himself he should have spent more time seeking her advice than the cabal of accountants and attorneys over the years.

He was watching her getting ready to put a peach pie in the oven. Flour dough dust covered the countertop. She had pinched the crust down round the edge and was now carefully venting the raw crust by knife into a leafy design. He levered himself out of the chair and walked into the kitchen.

"Momma, before you put that in the oven, why don't we go for a ride?"

"Oh, I don't have time."

"Sure we do. We should make the time. The fall colors are starting to get real pretty. Come on, let's hop in the jeep, get bundled up and take ol' Lizzy for a ride." The dog, already at their feet, pitched her ears forward at the sound of her name. Bobby reached over to her and put his arms around Vera and looked into her sweet face.

"I love you, ya' know. You've been a heck of a wife. I never felt I deserved you, but I'm sure glad I got you". She bathed in this and smiled back at him.

"You weren't such a bad catch, yourself," she toyed with him. His hands behind her, he pulled on the bow of her apron and it loosened. "Come on, let's go for a ride".

"Oh all right. I'll put this in the oven when we get back. Lizzy, are you ready to go for a ride?" she said, addressing the canine at her feet. At this the dog visibly shed half its age and began prancing up and down in place, wearing a dog smile.

There was still a few hours of daylight left. It would be a beautiful drive. They bundled up, with hats and coats and hopped in the old Willys jeep, Lizzy in the back cargo area. He drove slow and easy along the road as it skirted between the forest on the right and the great pasture, both irrigated and dry, on the left. The mountain engulfed the eastern horizon as always. They turned up the gully driving through 'Tall Trees', as magical as ever. Soon, the little un-named creek came alongside the road and the mixed deciduous trees began to show their colors, yellow and crimson, burnt amber and orange that looked almost neon in brilliance.

They smiled at each other the smile that forty plus years of marriage can bring to people who have always loved each other, been best friends and watched the years add wrinkles, pain and wisdom to a face. Lizzy's head came between them as if sensing the moment she was entitled to be a part of. They laughed at her, sharing thoughts without words. Soon the road turned away from the creek and began the long series of switchbacks, climbing in and out of gullies and across slopes and up ridge lines until it reached a large flat on top. It was nearly 2,000 feet above the valley floor. Bobby stopped the jeep on the flat and aimed it toward the mountain. They never tired of seeing the Shasta Valley from this great height. Its land forms and water courses, lakes and lines of trees were miniaturized. It was as if they were looking down upon the earth from parted clouds. They said nothing, but just gazed out.

They had parked here many times. It was among their favorite spots on the ranch. They climbed out of the jeep and met at the front bumper where he embraced her from behind. Lizzy wandered around sniffing for a place to pee. He perched his head on her shoulder and took in the wonderful smell of her neck and hair. She stood in his embrace and thought how lucky she was. She had never cared for more money than what she needed, yet she was blessed with plenty. She, like any of the O'Hares, never displayed wealth. They had it. They used it. But showing it was considered in poor taste. Yet, it was never said.

The man that held her in his arms had provided for them magnificently. They had four kids, all good she thought, despite the upheaval with Patrick. She loved each of them. Though the ranch was inherited, their period of custodial service had seen so much improvement, such advancement. The house had been modernized while never becoming modern. Thousands of acres had been added by lots of small acquisitions over a long time; both pasture and timber. Bobby was something of a timber expert without the benefit of the college degree he wanted long ago but never had time to get. The cattle herd had grown in numbers and for years now, he and the boys were narrowing the bloodline and perfecting an organic herd. She was proud of them all.

Matthew loved the cattle business. He and Sandy had given her three grandchildren. Angelina was happy in her busy life as a teacher. Her husband was a great guy and doted on her. They had given her two more grandchildren. JC was still single, but he was so dynamic and was now running the whole operation with Bobby now limited to offering advice and signing documents. She wished he'd find a good woman. There had been several nice girls, she thought, but none he was willing to call his wife. Patrick and Marie now had a child, and so there was another grandchild, but she could not know when she would, if ever, see this child. She thought how she wished things could be mended. He snuggled her and she wrapped his hands in her own.

"It's beautiful isn't it?" she said. They were the same words, the same sentiment that 110 years earlier Melissa Brennerman (Grady) had said to John Brennerman at their Nebraska homestead.

"I think you are what is beautiful." She smiled and he chuckled into her neck. The afternoon sun waned and the top of the mountain began to glow pink. Clouds that were moments ago invisible now magically appeared in the sky illuminated by the severe angle of the setting sun. First a slight gilding of pink, then deepening to fiery red and purples. Only the glaciers atop Mt. Shasta had remaining snow after the long summer. But those glaciers now reflected the laser intense colors of the sky above them. It was interplay between sky and earth and they both watched it speechlessly. They stood at the front of the jeep, Lizzy on her haunches beside them, also looking at the view, frozen by the stunning pallet of sky and land. Slowly, the sky turned gray and the mountain top with it.

"Well, we better get back down," Bobby whispered in her ear.

"Come on. Let's go." They got in and Lizzy took her position, snout between them. They bundled up as they felt the temperature begin to drop. The jeep swung around and began its descent. The shadows were long on the ridgetops. The gullies were nearly dark. Unknown to them the cotter pin holding the steering arm to the tie rod had rusted through and the nut was working its way down the threads. They stopped for a monstrous buck that stood in the road. It was unperturbed by their pressing upon him. Lizzy barked safely from her perch. Bobby tapped the horn and the buck descended down the bank below the road with deliberate slowness. They proceeded across the steep slope and began the series of switchbacks. With every rotation of the steering wheel, the nut worked its way down the threads, now holding on by only half itself. They went around a hard right corner and Bobby frowned. The wheel seemed loose. Vera picked up on his expression.

"What's wrong?" she asked.

"Not sure. The wheel feels a little sloppy. I'll want to look at it when we get back down."

"Is it okay?"

"Yeah, I think so." He cranked the wheel hard left going around another switchback, then it was straight for about a hundred yards. They ambled down the road only about ten miles per hour as the nut fell off. The steering linkage was held together only by grease, dirt and friction. The next hair pin was hard right and Bobby swung the wheel and the jeep edged its way around the turn. They were coming up to the last of the bad switchbacks. It was nearly a 190 degree turn. Miraculously, the linkage had held on. They entered the turn. As they did, the tie-rod dropped off the pin holding the linkage to the steering column. Though their eyes lead down the road, the tires straightened at the apex of the turn and the jeep went over the edge before they could stop. The steep angle down through the broken forest was nearly vertical. Vera screamed as Lizzy was pitched over the windscreen in front of the vehicle. Bobby slammed the brake pedal to the floor.

"Hold on!" he yelled.

"Oh God, no!"

The wheels locked, but the jeep was nearly in free fall sliding on the loose gravel, dust flew up into the air and filled their nostrils, choking them. The jeep crashed over brush five feet high, nearly throwing them from the vehicle, but the lap belts held them in place. Bobby tried to hold the wheel straight to avoid rolling the vehicle which would kill them certainly either by ejection or crushing. His mind was racing, 'could they exit the vehicle? No!' In a split second they were upon a downed log across the path of the cascading jeep.

"Oh sweet Jesus," he spat through his teeth bracing the steering wheel. The tires hit simultaneously and the jeep nearly stopped and time stood still. In that moment, the rear of the jeep cartwheeled upward. In the slow motion that the mind sees in, when one's own death is at hand, the world went silent and they felt the slow rotation of the jeep coming over the log. It was nearly vertical when the tires actually crested over the top of the log, and the jeep's front wheels slid off the log and began to roll down the slope again. The jeep would have slammed back to the ground but for the severe slope. The vehicle took off again, racing out of control. It accelerated rapidly down the slope, the thick forest below them. Bobby had barely veered the jeep, avoiding several large trees. He knew that only a tree would stop them now. But that, fatally. The end of the brushy, more barren slope was coming. At its bottom, the forest approached like a wall of green and brown.

"Jump!" he yelled. But Vera was frozen.

"Seat belt, then jump!" he screamed. There was only another moment or two. Bobby knew he could not undo his own lap belt and hold the wheel that wrenched violently in his hands. Vera was already gone. She was white like the flour she had kneaded only an hour earlier. She looked calmly at Bobby, with total serenity and said, "I love you".

And now he saw it as well. It was hopeless. They were careening down the slope and the massive tree trunks awaited them.

———

JC looked over at the main house from his modest home three hundred yards away and noticed no lights on. It was now dark. He thought to himself: Mom and dad weren't going out. At least not that he knew of. He quickly called them, but there was no answer. He jumped into his pickup and dashed over.

On the kitchen table was a pie. He sniffed. "Peach". Something was wrong. He'd seen them cooling and left, but never left unbaked.

"Mom? Dad?" he called. Nothing. Lizzy. 'Where was Lizzy?' he thought. He made rounds through the house, upstairs, in the bedrooms, calling as he went. Silence answered him. He broke out onto the covered porch and yelled again, calling them. The wind in his ears was all he heard.

"Lizzy", he yelled and looked toward the barn where she sometimes napped too long. Nothing. He went to the phone and called Matt.

"Yeah, listen. Were mom and dad doing something tonight?"

"No. Not that I know of. Why?"

"Well, there is nobody here. The house is dark. Lizzy's gone. The car and truck are here."

"How about the jeep? Sometimes they'll take it for a ride."

"Let me look. Hold on." He stepped outside and surveyed the shadows of the shed where the jeep would normally be parked.

"Its gone, all right."

"Well, then they went for a ride, but uh........ They're usually in by this time. I'm coming over."

"Okay, see ya in a minute". JC hung up and went out to the sheds and barn looking for anything out of the ordinary. His mind was racing. Had there been someone here. Could they ...... He didn't like where his mind took him. Matt's headlights swung into the yard. He had obviously flown over there.

"Anything?"

"Nothing."

"Did you look for a note?"

"No. But I didn't see anything and besides they don't usually leave notes."

"Let's check the house for wallets and purses."

They quickly found that all was in order. The ranch jackets were missing, so they had left anticipating some cold.

"Call Pepe and see if he knows anything."

Matt called Pepe, but he knew nothing. He was just finishing dinner with the family and said he'd be right over. Mere minutes later, his old pickup's lights were heading up the long private road. Pepe came through the door.

"No word yet?"

"Nope."

The three men shared each others company after making some phone calls to neighbors and friends, but they didn't really expect a positive reply. By ten o'clock, the living room had filled with friends and family, nearly thirty people were pouring over maps and deciding what to do. It was concluded that they were probably on the ranch.

They formed up search teams, maps, flashlights, blankets in case they found them cold, first aid kits with each team in case of injury. One neighbor brought an air-horn, which accidentally went off in the room and just about caused several coronaries. JC had taken charge.

"Pepe, you take Gus and Chet and search the west side of Eddy draw. Matt, take Jimmy and Paul and parallel them on the east side. Frank, you and Verne head up the left fork beyond Tall Trees. Josh and I will take the right fork. We'll go up on top. Make sure your batteries are good. Set your radios to channel six. Let's test 'em now, and take a thermos of coffee."

Matt added: "Go slow and call out often. They might be off the roads."

By eleven o'clock, the search parties left. In a caravan of pickup trucks, all lights were deployed. They left the barnyard in single file, along the main road that skirted the big pasture at the edge of the timber. Frank and JC's trucks turned up to Tall Trees, while Pepe and Matt's kept along the main road. Chatter started immediately upon this initial separation. Everyone was shining their high intensity beams and large maglights up into the woods and outward from the road.

Radios squelched all night, from time to time. The constant report was 'nothing'. To this, came the reply "Keep going."

By 2:30 am, everyone had reached the ends of their assigned roads and were heading back. JC had gone up and stopped at the flat. The lights of the farms and ranches twinkled in the cold night air. He and Josh combed the ground as they had seen fresh jeep tracks.

"It looks like them, all right", said Josh, the neighboring ranch's best hand.

"Look at this, JC. It looks like they parked out here near the edge. Now follow this. They backed up over to here and took off that way. See how the one track rolled over the other?"

"Yeah. You're right Josh."

They followed the track, but it lead them to the road where it went back down.

283

"Okay, we got something here. I don't understand how we could miss it but they definitely came up here and went back down. Get on the radio and get everybody over here. We'll go back down real slow. Try to watch the tracks."

They headed for the pickup, while Josh called on the radio. Everybody got the word and were headed their direction in a hurry.

They were following the tracks, but they were becoming indistinct on the road. Too much travel. As they rounded the switchbacks, they could see the truck lights in a caravan coming up the draw way below them. They crossed the slopes and went down the ridge, to the switchbacks that descended to the draw. They were going slow.

"Stop!" yelled Josh.

"What?" But then he saw it too. Just as they went around the corner, they saw where two tire tracks had parted the soft berm that accumulates over years on the outside of the turn. Josh was on the radio as they both exited the truck. JC knew this terrain and a horrible feeling came into his gut. They could hear the engines cranking up speed below them as everyone rushed to the scene. The two men went to the edge and peered down into a black darkness. What they saw turned their stomach, as the tracks lead straight down the hill.

They yelled down and then listened for a reply. None came.

"Josh, take the truck and go down to where the road nears the creek. You should meet the rest of the men down there. Then track toward the creek, looking upslope. Get everybody searching. I'll follow the tracks. Gimme your radio."

"Got it." Josh was gone, flying down the road, faster than he should. JC went over the edge. With every step downward he slid down several more feet on the loose gravel and cobble. His stomach sickened as he passed by long stretches of slope where the airborne jeep left no track. His maglight was panning back and forth across the downward slope. It stopped as it fell upon an object hung up in the tall brush. Perhaps a rag or shirt. It was black and white. He slid on the loose gravel going down the slope until he got closer. He saw now; it was Lizzy. She was upside down like a stuffed animal tossed of the vehicle. Her head had smashed the top of the windscreen frame when she was pitched forward of the car. He paused for a moment, then continued downhill.

It was steep as hell, and his pace hurried. He passed through a field of brush and saw the tracks go right through or over a bush, the splintered trunk remained the evidence of its being crushed. His light was panning across the bottom, still several hundred yards below him, when he saw a red flicker. He washed the area again with his light. There it was again. Yes, two of them; the tail light reflectors! He recognized them as the jeep. He bowled himself pell-mell down the slope until he came across a log. His light picked up the crash marks, but he had the jeep sighted, so he kept moving. 'Oh God, please save them', he thought as he crashed down the slope. Now he saw a dozen lights and lanterns coming from the woods to his left toward the jeep below him.

"Hey, straight ahead of you!" he hollered down, but his own voice sounded faint in his breathlessness. They were coming toward it and so was he, only a hundred yards below him. More brush. The jeep had flown through nearly six feet high manzanita, so he went around. Now he saw lights hitting the jeep and men's voices in the dark, talking animated, excited. He pressed downward to them. He saw in the flickering of the lights two still silhouettes, hanging slightly out of the jeep to either side. His heart now sank. Frank Johnson was making his way up to him. He could tell by the silhouette of Frank's worn cowboy hat. Only forty feet from the jeep, Frank blocked him squarely.

"Son, you don't need to go down there. Your parents have passed on JC... I'm sorry son. I don't know what to say. Your folks were the salt o' the earth. They don't come any better."

JC looked around Frank to see the scene.

"I need to....." He moved to step around Frank, but Frank moved to block him sternly, and he put a firm hand to JC's shoulder that said two things. One, was Frank's obvious affection for him and his family, especially Bobby and Vera. The other was a firmness that said: 'I really think you shouldn't go down there.'

"JC, you don't want to see them like this. We'll get 'em out of here. Pepe sent somebody to go call the coroner. You can just sit down right here and do whatever it is you gotta' do."

Somebody was putting wool army blankets over the bodies, and someone came and put a blanket over JC's shoulders. He just collapsed on the slope and Frank sat with him and they wept together. The men's voices spoke softly, reverently, just feet below them. Slowly, they carried the bodies away as the first diffused light of morning chased the pitch black away. He didn't know how long they had been there. There weren't any words for a long time. Pepe came up and poured a cup of coffee from a thermos and handed it to JC.

"I'm sorry, JC."

"Thanks, Pepe", he muffled. He got to his feet, Frank and Pepe at his side. He slugged down the coffee and walked down to the jeep. It had center-punched a two foot diameter Douglas Fir. It had put a horseshoe dent into the front that set the engine nearly back into the front seat. The glass was shattered and green radiator fluid ran down the hill until it disappeared into the thick duff.

Both seats were full of blood as was the hood. He could see the crash in his mind. They both slammed into the windshield frame, crushing both their faces, breaking the necks and backs. He saw the steering wheel broken off from three to nine o'clock and the column itself messed with blood and organ material. He turned and vomited. The men gave him his space, and just looked at each other. Through the bile and vomit rushed a new wave of tears and anguish.

"Mom......Dad", he choked. Pepe and Frank filled with their own emotions looked away with glossy eyes, giving him some space.

—

Vera was being pulled to the surface. She saw light coming toward her through water. Or was it a tunnel. Her heart beat rapidly in anticipation. She saw her hand in his; Bobby's hand. Suddenly, she broke through and they were together, somehow on a mountain top. 'What has happened?', she thought. Bobby was smiling big as ever, and-Oh my God, he was thirty years younger. He was in his prime, like when all the kids were young. They had been in the jeep. They were going to crash into a tree. The scene flooded back into her mind for a moment. But now they were back on the flat overlooking the valley again. How could this?....... Wait. It wasn't quite the same. Bobby was laughing like a child, as the fog quickly lifted from her mind and the realization took hold. Now the flat was filled with people. Family and friends and now the crowd pressed around them in love and lay their hands upon them and it was the most glorious touch she had ever felt. She and Bobby were surrounded. The love that emanated from this group whom she could not judge the number of, was like a tidal wave beneath them. Then

Connor broke through to them and embraced them. He himself was younger than she remembered him, yet it was clearly him.

"He's waiting for you".

"Who?" she asked of Connor.

"Jesus, of course. Who else?"

"I want to go to Him."

She looked around and it was Earth. It was the land she knew, but it was different. It was like a mirror image of what she knew, but this now seemed the real one, and her life had been spent in the reflected one. This one was crisp and freshness permeated her being. They were swept along, walking, yet more transported than step by step. She looked at the sky and it was like the most beautiful colored sunset of golds and crimsons in water colors on a pallet of blues from pale aquamarines to deep azure. But this did not fade. It changed constantly, but never faded. The mountains of the distance were different than the peaks she had known. They were more striking, more majestic, like the Alps, with snowy caps above the timberline. The clarity with which all things appeared was striking. She reached up and pulled a sprig off a fir tree and looked at it intently in the palm of her hand. It was a nothing of a sprig, only four inches long. Yet, it was so beautiful and so fragrant, her eyes began to tear up.

"This is heaven, isn't it?"

"Yes", the younger woman at her shoulder said. I am your great grandmother. All these people are your family, all saved by Christ. The reason you cry at the sprig is that your heart sees a resurrected world. Earth. The whole universe has been made new. This was done on the cross, by He who waits to see you and welcome you."

"Oh my God!"

"Yes. Exactly!"

BOOK 3-CHAPTER 1

The sun set into the bay and the lights on the bridges came into full relief in the growing gloom. The picture windows stretched for forty feet in a sweeping arc. The panoramic view was from high up in the Oakland hills. Eucalyptus trees towered a hundred feet high. The property was several acres in size. Two lion statues guarded the gated entrance and lengthy drive that wound its way to the house on the top of the knoll. Patrick O'Hare drank in the incredible view, the Bay Bridge lights twinkling now. Off in the distance the Golden Gate. The San Francisco skyline at the moment past sunset was breathtaking. Ships made their way up the bay to Vallejo, tankers and dry bulk cargo. He knocked the twenty-five year old scotch to the back of his throat and swallowed. Turning to the man at the private bar, he said, "That's good scotch, Ben. I believe I'll have another"

"Why not................ Senator O'Hare". He raised his glass to salute the new status of his guest. He pushed the velveted bottle toward Patrick. "That was a hell of a campaign you ran. You did well.

"And I certainly thank you, Ben, for your guidance and support. I couldn't have done it without you. I know that." The man smiled, and it spoke 'your damned right'. Benjamin Geiss was dressed in a black turtle-neck that had a loose, almost floppy collar. The sleeves pushed up to three-quarter length. The rounded wire rim glasses sat atop the gray hair, which flowed down to his shoulders. He was gaunt, a gaunt vegan, his face slender and boney.

"There is so much work to do. But tonight ...., tonight we want to celebrate the victory."

"I thought that was what the big bash last night was all about?"

"It was. It was. But that was for the photo op and the public. I thought tonight should be celebratory, yet reflective. We can talk of cabbages and kings, and the things to come". He grinned and poured himself another drink, after Patrick.

"This view is incredible, Ben."

"Yeah, I like it. When you see the bay and the city from up here and the darkness of the trees all around us, you feel like you're part of it, but separated."

"Looking down upon the mere mortals, eh?" Quipped Patrick. Ben smiled but said nothing. He held out his glass to toast the new United States Senator from California.

"To progress."

"Progress".

They went over and sat in two comfortable chairs near the windows with the view. A Steinway grand piano's ebony polish gleamed in the light of the room. It was there for guests. Ben and his common law wife didn't play.

"Patrick, we have two major themes that will both propel and maintain your power base and allow this country to progress: the environment, and social justice. You stay within that framework and this state is yours for as long as you want it-provided you don't screw up. Every time, and I mean every time opportunity presents itself, you must make a point of being heard. If its global warming, or global cooling it doesn't make any difference. The point is control. We need progressive thinkers in charge of industry, instead of these thieving bastards on Wall Street."

"We got a lot of support from Wall Street, Ben".

"Your damned right we did........, from *our* thieving bastards. They're all right. They are with us, Pat. They see things
the same way. We can make a better world, but we need
to get the right people into the right places. That is what
its all about. And tonight, we're another step closer. It is
important to set up regulations for pollution control, car
emissions, smokestack industry, coal, public transit, I don't
give a shit-even light bulbs. It is the promise and hope of
a better world, because enlightened people will run it. I
know we've already got laws on the books, but here is
the deal. When those laws, reasonable at first, then later,
are so onerous that no one can live with them, or they simply don't know how to comply, they'll come to us. That's
power, Patrick. That is where the rubber meets the vagi-
na". Both men laughed.

"The social justice thing is a piece of cake. Every minority is your cause. Here is the thing. When you add up
all the minority votes-and believe me they stand with
each other when compared to whites, they, together
with the *liberal* whites are an unassailable majority. Certainly in this state. Watch the Hispanic thing. Its growing
like a weed. We must be seen as supportive of all things
pertaining to them. Immigration, health care, education
and child care; these we can use to steamroll the Neanderthals that hold us back. Let them talk about their
'markets' and individualism, their invisible hand. It is no
match for a visible handout. Eventually, that will become
a fist that will smash them into irrelevancy. We don't want
the opposition destroyed, we want it neutered, unable to
reproduce. We want it visible, shown to be impotent and
ineffective; an object of ridicule, laughter and scorn: a
reproach."

"There is one other fundamental concept, I'm sure
your aware of, but its worth being clear about, here and
now. Property, or rather I should say property rights. This

is the key to wealth. It doesn't matter who owns a thing. It is the control that gives it its wealth factor and thus, power. Now this plays into the environmental movement, through the Endangered Species Act, Clean Water, Clean Air, next will be Clean Garbage, Clean Energy, Clean anything. Once this notion is firmly planted in their minds and they vote accordingly, we can control, for the benefit of all mankind, the key factors of production; land and capital. Once people accept that owning property is a obligation to all, all other property rights are weakened. Thus, the economy is more malleable, more manageable to our cause. The chaos of the markets can be diminished and there will, in the long run be less economic suffering. We must look at ourselves not as Americans, but as global citizens. As long as we look at the world from nationalistic viewpoints, we will constantly see our differences and this promotes conflicts. Erasing the boundaries of nations will promote a peaceful world, and that, in itself, means an economically more productive world."

"Ben, I was raised on a ranch. So I know what I am talking about when I say, that the property rights issue is going to be a hard sell. All of middle America, the 'red' states, the land owners, live off of those rights and you are not going to sell them on your plan."

"Of course, not. Patrick, we're never going to convince them. The people to convince are the urbanites, the college students, the celebrity class in Hollywood, the minorities who are metro and urbanized dependents on our system. There is a hell of a lot more of them than those acreage bound landowners. For those people, we just need a few converts. We just shoehorn them into it nice and gentle. The trend will take hold, and the end is inevitable. Its already begun."

"You don't know those people like I do. My dad was one of them. He died about ten years back."

"Yes, I know who your father was. I researched you thoroughly."

"Well there are still people just like him. My two brothers are among them."

"Its interesting you should bring them up. I have something to show you." Ben left the room, while Patrick sipped at the scotch. A minute later, Ben returned with a file folder. He removed a sheaf of papers, clipped by a large spring at the top. He flipped over what must have been half of the paper, an inch thick and then searched page by page.

"Here it is. Now before you look at this, I want you to know that we have a great deal of support already in congress. Adding yours, particularly, will increase the momentum. This is a United Nations Initiative. Its been running for about twenty years already and nearly every country has made contributions of historical places, or natural wonders. These unique places become the property of the United Nations, in trust for the people of the world. They also come under our laws, much a diplomatic embassy in a foreign country. We're constantly looking for new candidates. Our satellite photography has brought us around to a small place, which we think fits right into the program. I think you'll agree. I hope so. I know you'll recognize it." Patrick put down his drink and took the papers and scanned quickly down to highlighted text.

"You've got to be kidding."

"We're not."

"You're in for nothing but trouble."

"But we'll be victorious in the end."

"It'll cost you dearly. It won't be easy."

"We're prepared. The question is: Do we have your support?"

Patrick shook his head as he read further down the page. He let the papers fall onto the floor and picked up his drink. He finished it in a single gulp.

"It won't be worth it", he said.

"Do we have your support? Yes, or no?"

Patrick looked at the man across from him. The lighting in the room caste his face in a different light and for a moment, he looked sinister, until Ben's facial muscles formed the inquiry, waiting for Patrick's reply.

"..............Yes."

"Good! To Tall Trees". Ben saluted and downed his own drink.

———

It was the Spring of 2001 and the millennium had rolled over without a hitch. JC sat on the covered porch at the end of the day, his boots up on the railing. He gazed across the ranch to the Cascade range and Mt. Shasta, as he had thousands of times. He was thinking back, how his life had turned out in ways he hadn't expected.

He was recalling, almost twelve years ago now, the death of his parents. Danny had come home for the funeral, but not Patrick. They had sent word, but got no reply except for a bouquet of flowers. Matt was pissed at his brother, he threatened to go down to Oakland and kick his butt. He was easily talked out of it, though. Danny had come back and spent a week with him at the ranch. It was a wonderful visit. He was so proud of his older brother. Danny's career had been stellar; twelve years with the Seals, including as an instructor/trainer. He then spent four years with the Undersecretary of Defense Intelligence in Washington DC. He had gone back to school at George Mason and got his Masters in Economics and later, a PHD. Now, he was an advisor to the Joint Chiefs. He had been so for the past six years and across two administrations.

JC relived the walk back down to the house from the little graveyard on the hill. It was getting full. In some ways, he thought, it was better that they went together, Bobby and Vera. They had become like one, anyway. Whenever he thought of the accident he had to shake visions out of his head, physically. He remembered walking down the little road when his grandpa Connor was buried. Everyone dressed a little better, but not fancy. The conversation somewhat hushed. People sharing private thoughts.

The last twelve years had brought many changes to his life. Not long after the accident, he met a girl, Janine Cook. They had started out friends and the friendship had grown. It had never been a hot love affair. More, it was a companionship agreement. He was getting old as a bachelor. She had been married once, had a child, but this prior marriage had been a disaster. The boy was a troubled youth and was sent to prison on a five year stint for armed burglary. The father was somewhere in Arizona, at forty-five, trying to live the life of an eternal twenty-three year old in tank tops and cutoffs.

The early days of the marriage had been sweet and comforting to both of them. They had a lot in common, seeing things the same way, both with an easy sense of humor. But their efforts at having a child of their own were thwarted. Yes, she was getting near the end of her biological clock, but the doctors said that wasn't the problem. They had the best infertility specialists that money could buy, but in the end, she could not give him a child. And this, he wanted more than anything. He loved Matt and Sandy and the kids, and Angelina's family too, but part of him, like every man, wants to see something of himself carry on. He swigged now on the tall neck beer bottle. Somewhere in the psyche, it seemed important that he was there. That he had lived on and walked upon the earth. The lasting proof is offspring. At times he wrestled with that demon, explaining to himself that the facts don't support that egocentric notion. The world gets along just fine without us, or our offspring. But now those pains were buried deep enough to be forgotten.

They had turned to adoption and adopted a young boy of two years old. The parent was an unwed mother, a young girl who consistently made bad, no atrocious, decisions in her life. The one thing she had done right was to give the child up for adoption. Her family was a mess, and her own drug and alcohol problems forced her to the decision. A friend of a friend had known Janine and, well, it happened. The problems started out pretty quick; some mild abnormalities of behavior. By the second grade, there were some significant learning disabilities. Fetal Alcohol Syndrome may have been the problem, or perhaps the mother had done more serious drugs during the pregnancy. He was a good kid, and JC loved him. He tried to do a lot of things normal dads do with their sons. Perhaps, he thought, there is no normalcy, when it comes to kids. There is only your kids and other peoples. Quinten, or Quint as he was called, made friends pretty easy and seemed to show some real promise from time to time, though his grades were typically mediocre at best. JC could handle the deficiencies of the boy because he also saw some promise. Janine, however, took all the failure, biological and otherwise upon herself. This was a mentally and emotionally flawed response. There is no heartbreak like a woman's when it comes to issues of infertility. It is simply on a level that men cannot understand, though they have their own issues with progeny.

Three years back, they received a phone call from the warden at Pelican Bay Correctional Facility. There had been trouble. Her only son had been killed; stabbed to death in the showers. No one saw any of the fifty-seven wounds take place. Epithets had been written on the wall, but the warden saw no point in going into details. An investigation was under way, the warden was saying, when Janine put the phone back down into the cradle. For the past two years Janine had fallen into a depression. Their marriage was nearly unbearable to JC, not because he didn't love her or care about her, but that there was no affection, no touching. To see her, haggard and sullen, eyes shrunk back into their sockets, he could more easily feel pity than love. She rarely ate, but he and Quint did their best to keep her in what health she had. They had moved into the main house, but now it seemed too big. The emptiness sometimes felt cavernous given the pain that emanated from the upstairs bedroom of Janine's.

The screen door opened and nine year old Quint came out.

"Pull up a chair, son, and sit down for awhile." He scooted a nearby chair up alongside JC's and then pushed it closer to the edge so his own boots would reach up the rail. He effected the same pose as his dad. JC smiled to himself.

"So how was school today?"

"Good."

"No trouble, eh?"

"No." He was quiet and looked out across the vista for a moment.

"Sam Jasperson tried to start a fight with me, though."

"Yeah? How come he would do that?"

"He's a jerk. That's why."

"Yep. That'll sure do it........... Every time. Well, what did you do?"

"Nothing............Then I hit him in the mouth."

"Hmmh............................. Should I be expecting a call from the school?"

"No.... Yeah.... Maybe. I don't know."

The phone rang in the house and JC looked at Quinten, a look of resignation on his face.

"Well, here we go." He got up and went in to answer it. As he did, a letter JC had half sat on, fell to the wooden porch floor. It had an important looking design on it, a seal. The United States Government was the sender. Quentin set it back down and waited for his dad's return, wondering the punishment that awaited him. Soon enough his dad strode back onto the porch and put his boots back up on the rail. Quint's head was down and he stole a sideways glance at his dad.

"Well it looks like you're going to get to spend a couple of extra days with me. There is plenty of work to do so plan on being busy." A faint smile broke across Quint's face as he realized his dad was being very understanding of this school business. Relaxing a bit himself, he scrunched down in the chair and put his own boots up on the rail.

"How is mom today?"

"'bout the same."

"What's the letter about, dad?"

"This?" he held up the opened envelope. "This is from a bunch of people that want to buy part of our property and make it a place where everyone can come and enjoy it."

"Part of our ranch?"

"Yes. Tall Trees. They want to make it part of the United Nations World Heritage Site program."

"But 'tall trees' belongs to us. They want to buy it? Are you going to sell the ranch?" he asked animatedly.

"No. We are not selling the ranch and we're not selling them a big part of the middle of it. There would be no way to keep our privacy here. They'd build a paved road into there, put in public restrooms, self-guided tours. I don't mind showing it to people. It is a miracle of God's. That's for sure. But we've taken good care of it for a hundred and twenty-five years. We've managed the forest around it, taken out any infested trees nearby. I figure we'll take care of it another hundred years, if the Lord don't come back first. Would you be willing to take care of the ranch after I'm gone, son?"

"I don't know, dad. It's a lot." JC laughed.

"Well, let's hope you don't have to worry about that for awhile yet. Meanwhile let's go fix your mom some dinner. Maybe we can get her to eat something. What do you say?"

"You bet."

"I feel like breakfast for dinner. Why don't we fix her pancakes, with sausage and eggs?" The boy instinctively rubbed his belly and affirmed that it was an excellent idea. They went into the kitchen and began making a decidedly happy mess, as only two males that don't belong in a kitchen can do. Their efforts were as much about bridging that gulf that sometimes spans between a father and his son; in seeking that place where the veil between them lifts and they discover a place, for a moment when they simply love each other.

———

It was several months later that a white suburban with tinted windows all around pulled into the driveway of Grady-O'Hare. An insignia emblazoned on the door. Two men got out, both in casual attire and came up onto the porch. JC had been in the office looking over dismal financial conditions. The cattle business was in what seemed a perpetual state of decline. Timber was equally bad, with a lot of foreign wood, subsidized by their respective governments, coming into the country. Simultaneously, the cost of local timber harvesting raised dramatically. The cost of compliance with laws and regulations, and sometimes lawsuits, overwhelmed the efficiencies produced by better machinery and procedures. The offramp properties were holding their own, but development there was at a standstill. He had heard the crunch of the gravel under the tires and made his way to the porch to see who the unexpected guests might be.

"Mr. O'Hare?"

"Yes, sir. What can I do for you gentlemen?"

"I'm Fred Ingman", said the larger man, "and this is Aaron Tilbow, my associate." The men shook hands and JC tried to pick off some of the words on the insignia on the car but couldn't.

"We're private citizens working on a program for the Department of Interior..... Parks and Recreation to be exact. Uh, could we talk with you for a minute?"

Warily, JC walked them down the porch to an entrance to his office.

"Sure. We can talk in my office." The men came in and sat down. The smaller man, Tilbow, was dressed in a deep blue long sleeve shirt with some meaningful brand mark up near the collar, wide wale corduroy pants and ankle high boots with fashionable swatches of color. He had a multi-pocketed vest of heavy canvas with gads of buttons and lanyards hanging from it. He was a very mild looking man, gentile in fact, as if sheltered. His manners bespoke intelligence. The other, larger fellow, had a large gut hanging over his belt, thick black hair that looked wet, was parted and combed hard to the other side of his head. They were a little bit like Laurel and Hardy in that they appeared an unlikely pairing.

"Now, how can I help you?", asked JC. The large man, Fred, spoke first.

"Mr. O'Hare, Parks and Recreation have been fortunate in the budget process and have sizable funding for improvements to our existing parks, and there is money for new acquisitions. The parks of the future will tend to be much smaller than the big national parks, like Yellowstone or Yosemite, for obvious reasons. Nevertheless, there is growing demand to preserve unique cultural and natural sites within our country. And this isn't just our country. This is really a world wide movement."

"Hold on, now. Are you fellows connected with these guys that want to buy Tall Trees?" The men looked quickly at each other.

"Only loosely, Mr. O'Hare. We are private people and we belong to a private organization. We have a contract with US Government to help them make acquisitions. We provide park design, property appraisals, negotiations, including offering some incredible tax benefits to people such as yourself. I'm guessing you like saving taxes. Who of us doesn't?" The two men tried to instigate a group chuckle.

Tilbow opened up. "Mr. O'Hare, some time back you were sent a letter regarding your property."

"I received your letter and long ago threw it away. Gentlemen, I am not interested in selling any portion of this ranch to you or anybody associated with you. I thank you for your time, but I see no point in continuing this conversation."

Tilbow continued. "I certainly understand, Mr. O'Hare; uh....., may I call you JC?" JC nodded for him to continue but a look of exasperation was coming upon his face.

"I researched the history of your family. It was very interesting. I am certain you want to leave a legacy to your son and the rest of your extended family. We can help you do that and do it in a very substantial way. We are in a position to protect this place, to allow you to carry on much of what you do here without any interference. We can be extremely generous in our appraisal of the assets we wish to buy. We can also be very ...very helpful in allowing some development down at the offramp. Due to special provisions in the law, which is a United Nations Treaty, we can treat the purchase tax free to you. There are a couple of hoops to go through but they're minor and we can guide you through them." There was silence as JC pondered this for a moment.

"Gentlemen, I thank you for your time and efforts here, but I'm not interested in your proposal or any of the benefits you've promised me. Anything you give me that I haven't acquired rightfully on my own can and will be used against me and this I understand fully."

"JC, I would ask you to please reconsider. We can be very generous here. But you should know there are means to acquire this property, legally, against your will, as a matter of public interest and that would be a shame. The public's good is all we're after here and I'm certain we can treat your family well and this place with respect."

"Mr. Tilbow, the answer is no! And I don't appreciate your veiled threats, nor your offer to give me preferential treatment at the hands of the tax code. I have no doubt that you've got plenty of money, mostly other peoples', whom you've managed to expropriate 'for the public good', but no part of Grady-O'Hare is for sale and especially not to you." The two men stood up and after a moment extended their hand.

"Just think about it, Mr. O'Hare. That is all we ask." JC, shook their hands and they left. He remained at his desk and thought about what just happened. He looked at the business cards, they left on his desk. The email address at the bottom was Tilbow's name @ Greenworld dot something slash something slash. He tossed it onto the desk. Though he had said his heart and spoken his mind, he sensed a certain darkness come over him. He did what he rarely did any more these days. He stepped from around his desk and very deliberately got down on his knees and began praying. Hard. Something in him compelled this act.

—

"Thank you................. Thank you.............................
Thanks............ Please be seated.............Thank you," said
the man at the podium. The huge crowd was enthusiastic. It was a symposium for global awareness. The banner
across the top of the stage said "Greenworld Now !" A
rock band had warmed up the crowd at the Cow Palace
in San Francisco. The press was there as the promoters had
lavished perks on them and promised good footage and
a special surprise. At the podium was the new president.
The cameras zoomed in on his perfect suit and classy tie.
The hair was immaculate. The grooming perfect. Former
Senator Patrick O'Hare accepted the office of President
of Greenworld dot USA. It had been a political gamble.
But this was his chance to have more of an international
platform, and he was able to hand pick is successor to the
Senate seat. The truth was that Byron Semensky, was little
more than a cardboard cutout for O'Hare and Benjamen
Geiss.

The crowd was a mixture of aged hippies, men and
women almost gender neutral, dreadlocks, everyday
housewives, walking mannequins from the display windows of LL Bean. But all were obviously enthusiastic and
committed to their goal. Their goal was ostensibly an environment free from the pollutants of industry, unshackled
from the despotism of over-population, where life sustain-
able as they imagine it, could be, and must be obtained.
And apparently, now. The crowd was fed the typical raw
meat of industrial and capitalist villains. Never mind they
all came by car, mostly Volvos, or public transportation;
hardly products of a pastoral agrarian utopia.

Their new leader led them through a canned chant,
showing pictures of Republican politicians or industrial
leaders, followed by some negative hyperbole. The crowd
was enjoying it and so was Patrick, when all of a sudden
the cameras on him swung to the left and then settled

on a half dozen people, both men and women, all painted green but otherwise naked, who streaked across the
stage. It was classic and the crowd erupted in approval.
Patrick just shook his head, while flashing the smile of acceptance though his head swayed gently in the negative. Finally he spoke as if his remarks were spontaneous.

"Forty years ago we had the 'Blue Meanies'. But to-
day, ... I think we just saw the ...." And here the
crowd dutifully answered to hilarious laughter. ".........., the
Green Weanies!" It took awhile to get things settled down
and then he began a serious speech. He talked about the
need for a new mindset, a global thinking to replace the
worn out thinking within national boundaries. He spoke
not only of personal sacrifice to make the world safe for
our children's children, but about political responsibility
to change the course of history. To remove the chains of
bondage to a capitalistic system which benefited only
the few at the expense of the many.

"With your help we can start a new beginning. The beginning of hope. Hope for the world man has dreamed of
since the beginning of time. A world free of war, or worry,
of hunger, of want. The world we, in this gathering, see
is a world where there is finally peace. Where we live in
harmony with the other creatures of the planet, where we
can act like the part of the earth that we are. No longer in
conflict with other species, or our own brothers and sisters,
whether they are black, green brown, yellow, Muslim, or
Buddhist, Hindu or Athiest." He droned on, as Ben Geiss
his political mentor, looked on from a monitor in a private
room back stage.

"He's good", he said to the men who sat in the darkness with him watching a panel of monitors. Several were
on Patrick, many more were on the crowd itself. Some on
the exits and key security positions. The heads nodded in
agreement.

———

JC was in his office on the first of September 2001 when a Fed Ex van pulled into the driveway. A young man jumped out in a hurry as JC came out on the porch. The man scanned the envelope and then another and handed them up to him, not coming all the way up on the porch.

"Thank you", said JC. "Two ?" he said.

"Yep. See ya Mr. O'Hare." He sped back down the long driveway.

He sat down at his desk and opened the LetterPaks with a pocket knife usually on his desk.

The first one was from a lawyer's office in San Francisco. He was being sued and the corporate ranch was being sued by Patrick O'Hare. It was for a partition action of the ranch or for a pay off of the sum of $6,500,000 for his 25% interest. He read on but that was the gist of it. 'That's crazy', he thought. 'The whole place is only worth eight to ten million, and this is a bad market and we've got some debt still.' Disgusted, he threw down the envelope and picked up the other and opened it.

It was from the United States Government. They were suing him for Tall Trees, under eminent domain. There was a court order to allow appraisers and foresters onto the property for purposes of establishing values.

"You sons of bitches," he cursed aloud.

These days became tense with meetings of attorneys, his own appraiser, accountants and discussions with politically connected friends. Pepe and Matt ran the day-to-day of the ranch. It seemed like his own life was being frittered away on fighting fights that shouldn't have to be fought and whose outcome was uncertain. This included Janine's ongoing depression, which was worsening. Quint was getting by, but just barely. Behavior issues continued at school and his academic performance was discouraging. Doctors had him on Ridalin and cocktail mixes of behavior altering drugs, but JC wondered if they weren't more the problem than the solution. Quint seemed to do better working on the ranch and not taking the drugs. The businesses he was engaged in seemed to be suffering downturns. All of them. Money was flowing out, not in. Fortunately, he had a reserve of several million dollars and credit. But this was dissipating quickly. Grady-O'Hare, according to his own estimations, was worth about nine million dollars and he owed about two and a half on it. He had just finished going over financial statements and poured himself some coffee. Discouraged, he walked in and turned on the TV for a few minutes of news. It was 9:05 am on September 11, 2001.

———

In the days, weeks, months and years that followed, America changed. The natural consequence of the attack on it's shores was an increase in security. This comes always at the expense of freedom. The country pulled together as it hadn't in decades, for about six months. Soon the partisan bickering returned. There is nothing quite so strong nor urgent as the need to take political advantage when opportunity allows. While the enemy was clearly the virulent strain of Islam, referred to as Jihadists, the debate droned on as to the causes; America's foreign policy, the Israeli-Palestinian issues, American military bases in Muslim territory (such as Saudi Arabia), economic disenfranchisement of the Arab street. To the left, it was, as always, America's fault-for whatever reason. Everyone wanted the country better protected, but groused at the mechanisms for doing so, which universally eroded liberties and privacy.

Soon, the country retaliated. The military engaged the enemy in Afghanistan, routing the Taliban. These were the drug dealing maniacal fundamentalists of Islam. They were driven from power very quickly, but then started the insurgency. In 2003, America attacked Iraq and overthrew Saddam Hussein. Then began the real war; part occupation, part nation building, part religious, part economic. It sometimes bordered on a civil war but always an insurgency. This went on through the end of the George W. Bush administration at which time, the country elected the most liberal US Senator then sitting, Barry Perkins on the political promise of change and hope.

His rise to power was nothing short of remarkable; spawned in the political crucible of south side Chicago. He was raised on the milk of political extremism on the left and steady diet of Black Liberation Theology. His associations bridged the shady and elegant, but always far to the political left. His political career was meteoric in that he went from street or community organizer, to the state senate, then to the US Senate. Part way through his first term, he ran for president and was elected, requiring someone else to finish the first term. He had never owned or ran a business, nor held any executive office. His only full term was as a state senator, a collaborative roll, not executive. Now he was the most powerful man in the world. His youth and inexperience would not register against a fawning press corps, a youthful electorate and many Americans who simply succumbed to his eloquence in the promises of change and hope.

At this time of world history, Russia was flexing its muscle as in the old days of the former Soviet Union. Now, flush with petrodollars from record high oil prices, they sought to reacquire power over, if not the actual, former states. A huge oil and gas pipeline project now fed western Europe and the Russians did not hesitate to turn off its spigot even in the dead of winter.

Where oil was concerned, the Arab states raked in trillions of dollars over a few short years, and with those funds supported and financed by the Wahabi strain of Sunni Islam. In Muslim countries they established and funded madrassas, schools of hatred and illiteracy, save for the Koran, the Hadith and Sharia law. They built mosques, established chairs of Islamic and Middle-Eastern studies at prestigious universities in the west. Eager for the money, the universities gladly let the camel's nose under the tent. This had gone on for several decades but accelerated when oil increased in value and price.

America fought what was misnamed 'a war on terror'. But terror is a tactic not an enemy, any more than one declares war against artillery. Such obfuscation on the most primary level only serves the cause of the enemy. The enemy is a group of people-always. Not a tactic. They are either of one or more nations, or of ideology and/or faith. By far the enemies with a nation, with real estate to protect, are easier to fight than those of ideological or religious persuasion. If no nation declares its formal support, then large military contingents such as possessed by superpowers, are doomed to fight difficult and asymmetrical wars.

America had a vast and open country and culture. Its weaknesses, easily exploited and its vulnerabilities difficult to protect. It's Jihadist enemies were both quick and skillful in taking advantage of the freedoms found in the west. They would use the democratic principles and processes to overthrow, though they would never allow them in their own notion of a Sharia driven caliphate.

The asymmetry was more than just the battle field of real estate. The west, including America, contended with a press that saw the world first from an anti-capitalist mentality, second, from an anti-semitical viewpoint. Unable to undergo withdrawal from some form of self loathing, the western press was a useful idiot to a committed enemy. The asymmetry of propaganda was Islam's greatest weapon against the west. And committed they were. Willing to fly airplanes into buildings, blow up commuter trains, subways, seeking weapons of mass destruction in order to subdue their enemy, their commitment to jihad and either the total submission (Islam means 'submission') or destruction of their enemy was absolute. They publicly beheaded their captors, innocent but infidels just the same.

This at a time of rampant lawsuits and debates over the ability of the government to listen to citizens' phone calls, or track them in ways not previously done. A prison of captured Jihadists was held offshore on America's portion of the island of Cuba, at Guantanimo Bay. In trying to keep them out of the United States courts, the former administration held them without any notion of release. Upon the taking of the oval office in 2009, the prison was to be closed. In the end, the Jihadists acquired the rights of a United States citizen precisely and only because they tried to kill them. Had they attempted to kill or war against any other group of citizens, they would never have been accorded such valuable personal rights. They never had the rights, and would never have them in their own country. Such was the now upside down war on 'terrorism'. Fleets of ACLU lawyers came to the rescue of the Guantanimo prisoners. The legal asymmetry was breathtaking. In the caves of Tora Bora, the Al-Queda stronghold, there were smiles and laughter. Around the palaces of Riyadh, there were smiles and winks.

———

CHAPTER 2

The Panic of '08 would ultimately become one of the worst economic events in world history. Leading houses of finance on both sides of the Atlantic fell with stunning speed, though they had survived the "great depression". The new administration of President Perkins and its Treasury Secretary would end up pumping nearly five trillion into the economic system. The politics of the era were that of a government claiming to be beneficent by beating the capitalist system to a pulp. Once again, the unholy alliance of a media in concert with the government controlled the perception of the ignorant masses. And in America, the masses were ignorant indeed. For decades, the schools had substituted folly for education. Most highschoolers knew little of history, particularly an honest history of America, but could drivel endlessly about equality of sexual orientations, or the culture of homophobia. They had been disconnected from the truth of their past, and so were cutoff from what should have been their destiny. Instead, their education was squandered on worthless opinions to be accepted, and regurgitated with an Orwellian disposition to group-think.

The economy no longer resembled capitalism after the mauling. It was an empty husk of its former self, only capable of being stood up like a tortured prisoner, to endure yet another round of transmogrification. This happened because its critics kept finding *human* faults and failures with capitalism and free markets. They kept pointing at elements of embezzlement and greed; a human failing in any and all systems.

People at the top were always overpaid, and at the bottom the line workers were under appreciated and recompensed. Those of an anti-capitalistic mentality pounded their fists, saying "No more!", then administered thirty nine more lashes of regulations to the only system that ever produced enough wealth to distribute it broadly, creating the largest and wealthiest middle class in history. And this same middle class fought more wars, sacrificing more of its children on behalf of freedom and has given more of that wealth away as a blessing to the poor of other nations than all the empires of history put together. This is the legacy of capitalism and free market economics........... to the extent they were allowed to exist.

World leaders were all in the same boat. The western European and Scandinavian nations were beginning to collapse under the weight of a half century of socialism. Blue eyed, blond haired septuagenarians eagerly waited for the retirement check for a lifetime spent in a bureaucracy that produced nothing. They had spent a lifetime creating regulation often diminishing the efforts of producers. Yet, they thought their contribution was equal. The problem was that two generations had come through the post WWII system, where they produced insufficient offspring, preferring instead a life devoted to self and selfishness; mandatory paid vacations of four to six weeks. Life was lived when one went on 'Holiday'. So while the happy recipients of the early generation of socialist largess largely got away with it, it was not to last long. Without sufficient children to pay into this Ponzi system and perform the country's labor, and put money in at the bottom, the labor had to be imported. This, largely from Islamic countries of the middle-east.

The liberal leaders held fast to their egalitarian principles and waved the banner of political correctness at any mention of impending trouble from the immigrant class. While most Muslims may have appreciated the wider freedoms and economic opportunities of western democracies, the radical Islamists among them did not. Terrorism became the daily occurrence with the Israelization of France, England, Spain, Germany, the Benelux countries, and all Scandinavia. It transformed the continent. The increasing tax burden necessary to maintain lifestyles of the ever larger anglo-retiree population would have to fall on the backs of their few and dwindling descendants and increasingly upon the burgeoning Muslim minority. It was a recipe for revolution.

All developed economies were suffering. Some nations sought to take advantage of the global turmoil to advance their own dreams of hegemony. The global recession became a depression in China, which had been the darling economy for a decade. There began a revolution as the freedom obtained through its golden, market oriented years, told its people how good life could be. That freedom, risk taking and capitalism was not the enemy but the way of the future. It started with riots over job losses and through the following two years would evolve to food riots and civil war. While it focused on its internal problems, it warned competitive nations on the world stage not to take advantage of any perceived vulnerabilities.

The trillions expended in 'stimulus' spending not only by the United States as the lead economy, but by western European, Asian and Latin American countries grew exponentially. The economic solution seemed to be more money. It didn't matter where it went as long as central banks issued more of it-lots more. Deficits would become meaningless at somewhere above forty trillion dollars. This was done in just over a year.

By mid 2010, the economic misery seemed to flatten out, owing to the bizillions of dollars and other currencies, having been pumped into the system. Stable prices started inching upward responding to the currency in circulation. Finally, in 2011, the stimulation took hold like a cartoon character's pinwheeling legs when they gain traction at last. The price indexes shot up on a near vertical trajectory. Fuel and foods doubled in less than three months, then settled back to fifteen percent per month. Within eight months, shortages of critical goods and medicines were unobtainable. Factories were trying to start up and there was tremendous demand for energy. This quickly jumped into the general price of all goods and services. The oil industry had been capping wells as the price of oil fell to $18 per barrel. It skyrocketed once again past $100 per barrel in weeks on its way to $300 per barrel. Soon the weakest currencies began to collapse. All of them suffered as commodity prices and precious metals soared. The previous gold high had been about $1,100 per ounce. It shot past $2,000 without flinching. Then $4000. Then $7,500 per ounce. With every economy trying to kick start itself, demand for energy was unprecedented. Unfortunately, the middle-east continued its long standing blood feud, between the sons of Isaac and Ishmael.

Soon the Euro, the pound sterling, the yen and the dollar all fell to new lows. Then it happened. The London Riots of 2011. Here, Muslim youths for nine days took control of Buckingham Palace and The House of Lords, kidnapping the prime minister. He was beheaded and the video posted on the internet. There was a sense of outrage, but no punishment for it. England had become too weak and it now sat down its head of state pro-tem, a devotee of political correctness and appeasement, to negotiate a new constitution for the country. A pathetic scene of a dying civilization pleading to live a little longer, a plea to defer its execution versus an ascending barbaric tribal power intent on inflicting its laws and customs on all under its dominion. Goodbye Magna Carta, hello Sharia Law.

The United Nations, happy that the London "issue" had been resolved 'peaceably', dusted off its hands, while Sharia Law was installed veritably between breakfast and lunch in what had been one of the world's greatest Christian empires. The sun had finally set on the British Empire ......forever.

Happily, they then took up the currency issue. It was unanimously resolved to abolish all national currencies into one currency. At last, the bureaucrats at the UN's economic department could boast they had resolved the seeming chaos of currency markets. No longer would robber barons make billions sitting around their computers trading yens for yuans, pesos for rubles. There would only be one currency-Global Units, or as they were affectionately called by the public relations firm that advised the commission "UNIs"

Those that had stashed away cash were given a brief time to convert. Soon after, they might as well burn their dollars.

The UNIs were backed by a basket of commodities. There were four components in the basket; precious metals, industrial metals, food stuffs, and energy. Each of the components had a subset component:

Precious metals, included 50% gold, 40% silver and 10 % platinum. The precious metals basket was 30% of the backing of the UNI.

The Industrial metals included 25% iron ore, 25% copper, 10% aluminum, and 40% of other metals, such as zinc, cadmium, nickel, etc. The Industrial basket was 25% of the backing.

The Food Stuffs basket was 30% various grains, 20% fertilizers, 35% corn and beans of all sorts, 15% citrus and juices. This basket was 20% of the backing of the UNI.

The Energy component was 65% oil, broken into several sub-types, 20% coal and 15% natural gas. The energy basket was 25% of the backing of the UNI.

While the currency was an improvement over the fiat currencies of the twentieth century, it did little to allay the fears of globalism that many people had, particularly among Americans. In America, the damage had already been done.

During 2009-2010, the American economy gasped for air. Bloated governments, from the federal to the hick towns in the sticks, could not pay their bills. Unlike the federal government, local political subdivision could not print their money. They were quick to cut back services, but reluctant to trim their rolls of workers. Soon the absurdity was apparent. Fewer work days was no answer to a budget crises. Riots broke out as the public servants in most rural areas were paid twice the median incomes of the residents they were to serve. Cutting back meant they didn't go to work and still earned the bulk of their pay checks... until the well went dry. Banks shut the door in the faces of mayors, governors and county administrators. The system went bankrupt. It wasn't long before the jails emptied for lack of paid officers and food.

———

JC and Quint went to Yreka, the county seat, in order to look at some deeds in the Recorder's Office. It was business for JC and something new and not-in-school for Quint, so he was happy to come along with dad. Sometimes living at the ranch for extended periods leaves one disconnected with the town life.

"Well now, this is unusual", said JC. "Normally, you can't find a parking place in front of the courthouse like this. Did I miss a holiday? Let's see". He thought for a moment.

"It's not a holiday, dad."

"Just our good luck I guess." They locked the pickup and walked up to the steps, where they saw a makeshift sign printed on standard copy paper and scotch taped to the door.

"Courthouse Closed
Tuesday-Thursday
Thank You."

They peered through the glass doors. It was dark. No one was there. It was Tuesday. So they drove around town. It had been awhile since they had come to Yreka, probably a month. The changes were depressing. Several of the old motels on the highway were closed, no longer willing to give it a go. As they drove around, numerous small retail stores were boarded up. Some had soaped their display windows. They decided to go get a bite to eat and headed off to Poor Henry's, a favorite place of theirs. They pulled up, but it was closed, too.

"Sweet Jesus, what has happened to this town?" asked JC to himself. Quint was silent but observant.

The Wal-Mart was open and several fast food outlets as well. It was nearly lunch time.

"Let's head on home. We'll fix us something there."

"Okay", said Quint. They eased the pickup back down the highway, mindful of gas consumption.

CHAPTER 3

Fall, 2011

In the weeks and months to pass, the State of California claimed a form of bankruptcy to become a ward of the federal government. A magistrate was put in charge. There were many other states also in financial as well as political bankruptcy, but California's was breathtaking. Its police, public works and judicial system was administered from Washington DC. Federal troops kept the highways safe. All public works projects stopped. Tribunals were set up to make quick work of the jammed courts. Non-violent criminals were set free and room was made for more violent criminals and people who did not pay their taxes. A special contempt existed in the courts where owed taxes would not or could not be paid. It mattered little, that a lifetime of productivity and consistent tax payments had issued forth from the citizen. It was about making examples of people. Murder convictions? Eight to twenty years. Tax evasion? Twenty years. Period.

Government from head to toe, went into crisis mode. Fire stations were abandoned throughout the state. Some tried to keep them going with qualified and well intentioned retired volunteers. But union laws were broken to accomplish it. Under threats of prison, the volunteers eventually went home, understanding the futility of simply trying to help. Unionism had reversed its dismal course in only a few years under the Perkins administration regaining great power, and wielding it. Policemen, too, walked off the job, no longer being paid. Finally, after all the critical people were cut, they let go the jobs that never had a real justification in the first place except to further some popular abstract social goal to fruition and bring all human enterprise into compliance with inane laws. Many of these laws long ago lost their purpose-certainly their relevance in a time of crisis. The absurdity blossomed fully. In nearly the same year the bureaucrats regulated the 100 watt light bulb out of existence, people were dying over 5 gallon cans of gasoline.

Retirement checks for the hundreds of thousands of state workers quit coming. There simply was nothing to pay them with. Riots in Sacramento brought to light the anger that these former state workers felt, but the only people to be mad at were the hapless taxpayers, who themselves, had suffered immeasurably and lived without even the pretense that they would be financially cared for. The mask of the greatest scheme of 'something for nothing' was coming off. It was a raw and ugly face underneath. In conclusion, it was the state itself and the state's workers and their unions that had gobbled up the reserves and drained every account. They had paid out what there was. Nothing was left. Like the last days of Rome: Everywhere one turned was the remaining facade of greatness that once was, but now was void of life, nourishment and vitality. It had all been lost. The game was over.

The ensuing months were extremely difficult in rural communities and areas like Siskiyou County. But the big city metro areas were worse. In San Francisco, the real estate market, had crashed long ago and the crime level was intolerable by many of its residents. It had turned into a squatter's paradise. Street people from the Tenderloin district, occupied homes for free that were once valued handsomely. Soon they turned them into crack homes, seedy flophouses, where the vilest of human acts occurred. What once was prime residential real estate was reduced to the equivalent of a glorified cardboard refrigerator box for the homeless.

As the decline accelerated, the remaining residents huddled as captives in their own dwellings. Soon the drug-crazed criminal class had burned through the goods and comforts they had commandeered. Then the nightly raiding parties began with forays into the adjoining neighborhoods. There was no law, only lawlessness-mayhem. What occurred there, to the families and elderly, frozen in fear of what lay one foot outside their own threshold, made the chaos of Hurricane Katrina appear as a boyscout summer camp. Here, there was no natural disaster. God could not and would not be blamed. This was purely the debauchery of man, inspired by willful evil. The marauding gangs, bodies diseased and crazed with drugs or the clenched jaws of withdrawal symptoms, roamed at will with crude weapons through the streets. Those that survived each night, would one-by-one walk from their homes the next day, no longer safe from being accosted on the street and unable to defend themselves due to the prohibition on guns which they had imposed upon themselves. Of course, those who had guns fared much better.

In Los Angeles, it was a war zone. Gangs asserted control over entire portions of the city. All over California, the social fabric strained by forty years of tolerance of any and every type of behavior except proper. It was coming apart. Not at the seams, but ripped and shredded in its entirety. The mass dismissal of less onerous criminals from the prisons, might have, under better circumstances, had kinder results. The society that had imprisoned them, now lay before them, as helpless as a constrained rape victim. It was too much, and it brought out the worst in them. Rape and pillage became a street side spectacle. Instead of redemption, there was only retribution.

Yet, for some, a few, life struggled on, stumbling forward out of shear momentum. If the job still existed, they were pressed to get up and go to work. But increasingly, it looked like it was becoming pointless. The society was crashing. At some point, it's not worth the risk to get to work. But economic momentum is a hard thing to stop, at least quickly. And the willingness, no, the need for things to appear as they were, was a powerful mental yearning.

——

Small towns in rural counties received the influx of refugees with wariness and alarm. Long used to the rigors of basic life and sustenance, the rural people could not cope with the numbers now flooding into their communities, looking for non-existent food, shelter, or some assurance that they would not perish. The stories of metro sacking spread quickly. Some refugees, were given some basics; food, a night or two of shelter and then told to move on. Food and water would rise to the premium in the market place, that it naturally possessed in the biological order. People died and would be killed for it.

In the evenings, the news channels were showing clips of tax revolts from workers and food riots from non-workers. Marshall law was declared in Washington DC, Atlanta and Los Angeles. News crews took national guard escorts into some California cities, especially where minority ethnic populations had been held by dependence on government. Now the dependence which acted as a narcotic upon the unassimilated was withdrawn in all practical forms. The reversion to a more anomic world was as swift as it was brutal.

As the situation worsened, Grady-O'Hare, like every rural dweller, went into fortress mode. Already, guns and ammunition were not to be found anywhere in the towns, as the stories of the cities spread in check out stands of grocery stores, post office lobbies and cushioned booths in the coffee shops. The gun shops were emptied in a day. All cash transactions. Everything they had. It became a fine and indistinguishable line between prudence and paranoia.

———

Pepe moved his family into JC's old bungalow, nearer the main house. Matthew's house nearby was boarded up and he and Sandy and the kids moved in with JC and Quint. Janine continued to deteriorate in the prison of her own mind, often alone for hours in her bedroom. It was a place whose darkness, broken only by thin dramatic shafts of light through the draperies, and depression was palpable. When entering her room, two things were noted, one, the dwindling lump under the covers, usually beyond recognition and two; that you had halted a single pace into the room as if your own being questioned whether you should proceed.

Interstate 5 became a place of terror, and soon, locals used only the back roads. Too many desperate people. They had once been 'normal', nestled within a society of social norms and material abundance. But now, they had seen the worst of mankind, had fled from it and were slowly morphing into it. Family men, out of gas and food, desperate and frightened beyond anything they had experienced, now wielded firearms or baseball bats. They commandeered other vehicles of similar families. Some were hit by cars, catapulted through the air. No one would stop. Gunfights erupted. While traffic passed by in one lane, life and death vignettes played out in the other lane. It was surreal and the myopic motorists looked away, wanting to flee in all haste.

Most retailers, who carried critical goods, were forced to hire private security. Armed guards, drafted from the local neighborhood, thwarted the now burgeoning criminal class, which grew by the week as the state's prisons emptied one after the other. Still, high level bureaucrats in every department continued to draw down their salaries, but now called in sick so as not to come to work. Everyone hunkered down, hoarding necessities and seeing their lives devolve to a second rate, if not third world nation. Here, life was going to get a lot cheaper, and 'things' a lot more expensive. Those who fared best were those who prepared best. In this time, the goal posts moved in the lives of men from getting ahead to getting by, from success, down to sustenance.

CHAPTER 4

July 30, 2012, Grady-O'Hare

It was a period of gathering. Modern life reverted to a 19th century model of scavenging and improvising. The electrical grid had suffered several major bombings in the Bonnieville area and in Washington State. Key nodes on the nations grid had been damaged. As fast as crews repaired the massive high-tension lines, secondary targets fell. The repair crews were now escorted by helicopter gunships of the National Guard, as the first repair crew all fell to sniper fire.

Electrical generators were traded for luxury cars, but only gold or silver would command a drum of gasoline. Here too, the kind of violence that had occurred in drug deals gone bad a few years earlier now rose to probability in the transfer of a five gallon can of fuel. All commodities were revalued in the grave new world. Consumables that sustained life were the most valuable. Processing goods or machinery plummeted in value. Manufacturing was nearly at a standstill. Pharmaceutical companies continued to operate at full swing under armed guards. Their parking lots looked more like a SWAT event than a day at the office.

At Grady-O'Hare, the gate had been drawn across the access road. Additional wood gathered and split. Old woodstoves, long ago placed in an old barn were re-welded and pressed into service in the house. The generator was rigged up on the back porch, with the exhaust sent out through the wall. Lately the power had been good, over five days without an interruption. In the pantry, there were endless jars of canned vegetables and even meats. In the root cellar were sacks of onions and potatoes. What couldn't be consumed could be traded.

Matt walked across the living room and stared out the big window across the pasture to the county road in the distance. Fewer cars passed by each day. The expenditure of fuel had to be justified by even the careless. The mail truck only came twice a week and there was talk about going down to once a week delivery. As he watched, the mail truck pulled up to the box down at the end of the road and made a deposit. He took a military web belt off the hook in the hallway made of horseshoes and strapped on his pistol, a Glock .45 caliber. He stepped out the door and began the near half-mile walk to the mail box. Halfway there, his eyes spotted yet another carcass of a dead cow. They were losing about three per week to rustling. People killed and butchered out the main portions and left the rest in the interest of speed and time. It occurred at night. There simply was no place to keep the cows that wasn't near a public road. It was one of the drawbacks that had surfaced in the way the world now worked. He shouted out of anger and partly to scare the buzzards and carrion eaters away from the remains. But they did little more than flap their wings a few times, then return to the feast before them.

JC was in his office and on the phone selling a few head of cattle to the local stores. The price had tripled in four months, but they were being stolen blind by the rustling. He figured better to sell some than have them stolen. Often, he bartered for other goods in the store; toilet paper, aspirin, toothpaste. He also traded four cows for a 55 gallon drum of gasoline and five more for a drum of diesel. He needed both. Quint had been busy downloading and printing some homeschool lessons off the internet that he and his dad had discovered and liked. The boy actually did love to learn. He simply needed to have it at his own pace, which seemed to speed up as the weeks went by. Sometimes the power was out for several days. So when it was up, it was time to get a couple of lessons ahead. The online banking, amazingly, continued to work. It was actually superior in reliability to all the things that could go wrong with a physical invoice, mailed payment or visit to the bank.

Pepe and his eldest son were in the shop welding up stronger gate security clasps. All the clasps on barn doors were beefed up as security rose to a new priority. His younger ones schooled with Quint. Sandy, Matt's wife, took special care these days for Janine, though she remained clinically depressed and her general health continued to degenerate.

In the evenings, the entire family sat down at the expanded dining room table and ate. The grace offered at the meal was a little longer than it used to be. It included things it didn't used to. There was no longer any sense that someone would sigh quietly in haste to eat, frustrated by the length of the prayer. No. There was plenty of time for prayer now.

If there was electricity, TV was watched in the big living room on the flat screen, a purchase just before the world seemed to stumble and fall. The news was bleak and the outlook for the economy dismal. The men rolled their eyes in near unison as the reporter explained the latest attempt by the government to 'fix' things.

JC closed a file on his desk and put it into the file cabinet. He had gone through it and figured that, given the way things are, he wouldn't need to worry about it anymore. It contained correspondence and court motions in the government's attempt to take Tall Trees by eminent domain. He recalled, as the metallic drawer slid shut, a heated conversation with Tilbow in the driveway.

They had gotten permission from a neighbor to go onto his property ostensibly for some bird watching. They were packing GPSs, camera and binoculars. They got away from the house and crossed over the fence line onto Grady-O'Hare, between the posted 'No Trespassing' signs, or so they claimed. It so happened they stumbled across Tall Trees and encompassed it with data points, outlining the stand of incredible timber. They had found Billy's old cabin and photographed it, but their day was made when they found an arrowhead near the back wall of the cabin, or what was left of it. The local tribe was contacted. Not the Shasta, which would have been the most likely, but the Karuk which had its own aggressive land use agenda, largely complicit with those of Greenworld and the United Nations program to restore wildlands.

Tilbow had shown up with what turned out to be a report not from bird watchers, but an anthropologist from Chico State and an archeologist from Berkeley. He showed up with a representative from the Karuk Tribe. They claimed jurisdiction over the land. It was not to be tread upon or entered until it was thoroughly researched. They would cordon off the entire area in order to determine what Indians lived there, how they lived and what practices they engaged in.

"This may be sacred ground, in fact, holy ground, Mr. O'Hare", said the tribal representative.

"We believed that Indians once camped and walked here".

JC spat "Your damned right there were Indians here. They were my grandfather's best friends. Old Billy was his name. He and his family lived up there. Hell, he helped build this log house and my family's logging business. This family took care of his family and they all lived together on this property. He's buried in our family cemetery."

Tilbow and the Indian looked at each other in astonishment.

"You have an Indian buried on your property, Mr. O'Hare?"

JC didn't like the tone. "Your damned right I do, and he's gonna' stay there." He was bursting inside with anger.

"And if you two don't get the hell of my property right now, I'm gonna' bury me another one."

The two men scurried to their SUV and shot down the driveway.

Sheriff Smiley had called the next morning.

"What all went on out there yesterday, JC?"

He explained to Everett Smiley, whom he went to high school with and was a strong supporter for sheriff. Smiley warned him to be careful with these types. They usually had friends in high places. But soon, the world's problems overcame this issue and it was falling into the category of another stupid battle that needn't and shouldn't have to be fought.

JC shut off the office lights. There was little business to do anymore. Business was the business of surviving. He shut the door and walked out to the living room where the family had gathered watching the late evening news. It was a large room. There was Pepe and his family, Sandy and Matt. A couple of their kids were laying on the floor with Quint. He grabbed the easy chair that everyone seemed to acknowledge was his alone.

The news anchor was saying that the NYSE had been closed for three weeks straight. Many other exchanges around the world were sporadically open. They usually hit arbitrary loss limits and closed within minutes of opening. Big cities around the world were struggling to keep law and order. Martial law had been declared in many capitals of Europe. Pakistan and India plunged into a media blackout. No one knew what was happening. There was a big crackdown on dissidents in China, who wanted more freedom. The government brutally put down their uprisings and issued communiqués which, in effect, said: 'We'll tell you how much freedom you can have and when you can have it-all in the name of national security and public safety'.

About 11:30, the TV was turned off and everybody started turning in for the night. Pepe and family had left earlier, about 10:00 and walked home to the bungalow. The lights were out over there. The mercury vapor light burned brightly out in the yard between the old log house and the barns, sheds and workshops all clustered together to make the farmstead. Quint's heavy bootsteps went upstairs to his bedroom.

JC pondered on the present circumstances. What had happened to the country he grew up in. How could it have come to this? How long would it be like this? Would it get worse before it got better? He had been taught since a kid what the Bible said and he believed the Bible, but in a way, he didn't want to. He didn't like the fact that he hoped it was not true and didn't like much the realization that he did believe it. The book of Daniel and the book of Revelation had a lot to say about End Times, and it was sure feeling like they were here. He thought to himself; 'If this isn't the Tribulation, I sure don't want any part of *it*.'

He sat in his chair and closed his eyes and prayed, saying nothing. Just thinking the thoughts. He decided he should start with a grateful heart, so he started thinking about all the things he was grateful to God for: He was grateful for his family, for Quint, even though he was not biologically his, for his parents and who they were, for Grady-O'Hare, the life he was blessed to live, even for the few happy years with Janine. He was grateful for his prosperity and health, and here, funny, he felt tears in the corners of his eyes. The means to pull the family together. Even in the turmoil of this present day, how he liked the fact that the family was closer than ever. He was grateful, really thankful that he was born in this country when he had. He knew that his sister, Angelina, was safe. He had talked to her just that day. The schools were closed for budgets, but she and her family were safe and prepared, close by in Yreka. He got to thinking about how God had blessed him and somewhere between that thought and the gift of the Bible, he nodded off to sleep. When he woke up, it was morning. The shaft of sunlight shot straight from the tops of the Cascades, where the sun peeked over the top, and then through the window and lit up his face. Had he seen his face at that moment, head bent, all facial muscle relaxed, his mouth slightly opened, he would have sworn it was his father in the chair.

He took a moment to wake himself and rubbed his face. He moved toward the kitchen in his socks and started to make a pot of coffee. He made some toast, much as his grandfather Connor had done every morning, but he didn't know that. He slipped on his boots and walked out onto the covered porch. The sun was clear of the mountains already, creeping ever skyward. Out on the county road at the end of the driveway, he watched three vehicles drive by, a white van, a blue van and large sedan, like an older Lincoln or something. He sipped the coffee. It was good. He made it stronger than the women did and he liked it that way. The cattle herd, now much smaller, were bunched up over near the hills. Even they had learned to get away from the highway at night. But they were beginning to graze back across the large pasture before him. He heard the cow bell and liked the sound. He sipped the coffee more fully as it began to cool. Again, the three vehicles passed by going in the opposite direction. Maybe it was that they seemed to drive more slowly than most people, and yet they maintained their distance between each other. Obviously they were together. They passed by, going south this time. He thought about them, suspiciously.

The beautiful long shadows of the pines on the pasture, were drawing themselves up, as the sun arced upward. The morning was warming nicely. Thank God, he thought, that God still does his part: The sun rises and sets each day. Rain falls, grass grows. The natural world is remarkably created and designed. It is man's clumsy efforts that do most of the damage to mankind. Even the natural disasters were at least significantly man's doing in terms of the damage to life and property.

People naturally want to live on rivers, coastlines and river deltas and seemed stunned that the rivers flood or that occasional tsunamis strike. Even with all the knowledge of earthquake faults, incredible amounts of capital and life are put at risk. The hurricane swamped city of New Orlean, sat below sea level. Hundreds of billions were spent to rebuild it right after Hurricane Catrina..., right where it was. No levy will hold a hurricane of sufficient force. The San Francisco Bay Area continues to develop, despite the known earthquake faults certain to destroy buildings in the future.

The house awakened and the day moved into production. The large garden, fallen into disuse and overgrown, was now re-established and was growing wonderfully. Sandy and Matt loved tending it. JC strolled through in the evenings and was impressed. Pepe had a garden for his family at JC's old bungalow. They had an old family friend living in the distant house that Sandy and Matt used to live in, over by Mel's cabin. Gerry Jessup and his wife, along with their Down Syndrome son, Jimmy, lived there. Gerry had been a log truck driver. But every year for the last fifteen, there were fewer logs being hauled to the mill out of the forests of Siskiyou County. The public lands were highly contentious as to logging. Environmental groups, both local and distant sued to stop logging. There was always some issue; some potentiality that prevented the project from going forward. Sometimes, evidence that some unbeknownst endangered specie might be present within the area of the logging operations. If that didn't work, issues about the amount of trees to be cut, or potential erosion into tributaries would stop it.

The logging outfits couldn't wait for the lengthy court issues to be resolved. Continuances, the bane of the courts, punished only one side. They confounded the economics of the project, so they would move on. When victory was had by the loggers, the appeals were filed immediately-prepared. The Forest Service, the administrator of those public lands, found themselves wasting their time in court, responding to accusations of procedural infractions or environmental findings, or worse... requests for *additional* environmental studies. Eventually the project was defeated, not on the merits, but because no private vendor could put up with the delays and uncertainty.

When it came to public lands, it was the tragedy of the commons in full bloom and display. Even after forest fires had decimated tens of thousands of acres, the environmental minions would not relent in their pursuit of how things must be. Despite the rotting timber and impending infestation from a host of insects attacking the now weakened and vulnerable timber, loggers could not get permission to 'salvage log' it, i.e., take out the timber while it was still (barely) merchantable, though charred. But the window for salvage is short. In a few years the bugs would finish off the good trees. More lawsuits were filed, the continuances granted and appellate briefs written. Soon all the people who worked in the woods just walked away. The bugs, of course, multiplied exponentially and then attacked the healthy forests adjacent to the burned areas, whether private or public. The bulldozers were silent, the logging equipment was parked. The environmentalists cheered their victories, having success though their pro-bono attorneys, while the rural economies tanked.

———

Private timber lands fared better. They still had strict procedures, but were generally not subject to the radical lawsuit syndrome. Gerry Jessup's log truck had been parked for months and it didn't look like it was ever going to be needed again. JC had told him not to worry about the rent, just keep the place up. It would be fine until things righted themselves.

There was an order for two beef steers in town, at the butcher shop. JC was loading them in a trailer behind the big pickup. Pepe's kids and Quint cut firewood all day. They had nearly ten cords split and stacked, after several long days of work. Everybody worked. Everybody did what they could to produce something or fix things. Pepe still tended to the irrigation.

The phone rang and JC picked it up in the office.

"Hello"

"JC, Ev Smiley here."

"Hi Sheriff, what can I do for you?"

"JC, I've got some bad news for you.

"How is that?, he said, quickly realizing all the family was there at the ranch except Angelina." Is Angelina OK?

"Yes. She's fine as far as I know. We've got a problem at the other house, where Gerry Jessup lives."

"Oh no, what happened?"

"We rolled on a 911, and man are we hoppin' busy with those lately. Anyway, it was an interrupted call. Traced it back to Gerry's place. I got a deputy standing in the living room right now on his cell phone."

"Yes, well what happened."

"It's one of the worst crime scenes he's ever seen. It's Bill Cooper and he's a good man, long time on the force. He walked out of there puking. They're all dead, JC. Murdered. The little boy too."

JC was speechless and sat back in the chair. He had known Gerry and Sarah Jessup nearly all his life. They went to their church in Weed. They were good folks, eager to help a friend or stranger. The sheriff was still talking, but JC missed some of it.

".....all bound and gagged, throats cut ear to ear, ...food taken, all valuables. It may be one of these roving gang groups that have made it up this far. You'll want to keep a sharp eye out.... counting heads and such ....."

JC wavered slightly on his feet, feeling unsteady for a moment. "Ev, is there anything I can do?"

"I don't think so. We'll have the tape up a couple of days, so just stay out. Bill Cooper says the place is trashed. I mean holes in the wall. There is a lot of blood. I mean a lot of blood. For God's sake don't let anybody see it that doesn't have to. Understand?"

"Yeah. Thanks Ev."

"I'm sure sorry to bring you this news. I know you and Gerry go back quite a ways."

"Yeah, I was partial to Sarah and that little boy of theirs too."

"You have any questions,.you gimme a call."

"Likewise Sheriff."

He hung up the phone and started counting heads. There was Matt and Sandy, Pepe's family, some in the wood yard, some in the garden. Quint was splitting wood. Pepe wasn't in yet. Probably still irrigating. He told Matt what happened and said to keep everybody in sight. Keep them in close to the house. Whoever had done this to the Jessups might still be around.

"I'm gonna check on Pepe. He should be up the draw about now."

He left Matt there and set his shotgun on the front seat, jumped in the ranch pickup and started along the road skirting the bottom of the hills and the big pasture. He turned up the draw. The irrigation ditch crossed the road just a short way up the draw. There was a valve there on the ditch with a big stem wheel that turned, opening the gate, letting the water through. There was Pepe's truck, an ancient Ford, the color of a robin's egg. Pepe was no-where to be seen. The hair on the back of his neck raised up as he pulled up along side the old truck and set his brake. He got out and quietly looked around with his truck door still open. His gut churned. He called out.

"Pepe!"

"Hey, boss" came the immediate reply from a few feet behind him, as Pepe walked out from behind a huge Sug-ar Pine, zipping himself up. JC practically jumped out of his skin.

"Jesus, Pepe. Don't scare me like that."

"Hey, remember.............., you called me", he said with a smile.

"I got bad news." He told Pepe what had happened.

"Those were good folks, JC. I don't know what to say."

"Let's get back. We need to secure this place tight as a tick's butt tonight."

"Let's go", said Pepe.

Back at the house, they gathered everybody together. They sat around the big dining table and the day's events were told to everyone. There was some quiet sobbing, and some determined talk. Everyone was going to have to keep their guard up. There was considerable talk about having Pepe's family move into the living room for a couple of days.....until this thing seemed past. It was agreed.

JC, Matt and Pepe all got a cup of coffee and walked out onto the porch and sat in the chairs. They sat in silence for awhile, just staring out across the pasture. Then JC saw something that made him stand up and come to the rail. Three cars were passing by down on the highway, going north, a white van, a blue van and the sedan he had seen earlier. His face flushed as he had forgotten about the unusual way they travelled together.

"Pepe, get me the binoculars, quick." He told them what he had seen that morning, and they each wondered if it had something to do with the Jessups.

"Naw. It wouldn't make sense for them to stick around the area, if they did that. It's probably a family cluster". There had been a number of those coming into the area looking for places to rent. Some place to weather the storm.

He quickly focused on the white van's driver but it too quickly passed behind trees. He got a brief but good look at the driver of the blue van; dark skinned, exuded a rough manner by something JC couldn't quite put his finger on. Then he, too, passed out of view. The sedan now came into focus and it had four people, for sure. It looked like all males. The driver appeared Hispanic and had something, perhaps a tattoo on his neck. He was looking right at JC, or at least the ranch house. He disappeared behind the trees. He put down the binoculars and flipped open his cell phone to call Ev Smiley.

"Yeah, I'll wait."

"Sheriff Smiley, here."

"Ev, this is JC.............., yeah we're all OK. Uh, huh. Listen, there was something I had forgotten about ...."

He told Ev about the three cars and the Sheriff promised to get somebody out there and try to find them, see who they were. You and your men be careful, Ev."

"Thanks. We will. I'll get back to you when I've got something."

They all sat out on the porch, talking quietly, but really, waiting to see if the mystery caravan passed by again. Soon, there was the nightly call for dinner by the women in the house. Pepe's wife Madalena made homemade tamales with the husks and all. A couple of tamales and a cold beer and the spirits picked up. The phone rang after dinner.

"JC, Ev here....."

"Yeah, Ev, what's up?" There was a moment of silence and JC heard a shuddering exhale.

"Are you OK, Ev?"

"We lost Tommy tonight..., and Paul Jackson" Tommy was Ev's son and a rookie on the force. Paul Jackson was seasoned, eighteen years as a sheriff's deputy. Ev Smiley was clearly holding back his tears.

"Ev. I'm so sorry. What happened?"

"They found those boys out there all right, just north of Gazelle on West Side Rd. It was a felony stop. They knew the situation and I'm sure they approached with guns drawn. Apparently Paul walked up to the car. There was an exchange of fire. Paul died there on the road. It looked like Tommy fired everything in his clip and moved around to the back of the patrol car for cover. That's where we found him. They took the pistols and the shotgun................ Bill Cooper is out there at the scene right now. I've got more guys coming, but........., but. Oh my God, he's dead JC, my little boy is gone." Everett Smiley wept to his long time friend.

JC was speechless, as he listened to a friend he'd gone to school with, hunted with, been in civic organizations with and who now had lost his son. Though he could not quit working with a constant state of emergency, he took that moment to cry in front of his friend.

"I'm sorry, Ev," said JC. Ev mentally picked himself up.

"We're gonna find these bastards, JC."

"You will, Ev," he encouraged him. "You always do. Is there anything we can do?"

"Yes. You can stay safe. Protect yourself. If you see anything suspicious, you call. We're gonna' double up out there, even though we're stretched damn thin. It's getting dark and we don't know where these guys are. We don't know how many. We do know they won't hesitate to murder anyone in their way."

"We'll take care of ourselves. Again, I'm just sick about Tommy."

"Thanks. We'll talk soon. Good night."

"Good night."

———

CHAPTER 5

Dusk was passing quickly into night. The long shadows of the late afternoon dissipated into ever lighter gray, then disappeared altogether. The moon was well up, but shrouded in clouds which were scooting quickly across the sky. The men waited in their cars for the nightfall to complete. They were up Forest Service Road 46N17, which accessed several sections of government land to the side of Grady-O'Hare. The radios were turned off as were the lights. The cars pulled alongside each other on the gravel road in the thick forest. Six men, all recently released from Pelican Bay Prison on the coast of far Northern California, were gathered, talking across to each other in their cars, as if they were stopped at a traffic light. A bottle of whiskey was passed back and forth between the cars. The stars were appearing in rapidity now. The moon was near full and seemed to brighten with the encroaching darkness.

There were giggles from inside the van, where two women drank with their boyfriends. The men had each gone to prison for the violence committed in the name of their gangs. Two for murder, one for manslaughter and three for armed robbery. All had rap sheets since their early teens for drugs, stealing, dealing and increasing violence. Four were in the United States illegally, two were citizens. When the 'purge of the prisons' occurred, the violent criminals were supposed to be retained. But the prison system is another bureaucracy. Mistakes were made, careless-

341

ness prevailed and the inevitable was ...well, inevitable. Hardened and vicious men were set free. While some citizen groups tried to exercise some oversight, the Hispanic lobby, championed by liberal legislators, including Senator Patrick O'Hare, claimed racism and insisted that citizens were not qualified to pick and choose who should be given "foregiveness of sins".

They spoke in Spanish. One man got out to relieve himself. He looked up into the night sky, the alcohol and drugs washing through him. They smoked pot and crack. He looked into the forest about him, and it both scared him and invited him. The shadows of the clouds below the moon moved through the trees and made the forest seem alive. He shuddered briefly, then shook himself and returned to the sedan.

The tall, skinny man with the tattoo of a flame erupting from his neckline stepped out of the car and shoved the pistol of Tom Smiley into his belt. A large knife was holstered on his hip.

He spoke sparingly, giving orders. The others piled out of the vehicles. Several had pistols. One had a shotgun. One had a baseball bat, caked with dried blood. Their looks became serious. The laughter had stopped. The girls were getting dressed and they weren't giggling anymore. Below them, perhaps two miles away, the mercury light burned in the farmyard of Grady-O'Hare. One van started up and swung around. They checked themselves for weapons and flashlights and went over the plan. The bottle went around a last time, each man pulling hard on it and hissing. Then it was thrown empty into the nearby woods.

Here was the plan: One van would take them all close by the front gate and drop them off, behind the trees. They would make their way under cover of darkness and trees to the big house. The moonlight would be bright enough to allow them to see. Once at the house, they would enter it, bind up whoever they found or kill them if necessary or desirable. Stay for a couple of days, load up on supplies and then move on. They were certain there would be food, maybe some new vehicles, guns and am-munition. They couldn't plan too much just yet. That would come when they got to the house. They entered into the back of the van, leaving the girls and the other vehicles behind. It started down the road, slow and deliberate.

——

Some of Pepe and Madalena's kids were playing cards with Matt and Sandy's kids at the table. Quint was upstairs finishing his online schoolwork. Matt and JC and Pepe were watching the news.

The big story was the riots in Europe. Over taxation, empty grocery stores and soaring fuel prices. The streets were full of protesters. Groups of protesters attacked each other. Muslim groups, not about to be saddled with the taxes necessary to keep the European retirees in comfort, rioted for the burden put upon them by the host society. The anglophile youths rampaged against them as for-eigners, unwelcome outsiders, who would subjugate their hosts with their Sharia law, and general intolerance of all that was not Islam. The native youths of western Europe were more interested in drinking and brawling over soccer matches than defending the culture and country of their forefathers. All sides blamed the government for bringing them to this point in history. It seemed that Europe would soon erupt as it had so many times before, into utter cha-os and war. The mass killing could not be far off. The so-cialist politicians of Europe could not sufficiently appease the rising tide of Muslim youth. The conservatives were pil-loried by the media and regarded as Neanderthals, for crying out against the usurpation of the culture and the failure to enforce the laws.

The men on the long couch watched in resigned despair of the world around them, and spoke offhandedly to each other about the good fortune to be where they were, by comparison. JC flipped across several of the remaining channels which still had broadcasts. It was the same dismal story, no matter what the particular story was.

Back home, the country seemed in lock-down mode. Everybody on defense and security. Trouble in the cities seemed out of control, and the despair and the violence of desperate people spread outward, in search of food and a place to ...be.

It was breathtaking how only a year or so ago, the nation jostled and wrestled with issues of high public policy such as universal health care, banking reform, protection of ever more endangered species, increased education subsidies. Now all that was gone, a distant speck in the rear view mirror.

JC looked over and saw that Pepe was nodding off, his head bobbing gently until his chin rested in his chest. He slapped him on the knee, to which he woke with a start. Matt and JC laughed, while he worked his mouth and rubbed his face.

"I'd say it was time you got to bed Pepe. You're gonna' start the last irrigation cycle tomorrow."

"I know, I know", he said in automation.

"You better come and get your husband, Madalena", teased Matt. Pepe got up a little too quick and fell back onto the long couch.

"Pepe, you been sneakin' the schnopps, again?" JC chided him. Matt laughed.

"Ha, ha, ha. Very funny", Pepe countered coldly. "I'm going to bed", he announced.

"I'll be along shortly, honey" said Madalena, continuing to play cards with the kids. Quint bounded down the stairs two at a time.

"What's going on?", he said as he flopped into Pepe's place on the couch.

"Same 'ol crap", said Matt.

"Yep", said JC. "How's the homework coming?"

"Fine."

"All done?"

"Yeah. Hey, any of that apple pie left?"

"No."

"You two ate it all?" he whined.

"Yep" came the reply in unison.

"No wonder you guys are getting fat."

"Matthew, I believe I detect a note of subdued hostility in my son."

"I'd say it was a little jealousy as well, JC."

Sandy came out of the kitchen. "Quint, there's a huge piece of pie left. Don't believe these liars", as she walked through the room.

Quint shot off the couch and flew to the kitchen while Matt and JC laughed at him.

"I believe I'll get a breath of fresh air", said Matt. "I'll join you", said JC.

The brothers walked out onto the covered porch in their thick socks. They stood at the railing and looked out over the land in the moonlight. In the distance they could see a few cars traveling on the freeway. The locals continued to man the offramps, keeping people moving through the area and on to Oregon. Unless they had relatives nearby, the local freeway posse would not let them off. It was done courteously, but without ambiguity.

They stood on the porch and farted at will. Not saying anything, but drinking in the beauty of the moonlit landscape. Down on the county road, a car passed by. They thought nothing of it.

"Darn shame about little Tommy Smiley. I coached him on my little league team", said Matt.

"Yeah, he was a good kid. Ev sounded pretty tore up. Maggie has got to be in hell right now."

"Sandy called over there, but the house was full of friends. Maggie just couldn't talk."

"Paul Jackson was in Rotary with me", said JC. For a cop, he sure had a wild sense of humor. Jeez, he was funny. I think he only had a year or so to go to retirement."

"You just never know what's coming, JC."

"No, ya don't. Paul's wife died a couple of years ago. Breast cancer, I think. No kids. It's a damn shame."

They both farted simultaneously, laughed. "Must be those tamales".

———

The men crouched as they made progress through the trees. The wind was picking up as it does on summer evenings sometimes. The clouds passing beneath the bright moon darkened the forest floor, then moved past, allowing them to see easily where to step. They gathered in the trees about two hundred feet from the house. They could see it well enough.

They spoke in strong whispers, though the wind was loud in their ears, buffeting them. From there they crept furtively toward the house, from across the driveway and farmyard. The tall one with the tattoo spoke to another. The power system was old and the breaker box was on the outside of the house. They would cut the power at the right time. They observed the phone line came in at the same place. That would be easy. Others would quietly approach each door. They would need one to enter quietly if possible. Perhaps a door would be open, or a window. Once inside, the others would be let in. Then the mayhem would begin. But first, they would have to wait until the house was dark. Plan B would be if they could not enter quietly. A window would be smashed and that would be the start of the assault. They would have to move quickly.

But for now, they cursed the wind and pulled their jackets and hoods over to protect themselves. They felt the drugs coursing through them. Their jaws clenched, their eyes dilated and wild. They wanted to go now, but the tall one kept them back.

———

"Tomorrow, we'll need to go down to the old house and see what to do", said JC. "Maybe we ought to bring some paint with us. I can't see destroying the house, yet ...hell, I don't know. Maybe we should. Who would want to rent it after what happened in there? I know I wouldn't want to sleep there. It's creepy."

"We'll just go on down there and see. Let's not try to figure it out now. OK?"

"Fine".

"I'm gonna' go check on Janine, see how she's doing."

"I'm gonna' keep workin' on this tamale".

"'ats a good idea." JC got up and went into the house. The game at the table was breaking up and people were heading to the assigned rooms for each family.

JC cracked open the door to her bedroom, came in and sat by her on the side of the bed and stroked her hair which had turned very gray, earlier than it should have. She looked drawn and haggard. Dark circles swallowed her eyes. She tried to smile up at him.

"Its not fair", she said softly.

"What, honey?"

"You deserve more than I've given you Jon Connor."

He tried to soothe her, 'sushing' her gently.

"No. You're a good man, still full of life. You deserve somebody who can love you, care for you. Look at me, for God's sake. I can't do anything. I'm no good to me and I'm no good to you. How can you even love me?"

"Honey, don't talk like this. I love you. That's all that matters."

"No", she sobbed. It's not enough. Love should be active, alive, doing, feeling, being there for you. Let me go, Jon." Now she looked up at him, her eyes begging him her frail frame quaking as she began to sob.

"Help me to go."

He stood up.

"Don't ask me to do that. I can't. Don't ever ask me that again, Janine. You mustn't." But she was out of bed, surprisingly fast, at his feet, holding him, begging him.

"Please let me go. Help me." He felt the salt choking him in his throat and his eyes welled. He slumped down to her on the floor.

"I can't", he whispered. "I can't". He looked away.

Downstairs, the TV was shut off and Quint was finishing some crumbs in the pie dish. He turned to head upstairs to his bedroom, as Matt came in from the porch.

"Quint, let's get these doors locked and throw the dead bolts, will you?"

"You got it, Uncle Matt".

There were four exterior doors to the house; front, on the front porch, rear door, at the driveway, a side door to the utility and laundry room which had a second door to the kitchen and then the door to JC's office which also had an interior door to the house.

Quint made his way round, locking the handles and throwing the dead bolts if they existed. As he did, he shut off the light in each room. He could hear bone rattling snoring coming from the den which Pepe and Madalena used with their youngsters. Their older boy bunked in Quint's room on a sleeping bag. To the children, it seemed an exciting adventure, and the adults were glad it was taken that way. But in each bedroom, was one or more guns, loaded. Normally, it was this way, but these days, they were at the ready. Matt was headed upstairs. He turned back to Quint.

"You get 'em all?"

"Yes, sir".

"Your dad's office door?"

"Oh sh...." He expelled.

"Come on Quint. This is serious."

"Sorry, Uncle Matt. I'll get it."

He went through the office, locked and bolted the door, then locked the interior door. Crossing the living room, he peered out the big picture window. The bushes were flailing the sides of the house in the wind. There were thumps and bumps as things gave way to its force. As he looked out, it was surreal sort of light outside. The moon was high and the shadows it cast were small. The shadows of clouds still moved across, dimming the landscape for several moments then allowing the moon's illumination to return.

He turned off the last light downstairs and bounded up the stairs to brush his teeth in the now emptying bathrooms.

—

Outside the men watched the procession of the lights. Now only an upstairs light or two were still on. It wouldn't be long now. They huddled together, anxious to move, tired of the wind biting them. The drugs impelling them forward. They wanted inside the house, now! But the tall one kept them. Finally the last light flicked off. Quint climbed into bed and checked the western style Colt SAA .45 Peace-maker and holstered it on his bed post. He had used it in his western style shooting competition. He said good night to his room mate, Zachary, and lay back in bed, thinking about the events of the day.

———

The men were moving, slowly, quietly through the last of the woods and they stayed at its edge, protected from sight. Nearly twenty minutes had now passed and they moved out, fanning across the barn yard and driveway to the house. They kept off the porch, walking on the lawns. The bushes and shrubs continued to flail at the siding and windows. Slowly, the electrical panel door was lifted by the short stocky man, built like a tank. Then the main switch was carefully, slowly flipped. The phone lines were bundled together neatly, near the office door. A military K-bar knife cut them instantly. The house was dark, without power, nor telephone land lines. The tall one gave the signal and each man found a door. The wind was perfect cover for the small sounds they made. They moved within the shadows, trying each door and window. Every door was locked, but a window was found in the dining room and the screen was pulled off. The man with a bushy mustache had winced at the sound it made and was immediately still and quiet. Quint had thought he heard something, unlike the constant brushing of the shrubs against the house. His hearing went into hypersensitivity. He waited. Matt heard it, too. Both men thought their minds were playing tricks on them. JC, was emotionally tired from Janine, who had finally fallen asleep. He thought he would sleep on the couch tonight. He closed the bedroom door behind him and tiptoed to the top of the stairs. The stairs creaked loudly, but he went down quietly, trying not to wake anyone. The living room was filled with moonlight. Outside, the shrubs waived frantically at him as if trying to warn him.

The window slid open. Standing on his comrade's shoulders, the man grabbed onto the sill and pulled himself halfway through. JC felt a blast of cool air hit him as he descended the stairs. 'Where was that coming from?', he thought. In the hallway were several pistols on belts and a gun case with a small armory. Now he thought he heard something. He moved toward the dining room, as the living room was secured. The door was bumping the jamb, not being closed. The Mexican had slithered onto the floor and was very quietly trying to get up, when JC saw him through the cracked open door. His mind raced, but his actions were smooth, as if practiced. He unholstered a model 1911 .45, hanging holstered on a peg in the hallway, chambered a round and stepped into the doorway. The man was on his feet, now aware of someone in the room. The muzzle flash illuminated the room in bright orange. From four feet away, the man exploded backward. In that flash of light, JC saw his face, a menace. The second flash followed in half a moment and it found its mark again in mid-chest. But the man's torso was already red and his face in shock. The third shot was almost a full second behind the first, and it pushed his red clothed visage backward through the window and onto the lawn outside.

Nothing awakens like a pistol shot in the house. Everyone was out of bed, grabbing pistols and shotguns. But there were no lights. Fortunately, the moonlight flooded into the bedrooms offering ambient light. Quickly flashlights were grabbed and the upstairs hallway was filling with family. Shotgun blasts now came from the kitchen as Plan A and B failed, Plan C was invoked; every man for himself. Go in and kill everybody. The tall man, walked in behind the man who shotgunned the doorlocks and walked boldly into the kitchen. The two men stood there while they heard glass windows breaking on the far side of the house.

Matt was creeping down the stairs, a shotgun readied. Quint behind him with his pistol. Zachary had his snake pistol, he used when out walking the ranch.

"JC, you there?", asked Matt. But JC didn't answer, he was watching shadows coming from the kitchen and the door opening slowly, creaking on its hinge. Matt and Quint stopped. JC brought the .45 up at arm's length aiming at the door and waited. The door opened back toward him and he saw the muzzle of the long gun peak out from behind. He knew it couldn't be anybody but intruders, more of them. But still, the doubt. Could it be Pepe? He must wait and confirm the target. Then Matt spoke again from up the stairway.

"JC?", he whispered loudly. The shotgun discharged at the stairway, but missed Matt and Quint who scampered back upstairs. In the moment it took for his mind to understand, the shot was meant for the sound of Matt's location, JC discharged three more rounds through the door, and heard men scream.

"Careful Matt. Quint, you stay up there." The sound of the man collapsing onto the floor, the standard issue police shotgun clattering beside his slumped body. The tall man, froze in the door jamb, the .40 caliber Glock that used to belong to Tommy Smiley, already cocked and ready for action. Now another gang member was coming across the living room toward the kitchen. He passed below the stairway and Matt discharged the shotgun. A horrible thud followed the brilliant blast of light into the room.

Outside, the man who helped his compadre through the window was fleeing back through the woods. Up on the Forest Service road, the women and one man were outside the cars and heard the shots. They pointed as they saw the house and flashes of light within it.

The tall one, only feet away and around the corner from JC, was backing his way out of the kitchen, carefully. The gun pointed at the doorway that JC was tucked behind; everyone listening, eyes dilated, hearts pounding. They heard the screen door slam and realized someone had left, but were there more inside, or surrounding the house? The den door opened with Pepe yelling: "It's me, it's me!" He, too, had a pistol and a large flashlight, which washed over the crumpled body on the living room floor. As he panned, his light fell upon the body in the kitchen door way.

The tall man pressed his cell phone speed dial and up on the Forest Service road it rang. They did not answer, just quickly started the van and took off down the road.

Inside the house, they continued to move slowly, clearing each and every room. Quint and Zachary moved outside and flipped on the electricity, which seemed incredibly bright, their eyes now accustomed to the dark. Sandy picked up the phone, but called out downstairs to say the line was dead. She got on her cell phone and prayed the sporadic service would be on tonight, dialed 911.

"Oh thank God you're, there".

"Yes, ma'm what is the nature of the problem?"

"We've had burglars, there's been shooting. Send out the police and ambulance to Grady-O'Hare ranch on the old highway."

"What's the address ma'm?

"Uh,...., its uh...., 61579 Old Highway. Please come quick!"

"Yes, ma'm, the Sheriff is on his way. Is anybody hurt?"

"Yes, I think so. They're downstairs. I'm not going down there."

"Just stay on the phone with me. The deputy should be there in three minutes."

Sandy called out to the downstairs "Sheriff and ambulance on the way". The men stood around not knowing what to do, uncomfortable with the corpses in the house, but not certain whether to move them.

"Best wait for the police", Matt said.

Pepe asked, "You suppose these are the guys that killed the Jessups?"

"I think so" said JC.

"These guys look like prison people", blurted out Quint. "Look at all those tattoos. It's just like what I've seen on TV shows about prisons. Looks just like 'em."

"Pepe, you and Matt go on down to the gate and open it up for the Sheriff. Watch yourselves. These guys left on foot. They might be right out there."

The two remaining gang members jumped into the open side door of the van and it sped away.

Even though it was just to the end of the driveway, they took the pickup. Two sheriff cruisers pulled up at the same time. The gate was opened and the police cars sped to the house. They could see the ambulance coming. So they waited and then secured the gate when all were in.

———

JC entered the darkened and quiet bedroom.

"Janine?", he called out, but the frail lump under the covers was still. He approached the bed slowly. "Janine? Honey?" And he sat on the bed and pulled back the covers. Her face was so peaked and white, yet beautiful and at peace. There was no torment in her eyes, which stared into space, fixed. The facial muscles were relaxed. He grabbed her hand and fell to his knees beside the bed and wept. He wept in sorrow for her passing, in happiness for her release, in relief for his own burden of her care.

When the others found them, the coroner took her. He said it looked like a heart attack, very peaceful, probably from all the shooting and commotion.

CHAPTER 6

Oakland, California-September 11, 2012

Benjamin Geiss stood in front of his massive picture windows looking westward across the bay. The Bay Bridge arched over the water to San Francisco's skyline. The Golden Gate Bridge was slightly off to his right and more distant. He noted the large cranes along the docks and the steady stream of traffic at 7:12 am.

Emilio Lopez had gotten a late start and was now paying dearly for it. He had come down I-80 from Vallejo and had even ventured, for a time, in the car pool lane though he was alone in his vehicle, a contractor's pickup with racks on top and a dent in the left rear side panel. As he approached Oakland, the traffic slowed to a crawl. The highway sign informed him of a 50 minute estimate to travel the 4 miles to the bridge's toll gates. He could see San Francisco's skyline through the passenger window.

About three hundred yards ahead of Emilio's lumber laden pickup were three rental trucks; all from different rental truck companies. Each was the size of a small moving van, with roll up doors at the rear.

Roberta Salazar manned her toll booth. She was glad to have the job. It paid well and the union seemed to extract ever greater benefits from the taxpayers. But, she thought, it might be better to go back to school and further her education. The job was boring; boring to tears. She was beginning to think of it as a stepping stone, though all her friends jealously told her what a great 'gig' it was. She was manning the cash lane which was usual for new hires. The more tenured of her employment simply sat in the heated kiosk of the quickpass lanes, where all vehicles simply passed through, the camera recognizing the stickers on the windshield saying they had paid in full.

Ben got himself a chai tea and took up the healthy sized roach in the ashtray. It was very good pot, strong, grown in the national forests of northern California by pods of Earthfirsters and Gaia worshipers; those of his kindred spirit. He held the hit in his lungs and immediately felt the wave of numbing, well-being, start in his brain and flush through his system.

"Poor asses", he said to himself and smirked, as he watched the one way traffic-jam that still was the morning commute across the Bay Bridge. You'd think with unemployment so high, that traffic-jams would be a thing of the past. But, they were the cockroach of modern transportation. Much else had indeed changed, but nothing eliminated them.

Eastbound, out of the city, it was open pavement. He exhaled. The capillaries in his eyes flushed red. Now arms encircled his waist. He smiled and felt the back of his neck being kissed. His common law wife had flown back to Vermont for a family visit two days ago. He tilted his head forward to expose his neck to the delicacy and watched as the hands around him slid down from his waist to his crotch and caressed him. The skin was clean of arm hair, having been plucked. He turned around and pushed the roach to the young boy's lips and his partner inhaled deeply. Ben looked into the dark eyes, Cleopatran eyes, beautiful eyes and returned the gentle squeeze. "Ready for another round?" asked the young man, grinning.

—

Emelio had inched forward in maddening halts and lurches. It was 7:41 am and he could see the bridge easily over to his right. Soon the bottleneck would open up and all four lanes would make the sweeping arc of a turn and come onto the easterly bridge abutment, heading for the toll booths. A U-Haul truck snapped up the space in front him left by the darting Mercedes that had been there. The moment of inattention on his part now cost him the view of the back of a dirty truck and door latch graffiti written in the dust. He pounded his steering wheel in frustration. He should have been walking onto his job site ten minutes ago. He was easily going to be another hour.

Roberta Salazar was bored. Even the joy of efficiently having the change in dollars stuck between her fingers in order to keep the line moving as smoothly as possible was now dull. Sometimes she would play a game in her mind, guessing by the car and its driver what denomination of money they would hand her and she would already have the correct change between her fingers. But, after several months, she was bored even with that. There was no way around the tedium of the job. It wasn't work as much as mental punishment. She leaned out to take the cash from the middle eastern looking man driving the orange rental truck. He was sweating. He handed her a ten dollar bill, as she notice two other similar sized trucks pulling through the tollbooths on the next outboard lanes. She gave six dollars back to the man and the truck lurched forward. The Chevy pickup pulled up next. She looked at the handsome Mexican man who flashed her a quick smile and a twenty dollar bill. Emelio thought her a very pretty girl and she was, but no time for flirting today. He was late. She got the proper change for the twenty, already pre-folded and began to hand it to him with a beautiful smile and near flawless white teeth.

"What the hell?" he said as he looked forward. Roberta was pushing sixteen dollars folded lengthwise back at him. She glanced over her left shoulder and saw three trucks about a thousand feet onto the bridge pulled crosswise to the traffic blocking all lanes, beyond the metering traffic lights. Her heart sank.

Emelio watched men with western clothing, but Arab head-dresses, jump out of the truck. Some commuters were caught in front of them. The anger of the halted commuters quickly turned to fear, then panic, as the gunmen now toting AK 47s let loose a blast of bullets into the cars, walking slowly back toward them. Roberta screamed as several of the rear windows of the cars filled with a red mist. Emelio looked into his rear view mirror and saw cars behind him jammed in like sardines as far as he could see. No one was moving forward. In that moment, there was silence except for the gunfire. People watched in disbelief as the gunmen went to the few cars near them and pulled survivors out who had ducked down on their seats. They pulled them out onto the pavement and executed them. Women, children; it didn't matter. And in that moment it seemed all the oxygen was sucked out of the air as if the earth had inhaled it. Then, it less loose with screams and pandemonium. In his rear view mirror, car doors flew open and people were running back off the bridge, some fell and were trampled. Their cars sat idling with the doors open. First by the scores, then hundreds, and within seconds...thousands.

Emelio saw that he could reverse directions by making a U-turn around the toll booths, through a break in the median, near the main toll station. He put the truck into gear when Roberta looked at him.

"Please take me with you", she begged.

"Get in. Get in quickly!" She ran around and noticed the news helicopters were flying overhead.

Ben and his young lover were embracing when Ben saw the television screen picture turn to the Bay Bridge. The mute was on. He spun around and looked out his picture window to the reality unfolding on the bridge.

"What's going on?" he said under his breath to no one. He turned up the volume as the traffic reporter in the Channel 4 helicopter was live broadcasting from above the bridge back to Dan Swell, at the anchor desk.

On the bridge, the roll up doors on the trucks opened. A dozen men in balaclavas, the favored dress of Hamas and Hezbolah terrorists, all with automatic weapons exited. They jumped over the median and, after shooting several motorists who careened off the guard rails, all traffic stopped. Quickly the stoppage backed up. Within three minutes it was all the way into the Treasure Island tunnel. In another four minutes, all the way to San Francisco, downtown exit, just as the police cars were getting onto the bridge. They were useless. Motorcycle units were then dispatched. Now the air buzzed with half dozen news copters and the CHP bird.

The young man stood naked in Ben Giess' home and picked up the expensive marine binoculars from the stand near the window. Slowly he twisted the focus ring until the bridge came into crystal clarity. It looked like the action was happening at the end of his arms. His lips slowly spread into a grin.

"Alahu Akbar (God is Great)."

The people in the east bound lanes were confused, but quickly cell phone calls went out, news wires were picking it up. On the Oakland side was mayhem, but the San Francisco side was still in a fog. Was it an accident? What the hell was going on?

Two of the rental trucks now started up and proceeded quickly side by side to the middle of the first span of the bridge, between Oakland and Treasure Island. The thousands of cars, now parked on the eastbound lanes, were in abject confusion as these two trucks ambled above them. When they reached the midpoint, they stopped and out of the back of the truck jumped gunmen. Eight of them, four on each side, attached nylon ropes, hooks and caribiners and repelled down to the eastbound deck of the bridge. They spread out along the side girders quickly a hundred yards apart. One man slowly walked over and through a bull horn spoke to the people in their cars, four lanes abreast. Windows cracked so they could hear. I-pods turned off. Radios muted. In halting English with a distinct accent, the bull horn blared.

"Remain in your cars. Do not panic. Do not run. Remain in your vehicles and you will be safe."

A young man in a Porsche slithered out of his door and crouching, began running backwards through traffic. He was spotted immediately and shot incessantly, sprawling across the hood of a station wagon with a family inside. Screaming and wailing began. Several others panicked and fled their cars. Every one of them shot as if in a shooting gallery. Now everything was frozen in surreal time. Cell phones flipped open, but the servers at Verizon and AT & T crashed as calls emanated outward from this point on the earth in exponentially increasing volume. People in New York were on the phone with someone they knew on the west coast. All television screens were turned to one news channel or another. It was only eleven minutes since Roberta had left her post in Emelio's pickup.

The plan was working out nearly perfectly. The bridge was locked up with traffic, the exits sealed. The entire world was watching from helicopters whose telephoto lenses produced a clear and terrifying image, with a slight jiggle that the gyros governing the cameras could not take out.

FoxNews, CBS, MSNBC, CNN, and ABC all had talking heads on immediately. What did this mean? Then suddenly on Channel 4 in the Bay Area, Dan Swell put his hand to his ear bud.

"We're getting reports now that the terrorists are in communication with the administration." The picture on the screen was of a man on the bridge pacing with a cell phone in his ear.

President Perkins had been called out of a meeting with senior Democratic leadership. It was a strategy session on the upcoming elections, now only two months away. He was comfortably ahead in the polls. Heels clicked on the polished hallway, as the President with three top advisors turned into the oval office. He sat at his desk, his top advisors seated around him. His Chief of Staff, Ken Johnson answered his blackberry.

"Hell no!" he spat into the phone.

"Shove this to me or Bill Sweeney. We're not letting these assholes talk directly to the President. The election is around the corner. We're not taking any chances." He snapped the lid and shoved it into his coat pocket.

"The terrorists want a direct line to you, sir. I don't think you should personally touch this. It's too risky right now. The political stakes are too high."

President Perkins had a stern look on his face, pressing the long fingers of his hand across his chin.

"Ken, the stakes might be a lot higher than just political." His eyes searched his advisors around the room. "Thoughts?" he queried.

They were still looking at the television screen in the oval office. A four foot by eight foot sign came out of the remaining truck still parked near the Oakland side. In bold red letters on a white background it said: 'Pick up the phone, Perkins.' The video showed bloody bodies strewn on the pavement. Two men came in and out of the truck with a crate on a sophisticated looking dolly.

"Oh shit!" gasped several men around the room. Perkins looked at Ken Johnson. Their eyes met.

Up at the midpoint of the bridge, suitcases were coming out of the trucks and they were opened and set across the west bound lanes above thousands of cars stuck on the east bound lanes. Oakland SWAT had finally worked their way to the toll booths and now took cover there. They were held off by only three men with machine guns. The stalemate never got passed the toll booth area. The chopper cameras were focusing on the suitcases, when the red phone on the President's desk pinged and a light flashed. Perkins looked around the room at his speechless advisors and slowly picked up the phone.

"This is the President. Yes. I understand, General. Are you certain? Yes, uh huh. Have your people got a plan?" Perkins swallowed the lump in his throat and the others in the room saw it.

"Yes. Thank you, General. Stand by. I'll let you know." And he hung up the phone.

"Our satellites and a drone are just now coming on scene both confirm; the suitcases appear to be nukes. Russian ones, stolen back in 1994 and 1995. They're not positive but they think so. The crate looks even more ominous, but we haven't gotten a good look at it yet. Our hi-def satellite should be coming up in just a few minutes.

The terrorist stood before the placard making obvious his cell phone at his ear. He pointed to the sign. This time the regular phone on his desk rang. His secretary, Charlene, told him the terrorists have been patched through.

"Should I put them through, sir?"

He sighed, looked at Ken Johnson. "Yes, I'll speak with them." Johnson held his breath.

"This is President Perkins."

"Mr. President Perkins, please listen carefully", said the voice in halting English. "You will meet our demands or many thousands of people will needlessly lose their lives."

"I'm sure we can work this out if we can talk......"

"Shut up and listen. I will do the talking. Do you understand?"

"I'm listening. Go ahead."

"You will prepare a public statement and read it before the world. These are the points you must make. First, you will denounce Israel as a terrorist state and withdraw all support effective immediately. Second, you will order all American troops, wherever they are overseas, back to American soil, effective immediately. This includes South Korea. You will then issue an apology to the world that ......"

"That is not going to happen Muhammed, or whatever your name is."

The voice briefly screamed in an emotional outburst. "We are happy to die for Allah. Are you willing that hundreds of thousands shall die with us? The time of the Great Satan has come to an end. Last, you will..."

Military aircraft were lifting off at Travis Air Force Base. Satellites were being re-oriented to focus on this pinpoint of land. Hank Belcher, a chopper pilot with CNN, was talking to the other chopper pilots.

"I think we ought to back away. Who knows what these guys have got and what they'll do."

So that no one would lose any news advantage, the chopper and camera teams after checking with their bosses, all simultaneously backed away from the bridge at least one mile.

"That's not realistic. I am the President, but I cannot dissolve Congress, nor ask for their mass resignations. It can't be done. Surely there is something else we can discuss. Look we can have a dialogue the middle east, Israel, whatever you want. Let's talk about it. No one has to die today."

"Mr. President Perkins. You do not understand. You are an arrogant man. You once worshipped Allah, now you worship as a Christian."

"Well, we can talk about that, too........."
"No! No more talking. Will you meet the demands or no?"
"I can't possibly............."
"Then the time has come. You will be contacted by another brother and he will restate the demands after we are finished here. Alahu Akbar, Alahu Akbar, Alahu Akbar." The line went dead, and he slowly returned the phone to the cradle.

All eyes returned to the flat panel TV. The men on the bridge were scurrying around the suitcases. They were flipping the sign over. There was more writing. Some of it in Arabic.

"I'm getting a bad feeling about this, Mr. President", said Johnson.

The chopper cameras were focusing on the men as they flipped the sign over but at that distance it was difficult to read.

Ben came up and the boy gave him the binoculars. Ben refocused and could see them clearly on the bridge. He couldn't see the sign as it was aimed toward the choppers which hovered off to the north. Finally the focus came in clear. The terrorists were all in radio contact with each other and they all moved onto clear pavement and bowed down toward Mecca and prayed to Allah. The sign said "So long America". It was an unusual way of saying it; very western, very homey.

The words had just entered their brains in the Oval Office when a stupendous explosion blinded everyone near the Bay Bridge for ten miles away. The enormous cloud erupted upwards. The suitcase bombs at mid-bridge had been spread across all lanes, both directions, in regular intervals. And then they went off in simultaneous detonation. People recoiled, who watched it on TV to shrieks of: "Oh my God! Oh my God! No!" These were low level tactical nuclear devices intended for battlefield significance, not world killers. The Bay Bridge severed as if cut on a perforated line.

While everyone and everything within a quarter mile was obliterated, now the bridge started collapsing. The upper deck fell. The lower deck, with sections half the length of a football field, fell into the sea, with the cars flying through the air like splinters in an explosion. The choppers, jolted severely in the air, fought to regain air control of their craft and tried to refocus the cameras back onto the bridge. Debris was flying through the air. A seventy foot long shrapnel of girder swatted the Channel 7 copter demolishing its rotor and sending it into San Francisco Bay. The others, partly of duty and somewhat in shock, could not look away and focused their cameras on the bridge. Other sections now began to collapse, and with them first a few dozens, then hundreds of cars, of screaming, people dying, falling through the air crashing into the cold hazel green water. The sea like a frothing monster, swallowed them up. Back at the station, the camera feeds were coming in, but no one could move, or say anything. Tears. Hands covering mouths.

The vehicles crashed upon each other in the broth of the sea. They bobbed for a moment then sank. But more kept coming. A few people dazed, not understanding how they were now swimming in the bay, soon died of shock and hypothermia. Some crushed by vehicles falling from the sky. Like dominoes; one collapsing section brought down the next, while the entire world watched; precisely as intended. No one could speak in the news rooms of America. The picture on the screen said it all. The bridge collapsed by the columns all the way back to Treasure Island and finally stopped. It was four and a half minutes of hell on earth.

The masked terrorists near the bridge toll were back on their feet waiving frantically to the choppers. Channel 2's chopper refocused on them and came in a little closer. The terrorists were on their knees surrounding the single device in the crate. The chopper pilots were chattering with each other as to whether to back off again. The lead terrorist, held the obvious detonator in his hand and made the overt slow motion action, like a mime, of pressing the button down. Each of the copter pilots shoved their sticks hard away from the bridge and accelerated full speed.

Ben was blinded from the flash, but now the nuclear blast flattened all Oakland and all of Berkeley. In an instant, he and his house were vaporized; heated to 3,000 degrees. The treed hillsides did not burn. They were denuded. They exploded. Nothing, for several miles backward through the Oakland hills survived.

The mushroom had just started to form at twelve thousand feet, as the San Francisco skyline was leveled to pure dirt, and the blast quickly worked its way outward down to the south bay. The world was vaporizing. The bridge disintegrated along with the thousands on it. Within seconds, the blast wave traveled outward sweeping buildings off their foundations. Concrete went into spontaneous combustion. Eight miles out from the blast some of the best buildings withstood the blast, but all organic life was ignited. Patrick O'Hare was on the 38th floor of the Transamerica Building at world headquarters of GreenWorld. He had watched it all-live through his office telescope. The blast incinerated the building and he was water vapor, over the Pacific one second later. All the aircraft in the air over the bridge was tossed like chaff in a tornado. Most of Marin was destroyed. The Golden Gate Bridge fell into the sea, after melting. The explosion downward into the water now forced an instant tsunami, localized within the bay and traveling at seventy miles per hour, ninety feet high in every direction. Every wooden boat in all the marinas were ignited and vaporized by the blast, then the wave came. For the stunned people at the far end of the north bay, it was as if hell had come to earth. If they were unaware of the drama on the Bay Bridge, which only lasted 17 minutes, then they were in their own little world one minute, meandering along the sidewalks window gazing into the exclusive shops, and in the next, their world was gone. Thousands died of shock, untreated.

———

Ken Johnson puked on the oval office floor. Everyone was sucking air but couldn't breath. President Perkins, like the others, looked as a child upon the incomprehensible, unwilling to accept the reality of it.

"Mr. President, Mr. President", the voice repeated in urgency. Perkins looked as if the voices were speaking to him from afar.

"The phone, sir."

"Huh?"

"The phone, sir. It is ringing." The red phone pinged and its light flickered in anger and urgency.

"Shall I get it for you, sir?" said one of his advisors.

"No." He picked it up.

"Yes, this is the President."

"Mr. President Perkins. This is Muhammed. I have a list of demands."

"Yes, what are they?"

"The same as before. Your government will stand down. Congress will be dissolved....."

"Listen you crazy bastard, that is not going to happen. We'll find you and kill you and everyone just like you."

"Mr. President Perkins. There are bombs in Houston, Seattle, Kansas City, Los Angeles, San Diego, Phoenix, Oklahoma City, Atlanta, Pensacola, Miami, Norfolk, Boston, New York, and ....Washington DC."

"Hello... Hello. Are you there Mr. President Perkins?"

"I'm here."

"If you wish to save your country, you must do as we say. You have one hour to decide."

The phone line went dead.

CHAPTER 7

Life had moved into the surreal routine of survival at Grady-O'Hare since that night. The night that each of them would remember forever. Sheriff Smiley and his deputies did catch up with the remaining gang members.

It had occurred out in the farm land of Montague, a cow town surrounded by good ranching country. The gang had broken into another farm, murdered an elderly couple, taken a car and pickup and were trying to head north. A neighbor hearing gunshots called and they finally caught up with them on a lonely stretch called Three Mile Lane. They were boxed in, a gun fight erupted, long rifles, private guns came out, shotguns and pistols. When it was over, not a deputy was shot and Everett Smiley made certain there would be no trials. All were dead at the scene. The man with the tattoos on his neck and Tommy Smiley's pistol, was .... very dead.

It would be wrong to call their life normal, but routines do give a sense of stability, and that is what was happening. That is, until the day that San Francisco disappeared. The word had come across the news, but not before ham radio operators who often scooped local stories well ahead of the media had reported it.

Groups had formed with the idea of an insurgency. Perkins had stood the country down. A new "Parliament of Cooperation" was formed. Willing participants of the former congress, together with important leaders of Islam, would form an alliance to govern. The President retained his title, but became more like an emissary, a secretary of state. Real power existed in the Mahdi Cabinet. They met secretly and issued laws directly from this body.

Rights of *dimmis* were set forth. These were infidels, or non-believers. They would have to bear an additional tax and they were not allowed to own property. All property was confiscated and redistributed. Resistance was met with swift and brutal execution-televised. The conversion rate to Islam was remarkable but not surprising. Death or servitude on one hand or the open arms of Allah on the other. Moderate Muslims were singled out for execution. Their ranks shrank quickly. Those bureaucrats who cooperated during this "conversion" period were rewarded with leases of very nice properties on generous terms.

The economy simply stopped. Everything ground to a halt. There was virtually no manufacturing. The country was dividing between those who would live under such a regime and those who would not. The biggest cities were the easiest to control and convert. The countryside would prove far more difficult. There was lots of space, lots of guns and not so many people willing to convert.

America's underclass of its past was morally compromised by being given the homes of others. The transfer of real property wealth from those who had owned it to those who received it at the gracious hand of Allah was everywhere, every city and town.

The television stations and journalists were prohibited from showing the pictures of the dispossessed, like the emigrants of World War II, with only their clothes on their backs. Factory owners, if not converted, were executed and the factory put under control of the next highest executive. If there was not cooperation, he was executed and the next was given the reigns of power. It didn't take long for the conversions, and the factories to start up, but there was no motivation to produce. Workers whispered to each other furtively, under the watchful eye of a well-paid 'production manager' from the local caliphate.

While the caliphate's plan appeared to produce the political effect of establishing their power, it did nothing for the economic output of the people. The country was broken; physically, emotionally, economically and spiritually.

The purge of journalists occurred shortly after. The literati, for years were effectively the friend of America's foes. They had thrown open the gates of Rome to its invaders. Quickly they were rounded up and executed without so much as a 'thank you'. Within days, only state run television and radio was seen or heard. Churches were closed. And then they began to burn them.

As always, this occurred in the cities, first and foremost. But soon enough, the firebrands of Allah came to the country.

As the churches were burned, or converted to mosques, the underground began to develop into an insurgency. Soon, covert ham radio broadcasts could be heard. The moderate Muslims would have easily lived alongside people of other religions, but they were among the first to be singled out. Their leaders, the subject of show trials in the Stalinist fashion. Their great numbers were sadly reduced to fear of their radical and evil cousins.

The Bay Area was as abandoned as the lost city of Atlantis. No effort was made to resettle. It was abandoned wholesale. The radioactive cloud blew eastward with the prevailing winds, dosing many who did not or could not leave the Sacramento area. The fallout dowsed the communities along the Sierra foothills. The last of it to settle in the Reno and Tahoe area, where the height of the

Sierra Nevada offered some resistance to the cloud of death.

The country was as two. Where the Jihadists reigned, Sharia law was implemented. Where their presence was not felt, a colonial spirit of resistance permeated. Fortunately, this was also a well-armed resistance, as many people in the country had more than one gun; rifles, pistols, shotguns. Unfortunately very few machine guns, though conversions were quickly made as the knowledge was disseminated.

———

Quint took off his hat when he entered the little cemetery on the hill overlooking the ranch. It seemed right to him. He had come back now because he was ready to talk to his mother, when no one else was around. It was quiet in this special place. The wind always seemed to move and it brushed the hair across his brow. The dirt, fresh a week ago, was beginning to subside. Someday soon, it would be level, just like the rest of them.

He thought about how different life was turning out. It almost made him sick to think what had happened even within the short span of his short life. When he was a youngster, there was an assumed assurance that America was strong. It would always be there. That life would go on as he had known it and as his parents, grand parents and generations of Americans had experienced. Now he realized that it was not so. The freedom they had known and assumed could never be assumed. It was hard won and easily lost within a few generations.

He now understood that people hated us. It didn't matter why; our wealth, our religion, or heathenism. Some thought we were religious tyrants, while others accused us of moral degradation. What Quint could not understand was why some of *us* hated us. Why some Americans hated the way we lived, or worshipped. And why, they would rather see the nation destroyed if it proved them right, than the country prosper in the admission of personal misperceptions and foolishly held beliefs.

There were people who constantly toiled in their minds on how to plan a society. How businesses should operate, how they treated their workers. They thought about how to structure society from arts, to parks, to bridges and the military. They were the self anointed 'brains' that knew how it all should be. And they were certain and understood the levers of power. Coming to power, they implemented their great ideas; their programs for the future. Preaching tolerance, they were intolerant. They promised gullible masses the things they wanted and freedom from their fears of want. All who argued were reactionary and were ridiculed by the media arm of the great social planners.

Quint understood that he was among the reactionaries and that was the tribe he belonged to. He accepted this, believed in the simple yet profound notion of an individual living freely. He had experienced that. Having tasted it, however briefly in his short life, he would have no other. But now, he and millions of others, if they could be organized, would have to claw their way back to what was once given them so long ago.

He crouched onto his haunches and wiped his palms on the thighs of his Levi's.

"Mom. I know you're in heaven now. I just want to say how sorry I am for the way your life turned out. I loved you when you were well and I loved you when you were sick. So did JC. He's a wonderful man. You picked a good one, there. You were the best mom I could ever have had. I'll try to make you proud, mom. I love you so much."

He stared at the little cross. It seemed humorous that the pocket knife carvings of her name and terminal points of life were in the same crude scratchings as that of Jon and Melissa's crosses. The ones in between had gotten somewhat fancier; in stone or marble. But now it was back to basics.

—

"Hello."

"JC, this is Ev Smiley."

"Hi, Ev."

"JC, there uh, is going to be a meeting tonight."

"What's it about? I'm not inclined to be leaving Grady-O'Hare after dark these days."

"I understand. But I'm getting calls from other Sheriffs and law enforcement both north and south of us. It appears our overlords are headed our way to enforce their new laws on us. As of tonight, I'm no longer Sheriff. I can't be. All of us; we're abandoning the station. We're stripping it of all equipment, weapons and ammo, radios-everything. We need to be part of a resistance. It needs to start now. Tonight. Will you come? I think it would mean a lot to the men of this community. None of us can stay in our homes and just wait for them."

"I understand. I'll be there."

—

Day 23 AC (after capitulation)

To listen to the news, one would think that a veil of stupidity had been lifted from the eyes of the Americans. The major media was reduced to just one source. The officially sanctioned news. Seeing now the light of Islam, Americans were swooning to convert. This, according to the press reports from all the reporters now dressed in robes and head dresses. Americans had come to their senses. After a flurry

374

of public executions, things were finally settling down. Women were certainly acting more chaste; afraid to go out uncovered and without a chaperon, for fear of the religious police constantly patrolling in the cities.

Movie houses shut down, clubs closed their doors. But the most traumatic change Americans complained of, in whispers, was that music was gone. Nobody played music. Well, almost no one.

Bill Paisley, was a young man in Detroit, Michigan, and worked for a chain of auto parts stores. He was a typical twenty-three year old; an average student in high school, emotionally traumatized by his only girl friend dumping him as soon as they graduated. His life was among his friends; watching sports, drinking beer and trying to live the life the TV commercials told him was acceptable. He was a good worker, exceptional at auto parts. His first and only job, at sixteen, was with the local parts store. Every mechanic knew and liked Bill. If you neede a part, Bill would get it right ....the first time. Life was best for Bill Paisley at a tail gate party in football season. He was a big Lions fan. He had been drinking the beer that he, like many others, had stashed away, after the prohibition was reinstated.

Sometime, after midnight, it had got the better of him. Quite drunk, he staggered out of the front porch of his little house in the modest neighborhood not far from downtown. His stereo system was blaring Lynard Skynard's 'Sweet Home Alabama' He was rockking out with his air guitar.

His friends had already left and he was tired of living underground in his own house. So out onto the sidewalk he stumbled, beer in one hand, while he played his air-guitar, and sang at the top of his lungs. He was pissed at the situation and worked an imaginary conversation with the religious police, in his mind. They were feared. They were his enemy.

"I don't give a fuck what you say. This is my country! You bastards can all kiss my ass." He was staggering badly now, talking to himself or imaginary oppressors. He gazed up into the night sky, the street lights illuminating his front yard. He tipped the can of Bud upside down into his mouth but it was already empty.

The Toyota pick up truck turned the corner and came down Bill's street with the lights off. The bed was jammed with 'protectors of religious adherence' all dressed in their Taliban type garb. The radio chattered in the cab and Bill's address was confirmed. But by now they could see him out in his yard. Lights in the nearby and adjacent houses turned off and soon, there was only Bill Paisley's. His was the only porch light on. The music was very loud and so was Bill.

"Aw crap. I think I'll get me another beer". He started to stumble back toward the house. He didn't see the pick-up pull up to the curb until the men jumped out, with rifles pointed at him.

"Stop!" shouted a man in all black, from the shadows. Bill turned toward them. "What the f....". He was unsteady. One of the men ran into the house and the music stopped. He came out onto the porch with Bill's stereo and threw it down the steps where it shattered.

"It is against the law to play this music. It is against the law to have alcohol. It is against the law to disturb the peace. You must come with us. Now!" But Bill had taken one step toward the man coming down the step that destroyed his stereo. With surprising speed for his heft and condition, Bill cold-cocked the turbaned Muslim. He went down fast and Bill was upon him. The rest of the mullah militia went into hyper-agitation screaming and pointing their rifles point blank, but the mix up on the lawn did not allow for a shot. Then the one who had shouted "Stop", who seemed to lead this bunch, drew an overtly large knife and when he got down into tussle shoved it into Bill Paisley's back, through to his left kidney. The set upon man scampered free and the rest fell on Bill, tying his hands and feet. The leader was talking on his radio as they brought him bound under the street light. He spoke in Arabic, then with agitation in his voice, clicked off the radio and went back to the truck. He motioned something to the other men and they immediately stood Bill Paisley up against a wooden telephone pole and tied him to it. He was bleeding but amazingly coherent and angry, perhaps not even realizing the extent of his injury. The amber street light illuminated the surreal scene as neighbors watched, peeking through blinds and curtains.

"Screw you camel jockeys. I hate you're guts. You bastards are gonna' pay for this someday. We're gonna kill all of you," he slobbered.

The man returned from the pickup truck with a sword and Bill saw it. For the first time, fear rushed into him.

"What's that?" he stammered.

"This is the sword of Allah. It is the sword of justice."

"You towel heads don't know anything about just......", but the man in the dark robe had shoved the long knife directly into Bill Paisley's larynx in mid sentence and that ended all speech. Now only a gurgling, bubbling frothiness from just below the adams apple.

"You have violated Sharia. You have insulted Islam and profaned Allah. The sentence is death. I sentence you to hell as an unbeliever for all eternity. Alahu Akbar!" With this he swung the sword with perfect accuracy striking just above the protruding hilt of his own knife. The sword sliced through the soft tissue of the neck, hardly slowing for the brain stem, through which it passed, finally lodging into the wood of the telephone pole. As it passed through him, Bill had a quizzical expression on his brow. His eyes then rolled up into the head, showing all white. Slowly, the head toppled to it's right, hung by ganglia and neck muscle for a moment, finally falling to the ground.

They put Bill's head on his front porch like a jack-o-lantern, while the headless body remained lashed to the pole in front of his house. They piled into the back of the truck and sped away.

Behind drawn curtains and blinds, neighbors sobbed and were terrorized in their darkened homes and apartments. Most of them had watched what they could of it. The day of capitulation had come for the government and the people were adjusting; some compliant, some to take advantage and try to befriend their oppressors. The military was visibly absent in wholesale. So, while the civilian government folded under the threat of more major cities being nuked, the military quite brilliantly and right out of the play book of Iraq, simply disappeared into the civilian population. The navy was ordered officially to surrender their ships. They did not. To his great credit, President Perkins was able to send a coded message to all commanders in the navy, air force and military: "Ignore all official orders with the Presidential Seal and Parliament of Cooperation! Resist! Resist! Resist independently as necessary."

———

CHAPTER 8

Day 39

The first shafts of dawn's light broke through the treetops at Grady-O'Hare. The colors of fall were sprinkled across the landscape of the ranch. The deep green of the conifers stretched above the tree tops of gold, yellow and red oak leaves. The brilliant yellow of aspen and birch groves traced the stream corridors. Mount Shasta had received an early snowfall and was draped in a thin but dazzling white veil. Hues of purple glinted off the glaciers of her upper slopes. Another of the days that seemed like a bad dream was beginning. The physical beauty was there; all around them, as it always had been. But the sense of loss and dread of what had come of their nation was, at times, simply overwhelming.

The resistance movements were strong in rural areas, but the urban populations couldn't seem to organize against the menacing Jihadists. There were pockets of resistance but they were more dramatic than effectual and were brutally put down. This was the focus of the occupiers; control the metro populations, the media, the money and government. The rest would fall later.

JC had joined with many of the local men and women and established an informal command structure and redundant communications systems, including getting in the pickup and driving over to deliver a message. Some technology was advanced. It just wasn't reliable.

Plans had been formulated to isolate the county from the coming menace by blowing up the bridge on Interstate 5 at Bridgebay. It was a long span over 800 feet and typically several hundred feet above the water, depending on the lake level. Several trestles on the mainline of the Southern Pacific tracks would also be blown up. These were the modern steel replacements which Jon O'Hare and Uncle Billy had felled the timber for the wooden originals.

The north entrance to Shasta Valley was across the Siskiyou Mountains and the Oregon border, also on Interstate 5. Its pass was just over 4,300 feet elevation. The pass cut through sheer rock walls a hundred feet high on both sides. Some old miners had offered up enough dynamite to close it for a good long period. Colestine Road, was an old road that was superseded by the freeway. It would have to be closed as well.

From the west the Klamath River Highway, a scenic but winding river road leading from the coast, was easily cut off as there were numerous bridges. It was decided to blow the bridge at Orleans, about 140 miles west of Yreka.

To the east, State Route 89 connected up the Reno and the Lassen area to the McCloud and Mt. Shasta part of Siskiyou County. Bridges were nearly non-existent, but tall timber along the highway was plentiful. So the logging began. Scores of trees were felled across the road.

Off in the northeast, in Butte Valley near Dorris, US Highway 97 linked Klamath Falls to Siskiyou County. There were too many farm roads that could bypass any of the low bridges over the marsh lands, so a small gap in the pass was targeted for demolition. It would seal off any vehicles from the northeast. Back road travelers would face sniping by local hunters who knew the area well.

Men had formed up teams. With their hunting rifles, shotguns and whatever weapons they had, they made their way to the assigned points. None was more important than the route up the Sacramento River canyon from Redding. Here is where the greatest force would enter; by road or rail, or both.

The convoy of military transports was nearly six miles long in fairly tight formation, heading north on I-5. Recent conscripts lead by a cadre of devoted Jihadis were dispersed among the vehicles. Night was falling and the convoy was pressing in to the south side of Redding, only a twenty minute drive below the bridge at Bridgebay.

———

The small boat bobbed up and down as the breeze make the lake surface choppy. Massive amounts of dynamite were wrapped around the huge reinforced concrete pillars.

"Hurry up, dammit!"

A grizzled old man, smoking a short and awful cigar, turned patiently to the young man who was in charge of the boat.

"Just how much of a hurry should I be in for a job like this?" he asked. "I'll be done when I'm done. I did this crap in Viet Nam, when you were a squirt in your daddy's pants."

The young man knew to say nothing, but it didn't ease his nervousness. There had already been sightings of Jihadis on the freeway; reconnaissance. They were surprised to find the bridge unprotected, but they weren't going to wait for a fix on the situation. Traffic was minimal these days. Word had come about the convoy when it left Sacramento. There were updates along the way. It was dusk now. The few boats on the lake were turning on their lights. The small aluminum craft at the base of the last support pillar started up its engine. The old man finally sat down in the bow with a look of contentment. His cell phone rang and he answered it.

"Yeah."

"Done. And you? Good."

He snapped the phone shut and the younger man turned the boat toward a quiet arm of the river where the hidden vehicle was parked. He started off slow trying not to draw attention. No lights. After some distance from the bridge, he opened up the Mercury 40 hp outboard. The bow came out of the water and the old man grinned; the stogey in the side of his mouth.

On the other end of that phone call was a team of resistance fighters, setting charges on the deck of the bridge. It had recently been rebuilt with new steel and re-inforced concrete. There were two lanes in each direction of travel. Seventy feet below the freeway deck were the railroad tracks. They drilled holes down into the concrete, wearing bright vests like road crews. Between the charges at the north abutment and the charge on the closest column; the bridge was going to disconnect from the hillside by 200 feet.

The teams were heading back north to positions where they could watch the bridge. It would be detonated by a cell phone, much as the IEDs of Iraq had been. JC, Quint, Bill Cooper and two other former sheriff deputies crouched behind the concrete wall at the Turntable Bay overpass a half mile north, but within view of the bridge.

———

In Redding, the convoy was moving past town and starting to head up toward the lake. Everyone was clear and now they waited.

Darkness had come as the convoy moved northward alone on the freeway. At 50 mph, they were in tight for-mation. It was time to rout the resistance that had been reported in the rural areas. It was spreading and they needed to put it down hard. What was needed was a brutal show of force, of terror. That is what the people feared. Then they would obey. Only then would they 'submit'.

The vehicles coming around the mountain on the highway, now approached the south abutment. Staggered at two abreast, there were about thirty vehicles on the bridge when the first one neared the north abutment. JC dialed the phone number on his cell phone. This dialed both phones used for detonation. He prayed the cell phone system would not go down. It had been up for a week solid. Still, it was risky.

The number was entered. JC's thumb slid to the 'send' button. 'Wait, wait......Now!' He pressed the button hard, but nothing happened. The lead HumVees were just passing back onto land when the deafening roar let go, and a tremendous orange fireball erupted three hundred feet in diameter. The ground shook and a cloud of dust and smoke cloaked the end of the bridge. The screams were not heard. The bending metal and crumbling concrete was hidden within the blast. Thick smoke curled upward illuminated in orange and white. As the plume cleared, vehicles at the edge of the precipice were still being shoved over the edge.

Their brakes screeching, the occupants screaming; over they went. One after the other; ten more vehicles fell to the water below. Finally the convoy stopped. People jumped out and just started running back across the bridge, abandoning their trucks, jeeps and HumVees. Perhaps they thought more was on the way. Slowly the remaining five miles of vehicles clogged the retreat. It was four in the morning when they finally cleared the bridge.

———

The next morning, several leaders of the resistance met at Grady-O'Hare. They were at the dining room table. There was talk that the military was planning something. Word was coming out of Klamath Falls, but this could not be confirmed.

They began planning more attacks. They could not know that the world was about to change. That by the next morning, entirely new calculations about life would have to be made. It was all about to change ....again.

CHAPTER 9

It didn't take long in the weeks following the capitulation, for the Jihadists to understand that the military was not going along. Communications were intentionally disintegrated by the military from the President which is how the Mullahs tried to govern. Many military installations were moved in haste to more remote locations. The Dakotas, Idaho, Nevada and other less populated areas saw a huge increase in military aircraft arriving. Naturally, much had to be abandoned at the primary bases. This caused great indecision amongst the Jihadis because their inclination was to destroy things, yet the thought of wielding such powerful machinery against the infidels who built it, all in the name of Allah, was too juicy an irony to let go of. They decided to guard them instead. There were some military pilots from Saudi Arabia and some from western countries, but totally deficient in numbers to be meaningful. Meanwhile, the military in exile (MIE) had established communications between themselves. United States ships stayed at sea, using as little fuel as possible, waiting for a plan to develop and a chance to help take the country back.

Day 41

Of course, there were no Jihadists to fly American military aircraft. Their expertise was in cutting off heads, stoning people, torture and exacting high graff from infidels. On day 41 of the capitulation, an Ohio Class (Trident)

Submarine surfaced at 023:38 hours, in the Indian Ocean. There was a dark sky and the crescent moon hung low, just over the water. The stars were brilliant. They had surfaced for communications, which were now reduced to satellite phones. Commander John Hightower, of the USS Dolphin had received covert orders from the MIE which was secretly based in Mountain Home, Idaho. Here, the small Air Force base was the temporary home of MIE. A non-descript hangar housed the unit of some thirty people who tried to wield a military force on a shoestring of infrastructure. The communications platform was tight and mobile and could move in forty-five minutes by plane to any location; a cave, a house, a hangar-anyplace. Colonel Danny O'Hare was special assistant to the Joint Chiefs. These top generals and admirals were separated for security reasons. They kept in contact by sat-phones and computers their attachés kept at their side. Danny sat beside Admiral Butz and his attaché, Frank Beemon, who held the laptop computer. Suddenly, Commander Hightower's image appeared on the screen. He was below decks in his stateroom with his Executive Officer at his side.

"Are we secure?"

"Yes, sir" someone off camera returned.

"Good evening from the Dolphin, gentlemen"

"Evening Commander" Admiral Butz said. Colonel O'Hare is running this operation. It has been his brainchild and inertia driving it. I will let him brief you."

"Yes, Colonel" responded the Dolphin Commander.

"Commander, we are sending the targeting codes by wide band and will confirm them with you before this call ends. Is your crew ready for this assignment?"

"Yes sir, we're prepared to go anywhere; do anything."

"Good. By morning, we will have jammed Riyadh, Istanbul, Damascus, and Teheran. The people of those nations will receive a looped broadcast warning them that their country, and the Hijaz (Muslim Holy Land, encompassing Mecca and Medina) will be turned to glass. Every Muslim capital in the Middle East, will be leveled by nuclear blasts. The world, as they know it, and we know it, will have come to an end. If they want to survive, they will have to overthrow their dictators and all radical Jihadi regimes. The message will be an offer of peaceful co-existence for the great majority of Muslim peoples. But America will either be free, or we will write the final chapter of the world. They will have twenty-four hours to act. If there is another American city lost: Five Muslim capitals will be immediately missing along with their entire populations. And we will proceed on a five-to-one ratio, until there is nothing left.

O'Hare continued, "Commander, you will have 24 critical targets coded by now. We'll confirm them in a minute. You need to know that we have fourteen other subs with as many targets. You are not alone in this terrible business. They are dispersed throughout the world. No nation will be unaffected by this. It is probable that no nation will survive in its current likeness." There was silence.

"By the way, Commander, if you are a believing man, then you know that the Bible says the world does not end in this way. I believe that. So, I'm believing that the hundreds of millions of good, decent Muslim people will rise up and take back their religion and give us back our country. God, I sure hope so."

"That's a hell of a bet, Colonel O'Hare. I believe in God, but I can't say as I've been a religious man in my life. I'll be praying like never before, that's for sure. God help us." intoned the Dolphin's Commander.

The target codes and launch protocols were set up and confirmed. They signed off quickly.

———

Day 42
Capitals of the Middle East

Throughout the world of Islam in the middle east, the Muezzins came to life. Their pre-dawn recorded calls to morning prayer stretched over the rooftops. People were waking, groggy, sleepy and shuffling through their dimly lighted homes, unrolling prayer rugs. Some were walking through the streets, anxious to get to the mosque in time. They greeted each other coming through the door in perfunctory salutations, "Peace be upon you", and formed into lines of worshipers.

In the palaces of Riyadh, young boys and beautiful women were being discretely escorted out via non-visible routes. The princelings of the House of Saud arose, after a night of debauchery, to prayers and a waiting gourmet breakfast. The call to prayers were heard throughout every city.

Four specialty AWAC aircraft were making their way over the middle east capitals. At 38,000 feet, their sophisticated jamming devices were ready to come online. Messages were being delivered to the heads of state, notifying them that foreign aircraft were currently transiting the air space over them. Saudi Air Force fighters went on 'red alert', ready to scramble. Phone lines were buzzing amid nations. 'Who was this?', and then all cell phones and land lines went dead. High level government officials and heads of state were pressing their redial buttons and inquiring into their phones, but there was nothing.

The prayers were getting started. The crescent moon, near the horizon began to slip away into another day of dusty brown haze. Military channels were jammed and the air forces were grounded-unable to receive orders. Airport towers could not talk to the coffee shop, let alone any aircraft. Civilian aircraft aloft was scrambling trying to find alternative channels as they realized they were cut off from the outside world. People all over this part of the world were getting very nervous as the minutes ticked by. They poured out onto the streets to ask their neighbors.

As the first prayers of the day were concluding and the mosques were emptying into the burgeoning streets now coming to vibrant life, people were talking to each other, their phones in their hands, waving about. They turned on television sets, which came to life on the Al-Jazira channel, with no more than white snow and loud static. They looked at each other and uncomfortable feelings were welling up. Then, across several channels on the television, came a clear picture of landscapes of the middle east, its colorful city lights, industrial sites, its mosques and desert scenes of artistic dunes. They were images that spoke to the hearts of the people they were intended for. A moderate voice came on; Farsi on one channel, Arabic, on another, French with English subtitles on a third.

"People of the middle east and the world. Those who are of the house of Islam. This is a message to you. We have control of all broadcast systems at this time. We bring you a message of the utmost importance."

"For over a thousand years, our civilizations have clashed. There have been periods of peace, but our world views have been diametrically opposed. We are a people that must have our freedom. Without it, we have no identity, nor worth. The capitulation and temporary occupation of American soil and foreign embassies by radical jihadists have brought human history to this point."

"It is now time for the many Muslim peoples, the vast majority of which can peacefully coexist with their fellow man, irrespective of religious beliefs, to take control. You must take control of your governments, your national wealth, and your religion. You must take to the streets as you have so many times in the past. But this time, it is not the foreigner you must protest. It is your own tyrannical leaders. They are the people who have suppressed you, maintaining your poverty and pointing the finger of blame at America or Israel or your neighbors. You know in your hearts that your national wealth is concentrated in families which are dynasties. This has been at the expense of your ancestors, you and will be so for your children."

"Today....., now, human history changes forever. The people of America wish to live in peace with you, but will not suffer occupation of their native land. If the regime of your country, is not brought down, humankind will come to its end by our hand. Nuclear missiles are aimed at your capital and every major city. All life will be lost. Every building incinerated and the land will be uninhabitable for a hundred years. All will be lost; for us and for you. The radicals on American soil must divulge and give up all weapons of mass destruction on US soil. They must be recalled to their country of origin. You have twenty four hours to save yourselves. You have twenty four hours, at which time we will observe the progress. You will hear from us through this channel, or you will see mushroom clouds as your last vision in this life."

And then the loop began to play again. Around the world, in and outside of Muslim countries, the story was immediately picked up. Ham radio operators relayed the message. The Internet, sporadically operating, went into hyper mode. Some were calling out for pre-emptive annihilation of America and all of the west. In Indonesia, Malaysia, phones worked as in all of Asia and most of Europe. Somewhere across Greece was the last effects of the jamming. There was no calling in or out of the middle east and its people sat stunned, angry, fearful, but pondering. 'Was this a bluff?'

Outside, there were the first gatherings in the 'Arab street'.

———

In the hangar at Mountain Home, the gear was be-ing packed up-on the double. The operation was mov-ing. On I-84, a caravan of black Escalades, moved east out of Boise, toward Mountain Home Air Force Base. Inside there was agitated chatter among the black turbaned occupants. To their rear were several military trucks with conscripted recent converts to Islam, traveling much more slowly. The group raced down the freeway, weav-ing through the cars they overtook. There was no regard for safety as they nearly collided with other motorists go-ing over a one hundred miles per hour. "Insha Allah", the lead driver kept whispering out loud; 'God willing'. In ten minutes they would be exiting the freeway and racing out to the base, ten miles southwest.

———

Men scrambled, loading the hard-cased luggage and containers out onto the runway to a waiting transport plane. A second aircraft for the high level personnel was also standing-by, together with two fighter jets to escort MIE HQ.

The black Escalade in the lead almost went past the exit, as it came upon it quickly. They exited the freeway and bolted through the stop sign at the bottom of the of-framp, tires squealing, at 60 mph. They beat on their horns unceasingly as they made their way through the town, careening off several hapless motorists in their way. In minutes they could see the tower stretching above the flat desert sagebrush that surrounded the base.

The last of the luggage was now on board. Admiral Butz and Colonel O'Hare climbed aboard the military Lear Jet. The cockpit glass lowered and snugged down on the two escort fighters as they prepared to taxi. Everyone was on board their respective aircraft as the two fighters taxied to the runway and hit their throttles, full bore and took off. The Lear Jet was next and turned slowly at the end of the runway. The small cargo plane with the HQ communications equipment was on deck.

The Escalade and four other SUVs slowed for the entrance to the main gate, but now guards opened fire on the vehicles. The driver of the Escalade was taken out by a sniper guessing the head position through the darkened glass. His turban exploded inside the cabin of the vehicle and the car accelerated into a concrete barrier and erupted into a fireball. The other vehicles screeched to a halt as they took on fire from positions to either side of the main gate. They ran behind their vehicles. The American snipers pinned them down. The trucks with infantry troops were pulling up onto the scene. The vehicles were arrayed along the road, at angles to the main gate for cover.

On the runway, the radio crackled the news at the main gate and the Lear Jet lurched forward. The pilot, letting it roll down the runway, then pushing the thrusters all the way forward. It literally pressed the air from their lungs. Admiral Butz' eyes widened as he struggled against his lungs. Danny fought for a deep breath and then let it slowly out as the jet screamed down the runway. Then the nose pointed straight up and its passengers felt they would pass out. Frank Beemon did.

Two rocket propelled grenade launchers exited the truck. They took aim at the gate positions held by Marines, and they exploded upon their targets. There was more fire and a second round of RPGs opened a gap in the defenses, destroying the gates and dislodging the concrete barriers. The lead SUV, now a Suburban filled with Jihadis, drove through the mangled gates heading for the runway. The other SUVs followed. They sped their way through the base heading for the tower, the only visible clue to the runways.

The propellers were finally revved up for takeoff and the brakes let go. The plane ambled down the runway, slow at first, but picking up speed quickly.

The Suburban and entourage bolted onto the airfield at the far end. They parked laterally to the field across the runway and the RPG launcher came out and was loaded. The plane, now approaching at over 110 mph. At 150 mph, they would lift off the ground, a slow moving target directly over the scrambling turbans at the end of the field. The pilot and copilot were unable to stop, unable to lift off. There was nothing left to do but pray and keep accelerating.

———

In Siskiyou County, as so many other rural areas of the country, a new paradigm had emerged. The focus of every effort was not only the provision of food, fuel and security, but constant planning and preparation for the insurgency effort. What were once the critical elements of local infrastructure were now the targets of potential attacks and destruction from roads to runways. But day 42 of the capitulation was different.

At Grady-O'Hare, everyone was gathered around the TV. News reports were interrupted by yet other news reports. Nothing seemed confirmed except a sense of chaos. Pepe took off his hat and scratched his head thoughtfully. Quint was tapping on the computer keyboard trying to access the internet. Matt walked into the room.

"Gas tank is filled up, so the generator should be good for eight hours if we need it. We've only got half a 55 gallon drum left."

JC replied, "We're only going to run the generator for a half hour, then shut it all down. We can try again later."

"What's going on, Dad?" asked Quint.

"Not sure. Not sure if any body else knows, but something is going on. That's for sure."

All over the country, people were tuned to the fact that something really big seemed in progress. The Internet had gone down ...again, frustrating millions. TV broadcasting was interrupted frequently by color bars and audio static. Still, everyone realized something was happening. They could sense it, feel it.

———

A cloud of dust marked the location of every crowd in the sat-photos until they joined onto the paved boulevards of the capitals of Islam. The crowds were growing. In the Saudi palace, the King's cell phone rang. It startled him and he wondered if things were returning to normal. It was a message delivered by the high altitude craft that continued to jam all frequencies over the middle east.

"King Fahd?"

"Yes."

"This is the United States Air Force. Your phone will be turned on in two hours, allowing you to make whatever calls you must make to effect a complete and total stand down of all Jihadis in America."

The king protested, "But that is impossible. They hate me as much as you. I have no power over them."

"You have twenty-two hours and fifteen minutes."

The king rose to his feet, from his throne. "Let me have communications now. Why make me wait two more hours. Perhaps there is something I can do."

There was no reply. He clicked off the phone and called in his brothers, cousins, sons and daughters for a family and national meeting.

The satellite imagery showed growing crowds enlarging at every confluence of streets throughout the Islamic capitals of the middle east. What they didn't show was the mind of the people in those streets. Were they radical Wahabbis happy to rid themselves of tyrannical Sauds and take over the national petroleum assets in a coup, or were they moderate Muslims anxious for peace with the west and afraid of the apocalyptic threat before them? Minute by minute people joined the throng marching down the main boulevards to their national seats of power. But satellite photos can only reveal so much. They cannot reveal the heart or the intentions. What was being seen were the largest demonstrations ever seen in so spontaneous a situation. But what would be the outcome. The observers of the images could not say.

—

Mountain Home, Idaho

Mohamed looked through the open cross-hairs of the RPG launcher at the lumbering aircraft coming closer. The men around him bantered and laughed at the ease of this target. It was shooting proverbial fish in a bucket. The only question was whether to fire before it got to them or directly overhead or as it passed them.

The F-16 was coming around as Captain Lucius Johnson put his target box on the gaggle of black robes at the end of the runway and it locked on; the target box flickering in red.

The pilot of the transport had his eyes closed in prayer as he pulled back the stick and felt the aircraft's nose come up. The men in robes were about to pass from view under the nose of his plane. 'Oh God', he thought.

Lucius Johnson tapped the red button on the side of his control stick and a hell-fire missile shot out from under his left wing.

They were all chanting now; "Alahu Akbar, Alahu Akbar, Ala.......", and were evaporated.

The aircraft jerked in the air as the pilot and copilot's eyeballs popped open as the explosion below them shoved at them from their seat. They looked up and saw the last of the vapor trail of the missile stretching down below them. The F-16 passed overhead at high speed. They looked at each other, astonished at their deliverance. They gained altitude and headed for Klamath Falls, Oregon, an old Air Force base which still had good runways.

Lucius Johnson radioed, "I'll catch up in a minute." to his wing man. He made a large circle and came back lining up on the road to the base, where the trucks were beginning to move toward the main gate. The conscripts in the back looked up as they heard the roar of the jet bearing down on them. Pointing frantically, they pounded on the cab to stop the truck so they could jump out and flee. Too late. The machine guns opened up on them and the road was pulverized, the vehicles and people disintegrated. Captain Johnson then banked right to join the MIE group.

———

In the White House, the mood was oppressive; a surreal combination of people dressed in garments between the ninth and twenty-first centuries. President Perkins was looking over the travel agenda prepared for him and the speeches he was to make. The drafts implored the American people to submit. It was submission to Allah, and was inevitable. The time for violence was now over. This, of course, was untrue. Every day violent acts were committed against the people who showed any resistance.

Ken Johnson, his senior advisor, bent to Perkins' ear and whispered for a long time. Perkins' stare was fixed as he nodded slowly.

"Mr. President, the United States military has targeted most of the capitals of Islamic countries, together with those who have been our enemies. They are delivering an ultimatum to the people of Islam to overthrow their radical regimes and make peace with the west. Sir: This is the ultimate ultimatum. They're prepared to launch from Tridents in 19 hours."

The doors to the Oval Office burst open and a very aggravated Arab man in a western suit, Ibn Al-Ijahari, strode over to the Perkins' desk with two armed men beside him. More stood outside the door.

"You think you can bluff us?" he screamed at Perkins. "You think this is some kind of game we are playing here?" Spittle formed at the corners of his mouth and spewed from him as he raged.

"I have no control over this." said Perkins calmly.

"The hell you don't!"

Now Perkins' children were marched into the room, his wife hysterical.

"I don't care how you do it. You had better find a way to communicate with your military people and call this off or they will be the first to die. You don't have 20 hours. You have one hour. He marched the family back out of the room. They were taken away, crying. Al-Ijihari returned with his guards.

"Well. You better get started!"

"There is nothing to do Mr. Al-Ijahari. I'm prepared to let fate take its course."

"I will kill your family before your eyes."

"I can't stop you from what you are going to do anymore than I can stop what is going to happen. You have brought this upon yourself. I've made my peace with my maker. I'm prepared for the next life, no matter how awful you make the end of this one. You're reign of terror is over. The world will come to its end for humankind in less than fifty days since you took over. All you hoped to gain is lost. I know the people running this and the destructive capability they possess. It is an end-of-world capability. There is only one option: You must stand down."

———

In Damascus, the throngs gathered in front of Assad's palace. Many Lebanese, yearning to be free, were among the crowd. There was a police line protecting it. They were face-to-face. Then, as the satellite imagery showed, an unexplainable wave of energy moved from the back to the front of the crowd and it bowled over the police line and thousands of people stormed up the steps into the palace. There were a few gun shots. Within minutes Assad was marched out onto the balcony high above the remaining multitude that clogged the streets. Arms were raised by the crowd chanting "Down with Assad" over and over.

His face was filled with terror, as the dozen men behind him lifted him up onto the balustrade, holding him only by the back of his belt. His shirt, pure white, opened several buttons at the collar. He was begging the people behind him, offering to step down; offering to allow a democratic process to begin. He only wanted his family spared. He begged in the name of Allah, just before he was pushed off the edge. His arms and legs flailed as the crowd parted below him, and his wife, back in the room, screamed.

High above, the jamming of communications was shut down. Now images were flooding in to middle east television sets from all over the world. It seemed every cell phone in the middle east rang as people started getting through. Twitter and Face Book servers crashed, but quickly recovered, as stories from around the world and their images flooded in.

By noon, Riyadh time, the house of Saud was offering the people of Saudi Arabia a new beginning. It was not necessary for their to be a revolution. The revolution was occurring and there would be meetings with people to establish a new form of government.

In Teheran, the Mullahs and leaders were overwhelmed by the largest crowds ever gathered in this part of the world. Some estimated it over two million. The young people of Iran had thrown down the theocracy and jailed its leaders and now they stood before flashing cameras. The world watched.

"We the people of Iran, where civilization began, have taken back our country. We are ready to create a world, where our own culture and history can be in harmony with the West. There is no other possibility. We must learn to live together. The tyrants who have ruled our country and those of our Arab brothers in the nations around us must step down or be thrown down. Accordingly, we implore the military of the United States of America, that we are no longer your enemy and all of us must step back from the brink of annihilation. We wish further to proclaim that we declare a state of peace with the people of Israel. We offer to begin talks as soon as possible. Talks which will establish a peaceful Israel for the Jewish people and we will work to establish a humanitarian assimilation of the Arabs living in Palestine."

———

Pyongyang, North Korea

The Supreme Leader, looked at the dispatches coming across his desk. Asia was never under the black out, so there had been a flurry of communications between North Korea and China and the Russia. They were formulating plans, but there was too much uncertainty. Was this a bluff? Did they really have the assets in place to pull this off? Who was in charge of America? Are they really that crazy?

Though satellite imagery was compromised, the Joint Chiefs were talking to each other about the obvious launch preparations being made in North Korea. The Japanese were watching it too, but what could they do?

The laptop on the desk in the hangar at Klamath Falls, had four of the Joint Chiefs on the screen. The consensus was that Pyongyang was rushing to launch mode. Perhaps they had not heard that their friends in Iran were already out of business.

—

The USS Tennessee was just off the coast of South Korea, in the Yellow Sea, steaming north at full speed. Two nuclear missiles were readied and the target codes were being entered. One was Pyongyang the other, a recently developed multiple launch facility ninety miles away.

The Taepodong-X and Taepondong 2 type missiles were being fueled on the launch pads. Three of them, now nearly complete. Kim Il Jung gulped hard on a glass of Scotch, and nodded his head to the assistant who stared back at him long and hard. Then turned and left the room. The order had been given. There would be a pre-emptive strike on America. He wasn't going to lose his chance at greatness. Now was the time for the little country of North Korea and Kim, personally, to assume the leadership of east Asia; Tokyo, Seoul and Singapore. He would also deal a lethal blow to the crippled United States. His targets were Los Angeles and Seattle. The new epoch of power had begun and he was ready to take his 'rightful' place in world history. The scotch now flushed through his system. He closed his eyes, feeling the warmth inside and imagining himself among the most powerful men in the world. No more would his small nation be an economic laughing stock. World leaders would bow down as he walked by. His every whim, the power and force of divine law.

The Tennessee, had come to full stop and now came to launch depth, eight miles offshore. At 13:05 hours, two trident nuclear missiles with multiple war heads burst from the ocean surface, only 58 miles from Pyongyang. One minute, twelve seconds later, North Korea no longer existed as a government, nor society.

———

Day 43

"Son, go start up the generator. Let's see what is going on," said JC. Quint went out the through the kitchen to the generator shed. The screen door slapped the jamb. JC had aged five years in the last six months. He sipped the hot black coffee made on the top of the wood stove. It was good. He looked across the pastures to the mountain and noted the ever dwindling herd. Pepe was on horseback, at the far edge of the field, hardly more than a speck. The women were already in the kitchen pulling out previously canned goods preparing for another day of 'feeding the troops'. Quint came back in and you could hear the generator in the distance as the door stood open briefly. The water tank to the house was now being refilled, and the clanging of dishes began.

The television screen came to life since it was on when the power shut off last.

"..... and our man Hank Johnson is there. Hank are you there?"

"I'm here, on the west lawn of the Whitehouse...."

JC came around to view the TV. He had already become accustomed, in only weeks, to hearing the highly scripted news casts, with reporters of a middle eastern accent. Only the Internet had offered alternative and insurgent news. 'What did this mean'.

"I think you all ought to come in here." he called out.

"There is something going ....look at this." They gathered around.

"It happened this morning. President Perkins came out and declared that the capitulation has ceased. He did not explain how. There were detailed discussions with the occupiers set for later today. We don't know the workings, but we are getting reports from Europe that there has been an entire shift in the middle east. Some say it is a paradigm shift between the east and the west, between Islam and the west. Oh ....what ....OK. Jeff they're telling me to send it back to you in the news room for other breaking news."

The screen flickered and went to color bars as it so often did, and the living room at Grady-O'Hare erupted with shouting, some stood trembling in tears of relief and happiness. Matt and JC, Magdalena, Sandy and Quint. The men shouted and jumped up and down like school boys. They hugged each other and fell upon one another laughing and crying. The emotions could not even be explained let alone controlled. It was not like anything they had ever experienced in their lives. JC finally sat down on the couch and put his head in his hands and sobbed openly. Quint sprinted out to the front porch with a shotgun and before he could pull the trigger to call Pepe back to the ranch house, he heard shots being fired and distant horns blaring. He hooted like a drunk teenager at a bonfire and pulled the trigger, ejected the shell and pulled again, until the gun emptied.

He saw in the distance Pepe flying across the meadow on his Palomino. In a few moments he brought the galloping horse to an abrupt halt at Quint's position, noting the smile on his face.

"It's over! It's over!, We're free again!" Pepe looked at him and then heard the cheering in the house. Matt staggered out the door and dropped to his knees in prayer on the patch of grass that passed for a lawn now. It was true and now Pepe saw that it was so. He crossed himself and climbed down off the horse straight to his knees. Quint was staring up into the sky, looking for God, to thank Him.

That's what they did on day 43. They prayed to the Lord and gave thanks, for His deliverance. They never thought it was their resistance or any act that they had committed that had saved them.

———

Klamath Falls, Oregon

In a nondescript corrugated metal hangar, twenty or so men in uniforms, none with any medals on display were huggi ng each other and shaking hands. They were the MIE command and they had just learned of the stand down of occupying forces in America. They, of course, knew before anyone else the fate of N. Korea. There would be grave concern for the nuclear fallout washing westward. A strong wind had spared the South Korean's from any significant effect.

Admiral Butz shook Danny O'Hare's hand firmly.

"Your country owes you an immeasurable debt, General."

Danny countered "I'm not a general, Admiral, but thank you. I don't need any debt owed me by my own people. I'm just glad its over."

"No. Trust me. You're a General, now. I'll see to it."

"Thank you, sir. Then that is what I'm going to retire at."

"Oh? You are leaving us? We are going to need you to rebuild." Butz looked pained.

"Oh, I'll be around ... for a little while. But you know, I was raised on a ranch not far from here. Just down the road, outside of Weed."

"Really? Well you can certainly take some time off."

"Yes, sir. I'd like to do that."

The next day, the military helicopter lifted off, at the Klamath Falls air base. Soon to be General Danny O'Hare saluted the chief officers on the ground. It crossed his mind as the bird flew low and fast across the wildlife refuge of the Lower Klamath and over the gap and into Butte Valley, that his great grandfather made the same trip a hundred and twenty odd years earlier. He was flying over the pines and sage that Jon O'Hare rode through on horseback at the close of the last war in the west with the Indians. He thought about that trip and how it had later formed the union with Melisa Grady and the whole ranch had started. In minutes they flew over Mt. Hebron Summit, veering off the flanks of Mt. Shasta. Then he could see it: Grady-O'Hare.

He was 62 years old and had never been married. He'd had several relationships with women. One which might have progressed to marriage except for a tragic car accident. In the end, the service was his wife, his mistress and his constant companion. He had sacrificed what most men want; a family, offspring, for what every free peoples need, a vigilant warrior at their gates. He had given up a lot and had long ago accepted that sacrifice. Today, he was resigned to that fate. He would be a good uncle, a brother, a leader, but most important; a free man. Yet, he wondered if love, or perhaps better put at this stage of life, companionship could still be found. Was there still time? Maybe. Lives were shattered and there would be much rebuilding.

The copter circled the main field below the ranch house. Every body heard the popping sound of the rotors and had come out to see. They saw the USAF insignia, but most of them eyed the nearest gun. It set down in the field, the cows scattering, and several dried cow paddies took off like frisbees. A man in civilian clothes hopped out with a small duffel bag. A crew cut, salt and peppered hair. He turned back and saluted the pilot. He trotted easily, bent over below the rotors until he had cleared them. Quint had never seen, only heard about Uncle Danny. JC and Pepe leaned on a split rail fence nearby, watching. JC recognized him. Pepe was about to as well.

"Pepe go kill the fatted calf. We're gonna' have a feast tonight." he smiled.

"Is that Danny?"

"It is and I'd say he's home."

EPILOGUE

The transformation was global and breathtaking in its speed. Israel was making good progress with the younger Muslim leaders surrounding it. The Jihadis were becoming increasingly marginalized. But they were still there-still trying to terrorize people. But now, mostly other Muslims, with whom they vehemently disagreed. Islam's violence turned back on itself. For a time the non-Muslim world was relatively safe.

There was a renewed spirit of cooperation amongst countries, that only walking to the brink could produce. Russia and China were more willing to cooperate. Would it last? No. But life is lived between the now and the inevitable. Couples made love, had children, raised them and married them off, grew old and died. Everything had changed and nothing had changed. History teaches that great civilizations and empires come and go like the wind: a conquering hegemony one moment, spent and dissipated the next.

America had lost almost everything. Years and trillions would be spent to rebuild the broken nation, but its confidence was broken. The concrete and steel was the easy part. More important was that it had lost its way. It had turned its back on the divinely inspired founding documents that had created, shaped and sustained the greatest civilization known to man. It produced the most free, the wealthiest and most charitable people in human history. Then it neutered itself with collectivism, devolving downward through democracy. At the end it was little more than a sham: Socialism cross-dressing as a free people. It was not the free market, or capitalism or liberty that had failed. The people had failed to protect those gifts, from those who diligently pursued their destruction.

When Congress was re-established, another revolution began. Springing up from the people themselves, who yearned to be free- not hyphenated Americans but 'Americans', who had treated freedoms cavalierly, given to them by others. They had lost them. Then and only then was their value realized. And now they were ready to rebuild, but it would start with the refounding of the republic. They would return to the chalkboard of freedom erasing everything they had found that did not work and arrived back at the U.S. Constitution and Bill of Rights. What was appended to those refreshed documents was a fraction of what it had cancerously become. They burned the tax code and served without pay. As the session began, they opened with a prayer. After the prayer, a chaplain began reading from Exodus and the Israelites in the wilderness. Rooted in the natural law of their God, they began again to found a great nation.

The End

Made in the USA
Charleston, SC
15 August 2010